NO
GOOD
DEED

NO GOOD DEED

LYNN S. HIGHTOWER

Delacorte  Press

Published by
Delacorte Press
Bantam Doubleday Dell Publishing Group, Inc.
1540 Broadway
New York, New York 10036

Library of Congress Cataloging in Publication Data

Hightower, Lynn S.
No good deed / by Lynn S. Hightower.
p.   cm.
ISBN 0-385-32359-X
I. Title.
PS3558.I372N6   1998
813'.54—dc21   97-52634
CIP

Manufactured in the United States of America
Published simultaneously in Canada

Book design by Susan Maksuta

May 1998

10   9   8   7   6   5   4   3   2   1

BVG

For Wendell Berry

1

"I tell you what, this horse business is more crooked than the car business ever thought of being."

Doug Campbell, car salesman and horse owner

THE FIRST TIME Sonora saw the farm, it was dusk, and there were horses running in the paddocks. It did not seem like the kind of place where a young girl of fifteen could saddle up a horse for an afternoon ride and never come back—though Sonora did not know what such a place might look like. Girl and horse had vanished sometime around three thirty that afternoon.

The child had not disappeared entirely without a trace. She had left blood, and a discarded riding boot.

Sonora turned the Pathfinder off the dark ribbon of back road, onto the long dirt driveway that led to the barn. The sky was black and blue, like a bruise. It would be dark soon.

Gritty dust rose from the grind of gravel beneath tires that were much in need of replacing. The Pathfinder hit the bottom of a pothole, and Sonora bounced. New shocks wouldn't be a bad idea either.

As soon as God and Visa allowed.

Three patrol cars were parked at odd angles at the end of the drive, and blue strobe lights arced across the face of a weathered twenty-stall barn. There were horses inside, looking out. Light blazed from the tiny barred stall windows.

Sonora parked her Pathfinder next to a gold Taurus. Sam was here, then, in the company car. Maybe he'd have it solved.

She put the Pathfinder in park, left the doors unlocked, paused to look out over the small ten-acre farm. The fencing was bad—slats broken, whole sections sagging, paint bleached from black to gray by the sun and the seasons. Sonora assumed the horses stayed in their paddocks because they wanted to.

There was an electric snap in the wind, like you got before a tornado or the advent of fall. Sonora felt rain and chilled air—a welcome change from the heat of a miserable, bug-ridden summer. Ants in the kitchen, mosquitoes at night. Silverfish in the drain of the bath.

Something spooked the horses in the front field and sent them cantering across the sparse grass and weed clumps, heads high, tails up.

Thirty minutes ago she'd been dog tired and ready to collapse, dreading the long drive out of Cincinnati's downtown into the suburbs of Blue Ash, counting her cash so she could bring the kids takeout. The cold air had revived her.

She checked her watch. Seven P.M. Her children were going hungry.

2

A UNIFORM stood outside the office door, looking bored but alert. Sonora flashed her ID, and the man relaxed his pose and stepped toward her.

"Officer Renquist, ma'am. Detective Delarosa told me to tell you he's out at the scene—"

"We got a body?" Sonora asked.

"No, ma'am. Just blood."

Renquist was an older man, with the red flush of high blood pressure across his cheeks. A lot of lines around the eye— worry or laugh lines, Sonora couldn't tell. He was on the portly side, but he'd be cuddly in a sweater. He reminded Sonora of her favorite uncle who used to drink her milk for her when her mom wasn't looking. Renquist looked tired but alert. It was not every day a whodunit crossed his path.

Sonora rubbed the back of her neck. "How much blood?"

"Officially speaking? A lot."

Sonora glanced over her shoulder at the array of Mazdas, Explorers, and Camrys that were parked in and around the police cars. "A lot of civilians around. Who are they?"

"Girl's father—"

"What's her name again?"

The officer flipped open his notebook but didn't need to

look. "Joelle Chauncey. Her dad, one Dixon Chauncey, came home from work around five thirty—he lives on the premises in a house trailer with two other children—anyway, he comes home and finds out that his oldest daughter, Joelle, went out riding and didn't come back. They put up a search, but the girl and the horse were gone."

"Gone? Disappeared, just like that?"

"Like what, I don't know, ma'am. But the girl and the horse are gone, and there's a lot of blood."

"Where's the father now?"

Renquist inclined his head toward the office door. "In there with some of the people who ride here. Lady that runs the place, she teaches lessons, boards horses."

"She around?"

"She was out at the scene talking to Detective Delarosa, but I think I saw her head back into the barn a minute or two ago. Her name is Donna Delaney."

Answered the question before she asked. Experience was a wonderful thing. "Give me one minute with the dad."

The office door stuck, and Renquist leaned over and yanked it open. A gust of wind blew Sonora's hair and set off the ting of wind chimes, a circle of pewter horses, hanging just outside the door.

The father was easy to spot.

Chauncey sat way back on the couch, knees tight, chin wobbly with the effort not to cry. Likely he had shaved that morning, but he was one of those men who would need to shave twice a day to stay presentable.

He was flanked by two women, parents of children in the riding program, Sonora guessed. They sat beside him offering the consolation of their presence, in exchange for their involvement, albeit on the sidelines, in a tragic but fascinating ordeal.

They would have brought baked goods and a ham, if they'd had sufficient notice.

Chauncey slid forward on the couch and stood quickly to shake Sonora's hand. He might be out of his mind with worry, but he would not neglect common courtesy.

"Police Specialist Blair. You're Dixon Chauncey?" Sonora showed him her badge, knowing he would find it a comfort. She wondered why he was not out looking for his daughter with the uniforms.

"Yes, ma'am. I'm Joelle's father."

His knees were wobbly, and he teetered forward. Which answered her question of why he wasn't out looking.

Sonora took his hand and nudged him back toward the couch. "Sit down, Mr. Chauncey."

He obeyed instantly.

He wasn't overweight by more than fifteen or twenty pounds, which would have been unnoticeable if he dressed with a certain amount of common sense. He didn't. He wore his pants tight and curved over his hips, and the length was an inch too short. Likely the pants had fit perfectly until washed.

He could have been attractive, but he wasn't. The least endearing thing about him was his posture, back slightly humped, shoulders curved and sloping, elbows bent, like Popeye. He wore a short-sleeved plaid shirt with a pack of Marlboros in the pocket. His hair was black, like shoe polish, and dull as if he dyed it. It sat on his head like a plastic cap. Sonora figured he combed it straight down with water every day.

"Have you met my partner, Detective Delarosa? He got here ahead of me, he drives faster than I do." Sonora smiled gently while she worked him, felt the ease of tension in the room. The rider mommies gave her a look of approval mixed with relief, and Chauncey braved a shy half smile.

Let him know there was a man on the case, Sonora thought, on the chance that he was one of those people who are particular about the gender of their cops. Give an air of competent professionalism and leaven it with "I'm just a regular Joe."

Confidence and a bit of comfort for him to hang on to

while they found the body of his kid and decided whether he'd had anything to do with it.

The tears looked genuine, at any rate.

The door leading into the barn proper slammed open, just grazing Sonora on the elbow. She heard a horse whinny and snort, then a thumping noise, as if the horse was pawing the ground.

"Shut that up, or you're going out." A woman's voice. Harsh. Inflection sounding kind of Chicago—Midwest, anyway.

The horse was instantly quiet, as was everyone else in the room.

The woman stood in the doorway, taking them all in. Her attention created a frisson of awareness that said watch-your-step. Her chin was pointed, face almost drawn, hair a cotton-white blond because she was worth it. She did not wear a lot of makeup, and her features were strong. She bordered pretty, if you liked them hard-looking. Her eyes, dark, flat, and judgmental, went back to Sonora, and she extended a hand.

"I'm Donna Delaney. This is my farm and my office."

Tiny lines, half-circle grooves like hoofprints, arced the corners of her mouth. She had thin slash lips and wore jeans and a flannel shirt that fit her loosely. She was thin, and she looked good in jeans. She scraped her feet on the doorsill. Her black rubber boots were crusted with mud, manure, and wood shavings, and her feet were long and slender. Her throat and shoulders were dark brown, the permanent tan of a woman who spent a lot of time outdoors no matter the heat.

"Detective Blair," Sonora said.

"So you come in pairs. I've talked to the other one already. Delarosa."

"I have a few questions—"

"I already talked to your partner."

Sonora was aware of the rapt attention of the women on the couch. "That so?" She smiled, keeping it lazy. "Ms. Delaney, did you see Joelle Chauncey this afternoon?"

Delaney's eyes narrowed, then she turned and headed for

the door, glancing back at Sonora over her shoulder. "It's past feeding time, and my horses are hungry. Want to walk along beside me while I work?"

"I won't keep you much longer," Sonora said.

Delaney hesitated.

"I can feed them, Donna." Chauncey stood up again, then leaned against the wall. His voice was small, sad, and brave.

"You can't even stand up," Delaney said.

"We'll do it." The two women got off the couch, looked at each other, nodded their heads. This was something they could handle. Glad to be of help.

Delaney gave them a mere flicker of attention. "Don't worry about the horses in the back stalls. And only give that pony a taste. He's pigfat as it is." She looked back at Sonora. "No. I didn't see Joelle today."

"Were you here? What's your usual schedule?"

"I get here in the morning, a little before eight. Leave around twelve thirty. Got back at six, today's Tuesday. I do private lessons on Tuesdays, usually in the evening. Other days I'm back by four."

"Is there usually anyone here between noon and four, or six on Tuesdays?"

"No. Unless I'm showing a horse for sale or something, it's usually dead around here in the afternoons. Picks up at night for lessons from five to eight, except Tuesdays, like I said. When I do private. Then I feed and bed the horses and go home. Joelle usually helps me."

"Was Joelle in the habit of riding out by herself in the afternoon?"

"Yeah, she'd usually ride after school for a little while, before lessons started. She wasn't really supposed to go out on Tuesdays, though, because nobody else is here. It's better if someone's around to keep an eye out. But one of the arrangements I have with Dixon is that his kids get to ride the horses. He's supposed to look after them, I'm not their baby-sitter."

Sonora glanced at Dixon Chauncey, wondering how Delaney's insensitivity would register.

Defensively.

"She wasn't supposed to ride by herself," he said quickly.

Sonora looked back at Chauncey. "She did, though, didn't she?"

"I should have been stricter with her about that. But she was a good rider."

"She could handle herself," Delaney said. High praise.

Joelle was only fifteen, Sonora thought. A lot of things could come up that a fifteen-year-old couldn't handle.

3

Dixon chauncey insisted on showing Sonora through the barn, as if she could not make it down the dirt-packed aisle on her own. The rider mommies manned a wheelbarrow, scooping feed through the bars of the stalls. The horses nickered, waiting impatiently, snorting when the grain hit the feed tub.

The musk of horse mixed pleasantly with emanations from the fresh cedar shavings that were piled all the way to the barn roof in an empty stall at the opposite end. Sonora found the noise of munching horses soothing. She peeped in through one barred window.

The horse, chestnut and skinny, did not lift his head from his dinner. The stall was rank with black muck and manure, cobwebs hanging in streams from the rafters.

A barn cat, tiger striped and skinny enough to show ribs, scooted in front of Dixon Chauncey. Sonora bent down absently and caught its tail as it went by, got a handful of cat fur and barn dust.

The barn doors were open. An outdoor light sent a weak yellow glow over the weed-edged, beaten-down path that led to a small riding ring. Dixon Chauncey pointed to the lit section of back field. Sonora saw the uniforms, Crime Scene Unit techs in heavy boots walking up and down the field, a man in jeans she thought might be Sam. Business as usual no matter where she went.

"Where's your trailer?" Sonora asked.

Chauncey pointed to the far left of the back field. Lights shone through tiny square windows, much like the barn but smaller.

"Mr. Chauncey, did Joelle leave any kind of a note?"

"No, ma'am, I don't think she did." He shook his head, eyes wide and wary. This was a concept he had not considered.

The trailer door opened, and a little girl walked out to the front step. She wore a faded red sweatshirt and shorts, though it was chilly out. Her shoulders drooped, and she rubbed her eyes, head tilted sharply to one side. Sonora thought she was crying.

"Mr. Chauncey, how old are your kids?"

"Seven, nine, and fifteen, counting Joelle."

Are we still counting Joelle? Sonora wondered. "They alone?"

He waved at the little girl, but she did not seem to see him. "Yeah. I really need to go and see to them."

"Hang right here, just for a moment." Sonora went around the front of the barn, called to Renquist.

He came toward her at a jog, which put him immediately out of breath. "Press is coming."

Sonora looked down the empty drive, wondered how Renquist knew. A car passed by on the two-lane road, switched on its lights. It would be full dark soon.

"They listen in on us. We return the favor."

Sonora nodded. "I'll send somebody out to watch the drive, I don't want them wandering. You I need."

Renquist followed as she walked back around the barn.

"Escort Mr. Chauncey back to his trailer—evidently this guy's got two other kids. Stay with him till I can get over there, go through Joelle's room myself. Let me know if he goes through her stuff, removes anything. Keep watch. In a sympathetic manner."

"I got you."

He understood, Sonora could tell by his tone of voice. He handed her his flashlight, a big black Mag-Lite, cop issue.

"It'll be dark soon, ma'am. You may need this."

She took it from him gratefully. Must be looking for a promotion. Age discrimination would sink him.

"Thanks, Renquist. I'll make sure it's returned."

She turned then, feeling the strong pull of the crime scene, and headed for the back field and Sam. She heard the murmur of voices over her shoulder as Renquist introduced himself to Chauncey and suggested they head for the trailer. Chauncey went like a lamb. Sonora gave them one backward look. Renquist moved like a Marine, maybe he'd been one. Chauncey had a peculiar walk, head down, one foot forward, the other scooting behind in a soft shuffle that whispered low self-esteem.

Sonora glanced back at the trailer. The little girl was gone. The porch light, dim already, flickered once and went out.

4

THE GATE to the paddock had been white some years ago. The bars had rusted through, two of them had separated, and the whole mechanism sagged crookedly, wedged in a mound of dirt. Sonora passed through and stepped into knee-high clumps of sawgrass, ironweed, and purple-topped thistles. She was wearing her newest Reeboks and the khakis that made her look skinny. She prayed to the god of detergents that she would not get anything on them that wouldn't come out.

No body, no smell.

It was a good walk to the end of the back field, and the sky was going darker. Sonora took a breath. You could almost taste the metallic hum in the air. They'd better get this crime scene processed—it would be raining soon.

Wind ruffled the bright yellow crime scene tape, a loose end flapping. One of the horses took exception to the tape and took off, stampeding them all.

Something had come through the fence, smashing through an entire eight-foot section. Broken slats, the wood raw and splintered, hung on either side like badly broken bones.

A riding boot lay in the grass, maybe eight to ten feet from the broken fence line.

Sonora ducked under the crime scene tape, looked around

till she spotted Sam—wearing jeans, so he'd already been home. He was studying the edges of a broken fence board. He'd lost weight, and she hadn't even noticed. Must be the jeans.

"Hey, buns of steel. You got a clue or something?"

He turned, and Sonora realized that either it was darker than she realized or her eyesight was going. Whoever he was, he wasn't Sam.

The man grinned. "Have we met?"

Sonora had lately been in the habit of looking at men and thinking up reasons why she was happy not to be married to them. She was missing romance, though, missing lust even more. And beginning to wonder if her heart had deadened somehow, from one too many extremes.

One look at this guy, and she knew she was all right.

She extended a hand. "Detective Blair. I'm sorry, I thought you were someone else. Who are you, anyway?" And what are you doing in my crime scene?

He had a firm handshake, as well as other things. He was tall and dark-haired and had brown eyes and broad shoulders and a lot of other things Sonora liked.

"Hal McCarty."

"What exactly are you doing, Mr. McCarty?"

"Interfering in your crime scene, detective. You look annoyed. Or maybe you're just embarrassed."

"Hard to tell, isn't it?"

"I'm a neighbor—I lease the barn next door." He nodded his head to the right, frowned, voice dropping. "Dixon stopped by my house earlier and asked me to help him find Joelle."

"What time was that?"

"A little before six."

She heard the swish of footsteps and turned. Sam. Still wearing the wrinkled khakis and sport coat he'd had on when they parted no more than two hours ago.

"Mr. McCarty, if you'll stand to the side over there, I'd like to ask you a few more questions, once I've come up to speed."

"Look, detective—"

But she was turning away. She saw, from the corner of her eye, that he did not look happy to be dismissed, but he moved away, turning once and giving her a second look over his shoulder to see if she was still watching.

She was.

"About time you got here." Sam ran a hand through his hair, which blew every which way in the wind. He had loosened his tie.

"That's mine," she said, pointing to said tie.

"You gave it to me."

"I did not."

He took her elbow, pulled her toward a knot of technicians—two she recognized.

"What are you eating?" Sonora asked.

"Starbursts."

"Give me a pink one."

"I ate the pink ones. I've got red ones, cherry okay? Want to see the blood?"

She nodded. "Yes I want to see the blood, and yes I want a red one."

He handed her a Starburst. "Over here."

She unwrapped the candy, thinking that as bloodstains went, she'd seen better. But this one belonged to a fifteen-year-old girl, and Sonora sighed deeply and stepped closer. She bent down, squinted. Blood had pooled thickly, soaking up loose dirt and making a puddle like black-red gelatin in an area about the size of a football. A worn black riding boot, knee-high, English, lay sideways about four feet away.

"More here, on the fence. We figure she fell off her horse, hit her head good, and went down."

Sonora stepped sideways and looked at the top of the fence line. The wood had an indentation, and the top was soaked with blood and clotted with bits of tissue and long brown hair.

"Just to confirm, but Joelle Chauncey *is* a brunette?"

Sam jerked a finger toward McCarty. "He says so."

"What does the *father* say?"

"He was in the office with the shakes, and McCarty was handy, okay?"

"Fine, okay. He just seems to be wandering pretty freely around my crime scene."

"It's my crime scene too."

"Yeah, Sam, but it ain't no party. He ID the boot?"

"Not definite. *You* notice shoes?"

"Sure."

"Yeah, but you're female."

Sonora looked over her shoulder at Mickey, strong, squat, working moulage impressions of something about a hundred yards away. Tire tracks? She flicked a finger at the fence line, the clots of hair, blood, and tissue. "CSU get samples of this?"

"Gosh no, Sonora, nobody does any work till *you* get here."

"Fine, but we got a track, Sam, and I don't see shepherds. You call canine?"

Sam put a hand on her shoulder. "Please don't be hurt when I tell you I took care of that already."

"How long till they get here?"

"Not coming. The shepherds look for broken grass, anything to tell them where the trail goes. This place is full of tracks—horses heading every which way. Impossible for the shepherds. We do have a chopper on the way. Infrared heat sensors and NVGs. They might spot something."

"And they might not." Sonora looked up at the sky, thinking about rain. A lot of acres here, and it was coming dark. The child could be anywhere.

She heard the horn of a train, the background roar of wheels on tracks. It sounded a long way away.

"We need Bella, Sam."

"That's a hell of an idea. Doesn't Mickey have an in with her handler?"

"Related, I think." Sonora looked at the downed section of fence, trying to imagine the scene. A young girl on horseback. Something had crashed through the wood. Spooked the horse, maybe, causing the fall. She looked at Sam, inclined her head. "What caused that, do you think?"

Sam shrugged. "Big enough for a pickup to go through. The ground's pretty soft from the rain we had over the week- end. Mickey's got tire tracks."

"Any chance the horse kicked it through? I bet a horse could break a fence down if it really wanted to. If it was scared."

Sam looked at her. "If a horse could break a fence through, then why are all these horses still penned up?"

"I think a horse could kick a fence down if it was really scared, Sam."

"Okay, girl, come see for yourself." He headed for the fence, and she followed. He handed her another Starburst. Lemon.

"You got tire tracks leading up to the break here—looks like the tread of a Dually pickup, there's two tire prints side by side there." He touched a splinter of wood. "Streaks of green paint, Sonora, which horses rarely leave. Plus, the wood is splintered on both ends." He held up a board that had been torn away. "The break is symmetrical. Similar lines of break- age on both sides, so the force of the impact is pretty evenly divided. A horse is going to break the wood on one side. And if you look closer here, there's no sign of mane or tail hairs, like a horse smashed a slat, then squeezed through, breaking the board off."

Sonora bent over, studying the wood. "And the break goes inward, toward the field. So somebody just drove up and crashed on through." Sonora looked at Sam. He was chewing. She smelled oranges.

She straightened up, touched the small of her back. "Did you notice McCarty?"

"I notice you did."

"His sleeve, Sam. Looks like blood to me. A few hours fresh. Go check and see what you think. I'm going to talk to Mickey."

"About the tracks?"

"About Bella."

* * *

Mickey was on his knees with a tape measure, inspecting a tire track. "Shoulda done this one. Would have come out crisper." He saw Sonora, got up. "What?"

"What do you mean 'what'?" Sonora asked.

"Don't mess with me, kid, I had a cavity filled this morning, and the Novocain is wearing off."

"Talk to me, Mickey."

He tilted his head to one side. "Big old Dually pickup. Four tires in the back, two in the front. And what looks like a new patch on the left front tire. Might check the repair places in the vicinity. And Sonora, pay attention. From the depth of the tracks, back ones in particular, I'd say the truck was pulling a load."

Sonora looked at him. "Load, as in . . . horse trailer?"

Mickey shrugged. "What better way to get rid of a horse?"

"So what you're saying is a truck and trailer ran through that fence."

"I'll get you the make, year, and model by tomorrow."

"You work miracles, get it by tonight."

"Tomorrow at the latest. Looks like there's at least two sets of tracks here, both trucks. And I got paint traces. Teal green. Paint can narrow the make down to two years at the worst. And clearly the truck that went through that fence is damaged."

"You're good, baby, I got to say it."

"If I had a dollar for every time a woman has told me that." He gave her a second look. "Wait a minute. That's the same tone of voice my ex-wife uses when she wants an advance on the child support."

"Do you give it to her?"

"Always."

"Did you know that you look down and then sideways to the right when you lie?"

"No kidding? I got to fix that. Usually I look to the left."

"You know Officer Murty, don't you? Isn't she a cousin of yours?"

"Daughter-in-law."

"She still working Bella?"

"Uh-huh." Mickey rubbed his chin. Looked out over the back paddock. "You know they got a chopper coming?"

"I heard that, yeah."

"But you want Bella?"

"I need her tonight. I can call Crick if you want, I don't mind going through channels. But you could get to her faster. If there's any chance this kid is still alive—"

He checked his watch. "Lucy will know where she is. Give me five."

She wanted to be sassy and say "five what?" but part of the detective's art was knowing when to shut up.

5

Sam had McCarty cornered by the fence and was waving Sonora over.

She went slowly, hands in her pockets. Looked pointedly at McCarty's rolled-up sleeve. Some killers can't resist being part of the investigation, she thought.

"Mr. McCarty able to explain the bloodstain on his sleeve to your satisfaction?"

"*Doctor* McCarty," Sam told her. "Guy's a vet."

"That makes it all better."

McCarty was unrolling the sleeve, holding it away from his arm so they could all take a look. "It's blood."

"Cut yourself shaving this morning?"

McCarty gave her a look. "And you looked so bright. This is Joelle's blood. I was the first one on the scene, remember?" He looked from Sonora to Sam. "You have a problem with this? Let's put your mind at rest. Search my house and barn. Feel free, I've got nothing to hide."

Sonora waited for him to say "trust me," but he didn't. She smiled at him. "The last guy who told me he had nothing to hide kept a torso in his Sears deep freeze. So thanks very much, we will search your house and barn."

"You talking about that district attorney?"

Sonora nodded. She almost felt like they were talking shop.

"In the meantime, you might want to put out an APB, or even set up roadblocks, to stop every horse van between here"—McCarty stopped to look at his watch—"and about a two-hundred-mile radius."

"That's a hell of a radius." Sonora cocked her head sideways. "What makes you think a horse van went through here?"

"It's a possibility, don't you think? With a horse missing? You got a guy looking at tracks, what does he think?"

"I want your shirt," Sonora said.

"Fine. If you wind up stopping vans, ask for a Coggins test. Anyone transporting horses is supposed to carry one. Very possible that whoever came through here won't have one."

"Thanks for your help," Sam said.

Sonora gave McCarty a hard stare. "We'll take the shirt, for now. And take you up on your offer to show us around. Your house and barn."

He held out his wrists. Smiled at Sonora. "You can handcuff me if you want."

"Some other time."

6

MCCARTY PAUSED outside a small and dingy cinder-block house that sat no more than fifty yards from a small concrete barn trimmed in red, about a third the size of Delaney's barn.

"It's not locked." McCarty waved a hand toward the front door of his house.

Sonora motioned the two uniforms she had grabbed to step back off the porch. "Take him on in," she told Sam.

McCarty nodded at her and walked in ahead of Sam without looking back.

Something about him.

Sonora turned to the uniforms. Both young, male, short haircuts, and on testosterone overload. She wished she hadn't sent Renquist off with Dixon Chauncey. She could use two or three of that man.

She started with their names, making them introduce themselves since she didn't know them. Majors was the black one. Hill was white.

"Officer Majors. Officer Hill. Let's start with what you already know. Female, fifteen years old, brown hair. You saw the blood. Likely severe head injury and God knows what else. Dr. McCarty is 'assisting' us in our investigation. That's information you will keep to yourselves."

Both of them nodded. Brows knit and on their toes.

"We have the owner's permission, and we have probable cause. What we don't have is a warrant, so don't take an ax to the place, you got me? But you make sure that there is no chance that a fifteen-year-old girl is in there listening to you walk through the halls, praying that you'll have the imagination to open the right door or check under the cellar stairs. That make sense?"

They nodded, heads synchronized, like puppets on a string.

"Go. And Hill?"

"Yes, ma'am?"

"Holster your weapon."

The house disappointed her. It was not the kind of house she would have pictured for McCarty.

The kitchen was small and would have been state of the art in the early sixties. The cabinets were yellow enamel over metal, and there was actually a dusty red-checked curtain above the small window over the sink, which was full of dishes. The countertops were clear, and there was an old-fashioned mixer that gave Sonora a pang. It was a big Bobbie, white enamel, with black trim. Her mom had one just like it when she was growing up.

McCarty waited for them on the front porch, leaning against the rust-stained cinder block, arms folded. He had surrendered the denim shirt and now wore a sweatshirt that said "Hawley-Cooke Booksellers" on the front. He waited with no sign of impatience while they went through the depressing bathroom, rust stains around the drain, and the small bedroom, which was dusty and held nothing more than a double bed, walnut frame, white chenille bedspread, a small dresser, and a red braided throw rug over the battered wooden floor.

He did not seem concerned at the number of times the uniforms tramped up and down the short hallway and went back through rooms, cabinets, and hallways they had been through minutes before. He waited with infinite patience until the uniforms were satisfied. Raised an eyebrow at Sonora when she followed the uniforms back out onto the porch.

"Right this way, officers. Part two of the evening tour. McCarty's barn."

The barn was small, eight stalls, well lit and clean, with a freshly swept asphalt breezeway. Sonora breathed in the tang of horse and fresh hay. Three of the stalls were occupied, and the horses nickered low in their throats when Sam and Sonora walked in. The doors were open on either side, and the wind blew through, making her shiver.

She opened a door into a tack room. Curious bits of leather and rope dangled from hooks on the wall. Pitchforks and shovels were wedged in a corner. A dark green feed bin hugged the front wall. Sonora lifted the lid—both sides were full of a yellow mixture of oats, pellets, and corn. She picked up a sticky handful and smelled it, tasted it with the tip of her tongue.

Sam looked over her shoulder. "Eat up, Sonora, I'm all out of Starbursts."

She rolled her eyes at him, wandered back into the aisleway, and slid a stall door open slowly, peering around the edge.

"Horse?" Sam asked.

Sonora gave him a look over her left shoulder. "Quit following me around and search the other side."

"Why? What do you think is in the stall across from this one? A pig?"

Sonora moved across in front of him and slid the door open.

The horse, ankle deep in pine-wood shavings, looked at them over his shoulder, then went back to munching from a rack of beige-gold hay. The stall was cozy, well bedded. Beads of water lined the lip of a bucket that had recently been filled with fresh water.

Sam opened the next door. "Another horse, Sonora."

"Stay with it, Sam. I'm going up in the hayloft."

She headed up wood slats nailed to the wall outside the tack room door. The ladder was made for longer-legged people than Sonora—she had to stretch to make each rung. She kept going slowly, thinking maybe she didn't like heights.

She pulled herself up and onto the wooden flooring. It was dim in the hayloft, dusty, a layer of old hay over aged wooden slats. A pitchfork rested against a splintered support beam, and strings of orange baling twine dangled from a nail. Hay bales were stacked to the edge of the loft, leaving an eight-inch ledge for walking.

Cozy.

Strips of dusky half light filtered in through cracks in the wood. Sonora squinted. Looked for hay bales that were disturbed, coated with blood, or bulging with body parts.

"Shit," Sam said below her. She heard him moving in and out of stalls. Then footsteps in the aisleway.

Sonora grabbed hold of a support beam and looked over the edge of the loft. Majors and Hill, with McCarty between them. McCarty lifted a hand and waved.

Sonora looked at her uniforms. "What?"

"Mickey said to tell you your kids have been calling. They're out of emergency meals and want to know what to do about dinner."

Sonora nodded. "Anything else?"

"Bella is here."

7

SONORA HEARD BELLA before she saw her—118 pounds of rust-red bloodhound, sitting on the seat of a little beige Mazda pickup. The dog had her head straining over the top of a half-open window. Her ears reached just below the bottom of her jaw, and her wrinkled face looked soft and touchable. Rivulets of saliva dripped from her jaw and slid down the glass of the window.

She was beautiful, Sonora thought.

"Sonora?" The driver's door slammed, and a woman walked around the back of the truck. She moved slowly, her gait off and clumsy.

"Helen?"

Helen Murty was in uniform, sort of, looking a very uncomfortable seven months pregnant. She had curly black hair, collar length, brown eyes, and a square jaw. Her face was memorable if not pretty, her skin a smooth deep brown.

Sonora stared at the belly. "Oh my God."

"If you were a guy, they could prosecute you for that remark."

"It's working with men that makes me act this way."

Murty put a hand to the small of her back. "There's always some way to blame it on 'em, right?"

"What I meant to say was congratulations, and don't you look fabulous." Sonora spoke with the two-faced relief of a woman who has been there and never plans to go back. Then headed, gratefully, back to business. "I need your dog, Helen, but you'll never keep up."

"I can handle it. Doctor says walking's good for me, it'll make my labor shorter."

"Yeah, they always say that. I've had two, so don't give me that macho pregnant bullshit. You up on the details of this situation?"

Helen waved a hand, and the dog jumped, toenails scrabbling the headrest. "Be good, Bella." The dog sat back down, but her nose was out the window. "We've got a missing girl, fifteen years old, *not* a runaway. Crime scene is clear, she went off a horse, and if she's not dead, she's hurt bad. Anything else?"

She's got two little sisters, Sonora thought, looking out over the farm. Dusk had thickened down to full dark.

"Where's the horse?" Helen asked.

"Disappeared, along with the girl."

Helen's mouth opened, closed. "Weird."

"She could be anywhere. Body stashed God knows where in the fields. Somebody may have stuffed her in a pickup and horse trailer and taken off, in which case—"

"Bella can still find her." Helen had that smug look, like a woman who knows her dog.

"They may have hit the interstate."

"Bella can still find her, even if she got stuffed in a car and driven for miles. We'll check every exit. Bella will know. She'll pick the scent up from the car's exhaust system. You can't fool this dog."

"What about the horse? Will that throw her off?"

"Not unless she's riding it, honey. Bella's trained to scent human."

"I'm everybody's straight man tonight," Sonora said. It was becoming a public service. "Helen, it's awfully dark out."

"Sonora, how long you been a cop? I always get called when

the sun goes down. Missing kids and felons rarely check my schedule.''

"I mean you."

"Main problem is me falling on my ass."

"Anybody else handle the dog?"

"You know better. Nobody can read her but me, Sonora. Quit worrying. Ernie will be going along for protection."

"And Ernie would be?"

"Shepherd. Can't remember the officer's name who runs him, but I called, they should be here any minute. In case we run into the guy took this kid. Bella will track this girl, and Ernie will eat up anybody who gets in our way." Helen patted the dog's head. "Your boyfriend's coming, isn't he, Bella?" She looked at Sonora, hand resting on the mound of belly. "It's a fifteen-year-old kid, you know? My first is almost fifteen. And it's getting cold out. We'll go."

"Did you just have a contraction?"

"Braxton-Hicks, fake labor, I been getting them for weeks. Sonora?"

"Yeah?"

"This doesn't work out, I have a friend who's got a bloodhound that's a good cadaver dog. Scent over water, anything. Just give it four or five days to cook."

8

Sᴏɴᴏʀᴀ ᴄᴏᴜʟᴅ ɴᴏᴛ remember where she had heard the adage that the more wrinkles in a bloodhound's soft face, the better a tracker the dog would be. Something about the folds of skin catching scent from the air.

She squatted down on her heels and watched the dog run in circles around Helen, who was buckling Bella into a leather harness. Bella's tail was wagging, and her head was up. She looked at Helen with adoration. Helen looked up at Sonora and grinned.

"The harness means time to go to work. And this dog loves to work."

Helen looked over her shoulder at a tall slender man with a pockmarked face and a sour attitude. A German shepherd sat at his feet with the air of being on coiled springs. "You ready, Ernie?"

"Yeah," the officer said, face going soft when he looked at his dog. "Ernie's ready. I am too."

"I wasn't worried about you, Officer Carl." Helen grinned and looked at Sonora. "You got that riding boot handy? We need to cast a scent."

Sonora pointed to the boot, which sat untouched in the dust. Helen led the dog close.

"Scent, Bella."

Bella was all over the boot, sniffing, circling, then sniffing again. Ernie sat at attention, ears pricked forward, watching Bella with what Sonora could have sworn was envy.

Bella sniffed the pool of blood, went paws up on the fence to sniff the hair, blood clots, and tissue. She circled among the bloodstain, the boot, and the fence line.

"Come on, girl, go get 'em. Let's go, girl, come on, let's get 'em." Helen glanced at Sonora. "Don't worry. She's in a big pool of scent right now. She'll find her way clear."

The dog veered right suddenly, toward the broken slats of fence. "She's got it!" Helen shouted, voice wavering as she moved out at breakneck speed with the dog. "Come on, Carl, get Ernie in gear."

There was clearly nothing the shepherd wanted more than to go after Bella and Helen. Officer Carl gave the command, and he and his dog headed off in the dark.

Sonora watched them go, feeling left out.

9

Sonora leaned back in the Taurus, closed her eyes.

"I found a box of macaroni and cheese," her son said over the cell phone. It was a good connection. His disgust came through loud and clear. "When are you going to the grocery store?"

"Soon," Sonora said.

"You always say that."

"Maybe you should go."

"I have homework."

"Oh, are you actually going to do it tonight?"

"Mom. Don't yell at me."

"There are Oreo cookies stashed under my bed."

"Not anymore. Look, I'm expecting a call. We'll eat the macaroni and cheese, I got to go. Oh. Heather has to stay after school tomorrow. Bye."

He hung up, and she saw Sam heading toward the trailer. Sonora slammed the Taurus door and ran after him.

"Sam!"

He stopped and waited. "Kids okay?"

"Scrounging up a box of macaroni and cheese for dinner."

"Mother of the year."

"Shut up. I have actual guilt here, and you're not helping."

She took a breath. The moon was coming up orange, an autumn moon, a harvest moon. Sonora turned her flashlight off, looked up at the sky. You could see a lot of stars without the competition of neon lights and city jazz.

"You look cold." Sam pulled her jacket up close around her neck. Buttoned the top button. "I left Donna Delaney on the phone with Crick. He put out an APB on a teal green Dually pickup with or without a horse trailer in tow. He's got a description of Joelle, but he wants something a little more specific than 'brown' for the horse."

Sonora folded her arms and took a deep breath, sucking in cold air. "McCarty's thing about the Coggins test sounded good."

"Yeah, I filled Crick in. He didn't have the slightest idea what I was talking about. Sonora, come on, let's wait in Delaney's office. At least it's warm in there."

"Let's hit Chauncey's trailer, take a look in Joelle's room." She switched the flashlight on, aiming the pool of yellow light at Sam's feet. "We can go through the paddock with the horses or walk all the way around past the barn."

"I can climb the fence if you can."

They headed across the field, feet noisy as they threaded through tall weeds.

"What do you think of McCarty?" Sam asked. "Keep the light still, Sonora, or give it here."

"He's cute."

"I mean the blood on his shirt."

"He could be lying; he could be telling the truth."

"Can't get nothing past you. Stop, Sonora."

"What?"

"Fence."

"I knew that. Take the light while I go over. I wonder where the horses are."

"Close enough to touch."

They were. Standing quietly, dark shapes over the fence, in bunches of two and three. Sonora heard a soft snort.

She started up the fence, careful of her pants. Her legs were short, so she had to go all the way up to the next-highest slat before she could swing her feet over. She teetered sideways.

"Need help?" Sam steadied her arm. The flash arced sideways, catching two of the horses, standing nearby. They shied, feet pounding.

"Great, Sam, now you've spooked the horses."

"It would have spooked them worse when you fell over the fence and landed on their necks. At least this way nobody gets hurt."

Sonora climbed down the other side of the fence. "Hard as hell to catch a horse at night, wouldn't you think? Especially if you wanted just one in particular?"

Sam handed her the flashlight. "What are you thinking?"

"Just that if someone wanted a fifteen-year-old girl, it would be easier to take her without the horse. Maybe they wanted the horse."

Sam's feet hit the ground, and he grabbed the flashlight. "So they come in the afternoon, when the place is usually dead."

"On a Tuesday, when nobody is supposed to be riding."

"And Joelle Chauncey just happens to be in the wrong place at the wrong time."

"Horse in jeopardy becomes kid in jeopardy."

"It's a theory."

Even in the dark, Sonora could tell that Dixon Chauncey had made the most of what he had. The cinder-block steps leading to the worn aluminum doorway had been whitewashed and recently swept. Six feet of weed and scrub around the trailer were starting to encroach, but a Weed Eater, propped next to the front step, indicated good intentions. Four bicycles and a scooter were stacked in a neat row to one side. Three of the bikes were rusty and old, one was brand new—silver and blue with pink plastic streamers hanging from the white rubber grips.

Somebody had a birthday, Sonora thought.

The bottom section of screen in the storm door was bowed out, as if a small child or dog habitually pressed against the ancient mesh. A hole in the center had recently been patched, the new square of metal dark and stiff.

Sam knocked so quietly, Sonora did not think they would be heard.

Renquist must have been watching for them. He opened the door immediately—thin wood with little arrow-shaped windows that filtered small amounts of light. Sonora found them depressing.

Renquist had that up-all-night look. Shirt slightly loose in the waistband, top collar unbuttoned, clothes wrinkled with the wear of a very long day. His face looked more heavily lined than it had earlier, and his eyes were dark circled.

"There's coffee," he said as they walked in the door.

The inside of the trailer had the hushed air of people sleeping. Sonora and Sam walked quietly. The floor creaked under their feet. The trailer had that mobile-home feel of fragility and impermanence. It would be cozy enough, except during tornadoes.

The carpet was new, the color of mushrooms, and far superior to what Sonora had in her house. The living room furniture was masculine and new, a brown leather sofa, matching recliner, and a rocking chair that had a tasseled green cushion on the seat. The television was state-of-the-art home theater, with a sound system that included separate speakers, a long slim presence by the screen. A bookshelf, oak pressboard, had a three-year collection of *Reader's Digest*. The top shelf was devoted entirely to Bryer horses.

The coffee smell was strong—the pot had likely been sitting on the burner for hours. There was a background presence of popcorn.

Chauncey came at them from the kitchen, limping a little, like his left hip was stiff and he'd gotten up too fast. He looked like he'd been crying—Renquist had had his hands full. The kitchen was tiny and very neat, and there were cards on the maple wood table—Chauncey and Renquist were playing double solitaire.

Chauncey was pulling out kitchen chairs as if they were visiting royalty.

"Mr. Chauncey, we haven't found your daughter yet, but—"

The sound of a helicopter made them all look up. Sam gave Sonora a look, and she nodded.

She pointed to the ceiling. "That's ours. The pilot has NVGs—"

"Night vision goggles?" Chauncey asked.

Sam nodded. "I know this guy. He's good."

Chauncey's eyes narrowed. "Are these starlight goggles? The AN-PVS 7s? Like they used in Desert Storm?"

Sonora caught Sam's quick look. Not a good idea to underestimate this guy. She didn't know if the pilot was using the starlight goggles or the heat-tracking thermals, but since the latter implied a search for a cadaver, she decided it would be good to move on. No sense discussing heat sources and decomposing bodies.

"We've also got a bloodhound on her trail."

Chauncey met her gaze full on. This man clearly put more stock in dogs than helicopters. She had not realized how bright a blue his eyes were. There was an odd quality about them she could not quite describe—but it was a look she associated with religious paintings and stained glass windows. She had never seen such a thing in the flesh.

She looked away, unable to hold his gaze.

10

CHAUNCEY STOOD in the hallway and waved a hand. "Right here."

Sam stepped ahead of him and opened the first door. "Oops. Think I've got the wrong one."

"That's Mary Claire and Kippie. Joelle's room is here, right next door."

Sonora stood on tiptoe and looked over Sam's shoulder. Two little girls sat on the bottom bunk of a white metal bunkbed. Sonora recognized the little one as the girl who had been standing on the front porch of the trailer in red sweatshirt and shorts. She had the warm, pink, well-scrubbed look of a child fresh from the tub. Her hair was golden and damp, and her tiny nose was running. She wiped it on the sleeve of the worn yellow plaid flannel men's shirt she wore as a nightgown. She was sitting cross-legged, back slumped, hugging a stuffed Winnie the Pooh.

"I'm sorry," Sam said. "We're in the wrong room."

"We're reading *Jemima Puddleduck*." This from the older child, a thin girl who had the air of being tall for her age. Her eyes were close together, and she wore glasses and a worried look. Her nose was a little large, her chin pointed, and her face held a haunted look of uncertainty that looked habitual.

The smaller, Kippie, was cute in the way of kittens, but it was the older girl that Sonora wanted to gather up and hug.

Mary Claire bit her bottom lip. "Are you going to find my sister?"

"That's why we're here," Sonora said. She did not want to lie, she did not want to raise false hopes, and she wanted to make it all better. "You don't have any idea where Joelle is, do you?" She felt, rather than saw, Chauncey going tense behind her in the short tight hallway.

"No, ma'am." Mary Claire's voice was soft and low. Kippie grabbed her hand and watched them with button brown eyes, and Sonora knew that they would not get a word out of this one.

"We'll let you get back to your book." She backed into the hallway. Heard Mary Claire say "Poppie" in a small voice.

"Be right back," Chauncey told her. He moved ahead of Sam, opened the door to Joelle's tiny bedroom, shook his head. "I'm sorry, it's a terrible mess." He spoke in a stage whisper so his voice would not carry through the thin door of the next bedroom, where the girls were looking at pictures of Jemima Puddleduck.

Sonora hated it when people whispered.

Renquist hung his head out of the kitchen. "Mr. Chauncey, can I make you a fresh pot of coffee?"

Chauncey shook his head. "I'm fine, really."

Wasn't going to budge, Sonora thought.

"Would you mind, then, if I made a new pot for the detectives?"

It was the first time Sonora had seen Chauncey look irritable. "Go on ahead, just help yourself."

"I know you showed me where the filters were, but—"

"Be right back." Chauncey headed back to the kitchen, moving quickly with his peculiar walk that hinted of a limp barely suppressed.

Sonora smiled to herself. Renquist really was good. Sam closed the door behind them.

The bedroom was compact, messy—the middle of the floor

clearly reserved for discarded clothing and schoolbooks. The
closet door bulged outward along the bottom, something red
stuffed under the crack next to the floor. Bookshelves ran
along all sides of the walls, and there were enough partially
full glasses of milk to make Sonora doubt there would be anything left to drink out of in the kitchen. On the windowsill, a
bean plant grew gloriously out of a Burger King cup.

It was clearly the year of the horse and Brad Pitt—with post-
ers of both crowding the walls for space. Men and horses.
Sonora could relate.

The kid was still into Disney. Mickey Mouse phone, Snow
White figurines, and an Aladdin pencil box.

Sonora stayed in the doorway, blocking Sam, taking it all in.
The room was dusty and ill kept, a depressing place to be for
hours and hours a day. She did not get a happy feel here.
What fifteen-year-old is happy? she wondered.

"You letting me in?" Sam nudged her gently, moving her to
one side. Hands on her shoulder, a quick squeeze, strong fingers.

Sonora thought of McCarty, who would probably turn out
to be some kind of sociopath—swelling the ranks of the de-
mented and the cute.

Mind back on the here and now. "I'll take the dresser and
the desk, Sam. You get the shelves."

He groaned. "This looks like Annie's room."

"Heather and Tim are worse."

"I've seen your house, Sonora, no contest."

There was makeup on the dresser—blue eyeshadow,
L'Oréal, Cover Girl lipstick, mascara from Maybelline. All of it
old and crusty, as if Joelle had tried it once or twice and let it
be. Fifteen years old. Experimenting.

Sonora's head was hurting.

The top dresser drawer jammed when she opened it, and
she yanked it hard. It was stuffed full—tights and pantyhose
snarled around cheap beaded necklaces and faux gold chains.
A white leather belt was intertwined with an Indian headband,
complete with crumpled feathers—the kind of thing you got

in roadside souvenir shops. A headless Barbie doll from by-gone days, cassette tapes of the Cranberries, Smashing Pump-kins, and a couple of groups Sonora's children would likely recognize. The soundtrack from *Babe*.

The second drawer held school papers and worn twisted bras, size 34A. The other drawers were almost empty, with the exception of a hunter green sweatshirt that said "Indian Hill Headhunters" in the bottom drawer. Sonora laughed under her breath. Empty drawers in the dresser. All her clothes on the floor.

She went to the desk, the surface crowded with books and an open statement from Community Trust Bank. Sonora opened the envelope and learned that Joelle Chauncey had eight dollars and thirty-seven cents in savings.

In the back of Sonora's mind were her own kids, Tim and Heather, with rooms much too much like this one.

Tim had about a year on Joelle, and on the rare occasions when she was in his room—usually when there were no more glasses or spoons left in the kitchen and she'd gone after his mold-encrusted collection—she'd seen the same disturbing mix. A bumper sticker touting the joys of the latest street drug (defiance from the son of a cop) alongside a pair of chopsticks from a dinner out. A plastic yellow duck and a sign that said "Start a Movement, Eat a Prune." And in a pile on the floor, three dirty pairs of socially correct blue jeans, three sizes too big.

Was Joelle Chauncey allowed to buy socially correct blue jeans? Or had Dixon Chauncey insisted on building character and ignoring teenage insecurities and snobberies and buying what was on sale?

Sonora sat at the desk and opened the drawers, hearing Sam moving things on and off the shelves, shifting the mat-tress on the bed. It was comfortable, having him in the room with her, knowing him so well that she could predict his move-ments with her back turned.

The desk drawer held magazines, *Seventeen* and *Sassy*, well read, judging by the rings of Coke, folds, and wrinkles. A catalog from Delia's. She shut the drawer, but it would not close, hitting something along the back.

In her experience, teenagers were elusive and secretive creatures—especially living in close quarters with too much family in a trailer home.

For a teenager, any family was too much.

Sonora pulled the center drawer out of its slot and fingered the inner recess of the desk.

Paper—an envelope. She pulled and it stuck, then peeled away.

"She's got something taped to the back of the desk." Sonora looked at Sam's back. He turned, brushed brown hair back out of his eyes with a familiar gesture that was curiously adolescent, crossed the room to take a look.

The envelope was addressed to End Point Farm and had been wadded, then smoothed. Sonora pictured Joelle removing it from the trash in Donna Delaney's office.

It was thick. She pulled out a sheaf of magazine and newspaper clippings, flipped through, scanning the headlines.

"Adoptive Son Finds Birth Mother in Homeless Shelter" . . . "Girl Finds Sister She Never Knew She Had" . . . a *National Enquirer* article called "The Search: Should You Look?" . . . "A Mother's Search" . . . "Adoption. What Happens to Your Child?" . . . "Who Am I?", *Seventeen* magazine.

Banded together with the articles was a stack of the kind of cards that come in the mail with advertisements, a coupon for an oil change on one side, the face of a missing child on the other. A big stack, maybe a hundred cards, a collection from the gallery of lost souls.

Sonora felt sweat break out on her temples, and her chest went tight, her stomach in a sudden flutter.

Sam tapped the *Enquirer* article. "Annie went through a phase like this when she was five maybe, or six. Every night when Shelly helped her wash her hair, she'd say, 'Tell me the truth, Mommy. I'm adopted, aren't I?' Did Heather—Sonora? You okay?"

She put her head in her hands. It had hit this way before, dealing with kids in situations like this one.

Sam rubbed the back of her neck, waiting her out. "Take deep breaths." He knew just to leave her alone.

11

O<small>UTSIDE THE TRAILER</small>, Sam and Sonora were met with cold air, the strobe lights of an ambulance, and Helen's voice, shrill, carrying in the darkness, as they scrambled over the fence and headed for the circus.

"I am *not* in labor, I am *not* going anywhere in an ambulance, and I am *not* going home."

As Sonora got closer, she could see that Helen was crying, tears of rage, and Ernie and Bella were much too excited, running in circles around Helen and Officer Carl.

The blades of the chopper were fading. Was he circling or leaving? Sonora wondered. Joelle was still not found.

Helen caught sight of Sonora. "She had the scent. She *had* it."

Carl folded his arms. "She lost it, Helen, admit it. And you're in labor, for God's sake."

Helen clenched her teeth. "*Braxton-Hicks,* you dumb shit, and a lot you know about it."

Sonora touched Helen's arm, motioned her away from the men.

"Take a breath."

"Sonora—"

"Take a breath, Helen, it's okay."

Helen pushed hair out of her eyes. Leaned against the fence.

"*Are* you in labor?" Sonora asked.

"Shit, I don't know, I don't think so."

"I went to the hospital three times with Heather before she finally came."

Helen took off her jacket. "It's hot, goddammit."

Sonora, shivering so much her voice shook, tried not to smile.

"I've been having these fucking contractions since September, but they don't hurt, so they're not the goods."

"When are you due?"

"Late in December. After Christmas."

"What happened with the dog?"

"We had the scent, Sonora, Bella was going strong. She got a little confused out on the road, that's all, then Officer Carl—"

Sonora waited. Looked at Helen. "Not so painless?"

"Not too bad."

"Look, Helen, your baby's not due for two months. Get off your feet, and don't push this."

"It's cold out, Sonora, for normal people who don't have a thousand hormones slogging through their bods. This girl could die of exposure tonight."

"We've got the chopper," Sonora said. Life was full of hard calls.

Helen grabbed her wrist. "Look, I'm going home awhile, put my feet up. Give it a couple to three hours. You meet me back out here daylight, I'm taking Bella out again. And we'll leave that asshole Carl behind. We got a deal?"

Sonora nodded. "Provided you don't have that baby tonight."

12

SONORA WAS SOAKING in a tepid bubble bath when the call came in.

She had the CD player sitting on the back of the toilet and was listening to Janis Joplin sing "Piece of My Heart," thinking BoyZ II Men might have been more restful in her present frame of mind. She was craving a cold Corona but had nixed the idea because one, she didn't have any, and two, a beer would have made her sleepy enough to drown in the tub.

The bubble bath, a Mother's Day gift from Heather, was a big success—a mango pineapple blend that produced firm, prolific bubbles. Sonora turned the hot water on full blast to warm up.

She had maybe a half hour left to sleep or loll in the tub before pretending to get the kids ready for school—wandering around sleepily while they did what they had to do.

The phone kept ringing. She couldn't think of anybody she wanted to talk to. She was getting too old for this up-all-night shit.

Sonora reached through a crest of white foam to grab the cordless phone. Janis segued over to "Summertime."

"What?"

"Blair? Sergeant Crick." He paused. "Is that Janis Joplin?"

"Yeah."

"Turn it down."

Sonora reached out and killed the music. She shivered, sank back down in the water.

"It's five thirty A.M., sir."

"If I want to know the time, Blair, there's a number I can call. You sound like you're down in a well."

"I'm taking a bubble bath, sir."

"Spare me the details of your personal life, detective, and dry off the rubber ducky."

Sonora sat up. "They found the kid."

"No. But there's—"

"Guy with the chopper still out?"

"They've called him in twice, man won't go home. Says he's got a stepson the same age."

Everyone was a parent under the skin.

"Sonora, pay attention. There's been an . . . incident."

Another one of the Chauncey children? Why was she so worried about them?

"An assault."

Sonora stood up, reached for a towel. Water sluiced down her skin. Her thick bath towel, navy blue and oversize, was missing. She grabbed the thin beach towel with the mermaid on it. She should have more towels. If she ever got rich, she would fill two closets with thick cotton towels, and washrags to match, more washrags than the kids could use in a month.

With her kids, that would be a lot of washrags.

"Blair? You with me here?"

"Yes, sir, I'm with you. What kind of incident? Who's the vic?"

"Donna Delaney."

He'd said assault. "How bad?"

"Bad. Call just came through from dispatch. EMTs have her en route to Jewish."

"What happened?"

"Nobody's sure. If I've got it straight . . . way I understand it, she was in her living room all night, doing paperwork, fell asleep on the couch. Woke up this morning to find her left hand bandaged and her right index finger gone.''

Sonora tucked the towel under her right arm. ''What do you mean, gone?''

''I mean somebody amputated the finger.''

''Cut it off?''

''That's what *amputated* means, Blair.''

''While she was asleep? How is that possible?''

''That's what we pay you for. EMT said it was a clean job, but she's in shock. You can hit the hospital later, see what the doctor says. Right now I want you to get over to her house and see what the hell's going on. This can't be a coincidence, coming on top of that missing kid.''

''No kidding. Sir.''

''Put some clothes on.'' He hung up before she did.

Sonora clicked the phone off and grabbed her robe, hanging from a brass hook on the back of the door. Her teeth chattered. She felt cold from the inside out. She belted the robe, shoulders hunched together.

She patted Clampett, the world's best dog, sound asleep outside the bathroom door. He opened and closed his eyes, snorting sleepily. He looked exhausted. Sonora peeped in at the kids, arms folded, her feet making wet prints on the carpet.

The hell with white shirts and ties, she was freezing. She was going to layer herself in two sweaters at least.

Sonora wondered what they had done with the finger.

13

SONORA WORE JEANS—they'd been black once, were now char-
coal, more formal than plain blue denim. Crick wouldn't like
it, but she wasn't going to risk the khakis out on the farm
looking for Joelle Chauncey. She found her favorite oversize
white shirt—Abercrombie & Fitch. After-Christmas sale, she
told everyone, though she'd actually paid full price. She had a
thing about white cotton shirts, but only if they were perfect.

She paused in front of the mirror, glanced over her shoulder at the bed, and debated whether or not to curl up, just for
a minute. She had pulled the new bedspread down, fluffed the
pillows, and laid her favorite quilt out so that she could go
straight from the bubble bath to a warm bed.

Clampett padded past her, jumped to the bed, and curled
up in the center, resting his nose on the quilt.

"What are you doing, dog?"

He snuggled deeper into the quilt, tail wagging.

Sonora wondered why people made jokes about a dog's life.

She went through her ties and found one that had fallen
down behind the lingerie bag, God knew when. She'd forgotten she had it. Hunter green print with just a touch of red. It
was still knotted from way back when, some boyfriend or another had done it for her, someday she'd have to learn to do it

for herself. She tried to learn one good skill from every man she dated.

Sonora tweaked the bottom flap of the tie, left the knot loose and comfortable. Pulled the sides of her hair back with a velvet clip and smeared the eye pencil under her eyes a little so Crick would see how tired she was and not complain about the jeans.

She grabbed a black sweatshirt and a zip cotton jacket that she'd stolen from the last guy who had asked her to marry him. He'd died soon after, caught in the crossfire of a case Sonora tried not to dream about. Bad timing all around. The relationship was coming to an angry end—a month later, and he would not have been a target.

She had been so furious with him.

She could look back now with a certain regret—his hats, his wardrobe, his assumption that he was the center of the universe. But he had not been particularly nice to her children— the cardinal sin, for a single mother. He had not realized what a privilege it was to be accepted into the fold. She wouldn't waste time feeling bad.

She wondered what happened to his clothes. He'd had some kick-ass jackets.

She headed for the kitchen. Food had not magically appeared. There was plenty of dog food for Clampett but next to nothing for the kids. Leftover macaroni and cheese for breakfast? No milk, no cereal, the bread was molded so it wouldn't work out, even toasted with blackberry jelly, which for some reason she had in spades—three unopened jars.

She tapped her finger on the countertop. She needed to get to Delaney's place, and she needed to meet Helen at the farm to look for Joelle. Two places at once.

But the kids had to be fed. And you couldn't send out for breakfast in the morning like it was pizza, and besides, she didn't have any cash.

Motherhood first.

She wound up at a Dairy Mart that had an ATM inside, got cash, and picked out Dunkin' Donuts and a glass bottle of

Tropicana orange juice to take back to the house. And some milk and Frosted Flakes. Broke a twenty—*the* twenty—so she could leave the kids lunch money.

No matter how late she worked tonight, she was going to have to hit the grocery store. She wondered, just for a moment, what other homicide cops did, then remembered that most of them had wives.

Sonora had hit upon a surefire method of staying awake when she was driving and dead tired—budget review and a plan for paying her bills, including short-term projections involving Visa, MasterCard, and the water company, plus a long-term question of how much it was going to cost to send Tim to college, if he changed his mind about his career direction from his current "do you want fries with that?"

It had rained again, and the pavement was drying black to gray. The reflection of headlights on wet asphalt created a hard-ass glare. Her eyes were going. Menopause would be next.

She leaned over the steering wheel and squinted. Reached for the caramel-iced doughnut that sat on a piece of tissue on top of her purse. Slammed on the brakes when the car in front of her changed into her lane and inexplicably slowed. The doughnut slid off the seat and landed next to the accelerator.

She grimaced. Kentucky tags. These people should either stay home or take a course in maniacal driving, like everyone else in Ohio.

Maybe you had to be born with the talent.

Someone honked. Sonora shrugged, leaned down to grab the doughnut. She waved it in the air, pretending that any dirt and dog hairs would magically fall off.

Sometimes you just had to have faith.

Donna Delaney lived in a four-plex off Elsted—not what Sonora expected. She'd pictured a farm of some kind, not the faded yellow brick that had looked snazzy in the seventies but was tired now. Not exactly suburbia either, more like aspirations to.

An asphalt drive ran up one side, to a backyard parking lot with covered carports and a sidewalk to a back door. Sonora left the Pathfinder next to a patrol car and a green Ford Escort. The crime scene van was at the foot of the driveway, blocking everyone in.

Sonora locked her car, glanced over her shoulder. The sun was coming up, the sky going dirty mocha brown. The pavement was still soaked—it had rained more here.

The screen door was propped open. Sonora went into the hallway, spotted muddy tread marks from the wheel of an ambulance gurney. Must have still been raining when the ambulance arrived. Sonora checked her watch. If Delaney had gone out on a stretcher, she'd gone out in shock. She wondered if the woman had been sedated. If she'd be too whacked to talk.

It would take some time, getting used to the idea of waking up with a bandage instead of a finger.

Sonora shook her head, but she was glad she had caught this case. Not the usual drug burn bullshit, marital squabbles, sweeps picking up glassy-eyed hookers on loads. This was one perp she wanted to meet.

If Crick was right and there was no such thing as coincidence, how did the assault on Donna Delaney connect to Joelle and the disappearing horse? There had to be a reason for the timing, a reason Donna Delaney had been attacked today, not yesterday or the day before.

Cause and effect. They were going to have some fun on this one.

A uniform stood outside the doorway—female, brown hairnet and a bun. Crisp and professional at six twenty-seven A.M. Sonora wiped caramel icing off her mouth, flashed the ID.

The woman looked at the doughnut and grinned. Sonora felt old and traditional. What did the new cops eat? Bagels?

"You here when the call came in?" Sonora peered at the

woman's name tag. Yolanda Sikes. "Officer Sikes? Were you here?"

The woman put her hands behind her back and took up the at-ease position you see in the military when soldiers aren't actually at ease.

"No, ma'am."

"All that for 'no, ma'am'?"

"No, sir?"

"Let up, Officer Sikes. I've got teenagers of my very own if I want bullshit this time of morning."

Sonora headed through the door, which opened onto a square slate foyer, four by four, tiny, tracked with mud. The living room branched from the left, old carpet that topsoil shade of beige favored by apartment complexes because it does not show dirt. Only this one was showing dirt—footprints. Sonora looked around the room. Three uniforms and two crime scene guys—Mickey and some guy she didn't know too well. Donald Finch, maybe? Couldn't remember names, a bad trait for a cop.

The living room was messy, layered with dust that had taken months to accumulate. The couch was khaki and faded, but it looked deep and comfortable for all that. A navy blue and yellow quilt was tangled at the bottom, and pillows were propped at the opposite end as if someone had slept there. The coffee table was stacked with magazines, *Equus, Arabian International, Michael Plumb Journal.* There were catalogs from State Line and Wiese. A leather buckle and strap sat next to two cans of Budweiser that Mickey was putting into a plastic Baggie.

Sonora peered at the couch, noticed droplets of blood freshly drying on the carpet and on the arm of the couch.

"Not too messy, considering."

"Considering what?" Mickey asked.

She hadn't realized she'd spoken out loud. "Considering they cut off the finger."

"I saw it," one of the uniforms said. He was a short guy, hair gelled in place, a square sort of head-and-neck arrangement that reminded her of football players.

"You saw the finger?" Sonora asked.

Mickey's head swiveled. "Why didn't you speak up, kid? We been going nuts, trying to find that thing."

"No, no, sir, I mean I saw her after. Saw her hand. It was all bandaged up, looked like a professional job. There wasn't like a pool of blood or nothing."

"Droplets down the side of the couch." Mickey inclined his head, and Sonora went to look.

The blood had already dried, but it looked fresh, just hours old. Not much, just speckles, on the khaki curtain that draped from the bottom of the couch to the floor.

"Not enough blood," Sonora said.

"Yeah, see, the guy taped it up," said the uniform.

Mickey exchanged looks with Sonora, looked back at the uniform. "What guy?"

The uniform frowned, hunched his shoulders together. "You know, the one that, umm, the one that done it. The perp."

"The perp bandaged it up?" Sonora looked back down at the tiny spray of blood, thinking you wouldn't even know it was there unless you looked for it.

The uniform was nodding. "Sick, ain't it?"

Sonora folded her arms. "Let me get this straight. Guy breaks in, cuts off Delaney's finger, and bandages it up, and she sleeps through the whole thing?"

Mickey opened his arms. "Hey, detective, we don't write the script, we just read the scene."

"Well, reread it, this isn't possible."

Mickey pointed to the coffee table. "Lookit, Blair. Two beers, one half full, the other almost three quarters."

"So there was another person."

"Yeah, plus she was drugged, don't you think?"

"What I think is, the whole thing is weirder than shit."

"Sherlock Holmes used to say the same thing all the time." Mickey looked at the uniform. "Put that in your report, kid—

'weirder than shit.' Maybe, if you drink your milk every day, you can grow up to be one of the greats like Blair here.''

Sonora shook her head. ''There's not enough blood, Mickey.''

''Don't look so disappointed, they were neat.''

''My kids should be so neat.''

''Rules out teenagers.''

The uniform opened his notebook. ''Perpetrator is over twenty-one.''

Sonora was beginning to like this kid. She stood up, touched the small of her back. ''Hair on the pillow, Mickey.''

''I'll get to it, Mom.''

Sonora looked over her shoulder at the square-necked uniform, caught his grin. ''You first on the scene?''

He nodded.

''She say anything?''

He referred to his notebook. '' 'Son of a bitch, son of a bitch, son of a bitch.' ''

''That it?'' Sonora asked.

''Like a mantra.''

''How'd the guy get in?''

The uniform led her into the kitchen, pointed to a ground-floor window that was still open, six to eight inches. ''Forced the window, climbed in.''

He pointed to streaks of mud on the windowsill. Sonora looked out. Hedge about waist high. A broken arm of foliage on the ground next to the grass.

''You check out there for footprints?''

''Got a toe smear,'' Mickey said. ''My guess is a male in Adidas, size eleven and a half. *Heavy*. Look for a big guy.''

''That narrows it down,'' Sonora said.

A green Tombstone pizza box, ripped open and empty, sat on the small maple kitchen table over a stack of old mail, newpapers, a pile of towels, and brushes one might use to groom a horse. A rusty hoof-pick sat next to the pizza box, like it had been used to rip the edges. The pizza was still on the stove, more than half of it, sausage, the edges dried and hard.

A stained, smeared pizza cutter was on the counter at the end of a trail of crumbs. Sonora bent over and squinted. Just pizza sauce and cheese.

Be awkward to remove a finger with a pizza cutter anyway, too much sawing. She wondered what the guy had used.

Something scalpel sharp.

Sonora went past Mickey, who was humming under his breath, past the uniform, and into the bedroom. The bed was made up. Sonora touched the edge, and it gave—a waterbed. Looked perfectly comfortable, so why had Delaney been sleeping on the couch? Drugged, Sonora remembered. So someone could cut off her finger.

The bedroom was crowded, too much furniture, like a person who has moved from a large house to a small apartment. None of the furniture was in particularly good condition, though some of the pieces were antiques. There were boxes in one corner, the one on top open. Sonora looked in, saw crumpled and faded ribbons—horse shows, greens, pinks, whites, the occasional blue and red. The box emitted the distinct odor of ancient cat urine.

There were pictures on the wall, of Donna Delaney with children—always around horses. Were they students? Children of her own? Somehow Sonora did not see her in the mommy role, but a little blond boy showed up in enough pictures to make Sonora wonder if the woman had a son.

The pictures looked old. Nothing since the last ten to fifteen years, judging from the clothes. The boy never seemed to grow older than eight, and he looked like Donna, particularly around the eyes.

The furniture was crammed in any which way, as if Delaney were storing things and had no intention of staying. The desk was a huge mahogany rolltop with a hutch of tiny drawers hidden behind stacks of mail. Sonora sat in a wooden chair that swiveled, the eighteenth-century precursor to the modern roll chair. The wood creaked. She scooted close to the desktop and began going through the mail.

Bills. Lots of them. Utility companies threatening cutoff at the barn address. Feed stores—Southern States closing her account. Tax liens from the state of Ohio.

Sonora felt a twinge. Some of this looked like her own stack at home.

She picked up an envelope with a clear plasticine window. Not a bill, a bill of sale. Donna Delaney had paid two thousand eighty-seven dollars for a saddle made by somebody named Kieffer. German?

Cash.

Sonora frowned at the stack of bills. A couple of the envelopes looked like they were from collection agencies.

Where had Delaney gotten that much cash? Why would she spend two thousand on a saddle if she owed so much? Was she expecting an influx of money? Would she make a horse disappear for the insurance money—as in the horse Joelle had been riding? Had the horse been insured?

But the horse, supposedly, had been an old brood mare, not worth much, used by the caretaker's kids as a trail horse.

From the living room, Sonora could hear Mickey singing a song she remembered from when the kids watched *Sesame Street* and every finger had a name.

" 'Where is Pointer? Where is Pointer?' "

14

SAM MET SONORA in the waiting room of Jewish Hospital with a cup of coffee. She handed it back to him.

"What?"

"It's cold, Sam."

"It wasn't cold forty minutes ago, which is when you were supposed to meet me."

"I went to Delaney's place on the way."

He leaned forward, drinking from her cup. "What was it like?"

"Dump."

"I'm not asking for the *Better Homes and Gardens* report."

"Forced entry through the kitchen window. A few specks of blood on the couch. Toe smear in the mud from a 'big guy,' and that's official, from Mickey. A lot of mud on the carpet, but most of that was from the cops and the ambulance crew."

"She say anything?"

" 'Son of a bitch, son of a bitch, son of a bitch.' "

Sam scratched his cheek. "Doctor says she's sedated and in shock, and he wants her vitals to stabilize before we talk to her."

"Who's the doctor? Not Malden, I hope."

"No, some new guy I don't know. Gillane."

"What kind of a name is that?"

"Where are you going?"

"After the doctor, Sam, let's get on with this."

Sonora headed for the desk, looked around for a familiar face. Why couldn't her bud Gracie be on duty? If she had to be working, so should everyone else.

The woman behind the desk wore blue polyester, shapeless, comfortable, and she did not look up from the computer.

Sonora flashed her ID. "Excuse me?"

"One minute."

"I don't have one minute." Sonora headed for the ER, pushed through the swing doors. She heard voices, Sam's mumble. *Who* was he talking to now? The man could make friends with anyone, anywhere.

She started looking into cubicles, twitching white curtains, trying not to rattle the plastic border at the top, which was impossible. Got a glimpse of a woman, highly pregnant—God, *that* made her stomach hurt. One who looked like a heart attack, a lot of doctors. She kept moving.

Found Donna Delaney sitting up on a metal table that was likely passed off as a bed, with a mattress not much thicker than a thumb. All for three hundred dollars a day. Delaney was huddled in a backless blue print gown, looking dopey and bewildered. Waiting to be admitted? Waiting to be released? Waiting.

Sonora pushed the curtain gently, and Donna Delaney gasped and looked up.

Whatever they'd used to sedate her wasn't working too well.

She looked bad. Chalk white. Sonora had not realized the woman was sun-freckled, but the brown marks stood out like leopard spots against her pallor.

Her hair was still tied back, but it looked slept on and tangled. An IV line was draped across her bruised wrist, connecting her to a metal pole and a plastic bag that was running on empty. Her legs were thin and well muscled. Covered with goose bumps.

Sonora moved in closely, quiet and soft. "Ms. Delaney?"

The woman stared, eyes dark shadowed like a corpse's. Her pupils were huge. Her hand was bandaged hugely, but the blood-flecked gauze did not disguise the space between her fingers.

"Ms. Delaney, I'm Detective Blair. We met yesterday afternoon. Do you remember meeting me?"

Delaney stared. Shivered. "Have you found her?"

The voice was flat, hard.

"Joelle's still missing."

"The horse. Have you found the bloody horse?"

"No." Sonora wondered again if the horse was insured—for a large sum of money. Maybe she was in foal to a valuable stallion. Sonora was out of her area here.

Delaney put her head in her hands, jarred the bandage. Pulled her hands away and stared at the gap between her fingers.

"Ms. Delaney, I'd like to ask you some questions."

The woman's teeth were chattering. "You've got to find her."

Sonora had the distinct feeling they were still talking about the horse. "You want a blanket, Donna? Are you cold?" Sonora knew her way around enough to find the linen closet. She could be there and back in minutes.

"Two blankets."

Sonora nodded, felt the first stir of rapport. She might actually get something out of this woman.

"Two blankets," she said. In exchange for some answers.

The linen closet had just been filled—the blankets were fresh out of the dryer, still warm. Sonora bundled two up, touched a corner to her cheek. They ought to use fabric softener. She headed back to Delaney's cubicle, moving quickly. Hoping the woman had not been admitted, or wheeled away for testing.

The seven A.M. shift was still doing their changeover, charting, chatting, in their own bubble world. Sonora scooted past the desk without being noticed, turned a corner, saw Sam standing outside Donna Delaney's white-curtained cubicle, facing a man who reminded Sonora of an undertaker she'd known when she was a child.

He had the self-important air of a newly minted M.D. He gave Sonora a glance over one shoulder, then turned to Sam.

Sonora scooted back into the cubicle with the bundle of blankets, half her attention on the medic, pontificating in the hallway.

Something about continuous single-lock sutures.

Sonora handed the blankets to Delaney, who took them with a surly ingratitude that made it easier for Sonora to look objectively at the bandaged hand.

From the hallway came the sound of bootheels and a shout for a nurse. The curtains were pushed to one side, metal rings scraping. Delaney raised her head, moving slow, groggy. But the light in her eyes was intense. Edgy, for a woman who was heavily sedated.

The man who stood and looked at her had to be a doctor, if you discounted the huge hiking boots and jeans. There were clues. A stethoscope around his neck, the pager on the belt, the Rolex on his wrist.

"You're tall," Sonora said, not thinking. He'd be six three in his thick white socks.

"You're not."

Sonora showed her ID. "I'm waiting for Dr. Gillane."

He flapped the white lapel, waving the name tag that said Gillane.

"I thought that was the guy in the hall."

"Ken doll with the waxy complexion, looks like an undertaker? That's Roth, LPN." He glanced at Delaney and frowned. "Why hasn't anybody replaced the bag on your IV?" His gaze went to Sonora, the blankets. Looked at the chart. "I see your buddy brought you some blankets, Donna—and they say there's never a cop around when you need one. Why don't you lie back . . ." He reached toward Sonora, and she handed over the blankets. "Let's put them both on, there you go. Let me elevate your feet there, Donna, get you warmed up. That better?"

Delaney turned her head to one side. Closed her eyes. Opened them.

"Dr. Gillane, I'd like to ask her a few questions." He would kick her out, Sonora thought.

"Ask away, I'd like to know what happened myself." He looked at Delaney. "You up for this?"

She didn't answer, and Sonora didn't wait.

"Ms. Delaney, do you know who cut—who your assailant was?"

Delaney looked away from Sonora. "No."

"No idea at all?"

"None. You deaf?"

Get your own blankets, Sonora thought. "Who was your visitor last night?"

"Just . . . no one. I was alone all night."

Gillane glanced at Sonora. Yes. That one was clearly a lie.

"Ms. Delaney, there were two cans of beer on your coffee table."

Delaney frowned. "I drank two beers."

"Did you cut off your finger yourself?"

"What the hell do you mean?"

"I mean that unless you cut your own finger off, you weren't alone all night, were you?"

"Son of a bitch," Delaney said.

"Oh, don't start that up again," Gillane said. Mildly. As if he didn't really care.

Sonora followed him out of the cubicle.

"Are you following me?"

"I'm trying, but you take big steps."

Gillane stopped and leaned up against the wall. Even slumped—and the man had terrible posture—he was a head and a half taller than Sonora.

Part of it was the worn Ropers. Maybe he rode horses too,

Sonora thought. Horse people were everywhere, once you started to look.

He folded his arms. "Are you a good witch or a bad witch?"

"I'm a witch with a badge."

"I don't like cops."

"I hate doctors."

"Really? What do you do when you're sick?"

"Suffer."

"What about lawyers?"

"Lawyers are okay." Sonora noticed that his eyes were very blue, and his face was tanned.

"I thought all cops hated lawyers. What are your thoughts on realtors?" As an afterthought. As if he really wanted to know.

"I don't have an opinion."

"Sell your house, you'll change your mind."

"Tell me about the finger. Tell me how you keep your tan this time of year. Didn't your mommy tell you that tanning beds cause skin cancer?"

"I spend a lot of time outdoors. And the finger is gone, what's to tell?"

"The wound, then, any thought on that?"

He cocked his head to one side. "They have real coffee down in the dungeon by the CAT scan machine."

"I'm on the clock," Sonora said.

"They pay you by the hour?"

"You been up all night like me, or you just stupid?"

Gillane smiled. "I'm always like this. 'Focus, Gillane.' People tell me that all the time. Ex-wives, professors, my cleaning lady. My last wife said that to me every day before she left."

"She left because you were unfocused?"

"No, she left because she said she could no longer stand being married to a cross dresser, and would I please return her lingerie."

"She must have been a big girl," Sonora said.

He smiled at her. Warmly. She liked him suddenly, except he was a doctor. It took a lot of self-confidence for a man to make a cross dresser joke, in a town like Cincinnati. People might believe you and send you to the sinning side of the river.

He winked. "Just kidding, of course."

"Darn, and me on my way to call vice."

"You're funny," he said. Frowning. "I'm funnier. I do my best standup in surgery."

"Go operate on somebody, you're wearing me out. I was up all night looking for a missing fifteen-year-old girl, and that's where I need to be right now. Looking. So—"

He put a finger to his lips and pointed upward to an imaginary sign. "This is a no-whining zone. But if you want to get into it, I got a kid upstairs in pediatrics—"

"Dr. Gillane?"

Sam. Laying a heavy left hand on Sonora's shoulder and shaking Gillane's hand with his right. His smile was lopsided, engaging the right side of his mouth, and Sonora recognized the universal good ole boy. "Nurse Roth tells me you worked two shifts straight, and we sure appreciate your staying extra to talk to us. Most doctors would have headed home and to hell with the cops."

Gillane looked at Sonora. "He's good."

"Damn right he's good, he's my partner. Don't patronize him."

Sam held up a hand. "Like I said, good of you—"

"Do you always repeat yourself?" Gillane cocked his head to one side.

"Over and over, till I get your attention."

"In that case, I'm yours. Here's my official diagnosis. The lady's finger was cut off."

"That official?" Sonora said. She was about to add moron, but Sam squeezed her shoulder.

Gillane waved a hand. "I'm about to use big words, so pay attention. Whoever it was had a bloody sharp knife with a thick edge, not serrated. It went clean through the tissue and bone, no tearing, which puts to mind some kind of a postmortem knife."

"Or scalpel?" Sonora asked.

"I don't think so. Most scalpels have a finer edge to them. Which means you should be on the lookout for a butcher, a surgeon, a soldier of fortune. Which a rude person might say exactly describes me."

Veterinarian, Sonora thought. That's what we're looking for. McCarty was a veterinarian.

Gillane shrugged. "Of course, anybody with money in his pocket can walk in off the streets and buy this stuff. Or order it on the Internet. Or out of a catalog. And excuse me, but if someone would make the effort to find this finger, I'd like to chance sewing it back on. The longer you wait—"

"Does she show any defense wounds?" Sonora asked.

Over her head the loudspeaker bonged, one of those oblique hospital signals. Someone wanted security, a doctor, a cup of coffee.

Gillane was shaking his head. "No other marks on her. Nothing on the palms, other fingers, face. The amputation was cleanly done and straight. She wasn't struggling when they did it. No tears in the flesh, no hesitation cuts or nicks, so I don't think she did it herself. She had to have been majorly doped when . . ." Sonora heard the soft shush of hospital footsteps, looked over her shoulder at Roth the Ken doll. Gillane was frowning. "Bo, you get results back yet from the drug screen?"

"I can check, but I doubt it."

"Any ideas on what they might have used to dope her?" Sam said.

Gillane shrugged. "Restoril comes in handy capsules, but it doesn't necessarily knock somebody out. She doesn't show any signs of respiratory distress, so that rules out a few. Chloral hydrate is an oldie but goodie that's making a comeback, for just that reason. Take a good gram to knock somebody out. She drinking coffee or anything when this happened?"

"Budweiser."

"That's not beer, but that'll work. Whoever pulled this off knew what he was doing."

"Why so?" Sam said.

"Stitched her up very professionally. Nylon four-oh continuous single-lock sutures—looks like a blanket stitch. Personally I'd have used simple interrupted sutures, individually tied stitches."

"Why didn't this guy?" Sonora asked.

"Blanket stitch is a lot faster, Slick there was probably in a hurry. He used lidocaine on the wound—we don't usually use that on extremities, the vasoconstriction will stop the local bleeding, but he was in a hurry, and he wasn't taking chances. Then he topped it off with a Xeroform gauze dressing for a nonstick covering. You know, if you guys want, we can run back in there—take the bandage off and look at it again. Take some more pictures. The uniform guy that came in with the patient took a whole roll. Let me know, will you, if any of them come out? I'd like some copies for my mom. Her son the doctor."

Sam looked at Sonora.

"He's a kidder," she said. "Thank you, Dr. Gillane."

"Does this mean you'll fix my next speeding ticket?"

"Gosh, that's one I never heard before," Sonora said.

Gillane watched her walk away, frowning and biting his lower lip. She'd gotten the last word. Sonora had a feeling he didn't like that.

15

THE HOSPITAL parking lot was packed, three cars jumbled at odd angles near admissions. A man, fiftyish, large-bellied, helped an elderly woman up to the curb. He held a powder blue suitcase in his left hand. The woman's eyes were dull and stoic.

Sonora remembered another reason why she hated hospitals.

Sam walked beside her to the car, gave her a sideways look, the kind he always gave her when she'd been flirting.

"I've never seen you like a doctor before."

Sonora wrinkled her nose. "I didn't like him."

"Whatever you say."

"Helen's probably at the barn, Sam, looking for Joelle. Why don't you follow me over?"

"Follow you? I need to be lost this early in the morning?" His cell phone rang. He reached into his jacket pocket, unfolded a tiny phone. "Delarosa. Yeah." He looked at Sonora, mouthed "Crick." "Yeah, I got a description of the horse last night from the Delaney woman. What? Shocky, but she'll be okay. She's not saying much. Part of that's the sedatives, but she's definitely up to something, could care less about the girl, and frantic over the horse. Yeah, I've got it. Hold on." He reached for his back pocket, pulled out the narrow spiral note-book. Flipped through some pages. "Okay. Brown—no, chest-nut. Three white socks, white snip from left nostril, and star blaze on nose. Frieze brand on the left side of the neck, under-neath the mane. That's unusual, according to Delaney, be-cause most horses, their manes rest on the right. What? Hell if I know. Now? Yeah, okay, better have him meet me there, I don't know a snip from a horsetail. Yes, sir." He glanced at Sonora. "No, I haven't seen her. She was headed to the farm. I'll catch up to her later."

He flipped the phone shut.

"Shielding me, Sam?"

"He's in a bad mood. Wants me to go out to a roadblock they got on I-65. Rounded up some horse trailers that fit the description of the truck—Dually, teal green, ninety-three. I'm supposed to go look at the horses and the headlights on the trucks. Guy from the mounted police is going to meet me there. Advise me."

Sonora looked at him.

"Come on, they've cleaned up their act."

"How many teal green Duallys can there be on the road in one day?"

"Three."

"Three? All with brown horses?"

"Chestnut, Sonora."

She took the gravel driveway of End Point Farm slowly, veer-ing into the grass to avoid the more cavernous of the potholes. It was farm visit number three, and the Pathfinder was coated with fine brown dust. She was glad her brother wasn't alive to see it. He'd have freaked to see the mud-caked tires, grimy wheel wells, and generalized farm dirt.

All she needed was hay bales in the back.

The weed-pocked gravel lot was empty. Sonora stood on the door ledge, staring past the barn toward Hal McCarty's house.

Porch light was still on. Probably forgotten. Or maybe he was still asleep.

Sonora checked her watch. After eight. Even normal people were off and running by now, your farm types would have been up hours ago. McCarty must have forgotten to turn off the light. Her own porch lights were on more during the day than at night, same reason.

She headed around the barn, moving toward the back fields. A black horse watched her from a barred window, giving her a throaty nicker. The wind came in fits, harsh then quiet. The crime scene was still roped off, yellow tape flapping.

No sign of Helen's little Mazda pickup. Was she around? In a hospital, in premature labor?

Sonora folded her arms, shivered. Zipped up her jacket, flipped the hood over her head, looked out over the fields. The Chaunceys' mobile home was dark and mummy silent, porch light off. Sonora pictured the children escaping in sleep, Joelle's bed unmade, the room already collecting a coat of dust and an air of abandonment. She thought of the secret cache of papers, articles on missing children, family reunions, milk carton kids. All tucked into a box on her desk. She would go through it again later.

She ducked under the tape, heading for the splintered fence line. Nothing moving except horses, and they weren't moving much, heads down, gnawing at short sparse tufts of sawgrass and weed. One lifted its head, watching her from the corner of one eye, like a bird.

Who was the focus of this crime, Sonora wondered, the child or the horse? Why take the horse, if it was the child Mr. Stranger Danger wanted? But why take the child if it was the horse?

She tripped over a depression in the ground, looked over her shoulder as a reflex, glad she was alone. If Helen had made it out at dawn, like she'd promised, where would she be? Where would she leave the car? Sonora shielded her eyes, squinting. No dog, no woman. No child.

The grass was wet, making the hem of her jeans go soggy.

Sonora stretched, fist in the small of her back. Bella had been a mile or two down the road when she'd lost the scent, or when Helen's contractions had become too much of a worry for the interfering Carl.

Sonora rubbed her eyes, carefully, so as not to smear her mascara. Helen had said the dog could pick up the scent from the exhaust of a car. Made sense. Joelle and the horse had likely been swept up by whoever drove the Dually pickup and trailer that had smashed through the fence. That was the only thing that made any sense.

Helen had described a two-lane road that bordered the other end of the pasture. That's where they'd be.

Easy to find, as the crow flies. In her Pathfinder was another matter. She wished Sam was around. But all she had to do was find the road, then look for Helen's car. Even she ought to be able to manage that one.

Sonora turned back, glancing sideways. McCarty's little house was quiet, but she could see a faint glow of light coming through the living room. She headed past his small eight-stall barn, peeped in a stall window. A horse, munching fresh hay. So he'd been up already, feeding his horses. Long gone, by now.

She went to the door, just to check. There was something off about this guy. She felt nosy. She rang the bell, the original ivory plastic baked yellow brown by age and exposure. Like she would be someday.

Something else to look forward to.

Silence after the bell. Sonora knocked on the door, waited. Knocked again. Looked into the living room window. Quiet and dusty inside. The light shone from the back of the house.

She went around the side. The ground was soggy. Sonora stood on tiptoe and peered into the kitchen window.

Light on over the sink. Same dishes on the counter as yesterday, when she and Sam had given the place the once-over. She did not believe that anyone had spent the night there. So where was he sleeping? Girlfriend, maybe?

Sonora frowned, retraced her steps till she was outside the bedroom. The blinds were open halfway.

She squinted into the morning dusk. No one had slept there. Nothing had changed since yesterday. The room had an air of depression and disuse.

She still could not picture McCarty living in this house. The clutter of useless things, cheap and dated, did not seem to suit him. Much too much down on his luck for a veterinarian.

And as such, he would have access to some very good knives. He would be able to remove a finger and stitch it up professionally, put a nice Teflon bandage on right and tight.

Was Joelle Chauncey somewhere in that house?

They'd gone through it carefully. She'd looked in every room herself.

But all of them had run across the jokers with the secret chambers, soundproofed and designed for long sweaty torture. How many times had the police been into John Gacy's house?

She'd known one of the officers who'd been first on the scene with Jeffrey Dahmer. Opened the refrigerator, routine drone, and found a head on a metal shelf.

If Joelle didn't turn up by late afternoon, she'd try for a search warrant and get hold of that construction guy who had helped her out last month. McCarty would bear looking into.

16

SONORA HEADED toward Donna Delaney's long overcrowded barn, thinking that now might be the perfect opportunity to look through it. Her jeans were getting wet to the knees now and going tight on her calves. Slim fit. She was resisting moving to the relaxed fit, like everyone else of her generation.

She bit her bottom lip, thinking about Helen. Maybe she should just hit the road.

She was halfway to her car, walking along the front of the barn, when a black horse stuck its nose to the window and nickered at Sonora, a low-key, affectionate-sounding plea.

All the horses were restless, calling softly. Had they been fed? Sonora frowned, walking more slowly. She had no idea what to feed horses or how much, but with Delaney in the emergency room, slowly coming out of shock, it could be hours before someone remembered them.

Maybe she could throw some clumps of hay into their stalls. There had to be hay in there somewhere—it was a barn.

The black horse watched her walk up the front stoop, then disappeared inside its stall.

"I'm coming," she said.

The office door was unlocked but stuck, and Sonora had to shove to get it open, setting off the wind chimes. She flicked a finger across the pewter horses. So much for the silent approach.

She half expected someone to be inside, but the lights were out, and the office was silent, smelling of mold and damp. There were cobwebs in the left corner, and water stains over a picture of a white Egyptian Arabian in full costume, silver and blue tassels hanging from a blue velvet saddle cover, breastplate catching the light.

The tile floor was liberally tracked with mud and manure and did not look like it had been swept since Nixon was in office. There was a heavy smell of wet dog and horse manure, old oily leather.

Sonora shut the door, pushing it closed with her butt. The office had an air of desolation, sweat, despair. Abandon hope, all ye who enter here.

She paused at the opening to the smaller office, where Delaney had her desk and files. The message light on the phone was bright cherry red. Number six in the digital display. The light was not blinking, someone had already picked them up.

The chair behind the desk was huge, a battered leather throne that smelled faintly of cigars. Sonora sat down, leather cracking, swiveled from left to right. The metal squeaked softly.

The desk was grimy, the only thing not dusty was the stack of crisp white bills on top of older yellowed ones. Sonora flipped through. Second and third notices. Water, electric, finances right down to the nub. Just like at her house.

Another interesting tack bill. A Corbette bridle, three hundred ninety-eight dollars, give or take change.

But water on the verge of shut-off.

Sonora hit the play button on the answering machine.

Donna. This is Eunice Foster, Kelly's mother. That girl I heard about on the news—wasn't that at your place? It's so terrible, I hope they find her okay. Ummm . . . will there still be lessons tomorrow afternoon?

That one had come through at ten P.M. the night before.

Ms. Delaney, Brian Fiore, Channel Three news. We'd like to ask you a couple questions if you could give me, or my assistant, Allison Vase, a call. . . .

Midnight, the night before.

Donna, this is Viv. How are you feeling this morning? I think we better talk, don't you?

Sonora sat forward. The call had come in at six forty-seven A.M. Weird time to call, even for horse people. *How are you feeling this morning?*

Viv. Vivian? Sonora looked for a Rolodex. Nothing. She opened the middle desk drawer, looking for an address book. Papers. Syringes. Pieces of metal and leather, and a tube of phenylbutazone. Horse aspirin.

No address book. There were phone numbers taped to the wall over the desk—vet, fire, police. Farrier. Donna Delaney's home phone in case of emergency.

Sonora sorted through the side drawer while the other messages played.

I bought a saddle horse named Addie's Way from you three months ago, did you not get my messages? We're having a bit of trouble handling him. Actually, we're having a lot of trouble. If you remember, we bought him for my daughter. I don't know if we're doing something wrong, but he doesn't seem as bombproof as you described. Anyway, to tell you the truth, my daughter is too scared to even get back up on this horse. Can you please give me a call, please, as soon as possible?

The last message concerned a child who had been bitten by a horse named Rebel, and would Donna please call back, this was the umpteenth time they'd called.

Sonora leaned back in the chair. No doubt somebody's attorney would be in touch.

She glanced around the room. There were ribbons on the office wall, and faded pictures of horses clipped, groomed, and in the show arena. All the ribbons dated from the seventies, many of them faded and grimy, as if they had been stored in boxes and moved around.

No computer. Nothing in the side drawer but mud-stained manila folders, hand labeled in pencil, Coggins tests, board agreements, lesson programs and policies.

Sonora checked her watch. Stood up. Opened the door that led into the barn. She had just a glimpse of light under the tack room door before it went out, leaving the barn dark. All the barn doors were shut, breezeway lights off.

Sonora stepped off the ledge into the dirt aisleway. Damp, chilly, the smell of horses, shavings, and cigar. The cigar smell was fresh.

Damn. Her gun was in her purse, locked securely in the car.

The light had gone out as soon as she shut the office door, so whoever it was knew she was there. And whoever it was had killed the light, not wanting to be found. They'd be listening, adjusting to the dark, expecting her to do the same. Best to move quickly.

It was not so dark she could not make her way. She moved quietly through the black gloom, tripping a little at an unexpected dip in the dirt flooring.

The horses, alerted by the smell and soft noises, made low throaty noises. From one of the stalls came the stomp of a pawing hoof. One of the horses was banging a bucket.

The tack room was across the aisle, to the far left of the barn, next to the mounds of cedar shavings. The sliding door was almost completely shut over the concrete lip. Was there a way out, other than through that door?

Sonora crossed the aisleway, inhaling the aroma of cedar and cigar. Absolutely no light coming under the doorway, nothing from the two-inch crack down the side where the door was not quite shut. If the room had a window, there'd be some ease of the darkness, it would be bathed in gray gloom and there would be light.

So, no window. Whoever was in there was trapped.

Sonora listened. Quiet. Pictured someone else on the other side of the door, in the dark, listening too.

She could identify herself and demand whoever it was come out.

In her mind's eye she saw the smashed fence, the pool of dried blood, Donna Delaney's thick bandages that did not mask the new gap between the fingers she had left.

She had children to raise. She'd wait it out.

Sonora kept her breathing slow and quiet. She did not like waiting. Even after all these years as a cop, keeping still and patient was the hardest part of her job.

She really ought to call her insurance agent and see about that twenty-year term policy the woman had been trying to sell her. If she died, the kids might want to go to college.

Sonora glanced over one shoulder. Saw the overturned wheelbarrow, the pitchfork against the wall next to the shavings; manure clumps and bits of cedar wedged between the tines.

She moved, soft but hurried. The noise of her feet shuffling the dirt was loud enough to be heard inside the tack room.

Sonora had the pitchfork in hand when the door slid open.

Dark inside and quiet. She squinted, noting the wooden arms bolted to the wall, draped with the dark shapes of leather saddles. Strings of reins and bridles hung from brackets, and shelves on the wall were crammed with the dim shapes of bottles, jars, hoof-picks and worn brushes. A pile of ancient blankets was stacked waist high, just inside the door.

That it was an odd place for a stack of blankets struck her just as the pile quaked sideways and tumbled forward. A large dark shape came toward her, moving fast.

Sonora registered the sideways fall of the blankets, a face in a ski mask, whites of the eyes weirdly circled by dark grubby knit. She swung the pitchfork and caught the man across his ribs, heard a groan and a word that sounded like guttural German.

She'd hit him hard enough to break bone. He checked, then came at her full bore, bowling her over with blankets, bulk, using the force of her swinging pitchfork to sling her sideways.

She lost her balance, crashing sideways into the tack room, hitting a saddle tree and going down in a tangle of leather stirrups and blankets, pulling the ski mask man with her.

It happened too fast. Off her feet and trying to hang on to the pitchfork. Her shoulder hit wood, head slammed into concrete, and she took it in the ribs when the man fell down on top of her.

He smelled horsy, or maybe it was the blankets. He reeked of cigars, old sweat, and a shaving lotion she remembered from her childhood—Old Spice. Only sold at your local drugstore.

He was punching before she caught her breath, but there were blankets between them, and they both realized at the same time that hits were useless.

She clawed the mask, missing his eyes and ripping the soft knit sideways. It slipped, blocking his vision, giving her a glimpse of a muscled, sun-bronzed neck, a swath of flaxen hair, collar length and shiny.

He grabbed a set of reins, held them like a bar across her throat—fast enough that she didn't have time to get a hand in between for protection. Her arms flailed, and she grabbed something small, sharp on one end. Hoof pick. She smashed the sharp end toward his left eye socket, felt a sickening crumple, resistance, then a juicy giving way.

A scream and a trail of blood in her fingers.

The pressure on her throat went slack, and she clawed the reins away, took a deep gasping breath.

She realized that he was up and off her, hand over one eye. Saw the foot—large, black barn boot, caked with mud and manure. She grabbed for it, but her hands slipped off his heels, and the boot came down toward her throat.

Sonora scrambled sideways, and the boot glanced across her temple, clipping her ear, catching her hair.

Her lip was swelling, and she tasted blood. He must have grazed her face.

He bent over her, reaching for something on the floor. Sonora caught him below the knees, shoving him off balance. Saw the gun lying sideways on the concrete. Smith & Wesson thirty-eight. Sam had one, and he'd let her fire it several times—southern country boys had a wealth of knowledge about weapons, pickup trucks, Rottweilers, and ways to make women smile.

Where the hell was Sam, anyway?

She felt strange, like she was walking around on the bottom of the ocean, like she'd taken one too many cold pills, but she kept her eye on the gun. Felt another kick, this one in the small of her back, and she smiled when she got hold of the Smith & Wesson, because she was going to shoot this son of a bitch.

She pushed the floor, made it to her knees, swaying forward, and her first shot caught him in the left knee, making his leg crumple, bringing him down.

He screamed and rolled sideways. Large cherry splats of blood blossomed against the concrete. The horses began to panic and call, some of them kicking. Sonora fired again, missed, heard the bullet thunk into wood. She'd always been a lousy shot.

He was up on his feet and galloping sideways, like a panicked crab, leg dragging and leaving a blood trail.

Sonora heard a shout, and the aisle flooded with light and noise as the metal barn doors opened behind her. A barn cat screeched, ran across in front of her, scrambling out of the barn into the light.

She squinted, saw the pickup parked at the dark end of the barn, took aim but did not fire. He was moving too fast, it was dark, and there was too much metal for ricochet.

He was in the truck. Must have left the keys in the ignition to get it started so fast. The barn filled with the noise of an eight-cylinder engine and the smell of exhaust. The metallic clang of gears grinding, the engine revving as the pickup tore backward in reverse, heading straight for her.

"Watch out!"

Someone, male, behind her, and she jumped sideways, back into the tack room, twisting her left knee, catching her balance on a tack trunk.

She pushed off the trunk, aimed her gun. Saw a blur of motion, the pickup going by, and ran after it, stumbling on the concrete lip into the dirt, almost too soon, close to harm's way, but in time to see the back tires—singles, not doubles.

This was not a Dually, this was not the truck that had gone through the fence in the back paddock where Joelle Chauncey had disappeared.

The pickup skidded sideways, then turned sharply out of the barn, wheels sliding in the mud.

Leaving tracks, Sonora thought. Go to it, asshole. See you in the ER.

The engine raced and the pickup fishtailed, got traction, and tore off. Sonora heard a bump as it hit one of the potholes and just missed her car.

No license plate. Highly illegal. She would ticket him at the first opportunity.

Another man was running toward her, Hal McCarty, and she was aware of disappointment. So he was definitely involved.

"Are you okay, you—"

"What the hell are you doing here, McCarty?" She leaned up against the wall outside the tack room, she was not feeling well, and it was hard to catch her breath.

"I came—" He almost laughed, as if surprised to have to come up with a story, under the circumstances. He had the well fed and crisp look of a man who'd had a hot shower and a good breakfast, two things she resented. "I came to feed the horses," he said.

"What timing. You and me both." She paused, breathing hard. "I'm taking you downtown, McCarty."

"Handcuffed if you like, but you better let me drive while you put some ice on the side of your head, it's already swelling up. Look, do you mind if I take that gun out of your hand?"

Her head ached. "I mind very much."

17

"AND YOUR GUN was where?"

Crick stood over Sonora, voice low. She knew him well enough to know that if she didn't look so bad, she'd be in a lot of trouble. She just didn't know him well enough to be sure she wasn't in a lot of trouble anyway.

She was sitting in the cigar stink of the leather office chair, elbows on the armrests, chin in her hands. She was bent forward to take the pressure off her lower back, where that son of a bitch had kicked her with his big-booted feet.

The door from the barn blew open, and Mickey came in shaking his head.

"That's one serious-looking blood trail."

"Yeah, and it was all from the other guy. Most of it anyway." Sam, coming in behind Mickey. "It's a good shoot, sir."

Crick looked at him. Did not deign to mention that Sam, being her partner, might not be the most unbiased judge.

"It was," Mickey said. Looked at Sonora. "Where was *your* gun?"

Crick's gaze was steady. Sonora looked at the floor. "In my purse."

"Which was where?"

"In my car. But the car was locked."

Sam winced.

"That keeps your weapon safe, but it doesn't do much for you," Mickey said.

"What brought you back in the barn?" Crick asked.

She looked up and saw Sam, standing behind Crick, shake his head slightly. As if she'd be stupid enough to admit she'd gone in to feed the horses.

"Instinct, intuition. Being nosy," Sonora said.

Sam nodded. "Good cop traits."

"We'll talk later." From Crick. He headed into the barn, Mickey on his heels.

Sam bent over her, muttered something about tagging along with Crick.

Going to make sure everybody came to the right conclusion, Sonora thought as he winked and headed out, leaving her alone with McCarty, two uniforms, and a woman from CSU who was bent over a clipboard, filling out one of the endless forms that are the curse of modern law enforcement.

Crick would look the scene over himself, Sonora thought. She did not know what he would say to her privately, but she did know that if he agreed with Mickey, he would watch her back with IAD. God help her if he didn't.

"I'd be glad to run to the house and get you some ice. If you don't want to go to a hospital. Which is where you should be." Hal McCarty's voice was kind.

The CSU woman looked up. "I'll drive you," she said softly.

Sonora shook her head, regretted it. "They'll just sit me on a metal table for six hours till some doctor comes in and tells me I have a concussion, which is something I already know."

The CSU technician, a tiny redhead who, in Sonora's memory, used to be brunette, nodded and went back to the form, which looked to be giving her trouble.

Sonora frowned hard. Kindness would undo her. It didn't sit well to get scared shitless, kicked in the head, and yelled at by the boss after being up all night.

There had to be a reason she was in this line of work.

She focused on McCarty, trying to come up with the right

questions. "You say Donna Delaney called and asked you to feed the horses?" She would get him on this one. Delaney hadn't called anybody.

He shifted in his seat and looked to the left. Prelude to a lie, Sonora thought.

"I haven't talked to Donna since . . . oh, last night. About the time you guys left."

He could be telling the truth, or he could know Delaney was incapacitated. "So what are you doing here, now, this morning?"

He leaned forward, hands on his knees. "I'm here every morning. The truth is, Donna likes to sleep in. She breezes in late all the time, so I come early and help Dixon feed the horses. She knows we're doing it, because there's feed missing, and it pisses her off, but she won't come out in the open and admit she isn't going to feed them herself, so Dixon's got her cornered. He started it. I just didn't think he'd be up to it today."

"You're telling me *she* doesn't feed them?"

"That's what I'm telling you."

Sonora held her head at an angle, to ease the throb in her temple. She had touched it once, a mistake, and she was afraid to look in a mirror. The miracle of makeup was not going to help her out of this one.

She rubbed her forehead. "So you just came over to feed the horses out of the goodness of your heart. And you do this every day?"

"No, I told you. Dixon does it." His smile was sympathetic. He knew the story was weak, and he knew her head hurt.

"Where did you spend the night, Mr. McCarty?"

"At home."

"Nope."

"Nope?"

"Did you take a shower this morning?"

"You working homicide or hygiene?"

"Answer the question."

"Yeah, I took a shower."

"What did you eat for breakfast?"

"Egg McMuffin."

"There isn't a McDonald's in five miles."

"Ma'am, when I want an Egg McMuffin, I'll get in the car and drive for it."

Sonora saw the smile flick across the CSU technician's face, but she frowned her down and the woman went back to the clipboard like she was glued to it.

"So you went out to breakfast?"

He shook his head. "No, this one was old and cold. Got it out of the fridge. Single guy syndrome."

Sonora did not believe him, but there was nowhere to go with this. She could ask him if he'd been to Delaney's place. Get him on record saying no. She checked her watch. Nine A.M. Only nine A.M. Shaping up to be a terrific kick-ass day.

"Did you go see Donna Delaney last night? Go to her home?"

He cocked his head to one side. "Nope."

"You won't mind coming down to the office, giving me a written account of where you were last night?"

"Not at all. But I wasn't there. You can trust me, detective. I've admitted to an Egg McMuffin. If I was a liar, I'd tell you I had bran flakes and a banana."

18

SONORA SHIFTED the ice cream sandwich up along her temple. The seam of thick white wrapping caught her skin, and she winced. "Did you even try to get ice?"

Sam glanced at her from the corner of his eye. "It was the most frozen thing I could find. Sure you don't want to go to the ER? You could flirt with Gillane some more."

"Maybe later. What did Helen say exactly?"

"How many fingers am I holding up?"

"One, Sam, and thanks for my morning obscenity. When did Helen call you?"

"She called Crick because she couldn't get you. You were supposed to meet her first thing, remember? Phone locked in the car with the weapon?"

"How many fingers am I holding up, Sam?"

"Crick took the call while we were following the blood trail of your latest victim. Helen was pretty excited. Said the dog was having a fit over a big pile of manure, and for us to bring a shovel and a pitchfork and get out there. Said there was a pitchfork up against the fence, but she was thinking it might be evidence, so she didn't want to touch it."

"My God, Sam, think about it. I'm excited. You're excited.

Helen and the dog are excited. Over manure. What kind of a job is this?"

Sam gave her a look. "You really got hit on the head." He checked over his shoulder, saw a pickup barreling toward them, pulled out anyway. Sonora hung on to the armrest.

"You sure you never saw the guy before?" Sam asked.

"What guy? The one in the ski mask?"

"Yeah, the one in the ski mask."

"How would I know if I ever saw him? He was in a ski mask, that's the point of ski masks. You don't see their face. But I have to say it weirded me out to find McCarty in the middle of everything."

Sam looked at her. "He your number-one suspect?"

"Where'd you get that idea?"

"Well. You did send him downtown."

"Let's see, he's got Joelle's blood all over his shirt, he's Johnny-on-the-spot when I run into that maniac in the barn—"

"Johnny-on-the-spot? I haven't heard that one in years."

"Plus he's a veterinarian. Which means he could be our finger ripper."

"Finger ripper, I like that."

"Are you paying attention at all?"

"Sort of, but I'm mainly looking for Helen's car."

"She knows we're coming?"

"Crick told her to hang on, we'd be right out. Told her you'd been delayed by a small case of dismemberment and a barn brawl."

"Nothing like the truth." She looked out the window. "Speaking of which. There's her pickup."

Sam hit the brakes, waited for a battered white Montero to blow past, and pulled the Taurus to the side of the road in front of the Mazda, which was half in and half out of a ditch.

Sonora opened the car door, looked over her shoulder at Sam. "You could have parked so the ditch was on your side."

"Climb over. The ice cream's melting. You going to eat it?"

She handed him the ice cream sandwich, slid across the

front seat of the car, and climbed out after him into the two-lane road. "Whch way from here, Sam?"

He unwrapped the white paper and took a quick bite of the ice cream, which was melty and sagged sideways. He pointed to a small square sign, red on white, a six mounted on a silvery metal stake.

"She said to look for a huge redbrick house, go down the gravel road that says 'Fire Gate number six,' and follow it back to the barn." He took another bite of ice cream.

Sonora looked across the road. Saw a large redbrick house that looked like it dated from the Civil War. If a brick house could sag, this one did.

She looked back at the sign. "It doesn't *say* 'Fire Gate.' "

"Yeah, but it says 'six.' "

"So 'Fire Gate' is implied? It's not on the sign?"

"I'm trying to remember if you were like this before you got hit on the head." Sam finished the ice cream in two large bites, rolled the wrapper into a sticky white ball, and handed it to Sonora. "I'll get the tools."

19

THE GRAVEL ROAD was narrow and looped to the right, leading to the fields behind the redbrick house. Sam and Sonora walked along the fence line, in the sparse grass on the shoulder of the drive, avoiding the muddy water pooled in tire ruts of mud and gray-white gravel dust. Sam carried a pitchfork and a scoop-shaped shovel over his left shoulder. Sonora carried her purse.

She touched the inside of her lip with her tongue. The tissue was swollen and huge, and she wondered if this was what collagen injections felt like. Too bad the swelling would not spread evenly so she could be sore but sexy.

They paid for this in L.A.

She frowned, because for some reason the lay of the land looked familiar. The pasture was pale brown and fading green, black four-plank horse fencing in excellent repair. The house, set back from the road on the right, was built in an L shape, with a porch running down one side and along the back. It had recently been whitewashed. Sonora pictured herself sitting there on a porch swing, drinking a glass of wine.

Maybe she would get a porch swing. That might be affordable.

"Sam, can you hang a porch swing?"

"I'm a guy, Sonora. If I say I can't hang a porch swing, I go down two notches on the belt loop of manhood. Your problem is—if you get me to hang a porch swing, will I do it right? Or will—" He looked over one shoulder. "This place look familiar to you?"

"The *belt loop* of manhood?" Sonora shook her head and moved ahead of him. The road completed its curve and straightened. On the left, the fields were fenced into five-acre paddocks, automatic concrete waterers in the center, circled by mud and churned-up sod.

The morning drear was giving way to patches of sun, and the wind was still at last. Sonora looked around, thinking how beautiful it looked, wishing herself away somewhere in the sun, dreading the short, dark days of winter ahead.

The road straightened and led to a huge black barn, with doors slid open. Cobwebs streamed from wooden rafters, pieces of rusty machinery were parked every which way.

Sonora heard a bleat, saw two black-faced sheep and a couple of goats in a pen on her right. One of the sheep had his head sideways under the bottom fence slat and chewed at the grass on the other side.

"Helen?" Sonora shouted.

She caught a streak of movement from the left—a dog, running toward them. Soft white with thick fur in a ruff around his neck. A shepherd-Akita mix.

"Tail's wagging." Sam held out a hand, and the dog went to him happily. Accepted a head rub, looked expectantly toward Sonora.

She scratched his ears. Looked at the tag. "Hello, Lincoln."

He grinned up at her, tongue sideways, then headed up toward the house.

"Watchdog?" Sam said.

"He's watching."

Sam pointed. "Helen said go around the back of the barn and head left along the fence line, couple hundred yards. We'll see her."

"She'll be hard to miss."

"I wouldn't say stuff like that within earshot."

They headed around the left-hand side of the barn, out of view of the house. The ground was spongy beneath their feet. The barn had small square windows, way high up, dark and impenetrable.

They rounded the side, both looking to catch sight of Helen. Wooden posts, twelve feet high, had been set in the ground behind the barn—skeletal, raw, promising. Someone planning an addition. A mound of freshly dug dirt was humped between the posts, and a wheelbarrow was tipped against a stack of twelve-foot slats of treated poplar.

Sonora hesitated at the edge of the barn, looked over her shoulder at Sam. Moved to the open door, took a small step inside. Barns were foreign territory.

It was cool inside, chilly and dark, sunlight pooling at the edge of the open doors. The dirt floor was uneven and sprinkled with straw and wood shavings.

The loft was full of hay on the right side, empty on the left. Pitchforks, shovels, rakes were hung on the walls. The right-hand side had stalls, with long mesh-metal doors.

"Sam," Sonora said. "Better get in here."

He set the fork and shovel against the barn door, came close enough to her that his hand brushed her back. Whistled, low and tuneless.

In the aisleway, next to a rusting manure spreader and a small yellow-and-rust John Deere tractor, was a teal green pickup.

Sam moved to the back of the truck. "I'll be damned. Double tires—Dually."

Sonora looked into the front seat. The floors were muddy, a wealth of forensic detail. "Keys in the ignition. Seems real strange."

"No, farmers do that all the time."

"Leave keys in the truck?"

"Sure." Sam pulled his head out of the cab, moved along the side. "Set up for a gooseneck horse trailer," Sam said.

"What's that mean?"

"Connects to the thing here in the truckbed, instead of a ball hitch on the bumper. Carries some serious weight."

"What you think he did with the horse trailer, Sam?"

"What you think he did with the horse?"

Sonora did not like to imagine such things. They went through the barn and out the back, blinking in the light. Sonora saw movement, caught sight of Helen leaning against the fence line where it turned to wire mesh, diamond shapes framed by black posts. She waved an arm at Sonora. Bella sat at her feet, planted in front of a composted manure pile that rose over Helen's head.

Sonora looked across the field, at the way the land sloped and dipped to the right. There would be a pond just over that hill, and a little knot of trees and brush.

"Sam. This is the Kidgwick place, isn't it? Halcyon Farm?"

He stopped, took the pitchfork and shovel off his shoulder. "That's what it is. I thought it looked familiar. I never got out here, but I saw the crime scene photos."

"You, me, and everyone else in the country."

Sam nodded. The crime scene photos had been leaked to the press. One of the secretaries had been fired—taking the fall for someone whose name was whispered but never said out loud.

"That was what, seven, eight years ago?"

"Somewhere around there. It was right before I went with homicide. You work that case?"

Sam grimaced. "We all worked that case. There's a pond over the hill. That's where they found the boy, half in and half out of the water. Ben Randolph. Sixteen years old, killed by his buddies for a 1973 Chevy Impala he bought used and rusty with money he saved bagging groceries all summer."

"He was killed by his buddies?"

"Two so-called friends, got him here to pick up Tammy Kidgwick, daughter of the house. Her parents were gone for the day—church retreat. The boys bashed his head in, and when that didn't do the trick, one stood on his back while the other stepped on his neck and held him underwater till he drowned."

Sonora remembered the crime scene photos. The back of the house. The pond. A shot of the boy, facedown in the mud, then another with him rolled onto his back, skin purplish white, lips blue, body stiff with rigor. They'd torn his back pocket when they'd taken his wallet and keys—Andy Rivett and Malcolm Sweetwater. Andy one year older than Ben, Malcolm eight months younger. Running with the crowd that attended classes sporadically, smoked pot, but stayed out of major trouble until they went straight to brutal murder along an unpredictable path that their peers, parents, teachers, and psychologists studied in detail, looking in vain for the warning signs of homicidal tendencies.

No one had a theory any more sophisticated than "shit happens."

The boy, friendly and trusting, had not had too many friends. It was a scenario that brought chills to any parent with children heading for the teen years.

"Sweetwater got out, shock probation," Sam said.

"He was the younger one."

"Yeah, but a real sociopath. I hear they're looking for him in Houston and North Carolina."

"What about the other two?"

"Andy Rivett is still in jail and will be for another twenty years. They measured his IQ around eighty-five or -six."

"The girl was cleared, wasn't she?"

"Not completely. Bristol was working juvie then, and he was pretty hard on her, but she cooperated and swore she didn't know what was in the works. She just hadn't stopped it. Died in a car accident two years after it happened. There was some suspicion of vehicular suicide, but the insurance company paid up."

Sonora glanced back up at the house. The porch had been painted in the last four weeks. Everything else looked worn, neglected, like the farm had been in stasis for several years. Now there was paint and a barn addition.

A new owner, she wondered, or the healing power of time? It would be nice to see someone on the recovery end.

Sonora took a look toward the pond, thinking they'd end up dragging or draining it. She followed Sam, felt soothed by his voice as he greeted Helen, talked to the dog. There was something comforting about the rhythms of his speech— maybe it was the southern thing.

She thought of Joelle's fine young face, round and un- formed. Tried not to think.

20

THERE WERE COWS close to the diamond mesh fence, attending to cow business, grazing. One lifted its head, looked in their direction. Sonora wondered if the cow had seen the killer. Cows as witness.

The compost pile had been there awhile, clumps of manure mixed with straw bedding. It was inoffensive, smelling faintly of horse and ammonia, with grass and weeds growing over the top, as if to convey respectability. A pitchfork lay on one side, tines facing down.

Bella sat near the edge of the pile, paws smeared with dirt, toenails crusty, tongue hanging from the side of her mouth. Her muzzle was flecked with white foam, her chest streaked with drool and dirt.

Helen murmured *good girl, good girl,* patted the dog's head. She smoothed a palm over the droopy, fur-wrinkled cheeks, looked sideways at Sam and Sonora. "I hate to be the bearer of bad news, but I think we maybe found your girl."

"You called CSU?" Sonora took the shovel from Sam.

Helen shook her head. "What if I'm wrong—and after that fiasco last night? Makes the dog look bad. Then some jerk calls an ambulance and sends me home, and I look bad. This time, if I'm wrong, me and Bella going to keep on looking, and I don't want interference."

"Teal green pickup in the barn," Sonora said, inclining her head. "Your credibility's intact."

"Yeah, I took a quick look. No trailer attached. You think it's the one?"

"It's a Dually. Fits the description."

Sam squeezed Sonora's shoulder. Handed her the pitchfork and kept the shovel. "Go at it easy, Sonora, small clumps of dirt in thin layers. Pile everything—Helen, get me that blue plastic tarp over there, will you? Put the dirt there, Sonora."

"This be the spot, I take it?" She pointed to the left-hand side of the mound. Raw compost with no vegetation in a four-by-three hump, dirt darker than the rest, newly crumbled, unsettled, aromatic.

"Yeah." He pointed. "You work that end, I'll take this."

Sonora had never used a pitchfork before, except a red plastic one she'd had with a Halloween costume when she was five. As she remembered, she'd chased her brother from one end of the house to the other, till her mother had taken the pitchfork away.

She took a quick look at the sky. More rain today?

Enough had fallen the night before to make the manure heavy and hard to move. She poked it carefully. Underneath the top layer, packed tight by the rain, the manure crumbled like fine ash.

"Composted," Sam said, wiping a hand across his forehead. "Nature at work."

"Don't you get it? If the stuff we're digging is composted right here at the top, then we're dealing with stuff that came from deep in the center of the pile. As in recently dug up."

"Then *say* recently dug up, don't get complicated."

Sonora adjusted the pitchfork in her hands. The wooden handle was smooth, annoyingly loose in the rusting metal joint that held it to the black crusty tines. Out of the corner of her eye, she watched Sam handle the shovel like he'd been born with one in his hands, moving half scoops of dirt onto the tarp at a rate that made her own efforts look pitiful.

She glanced back at the house. Still no one. Maybe they were at work. Did they have a regular schedule of leaving the farm every day? Had the killer known he was safe here?

If so, that would most likely make him a local boy.

Sam stopped shoveling, went to his knees, and reached into the dirt.

Sonora leaned on the wooden handle of the pitchfork. Took a quick look at her palms, hot and pink, with gritty lines of sweat. She was raising blisters. "Something, Sam?"

"Rock, maybe."

Sam scooped dirt with the palms of his hands, brushed a clod of manure and straw to one side. Squinted. Looked over his shoulder at Sonora.

She had always liked the laugh lines that creased the corners of his eyes. Today they looked like grief. There was a smudge on his forehead and a look in his eyes she had seen before.

"See it?"

The toe of the riding boot was well camouflaged by the compost beneath Sam's blunt fingertips. Black leather, like the one they'd found in the dust and blood at Delaney's place.

Sonora squatted behind Sam. They got their rhythm almost immediately, one scooping dirt, one dumping dirt, back and forth, moving quickly. In her heart, she knew there was no need to rush. She hurried anyway, hands weirdly padded by the white water-filled blisters rising on the reddened flesh of her palms. She was sweating, a tiny film along her spine.

Visible beneath the dirt was a riding boot, toes up, and the lower part of a blue-jean-clad leg. Dirt caked the boot laces, settling deep into the metal grommets and eyelets of the speed laces. The hem of an old green blanket covered the corpse to the knees. She could hear Helen, several feet away, talking softly to the dog, a calf bawling—scared? Hungry? Looking for its mom?

Sonora touched the back of the leg, along the calf muscles, over the loose black boot. Found it firm, like frozen meat.

"Rigor?" Sam asked.

"Advanced. I would have guessed she's been dead a minimum of twenty-four hours, except she didn't go missing till yesterday around three-thirty."

"So they say. I wonder if she was actually at school."

"Something to check."

"Y'all got something?" Helen. Bella whined, and Helen murmured something comforting under her breath. She moved toward them slowly, fingers twined in the dog's loopy ears. Helen was smiling a little, but it was a smile Sonora had seen on the face of other detectives, a smile because the awful but expected was coming true, and you could smile or laugh or cry, it meant nothing more than a release of tense expectations.

Sonora stood up, spit on the sweat-and-dirt-stained blisters, rubbed her hands on the belly of her shirt. "Looks like Bella was right."

"I'll call Crick," Sam said. "Get CSU down here."

The dog sat on her haunches, jowls hanging, eyebrows arching as she looked at each of them in turn.

"Good girl," Sonora said, touching a long silky ear.

21

THE CURTAINS had twitched once or twice in the house up the road.

"They're home," Sonora said.

"Who?"

Sonora inclined her head. "The people who live here, Sam."

"It'll be a while before Mickey gets his butt in gear. Now might be a good time for a talk."

"It's their truck."

Sam, walking toward the house, threw a look at her over his left shoulder. "You think they're involved?"

Sonora cocked her head to one side. "I'm having trouble wrapping my mind around the kind of person who would commit a murder and bury the body in their backyard."

"It's the fast-food generation. Backyard's convenient."

"And park the getaway truck in the barn?"

Sam shrugged. "We got to ask."

"Whoever pulled this thing off knew about that truck."

Sam arched his back and stretched. "Know what I think?"

"No. What do you think?"

"I think this place is bad luck."

* * *

Sam was a back-door person, so they went up the newly whitewashed porch. The concrete base had been painted a thick coat of slate blue, which made Sonora think of her grandmother's front porch.

The wooden door was shredding and splintered, and it opened before they knocked. The trim had been painted half-way up. A work in progress.

The woman who stood in the doorway was tall and thin and had reddish-blond hair that hung thick down her back. She wore slim-fit jeans and a long sleeved T-shirt with "Calvin & Hobbes" on the front.

Sonora could hear music coming in from the kitchen—bells and chimes and trickly noises that she recognized as a lead into a seriously tedious New Age CD. She had noticed, in her career, that people who listened to New Age music were often people who seriously needed to feel better.

The Kidgwicks certainly had a legitimate need.

Sonora flashed her ID. "Detectives Blair and Delarosa, Cincinnati PD."

Mrs. Kidgwick walked onto the porch, smiling, as if she had heard Sonora but her mind was a beat or two behind in processing the words. She looked at the porch swing, and Sonora had the distinct feeling the woman was going to invite them to have a seat.

Sonora took a quick look down the road. The crime scene unit and a coroner's van would be coming soon, but there was nothing in sight now, except fields, and sunlight on the water-filled ruts that gouged the gravel drive.

Mrs. Kidgwick kept smiling, but her face took on a set, mask-like tautness. The public face. She motioned toward the door.

"Did you want to come in?" Her voice was low and scratchy-sounding—you would love it or hate it. She had the slimness and muscle tone of a woman who took her gym membership seriously. Her face was still nicely brown, tanning-bed perfect, but even the careful makeup could not cover the seams and pouches around her eyes. She would look tired for the rest of her life.

Sam glanced at Sonora. Wiped his feet on a rubber mat that had a red jumping horse etched into the black center.

"We won't keep you too long," he promised, waving the woman ahead.

She slid inside quickly, feet soft. "Van. It's the police." The restraint in her voice brought tension into the room like a match to gasoline.

"Is there a problem?" He was with them immediately, breathless, though Sonora did not think he had done anything more than walk a step or two. The voice was young and did not match the ancient weariness in his eyes.

"I'm afraid so," Sonora said. She waited for them to move together, for comfort, but they exchanged looks and held position.

The ensuing pause was a long one.

"Will you sit?" the man asked. His hair was thin, totally white over a face that could have been thirty or three hundred, skin healthy and taut but webbed with lines of worry.

Sonora did not think he was aware of the lack of graciousness in his invitation. It was as if he were holding his breath and those words were only ones he could manage.

Tragedy had marked them with the knowing aura of people who have learned that bad things happen without warning. Sonora heard it in the softness of their voices, saw it in the care they took to pay attention. They had the air of small cats in a big jungle. They would walk quietly, move in the shadows, and look over their shoulders at regular intervals.

Sam and Sonora headed for the couch.

The living room had an open peaceful feel. There was just enough furniture, all of it heavy, dark, and simple. A blue and white rug, threadbare, made a square of color on the dark, well-scuffed pine floor. The room smelled lemony, as if someone had just been dusting.

Behind the couch, French doors opened out onto a concrete patio that was bare, except for an empty flowerpot and a rusted-out gas grill.

Sonora moved closer to Sam. The Kidgwicks exchanged

looks, then each took a chair. Sonora would have been willing to bet that each one knew exactly what the other was thinking—they had the closeness of people who had been through unspeakable things.

She had seen grief cut like an amputation in one relationship after another. It was interesting to see one where it had strengthened the bond.

"Either one of you know a teenage girl by the name of Joelle? Joelle Chauncey?" Sam leaned back into the couch and crossed one foot over his knee, just like he was passing the time of day. He started a tape recorder, winked at the Kidgwicks, and set it on the coffee table, as if it were the most socially acceptable thing in the world.

Van looked at the recorder and flinched. He smiled brilliantly at Sonora and looked at her with an intensity that was like hunger. She looked away.

"No." Mrs. Kidgwick, answering Sam's question. She had not bothered to look at her husband for this one. Her face was merely blank.

Sam picked the heel of his shoe. "You familiar with a Donna Delaney, runs End Point Farm?"

Two no's, blank looks, shaking heads.

"Is the girl missing?"

"Did she run away from home?"

Why are you asking us? was a question neither of them asked, but its presence was there in their voices.

"Do you own a truck?" Sonora asked.

The woman was wary now, moving sideways in her chair. "We have an F-350."

"Describe it, would you?" Sam.

"Did something happen to the truck?"

"Mrs. Kidgwick, can you give me a description of the truck?"

"Blue-green," she said.

"It's an F-350, Dually pickup, gooseneck hookup in the bed." This from Van. "What's going on, did something happen to the truck?"

"Do you own a trailer?"

"White Sundowner, maroon trim."

"Can you tell me where the truck and trailer are right now?" Sonora asked.

The woman stood up and headed for the door, wiping her hands absently on the T-shirt as if it were a hand towel. "They're *supposed* to be in the barn—that's where we left them. Where are they now?"

Sonora waited and watched, wondering if the woman would leave them and head to the barn. So far the Kidgwicks rang true. They might never have known that their truck was used to commit a murder.

Bad truck.

Mrs. Kidgwick turned and looked at Sonora, shirt bunched in her left fist. "It was stolen, wasn't it?" Her voice was flat, annoyed. "This girl you're asking about? She took our truck?"

"Did she wreck it?" Van asked.

"Is she okay?"

"Where do you keep the keys?" Sam asked.

The two of them exchanged guilty looks.

"I've got a spare set up in my top dresser drawer. But they're still there, I saw them this morning." Van looked at his wife, and her chin went up.

"We keep a key in the ignition. We always kept the keys in the truck on my daddy's farm. You never know who's going to use it next, and sometimes you need it fast."

Truer words never spoken, Sonora thought.

Sam smiled at Mrs. Kidgwick. "And that's how most farm kids teach their own selves to drive at a very early age."

She gave him a crooked sideways smile. "I used to stand up in the seat while my brother laid on the floor to work the pedals."

Sonora shuddered. Her son had been driving only a couple of months, and he had already claimed two fenders, managed one nonmoving violation, and decapitated a duck.

He had been very sorry about the duck.

Van stood up. "Is the truck okay?"

"Did the girl get hurt?"

It was on the tip of Sonora's tongue to make some tiny comment about leaving keys in the ignition, but she caught herself. These were the parents of a girl who had been dragged by outlaw children into brutality at the tender age of thirteen. A sixteen-year-old boy had been murdered on their property. These people did not need to be reminded or patronized.

"Where's the truck now?" Sonora asked.

The woman put her hands on her hips. "I told you, it's supposed to be in the barn. My guess is it's not?"

"When's the last time you drove it?"

"Can you please just tell us what's going on?"

Sonora glanced at the floor. Took a second. "Mrs. Kidgwick, I'd appreciate it very much if you'd bear with us for just a few minutes more and answer the rest of our questions."

She had not meant to sound so harsh. It was hard to keep the steel out of your voice when investigating the death of a child.

The husband took over. "We used the truck about ten days ago to pick up some paint for the porch. And I was in the barn about—oh, three days ago. Sunday, I think. And the truck was there."

"You remember exactly where you parked it?"

"I put it dead to the right, so I could get to a stack of lumber I got out there."

Sonora looked at Sam. She could not remember how the truck was parked. They would have to go look.

Sam slid forward on the couch. "I'm sorry, Mr. and Mrs. Kidgwick, but we're going to have to impound your vehicle."

"My truck? *But why?*"

Sonora kept her voice gentle. She knew that a pickup truck was a thing near and dear to a man's heart.

"Sir. We believe your truck was used in the commission of a felony."

"Drugs?" The word was like vinegar on his tongue.

His wife sighed softly. "They'll rip it to shreds."

"Not drugs." Sonora hated being called "they."

Sam pulled a picture out of his coat pocket—a school picture of Joelle, from last year. "You're sure you've never seen this girl before?"

Van Kidgwick took the picture, face blank, then frowned. His wife moved across the room to stand at his shoulder. He looked at her. A question.

She looked at Sonora. "Is this the one you were asking us about?"

"Yes. Joelle Chauncey."

"We didn't know her name. But we've seen her several times. She hangs out down by the pond sometimes."

"Why is that?" Sam asked. The Kidgwick farm was a good two miles from Joelle's mobile home, maybe a mile and a half as the crow flies.

Van rubbed his hand on his knee. "I talked to her a couple of times. We used to get people on the property a lot. Curious, ghoulish. I run most of those kind off. Do you know who we are?"

Sonora nodded.

"So you know what happened here? You know the pond was where they murdered Ben Randolph."

"Yes."

"Our daughter. Our daughter was involved, but—"

His wife pursed her lips. "You don't need to go into that."

She might never have spoken.

"She's dead now, our daughter. When it happened, she was probably about the age of this girl. That's why—that's why I didn't get after her for coming around. And she said she lived nearby, so she was sort of a neighbor. And Ben's parents came for a while. But that didn't work out."

"They blamed us," Mrs. Kidgwick said. "It got awkward. And it didn't seem to be good for them. The wife used to just crumple up, and the husband would about have to carry her out. And one day I saw Tammy watching them out the porch window, and we had to ask them not to come anymore. It was bad for her. She never . . . She's dead now, of course."

"What was Joelle doing on the property?" Sonora asked.

Van looked at the toe of his hiking boot. "She just sat by the pond and wrote in this little book. She'd come in the afternoons sometimes, after school. Just sit and look at the water and write in her little book. We didn't talk to her much. I'd look out the back window sometimes, and there she'd be.

"You know teenagers, they need a place to be by themselves. Once in a while I'd look out and think just for a minute that it was Tammy. You forget, you know, and you look up and expect to see her."

Sonora nodded. She still half expected to hear her brother's voice on the answering machine when she wasn't thinking. Not so much lately. Which made him seem further away.

Mrs. Kidgwick folded her arms and leaned against the door. "It's a funny spot, down by that pond. The animals won't go down there."

"Honey." This from Van.

"It's true. The cows used to drink out of it all the time. Now they won't go near it."

"Lincoln will."

"Lincoln was Tammy's dog. He goes everywhere."

"Lincoln doesn't mind ghosts." Van lifted his head. Looked at Sonora. "This Joelle Chauncey. She never did anything but sit by that pond. I'll tell you right now, she doesn't seem like the kind of little girl who would steal a truck."

Sonora took the picture back, handed it to Sam. "She wasn't."

22

"You think they were involved," Sam said.

Sonora leaned back into the seat of the official-issue Taurus she and Sam shared. As usual, she was too short for the head-rest to do anything but throw her neck into an awkward position, so she slumped sideways, cheek against the window.

"God, no. Still. We better check everything out."

"Get some uniforms to go over the property. That's a big pond."

"I wonder how deep it is?"

"We may have to drag it, I'll talk to Mickey."

"Of course we have to drag it, or did you just want to bide your time in case something surfaces in the spring?"

"Don't be cranky, Sonora." Sam started the engine. The car snagged in the mud, then broke free.

Sonora rubbed her eyes. "Why does Crick want us right now? Didn't you tell him we found the girl?"

Sam glanced at her. "I'm going to leave that out? He said there'd been developments, and we could come into the bull-pen while CSU does the excavation—which will take a while, Crick told Mickey to be meticulous."

"Mickey meticulous. That's scary. He'll be there till my kids start college."

"Don't sit like that, Sonora. If we have a wreck, you're going to slide right out of that shoulder harness and through the windshield."

"I'll be a violent projectile."

"Makes you sound like vomit."

Sonora studied the dirt-creased blisters on the inside of her palm. "Wonder what it's like to be murdered at the age of fifteen?"

Sam looked at her hands. "You got blisters, Sonora? After ten minutes with a pitchfork?"

Male. Conflict avoidance. Sonora looked back at her hands.

"I'm delicate, Sam."

"Spit on 'em."

"Spit on them? Don't explain, Sam, no doubt it's a guy thing." She glanced out the window, pushed her hair out of her face. "Listen, this is nuts. I don't like all this driving around, we're wasting time. We need to arrest somebody."

"You did already. That's why Crick wants us downtown."

"Are you talking about McCarty? I didn't arrest him, Sam, he's being held."

"I'm sure he appreciates the distinction."

Sonora spit on the palms of her hands, rubbed them together, which immediately made them more painful. So much for guy traditions.

"What did Crick say exactly?"

"I told you already. Why don't you talk to him yourself next time?"

"I don't like talking to him."

"Look, it wasn't what he said so much as his tone of voice. Something to do with McCarty, which might be good news, since it didn't have anything to do with your shoot."

"Are we in trouble?"

Sam gave her a sideways look. "*I'm* not."

"You're my partner, Sam. When I'm in trouble, we're in trouble."

* * *

They parked next to the chain-link fence at the back of the lot a block down from the Board of Elections building. It wasn't a marked parking space, but it would do. The lot was full. The shift was in full swing, and downtown was replete with weekday workers.

The sidewalks were wet, so it had been raining here too. The wind blew. Sonora knew her hair was curly and loose. She brushed dirt off her shirt front.

A woman in a navy suit walked by, her heels low and sensible. But she wore large silver hoops in her ears. Sonora glanced over her shoulder, bit her lip. The dress code changed every year, but big earrings were never okay. Too many cops had had their earlobes ripped open or off by perps in a scuffle. Dangerous enough to have long hair.

Sonora thought she might like to have a nice navy business suit, except that she wasn't through with back-to-school expenses, which meant backpacks, book fees, oversize and overpriced jeans, and long lists from teachers who knew exactly what they wanted down to size, brand, and color of folders.

She looked at Sam to see if he was watching the woman. "We smell like manure."

"We're hardworking, honest cops. Let 'em smell that."

She followed him into the building. "Believe me, they will."

The elevator was slow. Sonora leaned back against the wall, met Sam's eyes. He looked tired. There were dirt stains on the knees of his khakis, one trailing up the left thigh. Hers didn't look much better.

"What?"

"Nothing."

"Straighten your tie," she told him.

"Just as soon as I put one on. I just wish we could go to bed."

"Together, or to sleep?"

The elevator opened. Sonora looked at Sam over one shoulder. Saw the wink.

The homicide offices were fully jazzed, bulletin board full of crimestoppers info, Janey waving from behind the glass partition.

Sonora opened the swing door into CSU, peeped into the offices. Skeleton staff. She squinted, looking to the back of the room. Field boots and overalls off their hooks, if she could trust her vision at that distance. Everyone out to recover Joelle Chauncey. Which was where she wanted to be.

The left swing door swayed. Sam, heading in to homicide. Sonora followed him through, smelled fresh coffee and the faint odor of cologne.

She checked the interview rooms out of habit. The light was on in Interview One, but the room was empty. Interview Two, next door, was dark.

Where had they put McCarty?

They better not have let him walk. Lawyer or no, Crick could have kept him. Should have kept him.

Sam stopped at his desk, leaned over the machine to pick up messages. Sonora passed her own desk, messy and depressing. Everyone looked crisp and pulled together this morning, or maybe she was just self-conscious because she smelled like manure.

There were green cans of Serge mixed with the usual Coke and Dr Pepper empties in the box outside the offices of the elite. Sonora grimaced. Her kids loved that stuff.

She wondered if Joelle Chauncey had been a Serge fan—all the rage with that age group.

The door to Crick's office was closed. Unusual. Sonora knocked, glanced once over her shoulder at the bullpen.

Sanders had changed her hair again. She was on the phone, but her eyes were focused on a spread of tarot cards laid across her desk.

And her skirt was shorter than her usual conservative two inches below the knee. Sonora frowned. Did that mean the married guy was back, God forbid? Tarot cards and 1–900-PSYCHIC. Long long talks over coffee and Cokes.

She had hoped the wailing and teeth gnashing were finally over.

"Get in here, Blair."

Crick's voice. Sounding angry, but he always sounded that way, and she wasn't too happy herself if he'd let her suspect go.

"How did you know it was me?" Sonora said.

Hal McCarty sat beside the desk parallel to Crick's. He had his left ankle across his knee, and he looked comfortable and more relaxed than anyone had a right to be, with Crick in the room. He was drinking coffee, and Crick had given him one of the beige mugs, a clean one, which was a sign of gracious camaraderie one might extend to another cop—certainly not a suspect in the disappearance and brutal murder of a fifteen-year-old girl.

"I can tell by the knock. Sounds more hollow when it comes from the lower half of the door."

A short joke. For all she knew, it was true. She sat, folded her arms. Whatever was going on, Crick had evidently decided that Hal McCarty was not a suspect.

Both men watched her, and she caught a hint of apologetic amusement from McCarty. Sonora felt her face go hot. It was feeling like good ole boy time.

"Is something funny? Mr. McCarty?"

He sat up in his chair. It was the tone of voice that made him wary.

"I'm sorry. Just your face when you walked in and saw me sitting here."

"Like a guest instead of a suspect?" Sonora looked at Crick. "This man is reading my mind."

"He's more of a colleague than a guest."

"*Is* he?" Sonora stood up so fast, the chair behind her went over on its side. She looked at her watch. "We're twenty-four hours into this investigation, and my prime suspect is a colleague? I don't think so. A *colleague* would identify himself first thing. A *colleague* wouldn't waste my time. A *colleague*—"

McCarty had set his coffee cup down on Crick's desk and was moving around behind her. She watched him from the corner of her eye.

"A colleague will pick up your chair." Which he did, dusting the seat with his hands. "Please. Please sit down."

Sonora took a breath. Sat down because she felt stupid standing up and she had nowhere to go with this. She looked at Crick. "You know the first twenty-four hours are the most critical."

McCarty held up a hand. "I know. You're right." He sat back down. "I made a judgment call, a bad one. I'm sorry."

Sonora folded her arms. Looked from one to the other. "So, who do you work for, Mr. McCarty? You undercover for the ASPCA?"

"He's a fed," Crick said. Set his coffee cup on the desk, next to a stack of printouts and a mess of folders.

"Oh, happy day," Sonora said.

"Thoroughbred Racing Commission," McCarty said.

"On a mission from God?"

"Higher than that. The Jockey Club."

"What are you doing in the middle of my homicide?"

McCarty spread his hands, let them rest on his lap.

Sonora nodded. Like most feds, McCarty would love to hear anything they could tell him. But he'd keep his own stuff to himself.

"Tell me about the horse she was riding," Sonora said.

McCarty gave Sonora a long look.

Something about his eyes, she thought. Something knowing. He was going to open up. Just a little.

"Good question. No, detective, don't set your lips, I'm going to talk to you. Joelle Chauncey. I can't wrap my mind around that part of it, but . . . you found the body?"

Sonora nodded.

"What about the horse?"

"Don't know yet."

"It makes a difference," McCarty said.

"You tell me why."

McCarty put the left ankle down, crossed the other foot over in the wide-legged way of large and confident men. He rubbed the bridge of his nose.

"I don't know what it is. But greedy people, helpless animals, and money—makes a bad combination, you know?"

Sonora sat sideways, watching him. She nodded. "Like the Calumet thing."

"The murder of Alandar? Never proven."

"And Jimmy Hoffa just got on the wrong bus."

McCarty gave her a half smile that was more of a grimace.

She looked at Crick. "Brilliant stallion, breeding seasons oversold years in advance, money already paid. Well insured. Horse maybe worth more dead than alive. Same horse coincidentally dies under mysterious circumstances—"

Crick was nodding.

McCarty waved a hand. "I'm not going to argue. You're right, it's just the kind of thing I'm talking about. Sponges in the nasal cavities of racehorses, fraudulent birth-date registrations of yearlings—"

"Delaney's involved in that kind of thing?"

"Birth dates?" He grinned, shook his head. "That's like chasing down people parking in handicapped spaces. Happens all the time, and you only go for the ones that are blatantly in your face."

Sonora leaned back in her chair. "How to put this politely."

Both men waited, neither looked patient.

"What's an undercover hotshot doing going after a Donna Delaney? She's small time and shoestring. If she generates as much as a couple thousand in income off that place every month, I'd be shocked."

"Last year she reported her income to the IRS as eighteen thousand nine hundred. Taxable income."

"Yeah?" Sonora said. The bill for the Kieffer saddle came to mind.

"She bought horses in excess of forty-eight thousand. Owns a brand-new F-350, free and clear. Spent a small fortune on tack and gear from horse catalogs."

"Her duplex doesn't show any sign of monetary good fortune," Sonora said. "And the barn and pasture—nobody's spending money there."

"No. But she's got it. Another expense last year—over eight thousand on antique teddy bears."

"Bears?" Crick said.

"Antiques."

"That still doesn't warrant a TRC undercover cop."

"No, Sonora, you're right. Delaney's strictly small time."

She liked the way he said her name. He was attractive as hell and had all the right nots—not a suspect, not a witness. Not married. No ring, anyway.

"She's our wedge against the big guys," McCarty said.

"Would one of these guys be a woman by the name of Vivian?" Sonora said.

McCarty raised an eyebrow. "What makes you say that?"

"Weird phone message on her machine. This Vivian called at, I don't know, some ungodly hour, six thirty or something, asking if Delaney was 'okay' and saying they needed to talk. I didn't like the sound of it."

"Good intuition," McCarty said. "Vivian and brother Cliff Bisky, of Bisky Saddlebreds."

"Even I've heard of them," Crick said. "What's the angle with the kid? You think they're involved here?"

"I'm not sure. If they are involved, it's over the horse. The little girl is incidental."

Sonora leaned forward, seeing the steaming manure, the toe of a riding boot, in her mind's eye. She tried not to imagine what was underneath. She would see the real thing soon enough.

"I'm not asking you to be sure, just tell me your theory."

McCarty looked at her. Thinking. He needed a shave, which Sonora found sexy on this man. He smiled at her. Capitulation.

"The mare Joelle Chauncey was riding when she disappeared belongs to Bisky Farms. Owned by a wealthy client of Bisky Farms."

"If the killer was after the horse, why involve the kid?" Crick's tone of voice said bullshit.

McCarty waved a hand. "We're just blue-skying here, okay?

Snatching the kid, killing her—makes no sense. Pulls in a lot of heat, which you know they don't want. Not logical, unless someone went after the horse and just got the kid too, in some kind of clusterfuck.

"Bisky Farms has a lot of rackets going—dirty rackets. By reputation to the average Joe, they're a top-notch breeding farm, well known on a national and to some degree even international level. They breed and train high-dollar Saddlebreds. Having a brood mare boarded on their farm is a matter of prestige in horsy circles.

"Their specialty is to take, say, Mr. and Mrs. Good Bucks from Nashville. Take their mare while it's in foal and charge fifteen hundred dollars a month for top-notch high-flight vet and daily care for this oh-so-valuable mare. And if Mr. and Mrs. Good Bucks are dabblers with a romantic notion about dipping even more of their wallets into the horse business, then Cliff Bisky, or his sister Vivian, might even have sold them the mare, or bred the mare, or sold them part interest in the mare. Or the foal. Could be any possible combination, tailored to how the clients want to spend their money.

"Now, there are twenty-one stalls available at the farm, each one of them beautiful mahogany wood, I wish I lived so good. But the thing is, most of them are full of Bisky's own horses, and he's one of those horse people who always has to be buying and selling. It's not interesting to him unless he's bringing in new horses every few months, so he's always got more stock than is good for him.

"No room for Mr. and Mrs. Good Bucks's little mare, so she goes out to a little hole-in-the-wall farm like Donna Delaney's place. Cliff Bisky pays Delaney some nontaxable cash and gives her the horse to keep till whenever, meanwhile raking in fifteen hundred a month on board and vet bills, not to mention incidentals. I'm sure Cliff tells Donna Delaney to give that mare top-quality feed and to keep her out of the fescue. And I'm sure that the mare gets nothing but piss-poor pasture and low-grade hay, if she's lucky."

"And Mr. and Mrs. Good Bucks don't have a clue? They don't check it out?"

"Sure they do. They blow into town for a visit, and the mare is brought in, cleaned up, put in a stall she's probably never seen before, goes to horse heaven for three days while Bisky rolls out the red carpet for the clients, who are probably shown a fabulous prospect they might want to invest in while they're in the neighborhood. And I'm sure this prospect is being personally trained by Cliff or Vivian Bisky, who may possibly be available to train the Good Bucks' impending foal, if they decide in plenty of time, because the Biskys are much in demand and the schedule is filling up. Mr. and Mrs. Good Bucks go home with a roll of film, the seed of the next business deal, and the clubby feeling of being in the glamorous, romantic saddlebred horse business with no more effort or expertise than it takes to write a check."

Crick scratched his neck. "So Delaney leads you to Bisky."

"Exactly." McCarty sipped cold coffee.

"I understand why Delaney's frantic to get the mare back," Sonora said. "I don't understand why she gets her finger cut off. Who does that? Bisky?"

McCarty nodded. "Bisky. Who has every reason to be upset with Ms. Delaney, who refuses to give up said mare. Wants more money, likely she thinks they owe her, or she's just desperate. She's on the verge of bankruptcy, which is par for people in the horse business."

"Boom or bust," Crick said.

"Not much boom for the bottom feeders like Delaney. Hardscrabble and marginal profits. It's possible to be honest in this business. I've even heard of it once or twice. If they could sell their egos, they'd all be wealthy. And don't kid yourself. Ego is a big part of the whole wheel here. Cash, personality, and horses. Top you up, Sonora?" McCarty glanced over his shoulder at the coffeepot that was, as usual, overheating behind her on top of Crick's metal file cabinet.

"Why kill the kid?" Sonora sat back in her chair. "I just

can't get past that. They've got to know it'll bring down a major shit storm.''

"We got three things," Crick said. "The death of the child, the disappearance of the horse, the attack on Delaney. How they relate, if they relate, is up to the two of you. Working together." He pointed a thick finger at McCarty. "You'll focus on the scam angle." He pointed at Sonora. "You'll work the murder. With the proviso''—he looked at McCarty—''that the murder investigation takes precedence. Right now, we don't know if Bisky Farms is involved in Joelle Chauncey's murder— for that matter, we don't even have a positive ID on the body.''

"It's her," Sonora said flatly.

"You'll know for sure soon enough." Crick leaned back in his chair, folded his arms. "No holding back, either of you. Share everything.''

Sonora said yes sir, wondered if Crick had actually winked at her, or if she'd imagined it.

Didn't matter. A good cop never trusted the feds. She knew it, and he knew she knew it.

Except it was a fine line to walk, over the death of a fifteen-year-old girl.

23

THERE HAD BEEN a sudden flurry of paperwork in Crick's office, an exchange of numbers and forms with TRC, which Sonora saw did not please McCarty so must mean Crick was watching their back. She had slipped away, nabbed Sam, decided to head back to the Kidgwick place; Halcyon Farm. It was never a good strategy to stay in Crick's frame.

Sonora looked at Sam as he eased the Taurus down the gravel and dust road to Halcyon Farm.

"This driving back and forth is killing us."

"We couldn't have done much till Mickey got here anyway." He parked the car, put the brake on.

"Just do me a favor, Sam. If your cell phone rings, ignore it." She got out of the car, moving away from him and everybody else. Hesitated at the perimeter of the crime scene tape.

POLICE LINE DO NOT CROSS.

Death seemed somehow quieter when it was cold. Mickey glanced her way, and his look of intensity was not lost on her. She was aware of the wind, gusting, rattling the tape, sending drifts of grit from the exposed interior of the manure pile into the breeze, her hair, her clothes.

The world in motion, the child so still. The noise, the chit-chat, deep voices, technicians, coroner's assistants, all faded to a background buzz. If someone asked her a question right then, she would not hear them.

She was listening, listening hard. Not to her colleagues. Not to the wind.

To the killer.

This was where he would talk to her. This was his or her strongest voice, the big statement, the death scene.

Sonora moved in closer, hands working to slide into the latex gloves. She moved sideways to the manure pile, still steaming from the center where Mickey's crew had foraged.

Joelle Chauncey had been buried more than sixteen inches deep, wrapped in a thin mud-stained, emerald green blanket that had been tucked around her arms the way a mother would bundle an infant. Her face was covered, the top of her head visible, a crown of thick brunette hair crusted with dried black blood.

Sonora nodded at Mickey, flipped back the edge of blanket that loosely covered the face.

There was dirt in the hair, cold hard manure, and Joelle's eyes were open and soiled. The sun on her face did not warm the blue-white cast of her skin. The right pupil was a huge black pool, like a bull's-eye, the left constricted to a tight pin-point. Brain hemorrhage, blunt trauma. But in that left eye, the blood vessels were thick, ropy, and red.

Sonora knelt beside the body. For an unexpected moment she could not seem to catch her breath, and she was enveloped in a panicky asthmalike sensation that promised her that no matter how much oxygen she sucked in, her lungs would ache and strain, unsatisfied.

"Sonora?"

She looked up, saw Sam. He crouched on Joelle Chauncey's right side, and they huddled together over the body.

Sonora felt sweat film the back of her neck, and then she was okay.

"Look at her eyes, Sam. Look at those blood vessels."

"Petechial hemorrhaging. She suffocated."

Sonora shone her tiny penlight into the child's nostrils,

looking for dirt and fiber. Touched the mannequinlike wrist, testing the stiffness, thinking about time of death. Had they all gone home while Joelle was breathing her last?

She studied the face, remarkably clean under the circumstances, no blood on the forehead, one smudge of dirt on the left cheek. The arms were folded neatly across the chest.

"Placement," Sam said.

"Yeah. Very deliberate. You think she was alive when this son of a bitch buried her?"

"Let's wait for the autopsy. Maybe we're wrong."

"Come on, Sam, don't duck out on me. You said it yourself. He tucked her in like a baby, while she was still alive, and she suffocated in the middle of a manure pile. How long did it take for her to die, do you think?"

"She wasn't conscious, Sonora, not with that kind of head injury."

Sonora thought of herself, soaking in a hot tub of bubbles, listening to Janis Joplin, while Joelle Chauncey, bundled in the emerald green blanket, waited for someone to come and help.

Sonora was sitting sideways in the car with the door open, filling out forms, trying not to watch while Mickey and an assistant she did not recognize tucked Joelle into the heavy black plastic body bag. She heard the metallic rasp of the coarse zipper, winced when it snagged on God knew what, and sighed when it shut, sealing Joelle Chauncey's young blue-white face away.

Sonora caught her breath, hit by a spasm of claustrophobia that made her chest go tight. She watched Mickey take the top end of the bundle, heaving Joelle's body gently onto a stretcher. He covered the bag with a white sheet, then strapped the bundle, working the buckles with the deft precision of someone going about a familiar task. He always covered the young ones personally and carefully.

The first raindrops fell as the stretcher was loaded into the back of the coroner's van.

Mickey turned to supervise the techs who were gathering the layers of dirt and manure that rested under the body. They moved quickly, trying to beat the weather.

A hand on her arm. "Sonora?" Sam leaned toward her, left arm braced on the roof of the Taurus.

Sonora put her chin on her elbow. She watched the strobe lights arc across Sam's face. He looked like he always did, boyish but not youthful, lines of experience, lines of trauma, giving his face a plane of character that was as attractive as it was comforting. She knew better than to ask how he was holding up. Deep down inside, he was a much nicer person than she was. She used to think it made him more vulnerable, but it seemed instead to lend him strength.

"It'll be easier on the dad if we just show him the picture."

"Why would we want to be easy on him?" Sonora said.

"You think the father did this?"

"I don't know. Placement says it was someone who cared about her. Covered her up, set her arms like they did."

"You think the dad took the horse? Cut off Donna Delaney's finger?" Sam shook his head. "If you want to kill your kid, there are easier ways. And I'm sorry, Sonora, that guy doesn't have the balls for something like this." Sam rubbed his chin. "Let's just take him the Polaroid. We haul him down to the morgue, and there'll be a big scene."

"He'll still have to go down there. He'll want to. They always want to go see for themselves."

"He can come down to the morgue later, with a friend, when he's got himself together. For now, let's just show him the shot, tell him as soft as we can, then get the hell out. This guy isn't exactly a rock, you know? Do it now, he may puke or pass out."

"That's what I want to know."

"What?"

"The reaction, Sam. I want to see it. Don't you?"

He rolled his eyes, went around the back of the car, and slid behind the wheel. Sonora closed her door against the rain, the mud, the arcing lights.

Sam started the engine, cranked it a couple of times though it had already caught. "Let's just play it by ear, okay, Sonora? Be nice. Taking him through that whole morgue thing—the guy's daughter just got murdered, let's go easy."

"It would be a mistake, Sam, to confuse me with somebody nice."

"You always say that."

24

SAM TURNED down the gravel drive to End Point Farm, serpenting the Taurus to avoid the worst of the rain-filled potholes. Sonora looked out the window. Even with the investigation in the infant, raw, and frantic state, the farm gave her that peculiar sensation of homecoming that she often got from crime scenes, so strongly did they permeate the landscape of her mind.

The small gravel lot in front of the barn was overflowing—white vans, Pintos, and Subarus. A baby Mazda pickup, teal green, sideways in the grass.

The press had arrived ahead of them.

Sonora ripped off her seat belt, listening to the snort and scream of horses who called to each other, restless in all the commotion.

"Wait till I park," Sam said.

"Just pull it off the road and come on. The van isn't even at the coroner's yet—how'd word get out so fast?"

"That we found her? What makes you think it did? They're just here over the vanishing. Girl and horse, gone like that." He snapped a finger, put the car in park. Patted his pocket. "You got the Polaroid?"

"I want to do the morgue thing."

"We're not doing the morgue."

*   *   *

Dixon Chauncey was standing on the steps of his mobile home, surrounded by a horseshoe of reporters with microphones that looked like thick, fur-covered bananas, camera operators standing stoically in the rain. The camera guys were the same as always, never a word, no animation crossing their face.

Chauncey was spelling his name, chest thrust out, till he caught sight of Sonora and Sam. He looked away, unwilling to meet their gaze. He seemed to shrink, head bobbing, like a hermit crab scuttling for the shell. His eyes were wide, and he gave Sonora a fleeting deer-in-the-headlights look before his attention was caught by Wyndham from Channel Ten.

"Ma'am?" he asked, ducking his head. "No, ma'am. I just would like whoever took my little girl to please just bring her back."

"Shades of Susan Smith?" Sonora muttered to Sam.

"Hush, Sonora. He didn't do this."

"Mr. Chauncey, have the police found any leads to your daughter's disappearance, other than the blood-soaked riding boot?"

"Uh, no, ma'am. Not so far as I know."

"Do you think your daughter is still alive?"

His eyes went to Sonora and Sam. A ripple of interest moved through the knot of newspersons. They were recognized.

Tracy Vandemeer from Channel Eighty-one went straight to Sonora. "Specialist Blair, from homicide, is here on the scene. Detective Blair, have you found any new leads in this case?"

Sam took the opportunity to race up the staircase, leaving Sonora to draw the fire. She wanted to be the one to race up the stairs, but it was too late, she was surrounded. Sam had Chauncey's elbow—the man seemed reluctant to give up his place on the porch, and he stumbled going into the house, causing a flurry of camera shots. Sonora was too short to see what happened next, but she heard a door open and close. They had left her behind.

A guy she didn't recognize, from Channel Twenty-six, thrust a microphone into her face.

"My superior officer, Sergeant Crick, may have a statement later today. I have no comment at this time." She looked at Brian Fiore from Three, waiting to catch his eye. Gave him what she hoped was a significant look. If she caught him in private, she would give him some copy. It was payback time, but she'd have to talk to Chauncey first.

"But you are working the Joelle Chauncey disappearance?"

"Yes," Sonora said.

"Have you found the horse?"

"Have you found the girl?"

"Have you found the other boot?"

They were going through the motions, wasting her time and theirs. They knew she could not make a statement unless it was cleared through the department, but they were compelled to push.

Sonora put her head down, folded her arms, and headed up the steps till she could hang on to the rail and look down. One of the cameramen had followed her up. Stoically, of course, but he'd followed.

She was very aware of the dirt stains on the knees of her khakis, the sleeves of her shirt. Her hair, frizzing in the rain, blowing every which way. Everything about her screamed "body, we found the body," but no one seemed to pick up on the evidence.

Why did they never catch her on a good hair day?

"We are pursuing more leads, yes to that question." Sonora held up a hand. "It would be inappropriate for me to comment further. Any inquiries should be directed toward Sergeant Crick of the Cincinnati Police Division."

"Detective?"

She turned her back and went into the house, heard someone commenting on her mud-stained knees. Likely there would be a close-up on the six o'clock news. She hoped they would call it mud and not something worse.

25

Sonora WENT THROUGH the front door with something more like speed than decorum. Sam and Chauncey were seated on the brown leather couches, both of them perched on the very edge. One slip, and they'd be on the floor, next to the children, who were cross-legged in front of the couch, working a book of puzzles and mazes in pencil. The little girls were much too quiet. They sat side by side and watched with wide eyes.

"See? The penguin is over here." Mary Claire spoke in a whisper, and Kippie nodded, but watched the room.

Mary Claire looked up at Sonora. "We didn't go to school today."

She wore blue jeans and a long-sleeved blue shirt, and her hair was not combed. Kippie, however, was neatly turned out in a pink and yellow jumper, and her hair had been put back in inexpert fashion with two red barrettes. Sonora guessed that Mary Claire was taking charge of her sister. Which made her wonder how Chauncey was holding up.

Not well, she decided.

Chauncey sat limply, shoulders slumped, large hands hanging loosely between his legs. She took a step backward to lock the door, and he looked up. For a minute his eyes were alive with a light and a focus that Sonora found hard to meet. She studied his hands, looking for scratches, wounds. Nothing but calluses that she could see.

Sonora tried to catch Sam's eye. Had he delivered the news? Surely not, with the children in the room.

"Guess who's been calling?" Sam said.

Sonora sat on the footstool in front of the wide easy chair that she was sure would be the room favorite. It seemed a bit more worn than the others, and something sticky had been spilled on the armrest. Looked like Coke.

"Montel Williams wants Mr. Chauncey for an interview."

Chauncey swallowed. "He wants me to appeal to the kidnappers—ask them to"—the voice broke—"to give me back my little girl."

Both children looked up sharply, watching him.

Look to your daughters, Sonora thought, appalled to find herself feeling such a mix of annoyance and impatience. Chauncey was soft, unpalatably soft, and she wanted to shake him. She did not like the way he stood like a lamb for the reporters, putting up a brave front. She did not like the way he crumpled down and waited. Where was the anger? Where was the fight?

Why was she such a hardass?

"When is the interview?" She wondered what Crick would say about a Montel show. Another media blot for Cincinnati, still trying to live down their jailing of a grandmother for a parking meter violation.

My hometown.

"I told them no," Chauncy said, lips tight. He did not want to talk about it.

Sonora did not argue. A plea to kidnappers was a moot point. This was a homicide now.

Sam looked at Sonora, and they stared at each other for a moment—who would lower the boom?

Sonora cleared her throat, voice low and quiet. "Mr. Chauncey, do you think that Mary Claire and Kippie could draw in their room for a few minutes while we talk."

He looked up, shoulders drawn. He started breathing

quickly, and Sonora saw sweat, slick and oily, break out across his forehead. His fingers trembled like butterflies against his knees.

She bit her bottom lip. She should have handled that better, should not have talked about the children as if they were not there. But it was too late. Mary Claire was snatching up colored pencils and the puzzle books and taking Kippie by the hand. It was too much for a small person. Four of the pencils dropped, and she turned a look on Chauncey that made Sonora wish she was anywhere but here.

"Looks like you could use some help, ma'am." Sam bent down and picked up pencils, and Mary Claire gave him a mesmerized look. It was likely the first time a strange man had called her ma'am. Sam held out his arms, and Kippie went to him, and he led the little girls down the hall.

Sonora waited for the bedroom door to close.

"Mr. Chauncey. We've found the body of a young girl, and I'm afraid that she matches pretty closely your description of Joelle."

Chauncey bowed his head and began to cry, tiny little sobs like hiccups of grief. Sonora noticed that his hair was thick, clean, and blacker than ever. She heard soft footsteps, saw that Sam was back in the room.

Sonora met his eyes, then looked back to Chauncey. "We need to make a formal identification as soon as possible."

"Do I have to?" Chauncey's voice was small. Childlike.

Sonora looked at Sam, who nodded. "I'm afraid so."

Chauncey's shoulders slumped. Acceptance, Sonora thought, wondering if this man always did as he was told.

"I don't think I can drive, I'm too upset."

"We'll give you a ride." Sam's voice was gentle.

"Do you want to go to your daughters for a while?" Sonora asked.

"No."

Sonora leaned toward him. "Can I get you something? A glass of water?"

He nodded. Looked up and mumbled something.

"What's that?" Sonora was appalled to hear the tinge of impatience in her voice.

Sam gave her a sideways look. "He said no ice."

"Okay." Sonora headed into the kitchen. The dishwasher was running, sounding like Sonora's old Nissan when it dropped a brake shoe. Chauncey, whose sobs had subsided while giving the specifics of his water, kicked in with some gusty crying that teetered on the edge of a hysteria that made Sonora wince. She and Sam usually made their exit before this stage. They were going to have to ride with this guy all the way downtown. Sam was going to kill her.

The kitchen was clean, countertops spotless. The stainless-steel sink was shiny, a tiny residue of scouring powder along the rim of the drain. Not a crumb in sight on the tablecloth, foam-backed plastic, lemon yellow.

Sonora opened cabinets, looking for a glass. Found canned goods, stacked for the most part in order of size and content, with a few variations. Soups, chowders, jars of spaghetti sauce. Cans of Slim•Fast—who was going on a torture diet? Dixon Chauncey, or the young Joelle?

She hoped it was Dixon and not Joelle. She hoped Joelle had eaten chocolate and pizza before she died.

Sonora opened another cabinet. All the dishes were perfect, glasses in rows, perfectly matched, unlike her own cabinets, with cups with plastic bird feet lined up next to her remaining three crystal wineglasses.

All of Chauncey's glasses were clean. Her own dishwasher was leaving dried residue on her dishes, which made the machine something of a moot point.

She filled a glass with water—no ice. Opened the freezer, in case he hadn't wanted her looking there, remembering the head found in Jeffrey Dahmer's refrigerator.

No body parts.

Lots of Tupperware though, all neatly labeled—meatballs, lasagna, chicken noodle pie bake. Chauncey had dinner cooked ahead for the next two weeks.

He bought Ore-Ida Shoe String Potatoes, Sealtest ice cream,

chocolate chip cookie dough by the gallon. The ice trays were uniformly filled—none of that pop-out-a-few-cubes-at-a-time behavior was acceptable in this kitchen.

The refrigerator was less than perfect—catsup spills on the egg trays, which were empty of eggs. It would have been hard to imagine a refrigerator any other way, with three kids in the house.

Two now.

No Styrofoam white squares of take-home leftovers—did they ever eat out? Chauncey seemed to have the domestic front well in hand. Maybe he always cooked.

Sonora set the glass of water on the counter. Opened the cabinet under the sink—childproof latch, each new design an IQ test, but she was an experienced mom, she had it open in no time, like a expert safecracker.

No cleaners under the sink, which was good, there were small children in the house. The trash can was overwhelmed by a black plastic garbage bag, lawn and garden size, that hung down the sides, yellow ties threaded through the top seams for efficient disposal later on. It rested on a sticky plastic mat that would attract ants in the summertime. Sonora put a fingertip on the edge and tipped it forward.

Coffee grounds, lumped and deposited on a filter that had gone from white to sepia brown. Apple peel, an empty spray bottle that still had a blue film of Windex, and a lone plastic glove, thin, stained reddish black.

Sonora pulled the trash can out, looked at the glove. Not blood, surely? She rattled the bag, saw the box of Van Hale's Shampoo-In Hair Color, shades of raven black.

He had dyed his hair, that morning or the night before.

She found a plastic evidence bag in her jacket pocket. Put a latex glove on, took the stained plastic glove and the box of hair dye, just for good measure. He had invited them into his home and agreed she could get him water. She should be okay on this. Best make sure that was really hair dye and nothing else on the glove.

Her pocket bulged, but Chauncey was not the type to make

a challenge. And if he wondered and was nervous, so much the better.

Sonora put the trash can back under the sink, took the glass of water off the counter. Grabbed a box of Puffs—hefty size— sitting in the kitchen window. Chauncey was crying steadily, she could hear him faintly over the grind of the dishwasher.

It was going to be a long ride into town.

26

INSIDE THE FAMILIAR CORRIDORS of the city morgue, Chauncey seemed to shrink and grow wooden. He walked between Sonora and Sam down the long linoleum corridor that led to the room with a view.

It was very like a hospital corridor, hollow and impersonal, moderately clean. Not a happy place. There was no comfort to be had from block concrete walls, no matter how recently they had been painted.

Chauncey surprised her. He had stopped crying when he talked to the children, handling them gently, rocking Kippie in his lap until a friend from work arrived to look after them for the duration. Mary Claire had sat stiffly by his side as he rocked her little sister, and all Sonora could do was look at the little girl and wonder who was going to rock her.

He had cried quietly all the way into town, but as soon as they'd parked the Taurus and he'd looked out the window, as if to see that yes, indeed, what was happening was real, they were on their way to the morgue, the tears had dried.

He was quiet now, head tucked down into the wings of his shoulder blades.

Sonora watched him out of the corner of one eye. He had not asked how Joelle had died. Which could mean he was in shock, that he was afraid to ask questions, that he was avoiding the knowledge, or that he already knew.

With this man, any explanation could apply.

Was he capable of such a brutal murder and disposal? A man who did exactly as he was told, whenever he was told?

She'd interviewed men who had committed heinous crimes—men who were small, whippet thin, and dorky. One of the worst killers she'd tracked had been a petite blonde with tiny soft hands. Sonora could still see her, smiling serenely in the interview room. It was not a vision she encouraged. It reminded her of people she did not want to think about. Not now, when she had to concentrate.

They passed the ME's office—Stella's door was open. Sonora let Sam and Chauncey walk on ahead and stuck her head in. The woman behind the desk was precision perfect, careful makeup, a tight chignon, crisply ironed hospital fatigues. Sonora had never seen Stella when she was not handling three things at once, but today she sat behind the desk, fingertips pressed into a black cork blotter pad, eyes squinted and dreamy. She had high cheekbones, and her skin was a rich and flawless mocha brown.

"Stella?"

"Hello, Sonora. Was that him?"

They had been on first-name basis for a couple of years now, a major concession from this very correct, meticulous superwoman, who handled job, children, husband, and committee work with dedication, attention to detail, and very little humor.

"Yes," Sonora said.

Stella Bellair touched her bottom lip. "I gave the child a quick preliminary look before Lee got her draped for viewing."

Most MEs would have said vic. Victim. Subject.

Sonora stepped into the office, lowered her voice. "I thought she was in a pretty advanced state of rigor for someone who was last seen at three o'clock yesterday afternoon."

"Yes, but she was buried in a manure pile. I talked to Mickey. That could have accelerated the process."

"I see."

Stella tapped an impossibly white fingernail on the edge of the desk. "This girl was how old?"

"Fifteen." Probably about a year younger than Stella's daughter, if Sonora remembered correctly. "Stella. Do you think she was alive when the killer buried her?"

Stella shook her head. "Way too early for me to comment. How's the father holding up?"

Sonora shrugged. That wasn't what Stella was really asking—she wanted to know if he was under suspicion.

"Not well. He's here now, making the ID." Sonora wondered how Stella kept her office so clean. Did she come in after hours and scrub it herself? Or perhaps she just frightened the cleaning crew?

Stella gave her a steady look. "You want me to get blood and hair samples for you? From the dad?"

Sonora thought for a moment, nodded. "Yeah. That would help."

Lee Eversley was wearing a thick cable-knit fisherman's sweater in a color that could be best described as Mercedes white. He was holding a hand up at Sam.

"Give me thirty seconds." He glanced back down the hallway, saw Sonora, and winked. His face had healed indifferently over the scourge of old acne scars, which gave him a rough, masculine look. He had big shoulders, and Sonora always wanted to hug him. She wondered about his love life.

She heard the door to the viewing room shut, a bolt slide into place, and she waited for the song and dance to begin. The procedure, developed by the age-old process of trial and error, was set in concrete.

Sam and Dixon Chauncey waited, backs to the wall. The ring of a shower curtain sliding across an aluminum bar made everyone go tense. The curtains framed a rectangular window, six by two, coffin sized, through which they would be able to see into the refrigerated room where Joelle Chauncey's mortal remains rested on a thinly padded gurney.

That there had to be a wall between the victim and his kin was established early by the understandable but evidence-compromising behavior of people who often flung themselves on the body of their loved ones. There were no doctors in sight, in the hope that relatives would feel inhibited about fainting or showing physical signs of distress.

Sam pinched Chauncey's elbow and encouraged him to move closer to the window. He nodded at Eversley, who pulled back the edge of the white sheet to show the small, vacant, blue-tinged face.

Watching Chauncey made Sonora think of old Greek legends where vengeful gods turned men into stone. He grew silent and still in a way she had never seen before.

"Is that Joelle?" Sam asked softly.

Chauncey nodded. It was understood by everyone that he would not be able to talk.

Eversley glanced at Sonora; he was wearing his solemn look. She nodded. He put the sheet carefully back over Joelle's face and shut the curtains slowly and quietly.

"Come on, Dixon," Sam said, leading him away.

27

IT HAD TAKEN ONLY a hint that "he was needed" for Dixon Chauncey to agree to go back with them to the bullpen.

He sat in Interview One, hands between his knees. Sonora studied him across the chipped brown Formica table. There was no indication, from his expression, attitude, or body language, that they were intruding when he needed time to grieve, that they were asking too much of a man who had just identified his daughter at the morgue. Nor was there any indication of the crusader, the burning rage of the newly bereaved, robbed of someone they love by deliberate hands, ready to put grief on hold till they exercise their anger on the responsible parties.

Sonora reminded herself that it was unfair to harbor stereotypical expectations.

Chauncey could be in shock or, more likely, denial. He could be a difficult man to read. She remembered herself at her mother's funeral, making arrangements, making jokes, grief like a storm at sea—you know it is coming, and you do everything you can to prepare before it hits. But until it does hit, numb is a nice place to be.

Sam set a can of Mountain Dew in front of Chauncey, sat next to him on the left, took off his jacket, and hung it over the back of the chair. Sonora turned on the recorder, stated the date, place, and time. Chauncey had a straw in his Mountain Dew. Where had Sam come up with a straw? It was the kind with crinkles in the top, like they have in hospitals, so it made a little crook for easy sipping.

And while Sonora murmured into the recorder, Chauncey pulled the drink forward and sucked on the straw in a way that made her give him a second look. He was like a hungry baby taking a bottle.

She moved her chair a little farther away.

"Let's start with yesterday." Sonora leaned forward, elbows on the desk. "Do you get the kids off to school, or do they get up on their own?" She thought of her own morning routine, a weird mix of both. Her intention was always to get up earlier than the kids, but the older they got, the less successful she was.

Chauncey met Sonora's eyes, then looked away. "I, uh, I get up early. Around six. Get them cereal and juice and pack lunch for all of us."

"Anything unusual about your routine yesterday morning?"

"No."

Silence settled. Chauncey sucked at the straw.

"So you got them breakfast . . ." Sam prompted.

"Joelle gets up first, then the little ones, Mary Claire and Kippie. Mary Claire helps Kippie get ready. Joelle's kind of slow. She won't eat breakfast anymore, either, but I set her out a cereal bowl just in case. She worries . . . she was always worrying about her weight."

The child wrapped in the blanket had seemed so small. But Sonora did not take issue. Even Heather, in the third grade and underweight for her height, was weirdly concerned with her thighs. Rare was the teenage girl who did not weigh in and worry.

Sonora glanced at Sam. He shrugged. Chauncey was not bubbling over with information. Maybe a tactical change?

"Mr. Chauncey," Sonora licked her bottom lip. "Was Joelle dating yet?"

He was drinking when she asked, sucking that straw. He swallowed in a panic, choking a little, like people do when they're out to dinner and the waiter asks them if they need something when their mouths are full.

Chauncey shook his head. "No, ma'am, not that I know of."

"Would you know?" Sonora had a teenager. She knew there was a lot of stuff you might not know.

Chauncey leaned close. "I keep good track of my girls. As much as I can. I try not to work overtime or double shifts so I can head right home. But I am a single dad. It's kind of hard."

His eyes were opaque, like hard little buttons. He did not look away, as Sonora expected, but returned her gaze as if he were hungry for the contact. She watched him, thinking that this was what a martyr looked like, in the actual flesh.

"I think she liked one of the boys at school, but she wouldn't ever talk to me about those things."

"Were boys calling the house?"

"Oh, no, ma'am." He took an unopened packet of Wrigley's Spearmint gum out of his left front pocket. He was wearing a maroon-and-green-plaid shirt, and it looked new, the cotton-polyester blend stiff and uncomfortable.

"Gum?" he asked.

Sonora looked at Sam. She shook her head, and Sam took a piece. Southern graciousness, she thought.

Sam tapped a finger on the edge of the desk. Chauncey swiveled his head in the direction of the small and irritating noise.

"Mr. Chauncey, what's going on out there at Donna Delaney's farm?"

Chauncey frowned. "Funny business. That's what you mean?"

"That's what I mean." Sam kept up the rhythm with the finger.

"Sometimes? There are people out there that . . . how should I put this? I don't like the looks of 'em." He leaned close. Ready to confide. "Ms. Delaney does a lot of business she doesn't explain about. Horses come and go without warning. Sometimes she says she's bought them, but how could that be, if she doesn't even pay her bills?''

"How do you know she doesn't pay her bills?'' This from Sonora.

"They're always cutting off the water or the electricity, and she has to go down and make a deposit to get them to turn things back on. I myself would be embarrassed.'' He retreated to the back of his chair. "That's only me, of course. I shouldn't judge.''

He'd actually dared to give an opinion, Sonora thought. Followed by immediate retreat and discomfort.

Sam leaned back in his chair. "Who's she do business with, you know any names?''

Chauncey looked at his feet. Looked sideways. "I know she does some kind of business with those people out at Bisky Farms.''

Sonora watched him. He had all the mannerisms of a man who is about to lie, but the business dealings with Bisky Farms had been suspected and confirmed by Hal McCarty. So Chauncey was telling the truth.

"What do you know about Bisky Farms?'' she asked.

"Who, me? I'm a line worker at P&G, these folks are too high up for a guy like me.'' He shifted sideways in his chair. "Course now, some of these types they hire to do the barn work, they look like rough types to me. Not that they've ever bothered me personally, I've just seen them out there. If I was Donna, you know, if it was my farm, and all those kids out there, I wouldn't let people like that come around.'' He curled his fingertips on the edge of the table, leaned forward, shoulders hunched together.

"Did any of 'those people' bother you, Dixon? Come to your door? Talk to Joelle, maybe?''

Chauncey pressed his fingers deeper into the table, as if to bury them in wood. "No, never. We're far enough from the barn, we don't get bothered that way.''

"You sure?''

"Pretty sure. I can't be there every minute, a man's got to earn a living. But I don't know of anything. Not for sure."

He looked down again, then off to the side. Sonora couldn't figure him out. Was there something he was afraid to talk about?

She remembered the envelope, full of the faces of missing children. What or who was Joelle looking for? Herself?

"I noticed that she had an interest in missing children, kidnapping, children finding their birth mother."

Chauncey blinked. Stared at her. Made no comment.

Sonora looked down at her nails. "Didn't she ever discuss this with you, Mr. Chauncey? Was Joelle afraid of being kidnapped?"

"Not that I know of. She never said anything about it that I heard."

"Where's Joelle's mother?"

He looked up, mouth sagging. "Her mama? She's not around. I mean, she died. She had cancer, breast cancer, when Joelle was just a toddler."

"So the other children—"

"She made it through the first bout, but she was sick a lot. Chemo. We almost went under with the medical bills. She got a lot better, even went back to work. Then Mary Claire came along, and a couple years later Kippie. It came back, the cancer did, when Kippie was a baby. It took her real fast then." His eyes turned red and watery, like he was grieving or smoking pot. "I don't know what I'd do without my girls, my three musketeers."

It was not clear that it had dawned on him that the musketeers were now two.

"How well do you know Donna Delaney?" Sam asked.

Chauncey wiped his eyes with a thick knuckle. "I guess pretty well, you know how you do. I've lived next door to the woman, her barn anyway, for a couple of years now. I'd say we're pretty close. Not *real* close, but tight, you know. We see each other every day, so I'd guess that we know each other pretty well."

"You're friends, then?"

"Sure, we're friends. Donna doesn't talk to me a whole lot, but she's not all that talkative anyway. She lets my kids ride the horses. Joelle, anyway. Mary Claire's just nine, and Kippie is only seven. You can see how she'd have a problem with the little ones under her feet."

"I'm a little unclear about your arrangements with Donna. Do you work for her, or pay her rent, or how does that go?" Sonora glanced at the recorder. Plenty of tape.

Chauncey scrubbed his knees with his fists. "She likes having somebody out there, living out there, it's just better for the horses. So I only pay her a little bit of rent. I pay my own utilities of course, that would only be fair. And what I do in return is I get up early and do the stalls before I go on shift at P&G. Help out if she's got a fence board down, a loose post or something. You know horses, they chew the wood or even kick."

Sam nodded, man to man. "Keeping that fence from falling down's about a full-time job in itself."

Chauncey laughed, too hard, sounding forced, with something very like gratitude.

Sonora folded her arms. "Mr. Chauncey, do you have any personal theories about what happened to your daughter?"

The smile faded. That it had ever been there surprised Sonora a little. But not a lot. Grief takes time to absorb. Sometimes the mind and body resist. She had seen months pass before the enormity of a loss hit home. Had it happen to her in exactly the same way.

Chauncey hung his head, and Sam and Sonora had to lean close to hear him. "No, ma'am, I do not."

"Nothing at all? No gut instincts? Nothing?"

He shook his head, staring at the tabletop.

"You haven't had any indication at all that things might not be right? Strange phone calls, hang-ups, calls from school?"

"No. No, ma'am."

"Was Joelle worried a lot? Depressed?"

Chauncey mumbled something.

"What?" Sonora asked.

"Maybe a little depressed."

She could barely hear him. "Mr. Chauncey, are you saying that Joelle seemed depressed?"

His head bobbed. "Yes, she did. She didn't kill herself?" He looked up at her, eyes full of fat pearly glycerin tears. He had a hopeful air, like a puppy in a cage at the pound.

She knew that he wanted her to pat his back, to comfort him. What she really wanted to do was leave the room.

Sonora glanced at Sam. No help there.

"Your daughter was murdered, Mr. Chauncey."

"I know."

"You know?"

"I know."

"How do you know?"

"You told me." He was crying now, head down, eyes on the floor, quiet steady sobs.

Sonora looked at Sam. His hands went up, waist level.

Time to stop.

Sonora came out of the women's bathroom, droplets of water glistening on her face, just in time to see Sam heading down the hallway. Chauncey, a puppy at his heels, did not see her.

She had bailed out and left Sam alone with the sobbing man.

She hadn't meant to make Chauncey cry, and it made her feel unclean. His breakdown had disturbed her in a way she could not quite explain. It came too pat, like a habit, a familiar groove. The harder she was on him, the more he put that head down and groveled. She had the uneasy suspicion that he liked it, that he wanted to be dominated.

She did not like the way he looked at her—eyes so bright and needy. He had wanted her to look at him, to notice him, to feel sorry for him. She did not like being in the same room with him. He was like bruised fruit—soft and whangy. When he opened his mouth, she could see the metal fillings in his teeth.

She could not get the faces of Mary Claire and Kippie out of her mind. She told herself that they would be okay, that Chauncey kept an immaculate house, cooked nutritious dinners, worked hard for hearth and home.

She watched him follow Sam down the hallway, heard Sam's voice, tones soothing, promising Chauncey a short wait in the lobby until a uniform would come to give him a ride home.

Chauncey walked like a little bird, arms clamped against his sides like wings, hands balled into fists. Even when he moved his arms, they were never more than six inches from his hips, as if they were under restraint.

Sonora leaned against the wall and closed her eyes. The bullpen was night-crew silent, Crick was God knew where, and her head ached. She had not called the kids or bought groceries, and at the time when a good mother would have been home supervising dinner and homework, she'd been parading Dixon Chauncey through the morgue.

Time to call it quits. In her mind she spun the fast food roulette, thinking that Wendy's was close.

28

Sonora was in at seven the next morning, an hour before her shift. She had gone home the night before to a hot shower and five Advil, falling hard asleep on the couch where she had curled up to read her horoscope and be in the same room with the kids, who had immediately left.

She was awake before daylight, thinking about Joelle Chauncey's collection of missing children.

In the office, she started with coffee, her mug one third full of cold old dregs. The cream, aged now, had gathered in the middle, forming a star shape, with streaks that stretched across the brown oily surface.

She poured the leftovers into Molliter's cup, which glistened, squeaky clean, inviting. These petty forms of revenge made her happy, a bad reflection on her character.

She made a fresh pot of coffee, washed out her mug, and waited while the plastic coffeemaker bubbled three quarters through the cycle, then filled her cup. A stream of coffee, still spewing and brewing, hissed against the brown grungy burner and filled the bullpen with the evocative scent of scorched coffee.

Not an unpleasant smell, to an addict like Sonora.

She eased herself into her chair very slowly, closed her eyes against the blinking lights on her answering machine, and took the first sip.

Disappointing. She hadn't put in enough cream. She was trying to cut down, but the coffee was too harsh, and she didn't like the color, it was too dark. Might as well drink it black if it was going to taste this bad.

"Yo, *Sonora*. You make that fella cry? Molliter worked night shift, and he said you were brutal."

Gruber. Tie askew as always, but freshly shaved. He was coming from the men's room, he kept his razor at work. The man grew hair like an orangutan.

The guys were spending ridiculous amounts of time in the john these days. The city had renovated the men's bath and locker room, and they were getting pretty comfortable. Sonora wondered when the women's room would get fixed up.

"Did you spend last night in the john, Gruber? What do you guys do in there for so long?"

Gruber grinned. "I could draw you a picture. Better still, why—"

Sonora put her fingers in her ears and turned away. Could not believe she'd given Gruber an opening like that. She must be more distracted than she thought.

"I missed you last night. McCarty called."

The voice, immediately recognizable, came from directly behind her. She turned her chair back around and faced Sergeant Crick, who stood in front of her desk.

"He's been working the horse angle. Horse and trailer. He wants you to meet him at this address today at three." Crick tossed a folded yellow triangle onto her desk. Looked just like the notes they'd passed in junior high.

Sonora unfolded the paper. Frowned. Where the hell was Samoyan? "Is this in Cincinnati?"

"You're a detective, you find out."

It was one of Sonora's least favorite lines. Cops and psychics took too much of that crap.

Crick moved away, then paused. "I don't get this body drop. It's not Delaney's place—that End Point Farm?"

"No, sir, Halcyon Farm, about two miles away. End Point is the primary. Likely she was fatally injured in that paddock out there where she was snatched. Halcyon is the secondary, where she was buried."

"Okay, the body's at Halcyon, what about the Dually?"

"Same place, the secondary. The truck actually belongs to the people who own Halcyon Farm. We think it was stolen and used in the commission of the crime at the primary, which is End Point Farm, and wound up back at Halcyon, the secondary."

"As long as you've got it straight," Crick said.

"We don't actually have confirmation this truck is the one used in the commission of the crime, Mickey's on it, but I'm telling you, it's the one."

"Horse trailer turned up?"

"No."

"I'm almost relieved. I'm not sure I could keep track of another farm."

"We're dragging the pond out at Halcyon to see if it's out there."

"And no horse?"

"Not yet."

"Halcyon. Why does that name sound familiar? You talk to the owners yet?"

"Yes, sir."

"They do it?"

"My crystal ball says no."

He turned a quarter turn and faced her.

"It's no wonder you remember them," Sonora said. "They're Tammy Kidgwick's parents. The Randolph boy was murdered by their pond, you remember?"

Crick dropped his arms, stuck his left hand in his pocket. His face had that faraway focused look they all knew and dreaded. If he came up with a connection you missed, you'd feel stupid. If he came up with an assignment, you got overtime.

"Talk to Barry Fellowes about that. You know Fellowes? He's downtown with the mayor now. He worked that case, on the Randolph boy."

Sonora nodded. Crick was always telling them to look up the old guys. Like they had the time.

Crick gave her a second look. "What have you accomplished with your morning, Blair?"

Sonora glanced at her watch. Seven-thirty A.M. "We're waiting on the autopsy, sir. We interviewed the father last night. He gave us a definite ID."

"And?"

"He wasn't a whole lot of help."

Crick folded his arms. Lifted one thumb to rub the rounded jut of his chin. "He have any theories at all?"

Sonora shook her head. "Nothing but some vague stuff about 'goings-on' out at Delaney's barn. Nothing specific."

"What *did* he say?"

"That he didn't like the looks of some of the people Donna Delaney dealt with, and that she did business with Bisky Farms."

"How well you think he knows her business? They close? They fucking?"

"Not even vaguely possible."

"Then who does he think killed his little girl?"

It wasn't just the way Crick said little girl, softly, without edges, but the fact that he'd said little girl and not kid—clearly the man was upset.

Sonora shook her head. "I'm telling you, he's got no theories."

"None?"

"None."

There was a look in Crick's eyes. Sonora wished she could read him better.

"This guy cry every time you ask him a difficult question?"

"Pretty much. Hard to tell if it's a trend, he'd had a rough day."

"I don't like it when they cry instead of helping."

"Me either."

He took a step away, then glanced back over his shoulder. "Have the proper compassion, Detective Blair."

29

JOELLE CHAUNCEY'S THINGS had been boxed up by Renquist, released by a bewildered Dixon Chauncey, and were now resting next to Sonora's desk. The box, originally, had been used to ship a case of chicken/liver-flavored Alpo.

The reduction of an important life.

Sonora flipped through the envelope of information on missing children, parental searches for a birth child.

Joelle had been obsessed. And Dixon Chauncey had flatly denied any interest on her part.

Kids kept a lot to themselves. Joelle was fifteen. How much had Sonora confided in her dad at that age?

Nothing at all.

She'd like to talk to the other children. Which would be touchy. She needed to go to Joelle's school, talk to her teachers and friends.

The Kidgwicks had mentioned Joelle writing in a little book. Sonora rooted through the box, came up with several spiral notebooks, one a washed-out red, one shimmery lavender, one with Cinderella on the front.

That was right. Joelle Chauncey was a Disney kid, still attached to the mouse. Sonora knew people who stayed that way their entire lives.

She opened a notebook, read a few lines. She had hit pay dirt. Joelle Chauncey kept journals.

Sonora frowned as she read the stained notepaper, pages full of boys who were cute enough to die for but did not even look at her in the hall. Teachers who were impatient, bored, focused on their "pets." Little sisters who drove her crazy and got into her things.

Sonora leaned back in her chair, glanced around the office for Crick, then put her feet up on her desk.

Joelle Chauncey worried a lot.

She'd made a list of things she did not like about herself. Her weight, right at the top. Her hair color. Thighs that were "lumpy," cheeks that were round, eyebrows too heavy to be like "the pretty ones." And bony knees.

Bony knees?

Sonora glanced at a picture of Joelle at age twelve. A pretty child by any standard. Dark eyes and hair and a look of intelligence.

Sonora glanced down the hallway, watching out for Sam. He was late.

She flipped through the pages, lines and lines of tedious angst. Someone should have told this child to lighten up. She flipped to an entry neatly labeled as written at Halcyon Farm.

Joelle had an almost obsessive interest in Ben Randolph, the boy murdered at the pond. If Sonora hadn't known better, she'd have assumed the two had been close for a lifetime.

Understandable. Like a crush on a rock star. Intense and distant.

There were real friends, thank goodness, living breathing school friends. Joelle called them Pistol and Bits. Likely not baptized that way.

The next entry got Sonora thinking.

I have bad dreams a lot at night, and I am scared in my dreams.

Scared in her dreams?

Last night I dreamed about tornadoes—I had Mary Claire and Kippie with me. I was holding Mary Claire's hand and carrying Kippie, and we were running in the rain, and no one would let us in.

We would go to the door of every house, and no one would want us.

I dream about Mama sometimes. It is always daylight in those Mama dreams, and the sun is so bright my eyes hurt, and I can't quite see, but I know it is her.

Do I look like her, I wonder? I do not think so, because I have this feeling she is so beautiful and I am not. But maybe I am like her some. I watch families, regular ones.

Regular ones. Interesting. But probably most teens felt that way.

. . . and it's not so much that they look alike, they just talk alike and move their hands around. It's in the way they stand, too. That's how you can tell a family.

Poppie says we are sisters because he is all of our dads, but he isn't my dad. I don't remember my dad, but I do remember it was just Mom and me for so long.

Sonora had been reaching for her coffee cup. She checked. Chauncey had described a close devoted family, the mother dying tragically after Kippie's birth. But Joelle would have been eight. She would have remembered. Had the Chaunceys separated for a while? Not surprising, really, that he wouldn't have brought it up. If that were the case.

If I run away, what will happen to the girls? They are so little. And they make me so mad I feel like I hate them, but truthfully, I guess I do love them. I have taken care of them all of their life. I am like their mom. I'm never going to have any kids of my own, those two are enough.

But it would be wrong to leave them. I don't think we can all get away. I could go and come back for them, but I don't know where to go. And Poppie moves so much, I might never find them again.

Sonora made a note to look into past moves. Made another note. Had Joelle been going through the typical teenage run-away thing, or had she felt threatened in some way? The feelings could not be discounted—being buried alive was not a typical teenage experience. And Sonora got the feeling that the girl had felt an unease in her family situation that was striking. But very, very typical at this age. Don't jump to conclusions, she told herself. Her son could be writing worse, if he kept a journal.

If I find my mama, maybe she could take us all.

Very odd, this. As if the woman were alive.

> *The law would never allow it, but we could all hide some-where. We wouldn't even have to go to school. I could teach Kippie, and Mary Claire is so smart, she could get it all out of books anyway.*
> *But we could all run away until we grow up and then we'll be safe.*

There it was again. The fear. *Then we'll be safe.* Was Chauncey molesting the girls? This did not have that feel to it, but she'd have to keep her eyes open.

> *If we lived in the country, maybe we could have a horse. I wish we could take the mare with us. Mrs. Delaney says she is a bitchy mare, but Sundance likes me because she knows I would not hurt her. I sneak her food like Poppie does, and I never smack her or shank her with a chain like mean dog Delaney.*
> *Poppie really does love the horses. If I do leave the girls, he will see they grow up okay.*

Sonora ditched the child molesting theory.

And Poppie loves us and takes care of us. It would kill him for me to run away. Maybe if my mom is rich, she could buy Sundance. Mrs. D. will do anything for money.

If my mom is really dead like Poppie says, then I don't want to even think about it. He says she had cancer and he cries and everybody feels sorry for him, but she's my *mom, why does he get all the attention? I have heard that cancer runs in families. I am afraid that means I will get it. But Mary Claire and Kippie are safe because they are not my real sisters.*

What was with this kid? Living in fantasy land? Losing it? Or something truly odd in the wind?

Maybe I'll get married. If Joshua Bender would notice me, we could get married. I could go to work at Taco Bell.

When I am eighteen, I can go to that place that helps you find your mother. But that's only if she gave me up for adoption.

I keep on trying to remember what happened. It seems like one day she was there, then she went on a trip and did not come back. And Poppie said we would find her when we moved, but we never did, then he says she died.

Sonora sighed. Had Dixon Chauncey made the colossal error in judgment and told his daughter that her mother had "gone on a trip" when she'd died? That would explain a lot.

But if she really died, why didn't I go to the funeral? I don't remember a funeral. You can't forget your own mother's funeral!!!!!!

But if she's alive, why doesn't she find me? Maybe she can't, because we move so much.

Maybe.

The phone rang, and Sonora jumped. "Shit," she said, pulling her feet off the desk, leaning forward in the chair.

"Homicide, Blair."

"Medicine, Gillane."

She frowned—he was out of context. Then remembered. The devastatingly attractive doctor in hiking boots.

"How are you, Cricket?"

"Why do—" No. She was not going to play that game.

But he was.

"Why do I call you Cricket? It's not to annoy you, if that's what you think. My favorite dog in all the world was named Cricket."

"How can I help you, doctor?"

"Boy, that takes the wind from me, you being polite. I called to tell you that I put a priority on those lab tests."

"And?"

"And what?"

"You got them back already?"

"My God, you're an optimistic woman. I just did the priority paperwork an hour ago."

"Well, gosh. Thanks and all that."

There was a pause. What did this man want? Courtesy?

Sonora leaned back in her chair, checked over her shoulder for Crick, put her feet up on the desk.

"So," Gillane said. "What's going on with you?"

"It's been a bad day. I'm going to learn to play the guitar and sing mournful songs."

"Be interesting to see which comes harder for you. Learning to play the guitar or learning to sing."

This was more like it. For a heart-stopping moment, she'd been afraid Gillane liked her. In middle school parlance.

"Good-bye, Gillane. Feel free to call next time you have a point."

"Good-bye, Cricket."

He sounded happy. Insults were good for this man.

30

Sonora went through the garage door into the house, arms full of plastic grocery sacks. The days of brown bags were fading. Today's trip had been a budget cruncher; muffin mix, ground chuck, Vidalia onions and things geared to please children—Dunkaroos, Gushers, kiwifruit, and strawberries.

The house was quiet, except for the thump of Clampett's tail as it knocked against the wall. He expressed his ecstasy in her company by licking her leg, just over the knee, until her khakis went soggy and dark brown in a two-inch strip.

The woman at the deli and the kid behind the cash register at the grocery store had stared at her face, reminding her that no amount of makeup covered those serious bruises and swellings. She could see the addition in their eyes—battered housewife.

This was what the world had come to.

She fingered her lip, which was still swollen, still sore. If, for example, Hal McCarty wanted to kiss her passionately, it would not be without pain.

Did she have the right to risk her life doing police work? Was it sensible? Most of her colleagues had a spouse to carry on, ex or no, a co-parent. Sonora was all that stood between her children and the big bad world.

Did she want that on her tombstone?

She Was Sensible

It was late for a career change. And the mortgage had to be paid, groceries bought, shoes, backpacks, cool sunglasses, and haircuts.

She let the bags scatter across the cabinets, wincing as one hit a puddle of sticky milk next to dried cornflakes that stuck like Band-Aids on the counter. Those would come up about as easily as concrete.

She stopped to rub Clampett under the chin, reached into the cabinet over the sink for his heartworm pill. She'd forgotten to give it to him last month. Should she give him two?

He took it like an angel because the kids had convinced him that the pills were dog treats. She rubbed his nose. He drooled happily.

Sonora checked her watch. She was supposed to meet Hal McCarty in forty minutes. Her children should be trailing in sometime in the next hour.

She'd take some time. Make a world-class meat loaf. Bake muffins. She checked her watch, wondering if she had time to put in a batch of homemade macaroni and cheese. Pushing it. She'd have to track McCarty down at that livestock auction sometime today. If Crick caught her being a good mommy in the middle of a high-profile murder investigation, she might become unemployed.

It would have to be the macaroni that came in boxes.

For the first time in a long time, Sonora met her children at the door when they got home from school.

Tim came first, fumbling for his key, when Sonora opened the door and let him in.

"What are you doing home?" he asked.

"I live here. Hello, Tim. Hello, whoever you are."

The girl trailing him smiled shyly. She seemed nice enough. No tattoos, no black lipstick, just baggy denim and a T-shirt with the *Curious George* monkey keeled over dead from poison.

"Janet just came over to hang out," Tim said.

Sonora nodded. Did she have a rule about girls visiting when parents weren't home? Did she need one?

In the old days, kids got in trouble after dark. Now it was after school.

"Muffins in the kitchen."

Heather was next, running into the kitchen while Sonora iced the top of the meatloaf with catsup, covered it with foil.

"Mama!" Heather grabbed her around the waist. "How come you're home?"

"I just stopped in to say hi. I made muffins. How come you're home? I thought you were staying after."

"I didn't have a ride."

Sonora winced. Guilt pang. "You hear me? I made muffins."

"I bet Tim ate all of them."

"I hid yours. They're wrapped in foil, under your bed. Don't let Clampett get them."

"Mommy?"

"Yeah?"

"I got a D on my math test. Multiplying fractions."

Sonora sat down at the table. "Study harder, kid. You want me to help you, later on tonight?" She wondered what the odds were of getting home on time.

"Last time you helped me, I got an F."

"F plus. Maybe Tim can help."

"Tim's a pig."

"A pig who's a whiz at fractions. And by the way. What is your bicycle helmet doing in the tub?"

"You didn't move it, did you? Babe was in there."

"Babe?"

"My newt!"

"Oh. I think he may be somewhere else now."

"Mommy, we have to find him, he might die!"

Sonora looked at Heather, gauging her attachment to the lizard. Pretty attached. She thought of Hal McCarty, waiting, a young girl buried alive—all of it shifting on the scales that working mothers kept active in their minds.

Motherhood won. She was off on the case of the missing newt, tension making her stomach hurt, wondering where the average newt would go, given a choice.

31

HAL MCCARTY was leaning up against a tan-on-rust pickup that had a maroon trailer attached to the bed by a metal contraption that looked like a question mark.

A gooseneck, Sam had explained to her earlier, when he was talking to her about pickup trucks, a subject of which men never seemed to tire. She could almost imagine herself driving one.

This case, clearly, was getting to her.

Sonora pushed a button, her window glided down. She smiled at McCarty. "I'm late."

McCarty unfolded his arms. "Just a couple hours." His grin was friendly. He wore a white T-shirt—Jockey? Hanes? Short-sleeved. Jeans and boots. "I was forty minutes late myself."

"Then I win."

"Just lock up your car and leave it. *What* are you wearing?"

"They're called khakis, McCarty, you find them everywhere. When was the last time you shopped—outside of the general store, that is?"

"Nobody wears khakis to sell a horse."

"Crick just told me to meet you here, he didn't mention the possibility of livestock."

"I guess, being a girl, you can get away with it."

"Real men don't wear khakis?" Sonora glanced at the trailer, which seemed heavier on the left-hand side. "That is a horse in the trailer, right?"

"Well, let's see." McCarty looked into the side window. "Mane, tail, four legs. Looks like a horse to me, detective."

"Where'd you steal it?"

"He's on loan from the mounted police. Think of him as your new partner. His name is Oklahoma."

"Is he from Oklahoma?"

"He didn't say. But don't pet him. He looks like a lamb, but they kind of warned me about him."

"What does he do?"

"Sort of charges you down and bites. They use him more for night shifts downtown than kiddie carnivals, if you get me."

Sonora looked into the window. Oklahoma looked back. He was a dark chestnut, with a pretty head, a long refined nose. "He's a big sucker."

"Sixteen hands. Come on, hop in, we're running late."

The door on the passenger's side of the pickup was heavy. It creaked. McCarty glanced across the seat and offered a hand up. She scrambled in, hanging on to the seat belt while she reached out and pulled the heavy door shut. Sonora's feet just barely touched the floorboard, which was muddy. A Bubbalicious wrapper, hot pink, was wadded in the right corner.

McCarty squeezed her fingers, let her hand slip away, and cranked the engine. He shifted into first and hit the gas.

The engine was loud, and McCarty was driving fast. Sonora hung on to the armrest. It was nice, being this high up.

"McCarty?"

"Yes, darlin'?"

"You ever driven a horse trailer before?" She looked back through the middle window, wondering how the horse was faring. Couldn't see a thing through the grille.

"I didn't figure you to be a nervous type."

"Yeah, well, now you know."

McCarty slowed at the curve. "We're going to the auction at

Aquitaine. Hold it every Tuesday and Thursday, noon till whenever. Timewise, this place would work out pretty good for Joelle's killer."

"If the horse was sold to slaughter, would they keep a record?"

"A lot number maybe. Be hard to track."

"Is that what you think happened? Do you think the horse went to slaughter?"

McCarty shrugged. "That's what I'd do, if I wanted to get rid of a horse. The closest slaughterhouses are in Wisconsin. I've called, had a guy from one of our field offices go out there. No luck, but that doesn't necessarily mean anything. One chestnut mare among a thousand others, and nobody asks any questions, they just pay in cash and move along."

"Yeah? Doesn't this mare have a frieze brand?"

"Yeah. Do you know what a frieze brand is?"

She looked over at him. "Actually, no."

"White markings like hieroglyphics under the mane. They're not in use very much anymore, they're expensive, and most people just tattoo the lip. Be going to DNA soon." He looked at her. "You an animal lover, Sonora?"

"Sure, aren't you?" She squinted. The sun was in her eyes.

"Yeah, but what I'm asking is, do you want me to spare you the detailed explanations, or do you want to know what's going on as it happens?"

"I want to know what's going on."

"Prepare to hang tough."

Sonora looked out the side window. Poor Sam. Missing all the fun.

The Aquitaine Stockyards were a good hour out of the city proper, past the pretend-perfect town of Lebanon, past tiny horse farms with black run-in sheds and automatic waterers in small eaten-down pastures.

"What's the matter with that horse?" Sonora asked, pointing.

"Nothing. They just body-clipped him in the saddle area. Try not to talk too much while we're here, okay?" McCarty looked at his watch. "Our timing ought to work out. We're an hour or two after the killer would have shown up—I'm guessing between four and six. When's the autopsy?"

"Tomorrow morning. Is this the only stockyard?"

"In driving range, with the time frames. The killer didn't get caught up in the dragnet, which means he was long gone or in the area. The horse isn't at any of the farms real close to Donna's place that I could see, but in all honesty, it could be anywhere. Guy could have dumped the horse and trailer over a cliff."

"Somebody would have found that and reported it."

"Maybe, maybe not. I'm hoping our guy was greedy. Sold the horse, made a little money, let it go at auction. Somebody'll have it penned up somewhere before they cut its head off."

"Do what?"

"Sell it to slaughter."

"Do they cut their heads off?"

"Yeah, but they kill them first."

"How do they do it?"

"Chainsaw."

"They kill them with a chainsaw?"

"No, they run them up a chute and shoot them. Sometimes they shock them with a cattle prod first. They don't use the chainsaws till they're dead."

"So you say." Sonora pictured frightened horses, running up a path, smelling blood and death. "Suppose they won't go?"

"Go where?"

"Up the chute."

McCarty looked at her. "It's not like they have a choice. If they won't budge, they'll poke them with something sharp till they do."

"And sell them for dog food?"

"More like to Europe or Japan. Horse meat is big over there."

"Why don't they just let them retire?"

"Why don't they let cows retire? Look, I don't like it any better than you do, believe me. People ride a horse for years, make a pet out of it, then sell it and don't look back. And a lot of those dealers will give you a story, to make it all go down better. They'll tell you anything, they'll say the horse is for their little granddaughter and will be loved for the rest of its life. People either don't know any better, or they don't care."

Sonora folded her arms, thinking betrayal. If she had a horse, she'd keep it forever.

When the man leaped onto the running board of the pickup, grinning in through the open window, Sonora half expected McCarty to speed up and shake him off. Instead, he eased back on the accelerator and slowed. All around them, in the dusty gravel lot, were horse trailers, stock trailers, men in dusty Wranglers, men who had forgotten to shave. Nine out of ten seemed to be smokers. The rest probably chewed.

Sonora stuck her head out the window, taking it all in. McCarty was right, she was out of place in her khakis. Most of the women were harsh yellow blondes or brunettes with tough fuzzy perms and the occasional tattoo.

She kept looking, found some normal females. She could blend.

"How you doing there, buddy?" The man was still at the window, face seamed and burnished, and in spite of his heft, which was considerable around the middle, the skin of his neck and cheeks sagged into careworn creases.

McCarty stopped the truck. "I'm pretty good. Yourself?"

"Fine, thanks for asking." Even balanced on the running board of the truck, the man managed to reach into a shirt pocket for a wrinkled pack of Camels.

Of course, it would be Camels. And Jack Daniel's, no doubt, in the glove compartment.

"You need a ride or something?" McCarty asked.

The guy grinned. "I just thought I might save you some trouble. I mean, you can take your horse through all that rigmarole at the auction, but I give you fifty dollars cash for it right now, and we can unload him and you be on your way."

"Don't you even want to look at him?" Sonora asked, leaning across the seat.

McCarty did not actually tell her to shut up, but she could see that the thought crossed his mind.

The Camel man cocked his head to one side. "It's a horse, ain't it? That's all I need to know."

"This is a pretty nice horse," McCarty said.

"They all nice. I'll take good care of him."

The trailer rocked suddenly, and there was a metallic thunk. Oklahoma was kicking.

Horses knew.

McCarty cut the engine, leaving the truck and trailer parked smack in the middle of the gravel lot. Sonora got out, jumping off the running board and sliding in the gravel. The man in the next truck, a Dodge Ram, had the radio up loud—an oldies station. "Little Red Riding Hood." Sonora smiled a little, went around the side.

McCarty was leaning against the door, elbow resting on the ledge of the open window, hip cocked to one side.

"A chestnut Saddlebred, in foal and as big as a house." The Camel man had backed away a couple steps, a wad of bills clutched in his right hand. Sonora noticed that his index finger was missing. The man shook his head, scanning the lot every few minutes. "Son, I buy a lot of horses, I wouldn't say this one rings a bell."

"Got a frieze brand on the left side of her neck."

Something flickered in the Camel man's eyes. "Her mane go to the left instead of the right?"

McCarty nodded. "Chestnut, white blaze. You see her?"

"Seems like I might remember a horse like that going through here day before yesterday. I didn't buy her, though."

"Who did?"

The man rubbed his forehead. "I wish I could help you out, but when the fella wouldn't deal, I moved on."

"Wouldn't deal with you?"

"Nope, he would not."

"Why not?"

"Wanted to sell the horse and trailer as a package." His eyes flickered to Sonora, and he lowered his voice. "Didn't want to see her go to slaughter."

"I tell you what . . . what was your name again, sir?"

"Beardsley. Sonny Beardsley."

"Mr. Beardsley, that mare was a favorite of my wife here." He inclined his head toward Sonora, then winked at Beardsley. "And it was a sort of a misunderstanding or difference of opinion—whatever you'd want to call it—between me and her on whether or not she ought to be sold. I'd really like to get her back."

"Son, I wish you luck. You might want to ask around a little." His gaze flicked behind McCarty and over Sonora's head, scouting prospects.

"There's a finder's fee in it, if you hear anything. Fifty for the information. A hundred if you find the horse."

"How's about that fella you got there in the back?"

"I'm thinking he may be a little too sweet for this place. I'm going to head on in and take a look."

"You going to be here awhile?" the man asked.

Hal nodded.

"You hang tight till I get back to you. I may be able to find something out about your mare."

Someone was selling puppies out of a big cardboard box. GOOD HOME/FREE was hand-lettered in hot pink highlighter on a piece of posterboard taped with masking tape along the side of the box.

"What kind are they?" McCarty asked.

The woman sitting behind the card table, piled with 4H and riding club brochures, grinned and shrugged. "Their mama was an Australian shepherd, and their daddy is a memory. My suspicion is boxer, from the looks of them, but your guess, you know? Want one? They're cute."

Sonora looked into the box.

The puppies were sleeping—little round balls like hedgehogs, sides going up and down with every little breath, eyes shut tight. They had tiny little tails. Were various blends of brown, black, and tan. Sonora counted seven.

What would Clampett think if she brought one home? Even the world's most easygoing dog would be green-eyed over a new puppy. And she didn't exactly need the complications.

"What you think?" McCarty. Smiling. He really did have nice eyes.

"Now's not the time," Sonora said.

One of the puppies whimpered, raised up on tiny paws. Shifted sideways and settled back in.

The woman grinned at her. "Honey, you make him get you a puppy. Take two, they can keep each other company."

McCarty gazed into Sonora's eyes. "She's the most tender-hearted thing in the world, so I better get her away, or we'll go home with that whole boxful."

Sonora waited till they were out of earshot. "I have to tell you, McCarty, this is the first time I've ever been called tender-hearted."

"Don't worry, I won't put the word out you're human."

"Where are you going? The auction's that way." Sonora pointed down a concrete ramp that dropped down toward gray swing doors. She heard a man's twang, the echo of a microphone.

"Let's go around the back. Never know what you might see."

32

THE BACK of the arena was a maze of cattle chutes, ramps, and dirt pathways cordoned off with gray metal piping. The ground was strewn with manure. Sonora looked around, inhaled the whang of frightened horses.

"Heads up," McCarty said.

Sonora plastered herself to the side rail, and an emaciated young man in Wranglers and a red denim shirt trotted a freckled gray horse up the path where they stood.

"Passing through," he said, friendly, trotting his horse. He rode a light brown Western saddle, no bridle, just a halter with thick white rope reins. The horse moved smartly, head down, the two of them in perfect harmony.

"You'll be okay, Ranger," the boy said, leaning low and rubbing the horse's neck. He sounded sad.

"Why is he selling that horse?" Sonora asked. Ranger had relaxed at the boy's voice, the touch on his neck.

"Probably has to. Ole Ranger looks a bit underfed," McCarty said.

"So does the kid. Will he be okay?"

McCarty looked at her. "Sure, he'll be fine. Somebody'll buy old Ranger and take him home, probably make a pet out of him."

"You're a pretty sorry liar, McCarty."

"I tried, anyway. You want to go wait in the car?"

"Don't girl me down."

McCarty pointed to a couple of men standing next to a small enclosure where three horses raced from corner to corner. "I'm going to talk to those guys over there. You want to come with me or look around?"

"Look around."

"Watch where you walk."

Sonora wandered in and out of the chutes, could not figure out how to make it into the arena through the maze of metal. She did see a path back toward the parking lot. She could go that way and head back around the front.

She veered right, avoiding a large stock trailer, red, with wide metal slats on each side. It was crammed full of horses, most of them quiet, heads hanging.

Sonora frowned. Wondered how long the horses had been stuck in the trailer, wondered if they were coming or going. A logo on the side of a rusted maroon pickup said "The Horseman's Buddy" in large black letters.

Sonora looked at the horses, pressed tight against the metal slats. They did not look like they had a buddy in the world.

A quick movement caught her eye, and a reddish-brown nose poked its way between the slats, one big brown eye watching her.

McCarty would probably lump this one in the chestnut category too, but he was very red, with a white blaze on his nose and a rubmark where black skin showed through. He was wearing a dusty leather halter that looked like it might disintegrate at any moment.

"Hey, boy."

The horse looked at her curiously. Stuck his nose out farther. She rubbed a hand up to his forelock, and he butted her fingers with his head as if he wanted to be scratched. She obliged. He butted harder, scooting up close to the edge of the trailer.

A muscular black horse with truly impressive hindquarters

and a short cresty neck decided that the red chestnut was getting too close. He penned his ears and lowered his head, and the chestnut's nose went straight up as he jumped back out of the way.

All the horses shifted nervously.

Sonora looked over her shoulder, wondered if anyone noticed that she was causing trouble.

"Take care, buddy." She headed out across the parking lot to the sound of microphones and frightened horses.

The arena had a dirt floor, fenced off at waist level, and a circle of seats rising gradually toward the ceiling. A man in stained brown workpants held a horse by a dingy white lead rope that ended in a chain that was threaded through an olive green nylon halter and wrapped over the horse's nose.

The horse stood with locked muscles, head high, sides quivering, weight rocked back ever so slightly on the hind legs. He kept an eye at all times on the man with the lead rope. Three fresh piles of manure lay in the dirt.

A child ran down the ramp from the concession stand, feet thumping. The horse jumped sideways.

"Whoa there, buddy." The man in brown pants gave the lead rope a vicious yank, and the chain racked the horse's nose. His head went higher, but he locked his muscles and was still. Sonora saw that his back left leg was scarred.

The microphone man, loose jeans, a T-shirt, and an impressive pot belly, shifted the John Deere hat back on his head. He was built wide and square like a dwarf, yellow-white tufts of hair fluffing from the sides of his cap.

"Now this fella's been a lesson horse for thirteen years, real gentle with beginners. Somebody needs to take him home."

Nobody seemed much interested.

Tables next to the first row of seats were crammed with saddles, blankets, bridles, and bits of leather gear that Sonora did not recognize but thought might be more appropriate to a catalog catering to the S&M crowd.

Cigarette smoke was heavy. Two or three men stood to the left of the arena, talking. A man in overalls sat down heavily in a chair next to Sonora and lit into a plastic tray of nachos covered with gluey orange cheese and green rings of jalapeño peppers.

The real buyers sat, smoking furiously, waiting for the next horse.

The man behind the microphone talked faster and louder, but nobody was bidding on this one.

Sonora looked down into the ring. She had always wanted a horse. And the man had said he was gentle. He didn't look all that gentle right now, but terror never made an animal easygoing.

"Not thinking of bidding, are you?" McCarty bent close, whispering in her ear.

"Just doing reconnaissance," she told him. "What you got?"

He grimaced. "One guy who thinks he remembers seeing another guy trying to sell a horse and a van, but he's sure the man had a stud colt, palomino quarter horse, which is about as far away from a chestnut brood mare as you can get."

"Welcome to the eyewitness two-step. What about the guy that was climbing all over the truck?"

"Beardsley? He's around. Hasn't got back to me yet."

"Yeah. But that's two people who remember a guy wanting to sell a horse and trailer. Do the times pan out?"

"Consistently. Late Tuesday afternoon."

"Could be our guy."

"Hell, he's taking off."

Sonora looked up, saw Beardsley heading through the swing door to the outside ramp.

McCarty looked at her over his shoulder. "Meet you in the lot. And don't buy anything."

Sonora looked back at the horse in time to see him being led away with a number on his back. He'd sold for three hundred dollars.

She hoped he was going to a good home.

33

Sonora sat on the hood of the pickup, wondering where McCarty had gotten to. She kept an eye on two cowboys who'd been giving her the look. She estimated sixty to ninety seconds before they'd be heading her way. She hopped down. She was attracting too much attention.

Really, she should work undercover more often.

She checked her watch, stomach tight with the feeling that time was moving and she wasn't. Forty-eight hours into the case, and they were foundering. Was this their best bet—tracking a mythical guy who had sold a horse and trailer as a package deal, refusing to let the horse go to slaughter?

She headed down the right side of the trailer, peered in the grilled window. Oklahoma ignored her, head down. She climbed down off the wheel well, dusted her hands off, saw that she'd gotten a stain on the leg of her pants.

She glanced at her watch, thinking maybe she should go looking for McCarty. She remembered a drink machine back inside the arean, had a sudden craving for grape soda. She got her jacket and purse out of the truck. The sun was going down.

Definitely getting colder.

She heard a shout, the clatter of shod hooves on asphalt,

moving fast. Someone yelled "Heads up," and Sonora walked out in front of the truck to see what was going on.

Found herself directly in the path of a horse who wheeled sideways and stopped on a dime, head bobbing, sides heaving. Tufts of white foam rimmed his sides like dirty meringue, and his legs were braced as if he knew the worst was yet to come.

The horse's coat was black with sweat, but Sonora recognized the red chestnut gelding from the stock trailer, same rub mark on his nose. His eyes were wide, and she could see the whites along the edge.

Sonora took a step toward him. He wheeled sideways, nostrils flared and blowing.

"Hold still there, honey, I'll get him."

Sonora did not much like being called honey. Darlin' was okay, she kind of liked that one. But there was something patronizing about honey.

"Ho there, buddy, hold on."

The man's voice brought the horse's head up. The gelding wheeled and crow-hopped sideways. Sonora, self-preservation uppermost in her mind, was moving away from the horse's hind end when he circled again, facing her.

She pitched her voice into easygoing, conversational tones. "How you doing, fella?"

He was trembling hard. She moved toward him a couple of steps, and he skittered sideways. She stopped. Waited. Tried one step. That he would tolerate.

Step and pause, then his halter was in reach. Sonora unclipped her purse strap from one end of the soft brown Italian leather—Enzo, she'd paid too much for it, especially if the strap was going to be used for a lead rope.

But she had him. The horse lowered his head. She touched his shoulder, felt his flesh shrink and quiver. His head came back up, and he snorted.

"It's okay, boy, I've got you. You'll be all right."

Another red chestnut in an auction full of horses, half or more of them chestnuts. How many chestnut mares went through this auction in one day? And she was trying to find one in particular—one she was not even sure had come this way?

Wrong direction. She was going in the wrong direction.

A man in Wranglers so loose on his hips he could have stepped right out of them reached out and grabbed the purse strap from Sonora.

"Thanks for your help." His lead rope was red faded to pink and topped by a long length of chain, which the man threaded through the horse's halter and over his nose.

The gelding backed away, and the man, black hair glistening with oil, gel, and sweat, snapped the rope sharply, racking the chain across the horse's nose.

"Is that necessary?" Sonora said, in a tone of voice her children dreaded. She did not want to be here, did not want any more of her time wasted, and where the hell was McCarty?

The man gave her a sour look over his left shoulder. "I guess since I'm the one bought and paid for this horse, I'll do what I want." But there were people watching, and he smirked. "Anyway, this is all I got handy. I left my purse in the truck."

The horse's head went up, and he circled the man, who snapped the lead shank again.

"You're just making it worse," Sonora said.

"Honey, I'll give you some advice won't cost you a thing. And that is you don't let no animal boss you around, 'cause otherwise they'll run right over you." He jerked the chain again. "Animal needs to learn respect. Thanks for catching him though."

"He'd been better off if I'd let him go."

"You have a strange idea of what horses like, if you think it would be better for him to get squished in traffic." The man studied her a minute, a shrewd look. He shifted his weight onto his right leg. "He's for sale, you know, you like him so much."

Sonora got that wary feeling. "I don't have the kind of life where you can own horses."

"Yeah, that's too bad, this ole boy picked you right out.

Surprises me that he come right up to you the way he did." He brought the horse a few steps closer. Within petting range.

Sonora reached out a hand and waited. The horse thought about it a long minute, then stretched his nose to touch the tip of her fingers, as if he could not resist her hand any more than her son could resist trying to get the last word in any argument. The horse snorted suddenly and blew mucus across her arm.

The man chuckled. "They always do that when you're cleaned up, don't they?"

Sonora nodded and in spite of herself enjoyed being included in a sort of knowing horsemen's camaraderie. She touched the gelding's neck. She liked the way horses smelled.

What would she do with a horse? Where would she keep it?

"You could just try him out for a while, you know. If you don't like him, I'll take him back." The man stood to one side, stroked the horse's shoulder. "He's awful nice, when he's not all worked up and scared." He shifted his weight to one leg. "Now, any horse with a brain's going to get worked up at an auction. It's going to be a real shame to take him off to the killers, but I haven't been able to sell him, what with one thing and another, and I can't afford to keep him around." The man looked at Sonora's face. "It's humane the way they do it. Over real quick."

Sonora felt a heavy sort of depression settle over her shoulders. All these people, this guy, the kid on the gray gelding he clearly loved, all of them seemed to think nothing of sending a horse straight to hell as soon as it became inconvenient. The guy with the mare they were tracking was a red herring. Joelle's killer would not have bothered to keep the horse alive.

Except that killers were quirky. And the mare was valuable. And there might be a reason to keep the horse around that Sonora hadn't thought of. He'd gone to the trouble to take it in the first place.

Sonora looked into the horse's eyes. Encountered a look of intelligence that surprised her. *Take me home. It'll work out, somehow. Please don't leave me behind.*

"How much?" she asked. Only curious. No way could she afford to get serious here.

"Well. This fella here is a full-blooded Arabian horse."

Sonora nodded, stroking the horse's neck. "Are they good first horses? For beginners?"

"There are as many opinions about that as there are horses and people who ride 'em. *I* think they are, 'cause they're so intelligent. And Arabians, you can ride 'em all day, they don't get tired. They got endurance. Easy keepers, too, live on almost nothing."

Sonora looked at the horse's jutting hips and sunken rump. This one had been living on almost nothing.

"I'd say eight hundred seems fair."

The horse in the arena had gone for three hundred.

"Too much," Sonora said.

"I guess, seeing that the two of you have bonded, I could go seven twenty-five."

"You already said you couldn't sell him."

"Killers pay by the pound."

Sonora opened her purse. Took out her checkbook and looked at the register. "I have six hundred dollars in my checking account and thirty-seven dollars in cash."

"You give me a check for six hundred, and twenty-five dollars of your cash, and honey, you got yourself a horse."

Sonora took a deep breath and tried not to think. There went the grocery money.

Sonora's hand shook when she wrote out the check. The man had said she could bring the horse back if she wanted, and she could probably clean him up and sell him herself, he was a full-blood Arabian, he'd have to be valuable.

"How old is he?" Sonora asked. She hadn't had such a mix of Christmas morning excitement and sheer terror since she'd gotten her first mortgage on a house.

"Oh, about eleven or twelve."

"What does he eat?"

The man did not seem the least surprised by her question. "Just run him round on a little patch of grass, throw him some hay when the weather gets cold, and a coffee can of grain a couple times of day, he'll do. Make sure he's got lots of fresh clean water." The man reached into his pocket, handed her a dirty, wrinkled card: THE HORSEMAN'S BUDDY. "You got any questions, he don't work out and you want to sell him back, you just give me a call. You got a trailer?"

She nodded and led him to the truck. Wondered if he expected her to put the horse in herself. She would just open that back door and hope the horse went in.

"Nice trailer," the man said. "You buy it new?"

"It's not mine. Belongs to a friend."

"You should of been here day before yesterday. Could of got you a horse and a trailer in one package deal."

Sonora thought of the missing mare. Beardsley, saying he saw a man with a horse and trailer.

"I could use one of my own," Sonora said. "You buy that one that went through here, I might be willing to take it off your hands."

He shook his head. "It was a honey, too, a Sundowner, white with a maroon stripe. Snazzy."

"Sounds just like what I want," Sonora said. With absolute truth.

"I tried to buy it, but the guy wouldn't do no business with me. I'd of given him a good price for the trailer and took the horse off his hands too, he was trying to work a package deal."

"What kind of horse was he selling?"

"Saddlebred brood mare, looking like she's about ready to bust. He seemed to think she was going to throw a pretty nice baby, but didn't look to me like she'd been much taken care of."

You ought to know, Sonora thought, resisting a look at the overcrowded stock trailer. When was the last time those horses had had any water?

"Took them all back home, then, did he? Maybe I could track him down."

"You'd be out of luck. I saw him sell the lot to a lady got a stable up near Lebanon. I believe she wanted that trailer more'n she wanted that horse he was sweatin'."

"What do you mean, sweating?"

He gave her a wary look. She was full of questions. Sonora gave him her innocent, wide-eyed look. And this was a man who loved to talk.

"He and me didn't come to terms on the whole, because he didn't want to see that mare go to the killers. I told him I might could sell her, seeing she was in foal. But he wouldn't take me up on it."

Sonora gave him a sideways look. She wouldn't have taken him up on it either. Odd to find herself siding with the killer. A man who would kill a teenage girl but balked at sending a horse to slaughter.

The man was still talking. "I tell you one thing. That poor ole mare'd be better off at the killers than out at the Four Wishes Farm. Joke about that place is the horses out there only got one wish, which is to get the heck out."

Four Wishes Farm. Lebanon, Ohio. Sonora committed it to memory, took a look at her horse. *Her* horse, God help her. His ears were pricked forward, curving in a little on the sides. She got the impression he was taking in every word.

"Get in the trailer," she told the horse, who made no indication that he heard.

The man smiled a little. "I'll load him up for you, honey. Who's that other fella you got in there? That's a nice-looking horse. You buy him here?" There was surprise in the voice.

Sonora didn't answer. Oklahoma shifted his weight but did not bother to turn and look.

Sonora felt suddenly shy about reaching out and touching the animal she had just cleaned out her checking account to buy. "He got a name?"

"All I know's his barn name. But I think they got the registered name stamped here on the halter." The man spit on his fingertip and rubbed the brass plate attached to the side of the leather halter. Squinted. "Looks like . . . Hell Z Poppin."

"What did they call him at the barn?" Sonora asked. "Poppin?"

The man grinned, showing a crooked front tooth. "As I remember, they called him Hell."

34

MCCARTY LIFTED a hand to Sonora, headed to the side of the trailer.

She leaned across the seat, opened the door. "I already checked, Hal. Oklahoma is fine."

He slid into the front seat of the pickup, gave Sonora a tired smile. "What are you looking so bright-eyed about? Glad to see me?"

Sonora didn't answer. She would tell him about Poppin once they were under way. Otherwise, he might talk her out of it. She did not want to be sensible. She did not want to see that horse stand, quivering, in the dirt-floored smoke-filled arena.

McCarty grabbed her wrist, glanced at her watch. "We better get Okie back to the barn." He took her wrist between his thumb and finger. "Your pulse is jumping."

He thought it was him. She'd bought a horse in a fit of insanity, and he thought she was excited by him.

Which wasn't to say she would not have been at this time yesterday, or wouldn't be at this time tomorrow. But just at the moment the horse was taking all available mindspace.

"So, McCarty, did you find out anything about our brood mare?"

He put the key in the ignition, put the truck in gear. "Nothing new. I think our killer was here—I've gotten it from more than one source that some guy was trying to sell a mare and trailer as a package deal late Tuesday afternoon, and that he wouldn't let the horse go to the killers or go to auction. I'm just having trouble pinning him down."

"They say what he looked like?"

"They *all* remember him perfectly. Brown hat, with those flappers on the side, that's consistent. Short and fat, only tall and thin." He turned the trailer, put on his turn indicator, waited his turn to get out of the lot. Gave her a lopsided grin. "Where'd you disappear to? I half expected this cab to be full of puppies by the time I got back."

"Puppies? I'm doing undercover work, and you accuse me of buying puppies?"

He waited till the road was clear, pulled out slowly. Frowned.

"I found a horse," Sonora said.

"Chestnut?"

"Yeah."

"Like two million others. Mare in foal, I'm hoping."

"Gelding."

He braked, watching the turns. "We're looking for a brood mare. Our killer may have sold it, he may have killed it, he may have taken it home to Mama, but I guarantee you he didn't give it a sex change."

Sonora pulled out the business card in her shirt pocket. "I talked to this guy, the Horseman's Buddy. He told me about a man that came to the auction Tuesday afternoon, guy was looking to sell a horse and trailer. Package deal."

"The Horseman's Buddy?"

"Why do they call him that?"

"It wouldn't be accurate to call him the horse's buddy, but he will take an animal or its corpse off *your* hands."

"I knew it."

"Knew what?"

"That he takes them to the killers."

"You use that tone of voice, I'm surprised he talked to you.

Those guys are always wary of pretty girls with soft hearts. Animal rights activists are annoying."

"McCarty, what exactly do you feed a horse?"

"Good pasture's best. Hay when they're in their stalls, or the grass is gone. Grain a couple times a day."

"Where do you buy it?"

"Grain? Feed store. Get hay from a farmer."

She didn't know any farmers.

"What do you feed those horses at your barn? Where'd they come from, anyway?"

"Those horses are police officers working undercover, I deputized them myself."

"There are four empty stalls in your barn."

The light turned from red to green, and McCarty pulled the truck onto the interstate. Be very difficult for him to turn around now, Sonora decided.

He gave her a look. "I think I'd have noticed if our killer put the mare in my barn. You searched it yourself, remember? When I was your prime suspect?"

"I was wondering if I could borrow a stall for a while."

He smiled at her. "Your kids getting out of hand?"

"You're not getting this, are you?"

He looked at her. Smile fading. She saw it hit him. Saw his brow go together in a monster of a frown. Saw the look he gave her, which she would have to classify as incredulous.

"Sonora. Tell me you didn't do what I'm afraid you're going to tell me you did."

"Here's what happened."

"Sonora."

"Somebody yelled 'Heads up,' a horse went by, and I caught it."

He took a breath. "Is that all? You didn't get stepped on or run over?"

"No. But it wouldn't be still, just holding that leather thing—"

"Halter."

"So I hooked my purse strap to the little ring under his chin, and that's when the guy and I got to talking."

"You and the Horseman's Buddy."

"That's right."

"I wish to God I'd been there."

"We were getting along okay till he put a chain across the horse's nose."

"Sonora, a horse is a large animal, in case you haven't noticed. You've got to get it under control. I bet this fella gave you an earful."

"Well, no, he told me I seemed to know my way around horses."

McCarty eased back on the accelerator. "I don't mean to hurt your feelings, but anyone who knows less about horses would be hard to imagine."

"That's not what the Horseman's Buddy said."

"It was a sales pitch, darlin'. Appeal to your ego, then unload the horse. He probably bought that horse this morning, and he was hoping to turn it around in a few hours, make a hundred dollars. That'd be a good profit for a guy like him."

"It was a full-blooded *Arabian*, McCarty, aren't they valuable? He said the horse had endurance and never got tired."

"When your horse is tearing around the paddock with you on its back and it won't stop, you'll start wishing for a horse that'll wear out."

Sonora leaned against the door sideways so she could face him. "But they're good beginner horses, aren't they?"

"No. They're too smart and too volatile. If you ever get into horses, Sonora, start with a quarter horse or a Morgan. And call me, I'll help you find something." He looked over and smiled, and the thought of seeing more of him later down the road had a definite appeal. "Sonora?"

"Yes, McCarty?"

"You didn't buy that horse, did you?"

35

McCARTY WAS SPEAKING to her again by the time they pulled into the farm. They'd already been downtown to unload Oklahoma, who had been glad to leave them. McCarty's initial comment about her new horse Poppin was that it would likely be grateful for someone to feed it.

As they turned into the drive that led to his farmhouse, Sonora noticed the CSU van in the gravel lot at Donna Delaney's. She sat up her seat, saw the Taurus. Sam was here.

McCarty looked sideways, hit a pothole. The trailer swayed, and Sonora heard her horse kicking metal. Her horse. Poppin. Hell Z Poppin.

It was just a name.

"McCarty, let me out, will you? I better see what's going on at Donna's."

"Oh, no you don't. Didn't you watch John Wayne movies when you were a kid? Got to see to the horse first. You just cowboy up to the barn here, and I'll show you how to bed a stall."

Even with her mind on the CSU van and whatever might be happening at End Point Farm, Sonora was surprised at how much she enjoyed the stall work. McCarty brought her three wheelbarrowloads of cedar shavings and dumped them in the center of the dirt floor. While she raked the cedar from corner to corner, he washed out a blue plastic water bucket, filled it with clean water, hooked it with a clip to an eye-ring wood-screw embedded in the wall.

"What you think?" McCarty asked.

"It smells like the world's biggest hamster cage."

A thick gray coating of cobwebs hung from the center of the stall and dangled from the corners. Sonora decided she'd ei-ther throw a hell of a Halloween party here or clean it up.

"There's grain in a trash can in the feed room, right down by that end stall. Just give him a handful in a feed tub—there's an extra one in there somewhere, black rubber. I'll get him a couple flakes of hay."

"A handful of grain isn't going to feed a whole horse," Sonora said.

"He can fill up on hay. We don't know what he's been get-ting—my guess is nothing. We don't want him colicking on us."

"Colic?"

"A horsy tummy ache, Sonora. Painful and sometimes fatal. Death by cramps."

"Oh."

"Get the feed out of the dark blue can on the far right. That's the Triple Crown Senior. That ought to do him."

"He's only ten."

"Yeah. Right."

The horse tripped backing out of the trailer but caught his balance and deposited two loads of manure for good measure. McCarty led him into the barn. Poppin was wide-eyed and cautious, and he paused outside of his stall, then rushed inside all at once and would have run right over McCarty except McCarty seemed to be expecting the rush and ran Poppin in circles a few times to get his attention.

"I don't think much of his manners," McCarty said. He

unclipped the lead rope, gave the horse a pat, and got out of the way.

"Shouldn't we take that leather thing off? It looks pretty grimy."

"Dirt on a horse, I can't imagine. No, Sonora, let's leave it on till we know him a little better."

Sonora thought Poppin would be more comfortable with the halter off, but since she wasn't sure how to get it back on, she let it be.

She pushed hair out of her eyes. "Sooner or later I'll figure all this out and do it my own way."

"Spoken like a true horsewoman."

"I'm learning already?"

"No, but you're opinionated."

36

Sonora left McCarty feeding his own horses—decided that she would head for Delaney's place by way of the back field so the two of them would be less likely to be seen together.

The barn doors were wide open, but she saw people not horses—a small knot of little girls in breeches and boots, and several women talking in a huddle. Delaney's voice was loud in the background, snapping out a command for whoever was in the wash rack to turn that water pump off, pronto.

Sonora stood in the doorway, taking it all in, looking for Sam. He was leaning up against a wall talking to a blue-shirted EMT. He turned, some sixth sense telling him she was there—it always worked like that between them—and raised his hand.

She waited for him to disengage from his conference with the paramedic. Donna Delaney and a distressed-looking woman in hunter green stretch pants stood next to Renquist, all in the aisleway of the barn. Every light was blazing.

A CSU man went back into a small room to the left. Sonora had not been in that room. She was getting curious.

"What's up?" she asked Sam.

He put an arm around her shoulders and led her out of earshot of the others.

The office door opened. McCarty did not look her way when he joined the huddle with Delaney and Renquist.

Well. He was undercover, after all. But it was weird to spend all day with him and then pretend not to know him. He'd fed those horses awfully fast.

"Where've you been all day?" Sam seemed perturbed.

"At the horse auction. Trying to find the mare."

Something in his voice. "Took all afternoon, did it?"

"Yes, Mom. And where have you been keeping yourself?"

"I was trying to palm Chauncey off on one of the uniforms, when we had a nine-one-one call from the barn."

"Somebody hurt?"

Sam hunkered close. "Yes and no. You remember that missing finger?"

"Yeah?"

"It turned up."

37

"You think this is funny, Sonora?" Sam stepped up onto the concrete lip of a small room that held cheap metal shelves and boxes of moldy, aromatic bits and pieces of worn, dirty leather. The room smelled of mildew. Bridles and whips hung from hooks and brackets along the back wall, reins dangling behind an old washer and dryer that overfilled the room and made it hard for two people to fit inside. A wooden ladder, built into the wall, led into the hayloft, and bits of hay and cobwebs hung over the opening.

"I'm sorry, Sam, it just sort of struck me that way. I'm ashamed."

"Come be ashamed in here." Sam squeezed behind the door, motioned Sonora in, and shut it behind.

"Crime scene guys done?" Sonora asked.

"Yeah."

"So what happened?"

Sam jerked his thumb toward the second shelf, crammed full of black velvet helmets, some with chin straps dangling, some without. One of the helmets had split, exposing the white casing. It looked very much like a skull.

"They keep the riding gloves in here, in the helmets." Sam pulled a helmet across the shelf—this one green velvet, sweat stained, and worn, a piece of dirty elastic stretched across for a make-do chin strap.

"Okay to pick it up?"

"Yeah, this isn't the one in question. CSU has that one."

She looked inside. Sleek black leather gloves, some with Velcro closures, some with elastic wrists, a couple pairs of white gloves, stained and rolled into wads. All made to fit tiny hands.

Sonora glanced up, saw Sam watching. "It was *in* the riding glove?"

Sam picked one up, splayed the worn black leather fingers. "Tucked down into the finger, like this. Poor little kid about had a heart attack—she couldn't be more than eleven or twelve. She pulls it on over her hand and feels something in the glove, so she peels it back. . . . Sonora, if you think this is funny, you've been a cop too long."

"Sorry, Sam, I just wish I'd been here. The kid go into shock or something?"

"No, she's fine. But she takes the glove and finger to her mom, and the mother passes out, hits her head, and gets concussed."

"She okay?"

"I just told you, she's got a concussion." He took her arm as she headed back out the door. "Stay put. I'm not letting you back out in that barn aisle, Sonora, till you get a better attitude."

"Boy, you're cranky. You miss lunch?"

"Yeah, as a matter of fact. What did you and McCarty come up with?"

"We hit the auction—held twice a week, Tuesday and Thursday, from three until whenever. Guy came in trying to sell a chestnut mare and a maroon-and-white Sundowner trailer the same afternoon Joelle Chauncey disappeared."

"Timing work out?"

"Looks like. And we know where the horse went."

"So great, let's saddle up and go."

Sonora folded her arms. "McCarty wants us to get a warrant to search Bisky Farms, just to cover all bases."

Sam scratched his cheek. "We might actually swing that, considering the age of the victim. But if you think that horse is out there, you're dreaming. McCarty going to help us look?"

"He can't, he's undercover. Where's Dixon Chauncey?"

"Home with his little girls."

"You want to try and hit Bisky Farms tonight?"

"You want to look for horses in the dark?"

"I don't want to look at the horses. They want to hide the horse, they'll hide it. I want to look at the people. But, Sam."

He looked at her. Waited. "You were saying?"

She looked out into the aisleway, closed the door. "I did something today . . . maybe I shouldn't have."

He narrowed his eyes. Folded his arms. "Does this involve McCarty?"

"Sam, did you ever want a horse of your own?"

He shrugged. "I did when I was a kid and watched *Mr. Ed.* I wanted a plane when I watched *Sky King.*"

She crooked her finger. "Take a minute. I got something to show you."

38

THE CHILDREN were waiting when Sonora walked into the kitchen from the garage. They had set the table, cleaned off the countertops, warmed brown-and-serve rolls.

"You're late," Tim said. He set a black ceramic bowl of congealed macaroni and cheese on the table, next to the foil-wrapped meat loaf. "Everything's cold."

He frowned at her. She had sinned.

Sonora set down her purse, took off her jacket. "You guys should have gone on and eaten."

"We wanted to wait." Tim's tone of voice said it all: *We waited for you, and our dinner got cold.* An attitude of moral superiority that can be be found only in teenagers trying to turn the tables on their parents, and militant activists in the right-to-life moment.

Sonora went to the television. Turned *The Simpsons* off as the phone rang. Tim answered, sounding delighted to hear from whoever was on the other end, a tone of voice he never used in conversation with her, a mere mother.

Sonora made a slitting motion across her throat. "Off."

Tim curled his lip. "Got to go eat dinner. My mom for once decided to come home and eat, so now we drop everything, *that's* fair."

Sonora sat down at the table. Smiled at Heather, who she realized was wearing a sweatshirt for the sixth or seventh day in a row.

"We should wash that," Sonora said.

"It doesn't matter, *okay?*" Heather glared at her.

"Bad mood?" Sonora asked.

"You'd be in a bad mood too if you had to come home from school to Tim every day."

Sonora poked the macaroni. Sticky. Got up to put the bowl in the microwave. "Off the phone, Tim, *now.*"

He slammed down the receiver. Sat at the table. Glared at the floor.

"Isn't anyone going to ask me what I did today?" The bell on the microwave dinged. Sonora stirred macaroni, put the bowl back in the center of the table.

No one answered. She got the catsup out of the refrigerator, reached for the Worcestershire sauce.

"You saw a body," Heather said, tone of voice implying big deal.

"You went to court."

"You caught a killer."

"Met an informant."

"Filled out paperwork for your casebook."

They were on a roll, voices full of boredom and scorn for the everyday activities of a single parent.

"Nope," Sonora said. They were still talking. "I bought a horse." They kept talking. She wondered how long before the words would sink in. Then wondered if they were going to sink in.

The phone rang. Dinner as usual.

Sonora wondered, as she headed out the door, locking it carefully, if she could pull this off every night and keep her job. She wondered if she wanted to.

Sam opened the driver's-side door of the Taurus, stuck his

head out. "You're going to need a heavier jacket, Sonora, it's getting cold."

"Thanks, Mom."

She slid into the seat behind him. He had the heater going, and it felt good.

"What's that on your shirt?"

Sonora looked down. "Meat loaf and catsup."

"Meat loaf? Did you cook?"

"I cooked."

Sam gave her a sideways look.

"What, Sam?"

"I didn't say a word."

She leaned back into the seat. Folded her arms. Closed her eyes, just for a moment.

"You asleep?"

"No."

"I was thinking maybe we throw Donna Delaney to the wolves."

Sonora sat sideways and looked at him. It was dark in the car. They passed through a row of streetlights; she got a glimpse of Sam's face in the glare. He had shaved.

"What'd you have for dinner?"

He glanced at her. "Chicken over rice."

"Shelly cook?"

"She always cooks."

"Was it good?"

"Yeah, she bakes it in this mushroom soup thing with white wine." He looked at her. "Why?"

"I was wondering what was on *your* shirt."

"There's nothing on my—"

"I know, I just wanted to see if I could make you look. What do you mean, throw Donna Delaney to the wolves? Where the hell are you going?"

"Bisky Farms. You want to drive?"

"Yeah."

"Tough. I mean we tell them she ratted them out."

"Tell 'em outright, or imply?"

Sam shrugged. "Play it by ear."

Pink neon flashed across the interior of the car. "You're liking Bisky Farms for this?"

"I talked to Mickey this afternoon, while you were off doing your thing with McCarty. That blanket we found wrapped around Joelle is something for horses called a cooler."

"What's a cooler?"

"I told you, it's a horse blanket. Lightweight. When a horse gets exercised and you cool them off, you walk them around in this blanket thing."

"Doesn't it make them hot?"

"See, Sonora, if you ever worked out, you would know that after intense physical exercise, some people get chilled."

"Other people just light a cigarette."

"Not that kind of exercise."

They passed a White Castle. The smell of onions and burgers wafted through the car.

"Look, Sam. Every horse farm in the world has coolers. Anyone can buy them. Donna Delaney probably has some in her tack room."

"This one was almost new, in excellent condition."

"That lets Delaney out." Sonora had been in that tack room. Seen nothing that was not threadbare and dirty. "Mickey got specifics?"

"Horsehair, and hairs that he thinks will belong to Joelle. He's just started, got a long way to go. But someone has removed a square of material, bottom right of the blanket."

"It's not just torn?"

"Mickey said it was cut away with scissors, and he says it happened probably the day of or the day before the murder."

"How does he know that?"

"Fiber fragments on the end. Come on, Sonora, you're quibbling. If it comes from Mickey, it's written in stone."

"That's an archaic expression, Sam. Nobody writes 'in stone' anymore."

"Fine, it's written in aluminum siding."

"Why cut a square out?"

"I'm thinking maybe a barn name, farm logo."

"The farms put the names on the blankets?"

"Yeah. The big ones do."

"To keep people from stealing them?" Sonora asked.

Sam laughed. "No. It's like monogrammed stationery. The little ones just write their name in the tag."

Sonora tapped a finger on the armrest. Sam gave her a quick look that meant he was annoyed. She kept tapping. "We use Delaney, it could screw up McCarty's investigation."

Sam did an imaginary scale, shifting weights from one open palm to the other.

"Keep your hands on the wheel, will you?"

"The point, Sonora, is do we care? Who else we got?"

"We got Dixon Chauncey."

Sam glanced at her. "There are three reasons at least why that doesn't make sense."

"I can give you three why it does."

"Name them."

"Placement. Opportunity."

"That's two, Sonora."

"He dyed his hair."

"Come again?"

"He dyed his hair the night Joelle went missing. The night before she was found. He's not out looking for the kid or sitting up worrying—he's in the bathroom dying his hair. Plus there are all those casseroles in the freezer."

"I'm having a little trouble with your logic, here."

"He's made a whole week's worth of dinners, all wrapped, labeled, and frozen. Like he knows he's going to be too busy to cook."

"He may do that all the time. Look at that mobile home, this guy could win the Suzy Homemaker award."

"Oh, and I couldn't?"

"How did you get into this, Sonora?"

"You just keep your societal expectations to yourself, I'm a working mother. I made meat loaf, and I had to sneak out this afternoon to do that."

Sam gave her a look. "I thought you were with McCarty all day."

"That's what you were supposed to think."

"You made meat loaf in the middle of a homicide investigation?"

Sonora turned sideways. "You people can't be pleased, can you? If I'm working, I should be at home putting chicken in a mushroom wine sauce. And if I'm making meat loaf, you look at me because I'm working a homicide."

Silence settled, like leaves falling. Sonora looked out the window, saw nothing she had not seen a thousand times before.

"Is it safe to talk again?" Sam asked, giving her a quick sideways look.

"Give me your three reasons why Dixon couldn't have killed Joelle."

"First off, the timing is wrong. What's the trigger, what's the motive? Why now and not next week, or last month, or two years from now? With Bisky Farms, we know why now. The horse, and Delaney not giving it up when the owner is due back. That's a big motive, if McCarty is right. One irate owner, one missing horse. Even if the Bisky people manage to explain it away, you think it looks good? You think people who haven't had their doubts before might not jump on it?"

"That doesn't mean Dixon didn't do it, it just means that Bisky might have."

"And another thing. This was planned, Sonora, somebody had a truck and trailer to transport that horse. Why transport a horse if you don't want a horse? If Dixon did it, how's he going to know the horse will spook and the kid will fall?"

"It just so happens that I own a horse now, and from my short but sweet dealings with this animal, I think you could count on *him* to spook at any available opportunity."

"Come on, Sonora, there are better, more definite ways. It's too iffy. Say you're right, which you're not, but say you are. Suppose Chauncey really is a planner. He dyes his hair—for what, efficiency?"

"For the television cameras."

"Okay, he dyes his hair for the press. And cooks meals ahead. And gets a truck and a trailer and has a plan on where to take it to get rid of the trailer and the horse. Every detail in place. And this same guy just hopes Joelle's horse spooks and the kid falls off and gets hurt?"

"Yeah, and it didn't exactly work, did it, Sam? Because she probably wasn't dead when he buried her."

"So why didn't he kill her? Strangle her, or shoot her?"

"He couldn't bring himself to do it. Have you ever met anybody less confrontational than Dixon Chauncey?"

"No, I haven't, which proves my point, not yours. What if Joelle doesn't even fall off the horse? What's he going to do, grab her and kill her? It's not in him. He doesn't have the balls for this kind of thing."

She looked out the window. They were moving quickly now, Sam driving fast, leaving the city behind. It was one of those weird night skies, clouds like fists sculling across a horizon with just enough moonlight to see by.

"You think we'll get anything out of those Bisky Farms people? Even if we threaten them with Delaney?"

"You think they'll talk if we don't?"

"And you don't care if we screw up McCarty's investigation?"

"It's just as likely we'll help it. But no, to answer your question, I don't care. Do you?"

She thought about McCarty squeezing her fingers before he'd said good-bye. The murder of a young girl, against the concerns of the Jockey Club.

"I guess not. But I don't think they'll tell us anything."

"Which tells us they've got something to hide. We're fishing, that's all. Aren't you the girl who always wants to see people's reactions?"

"I hate it when you make me eat my words."

39

SONORA SIGHED when Sam turned off the four-lane limited-access highway onto the wide asphalt drive. It was the kind of farm that made you catch your breath.

A small sign, professionally painted, swung in the breeze, making a slight creaking noise.

BISKY FARMS
CLIFF BISKY, VIVIAN BISKY
OWNERS, TRAINERS
WELCOME

Sonora, embryo horse owner that she was, felt a wash of envy and wistful admiration.

A small, well-lit guard booth was empty. Sonora hung her head out the window. The booth was generously built; it had the look and fragrance of fresh raw wood. It was cute inside, like the little playhouse that the girl who had grown up across the street from Sonora had had delivered on her eighth birthday, causing Sonora much envy and distress when the girl would only permit her to stand in the doorway and look inside.

A phone, a neat desk, an intercom. A small brown bag with a sandwich made of white bread resting in a Baggie on the top.

"What kind of sandwich is that?" Sonora said.

Sam leaned out the window. "Definitely chicken salad."

"Could be tuna."

"Tuna's darker."

A radio played softly. Country music. Sonora listened for a moment, thought of her brother, Stuart, killed by a female serial killer Sonora had been stalking, only to find herself on the receiving end of the attention. His had not been a pretty death.

It was his kind of music, country, and hearing it always made him seem close.

"Sonora?" Sam said. "You with me here?"

"What?"

"I was wondering where the guard is."

"I dunno. In the john somewhere is my guess." She focused on the song lyrics—some woman had reached the enormous age of thirty-four without saying the *I do* word. "Listen, Sam?"

"What?"

"If we stay to the end of this song, I may have to kill myself."

He gave her his sideways smile, accelerated gently.

The acreage rolled off into the darkness, enclosed by a double row of four-plank fencing separated by a thick, perfectly trimmed hedge. There were no corners, just rounded edges.

The drive, which looked like it had been freshly paved within the last two weeks, curved toward a house that had the sort of sprawling presence one might find with a Spanish ranchero heavily influenced by *Architectural Digest*.

In the distance, Sonora could see the dark hulking presence of a row of large barns, some of them well lit. Barns with skylights.

She was in an agony to see them up close, to see what kind of horses would occupy such stalls, and for a minute she forgot why she was there.

But only for a minute.

"Come on, Sam, let's get this wrapped up. We got Joelle's autopsy first thing in the morning."

He nodded. It was something they were both dreading.

Sam parked the Taurus in a small, perfectly paved lot to the left of the house. A darkened section to the right, wooden stairs leading up to a double door, was clearly a daytime office. They got out of the car, shutting the doors softly.

The living quarters were brightly lit.

They could see a woman through the front windows, plantation shutters wide open, in a room that was a living room, or a study, or a den. The sound of cicadas rose and fell. The porch was wide, wooden plank, and on the right, facing sideways, was a white wicker porch swing.

Sonora was surprised by the open shutters. She had been a cop too long to understand such innocence.

Not innocence, she realized. Freedom, thanks to a buffer of privacy afforded by green velvet acres.

They headed up the porch steps, both of them walking quietly. She could make out a small kitchen alcove on the left, surrounded by a horseshoe of cabinets, the room making a long sweeping L shape. There was a fireplace on the right, a desk against French windows that ran along the back, a couch, and a rocking chair.

A woman reclined on the couch. A small fire glowed in the fireplace, Sonora could smell the smoke. Real logs, not natural gas. A blue oriental rug had been thrown over thick wheat-colored carpet.

Outside looking in, a beautiful room. Books on shelves that were built into the walls. The desk, cherry wood, the chair, more cherry wood and violet cushions. Sonora had to squint here, but it was definitely violet. Startling. Pretty. Eccentric. It made her long to own a violet chair.

Sam knocked, and Sonora had the quick reflexive clench of her gut she always got when she went to someone's front door. More cops were killed on doorsteps than anywhere else.

Sam and Sonora exchanged looks, waiting with a polite patience and a pretended indifference to the way the woman glanced at her watch, made a note, and put a bookmark in the book she had been leafing through. She took a sip from a glass of wine, stared into space for a moment. Then went to the door, moving slowly, in spite of the open shutters that exposed her every move to Sam and Sonora from a distance of less than six feet.

If the woman had been racing around the room, hiding dirty laundry, flushing used condoms, emptying ashtrays, Sonora might have liked her better.

Maybe Sam was right. Maybe these people had killed Joelle Chauncey. She began her mental list with "pretentious."

The woman opened the door slowly. It was, in fact, a beautiful door, oak with a stained glass window. Sonora had priced one once. Over a thousand. This one had probably cost more, like everything else on this farm.

Sam had his ID at the ready, so Sonora left hers in her purse. "We're Detectives Blair and Delarosa, Cincinnati Police Department."

The woman looked at them with a mild and unenthusiastic curiosity. She cocked her head to the left, one leg bent, the other toe to the floor, like a ballerina. An odd stance, though she looked comfortable.

"I'm surprised"—she dragged the word out—"that Mr. Hoiken didn't announce you. Mr. Hoiken is our . . . *security* guard." She cocked her head in the other direction, giving them her full regard. "Cliff's not here. But I'm here. Do you want me?"

Sam was smiling, as if he couldn't help himself, and Sonora wondered what he thought was so funny.

"And you are?" Sonora asked.

The woman looked at her. Languidly. She had, Sonora thought, the largest nostrils she'd ever seen on any living creature who was not also on exhibit at a zoo.

"It's such a *funny* thing, when someone comes to your own doooor, then wants to know who you are." She had the kind of southern accent one rarely heard outside of movies like *Gone With the Wind*. The drawl was clearly an ingrained habit, and it slowed conversation. One simply had to wait for her to get the words out. "But I don't *mind* introducing myself. I'm Vivian Bisky." She held out a hand for both of them to shake, which they did.

Her hand once more her own, she ran her fingers through hair that was a flat-looking meld of brown and gray. Sonora wondered why Vivian Bisky did not go to a drugstore and pick a number. On the plus side, the hair was cut short, over the top of her neck, full, and soft. Her eyes were brown, deep socketed, and made up with brown eye pencil, eyebrows plucked and filled back in. Her skin looked tissue-thin and fragile, likely oiled by something expensive every night, but her wrinkles were deeply etched into a permanent freckled tan, that was, oddly, the most attractive part about her.

"Why don't the two of you come in and tell me what it is you're doing on my doorstep this time of night. It must be important, for you to come all this way and not call first." She waved a hand and opened the door wide. Sonora half expected her to precede them into the room and was almost disappointed when the woman's notions of courtesy kept her in the small well-lit foyer while the two of them filed inside.

"Please, sit down, if you want. I was just having a glass of wine before bed, it helps me relax. Can I get you something? I have hot tea, if you don't drink."

Sonora caught Sam's look. A *tea drinker.*

Vivian Bisky left the front door open to the night. Sonora was annoyed. Doors needed to be closed after dark.

The woman paused in front of the kitchen. She was not one of those hostesses who cared whether you drank or not. She would go through the motions, check, checkmate. None of this "try my fried chicken or my feelings will be hurt" that seemed common to the southerners Sonora had met in the past.

But in spite of the accent, which sounded more like affectation than anything else, Sonora recognized a true woman of the South. Though clearly intelligent, she might well pretend otherwise, and there was no way in the world that she would be hurried. Sonora gritted her teeth and prepared to be patient. Vivian Bisky was a Tennessee Williams character come to life—and if she was aware that she was not in the Deep South of the forties and fifties, she did not show it.

Perhaps she had not yet noticed.

Sam and Sonora both declined the woman's hospitality. Sonora chose the couch where the woman had been sitting, and Sam raised an eyebrow at her but sat beside her, fishing the book up from between the deep cushions and setting it on the coffee table.

The Man Who Listens to Horses, by Monty Roberts.

Vivian Bisky took her glass of wine and settled into the rocking chair. "Have you read that?" she asked, sounding almost human. "If you love horses, you have to read this book. Are you just police officers, or are you horse lovers too?"

The question, as Sonora saw it, was, are you one of them or one of us?

"I have a horse," she said. Saw Sam roll his eyes, which made her decide to hit him the moment they were alone together in the car. He pulled out the mini-recorder and set up a tape, and Vivian Bisky pretended not to notice.

She leaned forward, causing the rocking chair to tip. "What kind of horse do you have?"

"Arabian."

The woman leaned back in her chair with a smile that was almost friendly. Waved a hand. "My brother and I raise Saddlebreds."

And there it was. The ranking. Just how good is your horse?

"Do you show him?" Bisky asked. Trying hard to control the interview.

"He's in training," Sonora said. It was sort of true. The first thing she was going to do was train him to walk quietly when she led him around the barn, and not bolt his food when he ate. But she made a mental note about that book.

Sam leaned forward. "I understand you do business with End Point Farm, with a woman named Donna Delaney?"

Vivian Bisky frowned, sighed deeply, leaned back in the

rocking chair. "I wouldn't put it that way. We do *try* to throw her a little something, from time to time. The horse industry, as you may already know"—this with a little nod toward Sonora—"is a bare-knuckle kind of business. Many people start up with nothing and end up with nothing. More people than you might think."

"I got the impression from Ms. Delaney that you do more than just a little business." Sonora did not bother to tamp down the hard edges.

Bisky curled her feet up beneath her knees. "I have not one doubt in the world that's the impression she tried to give you."

"You mean she was name dropping?" Sam asked gently.

Bisky gave him her smile, a rare offering. "I don't want to say we've never done *any* business with the woman, I'm not trying to make a liar out of her. Let's just say our business is *limited*. Really, the person you need to talk to is Cliff. He takes care of that end." She waved a hand. "I'm more the books and accounting stuff, the boring parts. And the entertaining, which one has to do in this business from time to time, that's more in my line. Clients or associates come into town to check on their horses—it's nice to have a little thing. But now, don't think I'm totally boring. I imprint all the babies, that's my particular specialty. It must be the *maternal* instinct."

Sonora glanced at Sam, wondering if he knew what she meant by "imprint the babies." He was nodding, in that knowledgeable way men have, whether they know what you're talking about or not.

"What is that, imprinting babies?"

Sam rolled his eyes at her, muttered, "You had to ask."

Sonora ignored him. She had a horse now. These were things she might need to know.

Vivian gave Sonora a smile that was friendly, if indulgent. "You just pick them up right after they're born and pet them, so they'll respect that people are powerful—they can pick you up, but they're safe, they pet you. Then they're much easier to deal with, more trusting, for the rest of their lives."

Sonora thought of the livestock auction. Wondered if horses

ought to be encouraged to trust people more than they naturally did. She thought not.

"Is your husband home?" Sam asked.

Vivian Bisky gave him a little smile. "I hope not, he's been dead for fifteen years." She sighed, and her sigh was state of the art, welling from deep within the diaphragm, swelling the lungs, then escaping through the nose. She breathed the way Sonora's junior high chorus teacher had always told them to. Outside of opera singers, Vivian Bisky was the only person Sonora had met who breathed that way. Not counting the junior high chorus teacher, who breathed that way too.

"It's a long time ago, detective, so don't feel the need to apologize for bringing it up, although I do miss him *terribly*. *Cliff* is my little brother—not so little, but then you'd have to meet him. But he's not here, he's in Saratoga."

"When's he due back?" Sonora asked.

"Day after tomorrow, if not sooner."

"Why sooner?" Sonora asked.

"I beg your pardon?"

"I said, why sooner? Is there a chance he'll be in tomorrow?"

Vivian Bisky smiled, but it wasn't pleasant. "It's possible he might come home early due to family business, detective. I probably shouldn't tell you this, but you *are* detectives, and one should cooperate with the police. Cliff's wife is not what I would call . . . self-sufficient. Cliff travels a good deal, as you might imagine, and every single time he's gone more than three hours, *she's* on the phone, trying to talk him into coming back home. Course, if I had sole charge of those kids of hers, I'd be on the phone too. They *ought* to get a nanny, or something, and keep her around with danger pay."

"What is the exact nature of your business with Ms. Delaney?"

Vivian Bisky smiled thinly. She was not intimidated by the question or the tape recorder. It was always difficult to convince wealthy people that they were subject to the rules like everybody else, often because they weren't.

"We might sell Donna a horse now and then, if we had something that just didn't work out. Something we could let go on the cheap. It's a little expensive out here to keep a lot of paddock pets, and it's not fair to the horse. If we have an animal that just doesn't cut it, then we'll sell it for a very reasonable price just so it goes to a good place."

"You consider End Point Farm a good place?" Sonora asked.

Vivian Bisky sat sideways, one eye on Sonora, like a crow. "I hear you, believe me, I hear what you're saying. Mostly we've sold Donna horses only when she had a buyer, somebody who might want a horse to show or a mare to breed. But like I said, I don't think Cliff does much business with Donna these days, and if you've been out there, I'm sure you can see why."

"You don't, by any chance, send her your overflow? Horses you don't have room to board?"

It was as if all the air had suddenly gone out of the room. Then the moment passed, and Vivian Bisky laughed with the enthusiasm she usually gave her sighs. "I tell you what, detective. I'm going to give you a midnight tour of one of our boarding barns, and then you can see how absolutely *ludicrous* that question is. Sit tight while I get my barn shoes."

40

VIVIAN BISKY'S barn shoes were a very sturdy pair of knee-high black rubber boots. They looked scuffed, worn, comfortable.

Bisky noticed Sonora looking. "Got them right out of the State Line tack catalog, dirt cheap, don't you just love them? Let me just grab my jacket, and we'll go."

Vivian Bisky shed the hothouse-orchid image as she led them down the front steps to the barns and paddocks. She could have passed for a stable hand, albeit a self-confident one. She walked differently in the boots, wearing a rough green jacket over a worn sweatshirt. The sweatshirt had a Bisky Farms logo, an F superimposed over a B, joining in a circle. Sonora noticed Sam looking.

Sonora lifted her chin, looked over her shoulders. She could see no horses in the neat square paddocks.

"We keep them up at night." Bisky waved an arm toward the barns. Her feet made small noises on the asphalt—Sam and Sonora's leather soles were louder.

"Why is that?"

Bisky stopped in the comfortably wide drive. "These are high-dollar horses, detective. They're *safer* up at night."

"What problems do you get at night?"

"Mosquitoes in the summer, which are not only pesky but

carry disease. Coyotes sometimes. They're not as bad as the dogs, neighborhood dogs, would you believe it? We had them going out at night running in a pack two years ago. Maimed a pregnant mare, and one of our stallions went through a fence after them, tore a tendon. We've spent a *ton* on vet bills, and he's still not right. Which doesn't keep him from his pleasure." She said it in an offhand way, as if she'd used the phrase many times.

Sonora heard a quiet engine. A pickup truck with the Bisky logo pulled up beside them, and a man in the blue and white of a rent-a-cop stuck his head out the window.

"Everything okay, Miz Bisky?"

"Fine, John. We're going to First Barn. Everything all right on the rounds?"

"Yes, ma'am, everything's fine."

"Did Mahan get that fence board fixed—over by the stallion barn, you know the spot?"

"Oh, yeah, he took care of that first thing this morning."

"Good, then. See you tomorrow."

He nodded. Drove on. Vivian Bisky talked faster when it came to business. Sonora liked her better that way.

Motion sensors activated floodlights as soon as they were within fifty feet of First Barn, which had been painted a deep hunter green and trimmed in burnt sienna—the Bisky Farms colors.

This was clearly the show barn, built to impress. The asphalt drive swept past, toward two other barns farther out, both built conventionally in long dormitorylike rectangles. But this barn, First Barn, was shaped like a horseshoe, the roof rising up in a vaulted arch that peaked in an enormous skylight.

Sonora could hear Sam and Bisky as they made their way down the barn aisle, Vivian almost flirty, Sam quietly questioning. She wondered if there were any coolers in this barn.

She moved quietly, breathed in the smell of horses, fresh bedding, leather tack. It was a surprising thing, how content she felt in a barn full of horses. Caught a glimpse of a horse quietly munching hay from a corner rack.

Had the chestnut mare gone from a stall like this one into the chewed-down, overcrowded pasture of End Point Farm? Had she gone from hay and grain three times a day to fighting for food in a herd of hungry, desperate horses? Had she wound up in a stock trailer like Poppin? Was she in some holding pen at a slaughterhouse? Was she at the bottom of the pond across from the dump site of Joelle Chauncey's body?

Surely, if they could find the horse, they could find the killer.

The tack room was open a crack, a bar of bright light over the concrete lip. Sonora could hear the faint sound of a radio, playing low. "Desperado." The Eagles.

She pushed the door gently.

The bright lights made her blink after the muted nighttime dimness of the barn aisle.

"Can I help you?"

The girl was college age, with the angular thinness one gets from missing meals rather than dieting. Barns were full of them, young girls trying to juggle school, tight budgets, and a passion for horses. She was flipping through a battered biology book propped up on a work table that held cleaning supplies—Leather Balm, glycerin soap, Byck's Leather Polish, a worn toothbrush with a yellow handle, and stained cotton rags.

"I'm looking for a cooler," Sonora said. Nothing like the truth.

"Sure, there should be one back here." The girl got up, went into the next room, flipped on a light. "This okay?"

The blanket was hunter green, worn but clean, folded in a neat square that showed the Bisky Farms logo in what Sonora was sure would be the lower right-hand side, when she unfolded it to double-check.

"Thanks," Sonora said.

The girl settled back with her book. "If you need anything else, just let me know."

Sonora headed out into the barn aisleway. Sometimes all you had to do was ask.

41

It was a dark time, a silent time.

All the lights in the house were off, even the porch lights and the ones out back that Sonora usually left on for security. She lay in bed, bundled in a ratty blue blanket that was as familiar as it was soft and worn. She thought of Joelle Chauncey on the autopsy table and felt cold. She had gotten up and put on a pair of thick white cotton socks, brand-new ones, she loved new socks. But she was still cold.

The weather was turning, fall into winter. Tim would be needing a heavier coat, Heather too, probably. Did she need to buy a blanket for her horse?

She had yet to seriously tell the kids about Poppin. They hadn't listened at dinner, and she thought it might be just as well. She might sell him. Best to keep this new horse to herself till she made up her mind.

She had been reading in Joelle's diary again that night. More of the same. It had been a mistake to go back through those pages. She had struggled to keep her eyes open, but as soon as she'd turned out the lights, she could think only of Joelle, her need for a mother, the daily hurts that were the lot of teenagers.

What had happened to Joelle's mother?

Sonora closed her eyes. Opened them. Two hours ago she had come in dog tired from Bisky Farms. She had drunk half a beer, but it had upset her stomach, and the alcohol had not put her to sleep.

She'd been turning the ceiling fan off and on, off and on, hoping that being cold and bundling in blankets would help her sleep. But she kept getting too cold, even with the socks, and Clampett, unable to sleep with her constant activity, had jumped off the bed and burrowed underneath with his secret cache of stolen socks and mangled stuffed animals.

He was snoring. Maybe she should eat dog food—it certainly worked for Clampett.

Her mind went back to her Poppin but could not quell that feeling in the pit of her stomach. What the hell was she going to do with a horse? Talk about your big animals.

And where was Joelle's horse? Was the animal alive? Sold to slaughter? Hidden away? Gone west with the night?

The panic was coming, a tightness in the chest, and she'd gone from cold to hot, sweat filming the back of her neck at the hairline. She sat up, swung her legs over the side of the bed, hung her head. Took a couple of deep breaths.

She went to the closet, rummaged in the pile of clothes at the bottom till she found her favorite sweatpants, pulled them on over the silk boxers she'd charged to her account at Victoria's Secret. Put on a jog bra and a loose black sweatshirt. She could not stand to wear anything tight when she had this panicky feeling.

Sonora tied her hair in a high ponytail, breathing with relief as it left her neck bare. She splashed water on her face. Looked in the mirror. Dark shadows beneath her eyes and a look of wide-eyed panic.

Definitely going crazy.

She padded downstairs, heard Clampett groan. She walked softly, careful not to wake Heather and Tim. Which became a moot point when she rounded the corner and saw the flickering light in the living room.

They were playing a video game, Heather in her oversize football jersey—"Go Bengals"—and Tim, barefoot and shirtless with goose bumps on his arms, jeans riding low showing his green plaid boxers.

Sonora sat on the couch and curled up in a blanket before they saw her. "Turn it off." Her voice was quiet but with the underlying steel of a very offended parent.

Tim and Heather exchanged panicked looks—Sonora was not sure whether their desperation came from being caught or being forced to abandon the game just when they'd defeated something called Gendermaye, thus acquiring a ticket to the City of Golden Tents.

The game went off without protest from the children, and Sonora was assured of her authority, a good feeling. The television screen went a vibrant shade of blue that meant it was in between—movies, cable, video games.

"What's going on?" she asked. Wondering how many nights this happened while she was working late.

"I couldn't sleep," Heather said.

"She was crying about her hair again, and I was trying to distract her." Tim smiled, disingenuous. "We didn't want to wake you up, man, we know how hard you've been working."

Sonora studied him. He would be a charming man when he grew up. He would excel as a salesman, politician, or attorney.

And Heather had been crying, her cheeks showed tear tracks, dry but unmistakable, and her eyelids were puffy. She had insisted on cutting her waist-length hair short two weeks ago and was mourning its loss, even though the new chin-length style was perfect for her small delicate face. Sonora's opinion, which was that the cut was adorable, carried absolutely no weight.

"I have a surprise," Sonora said, matter of fact. They looked at her, kind of a sideways thing. "A good surprise. I bought us a horse."

* * *

Sonora was blaming the night on the full moon. It was almost full, more of an oval than a circle, but good enough. And she hadn't had a family outing with the kids for way too long.

Nobody was sleeping anyway.

She sat on a hay bale and watched Tim and Heather petting the latest addition to their family. Clampett was pressed against her leg, watching the horse like it might explode.

The lights in the barn were achingly bright, here at two o'clock in the morning. It was chilly and breezy, and Sonora wore a knit jacket over her sweatshirt, two pair of socks, and her oldest Reeboks. Heather's cheeks were pink, whether from the cold or excitement, Sonora could not tell.

The barn had that Christmas morning aura of magic and breathless expectations.

Poppin was, if nothing else, a friendly and curious horse. He had been standing in his stall, head down, hind leg cocked, eyes sleepy, but seemed quite willing to stick his head out the stall door and accept pats in the middle of the night.

"I can't believe this, Mommy, it's like a dream come true."

"Yeah, Heather, but that dream will bite, so step back a little, and don't let him put his mouth on you like that."

Tim grinned. "Can I ride him to school tomorrow?"

"All in due time." Sonora listened to herself, thinking that she sounded sensible, just like a grown-up, just like her mother. Except it was two A.M. and she'd not only bought a horse but was bringing the kids in for a visit in the middle of the night.

Sonora held up a plain white paper bag. "Hamburgers, anybody? There's eight left."

No one answered except Clampett.

They had stopped at White Castle along the way, which was how Sonora had celebrated all important events in her childhood. She was aware that more sophisticated people drank champagne.

Looking back with the eyes of an adult, she thought her mother might have preferred the champagne, or at least food that did not come in square cardboard boxes, but she could not get over the childhood conditioning that White Castle was exciting.

She closed her eyes, conjuring late summer nights, heated pavement, the smell of gasoline fumes. She could see the car headlights haloed by moths and mosquitoes, feel the up-past-bedtime excitement, and she was back in the backseat of the '56 Buick with her brother Stuart, their legs brown with sun, hands glazed with grime, soles of their feet black from going barefoot on hot, tar-sticky pavement.

Sonora had a sudden and strong sense of her brother, as if he were there in the barn and not long gone into that not-so-good night. Clampett nudged her knee, and she fed him a hamburger. In the efficient way of large dogs, he ate the box it came in as well.

42

SONORA LEANED against the wall of the hallway in the morgue, holding a styrofoam cup of coffee that Sam had just handed her. She took a small sip. A mistake.

Was the ulcer coming back? She hadn't had a twinge in over a year.

Maybe not. Her stomach was often upset this early in the A.M. if she'd had a pretty sleepless night, like she had last night.

Sam picked a piece of hay out of her hair. "What's this?"

"I had to get up at five A.M. to feed that horse."

"Wouldn't McCarty feed it?"

"Yeah, but I wanted to check on him myself. See if he was okay. Put some more shavings in his stall." McCarty was going to kill her when he saw how many shavings she'd used, Bisky inspired, to bed out Poppin's stall. She wondered how much they cost. Figured she'd be finding out soon enough.

"Was he?"

"Was who?"

"The horse, Sonora. Was he okay?"

"He was nervous. He's like that a lot."

Sam patted her shoulder. "He'll settle in."

"I can't drink this, Sam. You want it?"

"I was raised not to let anything go to waste." He took the cup and went through the motions, but his mind was elsewhere. Like hers.

"I haven't felt like this since my first autopsy."

Sam put his hands on her shoulders, massaged the muscles. She touched the top of his hands. Strong fingers, masculine, vibrant with tensile strength.

She was getting that feeling again, like she couldn't breathe.

Eversley nodded at them as he passed in the hallway. He stopped by the metal cart that sat outside the steel swing doors that led into the lab where the autopsy would be performed.

"Sam. Why do they say performed?"

He stopped rubbing her shoulders. "What?"

"When they talk about autopsies. Why do they say performed? Why not . . . executed?"

"Because the victim is already dead."

Stella Bellair passed them next, heading down the hall with her entourage of indentured servants otherwise known as medical students.

Stella inclined her head. Then the hallway was quiet, save the soft echo of rubber-shod feet and the swing of the steel door as everyone went into the autopsy room.

Sonora looked at Sam. Time.

43

SONORA COULD HEAR the faint rise and fall of Sam's breath, realized they were breathing together in rhythm.

She sat next to Sam in Interview One. Their knees touched.

The door was open. They could hear Crick's hand slide up and down the wall as he fumbled for the switch. The light was harsh and sudden, but neither Sam nor Sonora flinched.

If Crick was surprised to see them sitting side by side in the dark, he did not comment, merely looked at his watch, muttered "two out of three," and left.

Sonora watched her coworkers walk past the open doorway, down the hall to the bullpen. She felt out of sync, as if they inhabited another universe. They walked back to their desks, did their paperwork, worked their shift. Drank coffee or Coke or Highbridge Springs Mountain Water. Mango Snapple. They answered the phone, listened to their messages, and filled out the endless cycle of forms that violent crime always engendered.

And she knew that some days, some times, all of them felt just like she did just then. She felt a quick touch of nostalgic sympathy for all of them, as if they were long-lost relatives she would never see again.

Crick came back through the door with his own personal

coffeepot, chipped enamel, harvest yellow, in which he made his own very bad coffee.

He had brought Sonora her mug, the half moon of lipstick like a brand on the side. She felt embarrassed. The guys kept their mugs cleaner than she did. Crick set a cup in front of Sam. Laid out spoons and the jar of dust-encrusted Cremora that had been sitting on his file cabinet since Sonora had come to work for him in homicide seven and a half years earlier.

Sonora gave the jar everything she had to get it open. Inside, the white powder looked gummy and gray, as if someone had left it out in the rain. Sonora dug out a chunk with a plastic spoon, put it in her cup. The coffee went from oily black to oily brown. Just needed to find a victim to feed it to.

"Want some?" She held the cup out to Sam. Who looked in the cup, then at Crick.

"How long has that creamer been sitting around?"

Crick looked at the ceiling. Frowned, making his eyebrows bunch thickly. "Have to be 1962."

Sonora wondered why it would *have* to be 1962. Knew it would be useless to ask, Crick would never explain. She believed he made statements like that one just to make people crazy.

Sam screwed the lid back on the jar. It made a grinding noise, like someone gritting their teeth. "None for me, y'all, but thanks just the same."

"Real cops drink it black." This from Mickey, who stood in the doorway, a brown accordion file under one arm, a legal pad dangling from his fingers, and a bottle of Jolt Cola in his right hand.

The bottle was one-third full. Mickey paused in the doorway to take a healthy swig, belched in polite understatement into the top of his fist, as if he were speaking into a microphone.

"Come in, Mickey." Crick did not bother to turn around.

Mickey raised the bottle over his head so he could scratch behind his ear with his little finger.

"He recognizes your voice," Sonora said.

"More like your belch." This from Sam.

"You can't say I'm not entertaining." Mickey joined them at the table, set his accordion folder down. Straddled a chair and pulled himself all the way to the edge of the table.

Crick scooted his chair closer in, the signal to begin. "Let's start with the autopsy. What you got?"

Sonora rubbed her finger on the edge of the table. She had only just realized that women who had really beautiful nails were likely wearing acrylics. It did not annoy her. It made her want to go out and get a pair of her own.

Joelle Chauncey had tiny little nails, bitten down to the quick, bluish-white where once they had been pink-tinged and healthy.

Sonora cleared her throat. "No foreign matter under the nails that would indicate she put up a struggle or fought an attacker. No defense wounds on the fingers or hands or arms."

"Cause of death?" Crick asked. He was making notes.

"Suffocation. Foreign matter in the nasal cavities, including fibers, which will be sent to Mickey for a match with the blanket she was wrapped in, indicating that she was buried alive." Sonora paused, looked at Crick, who held up a finger.

"The blow to the head was not the cause of death?"

Sam rubbed the back of his neck. "Dr. Bellair said the head trauma would have eventually been fatal, but that Joelle was alive when she was buried in the manure pile."

"Not conscious?" Crick asked.

"No. And no sign she woke up and struggled—her hands were clean." Sam looked at Mickey.

"Yeah, crossed over her chest. Like this." Mickey crossed his arms, a palm on each shoulder in classic undertaker pose.

"Placement," Crick said, opening a file and laying out black and whites from the secondary crime scene.

Sonora looked up and nodded. "Very much so."

Mickey opened the accordion folder, began adding pictures to Crick's pile.

"Stella thinks the killer washed Joelle's face."

Crick met Sonora's eyes. "That so?" He pulled a photo across the desk. Sonora leaned forward, recognized Joelle Chauncey wrapped in hunter green.

"She found traces of the kind of residue you'd find on commercial wet wipes," she told him.

"What about the blanket?"

"Horse cooler," Sam said. "A lot of hairs on it, some horse, some human."

Crick pulled up another picture. Put it down. "Time of death?"

Sonora pulled the hair off the back of her neck, which was filmed with sweat. It had been hot in the autopsy room. Stella kept it overheated, as if her patients could feel the cold as they lay flaccid and unprotected on the wet steel table, their bodily fluids running like a river down the troughs along the side.

Sonora frowned. "Time of death is complicated."

"When is it not?" Mickey, drinking from his cola bottle.

"Stomach contents were chicken nuggets, French fries, and pineapple chunks, all about three and a half to four hours digested. Canned ravioli was eaten just before death, almost no digestion. We checked with the school cafeteria, and the chicken nuggets, et cetera, pan out. Rigor was further along than you'd expect, looking at the stomach contents. If you go by rigor and body temperature, she died around ten A.M.

"If you go by the stomach contents, say three-thirty to five P.M., which is more in line with everything we've gotten from witnesses. Stella thinks that Joelle was knocked unconscious, and the trauma stopped the digestive process. And that the heat of the manure pile accelerated the rigor. Her estimate for time of death is between three-thirty and seven-thirty P.M."

Crick looked at Mickey. Waiting.

"We're not ready to close the case book here"—Mickey opened his arms—"but preliminaries tell me the pickup truck at the secondary crime scene is a match for the one that went through the fence at the primary scene. So, in my opinion, what we got is the vehicle used in the commission of the crime."

Crick folded his arms and nodded. He looked at Sam and Sonora. "What's your take on the people who own the truck? Alridge, isn't that the name?"

"Kidgwick," Sonora said.

Sam scratched his cheek. "My take is that they're about the unluckiest couple who ever walked the face of the earth, or that property they got is bad luck. Really bad."

"You superstitious?" Crick asked.

"Wasn't. Am now."

"You know the place," Sonora said. "Where the Randolph boy was murdered."

Crick was nodding. It was always annoying to tell him things, Sonora thought, since he already knew everything already. A sort of teenager for life.

"They had a daughter who was involved, didn't they?" Crick said.

"She died," Sam said. "Car wreck, single car, suspected vehicular suicide."

"How'd they hold up?"

"They play New Age music," Sonora explained.

For some reason, this description satisfied Crick. "And while they were listening to those harps, bells, and whistles, did they happen to notice that their truck was missing? Did they manage to see a guy burying a little girl in the manure pile behind their house?"

"The barn kind of hides it from view," Sonora said.

Crick rolled his eyes.

"They work," Sam explained. "They probably weren't home."

Crick shrugged. "Get their schedule down. I'm guessing our killer did his bad deeds while the Kidgwicks were doing their nine-to-fives. Which means he's pretty comfortable, pretty familiar with the area. And that the killing was planned."

Sonora frowned. "That doesn't fit the Bisky Farms theory."

"Blair. Be radical. Get the facts before the theory."

She sighed. Crick found a way to use that line in every single investigation. He was like a parent, mouthing the same irritating strictures over and over and over.

Crick leaned into the table, supporting his weight on both elbows, Mickey the object of his intensity. "Was Joelle Chauncey transported in that truck?"

Mickey leaned back in his chair. He had an expression on his face that Sonora called "that backpedaling look," so she expected bad news.

"So far, I've got nothing."

"No hair, no fiber, no—"

"Nothing. Dirt in the carpet, driver's side, but not too much of that. I figured that blanket she was wrapped in might leave some fibers on the front seat. But, hey,"—he held up a hand—"it's early days yet. I'm still looking. My opinion? She didn't get transported in the truck."

"Killer could have put her in the trailer with the horse," Sam said.

Sonora pictured it. A horse on one side of the divide, a green-blanketed bundle on the other.

"Makes sense, in case he gets pulled over." This from Mickey. "Guy gets pulled over, it's a lot better to have her in the back of the van than lying out in the backseat. You want a wish list, get me that trailer, I promise not to ask for anything else."

"Come to Santa," Sam said.

"Nothing from the uniforms?" Sonora asked, looking at Sam.

Crick shook his head. "We've concentrated on an area with a thirty-mile radius. Nobody's found nothing. So far. Horse and trailer could be anywhere."

"He could have sent them over a cliff," Mickey said.

Sonora threw up her hands. "If you found a dead horse and trailer, wouldn't you tell somebody?"

Mickey shrugged. "Unless I wanted the trailer?"

"Somebody would talk," Sam said. "If they found it. Sonora's got the best lead on the horse and the trailer."

Crick folded his arms. "I'm glad something productive came out of yesterday afternoon."

Sonora opened her mouth, closed it. Crick's tone of voice implied dissatisfaction. The case was three days old, unsolved. A profile case at that. Had Crick found out that she'd bought a horse? Did he know she'd gone home to make meat loaf? Was he dissatisfied with her results, or did he think she wasn't working it hard? She felt guilty about all of it, buying the horse, cooking the meat loaf, tracking the newt, wasting so much time at the auction.

Speaking of which. Sonora traced a finger on the table. "We went to an auction, there's one every Tuesday and Thursday afternoon at the Acquitane Stockyards over past Lebanon."

"*Milk Money* town," Crick said.

"Tuesdays and Thursdays are their days for horses, tack, whatever. Low-end kind of stuff. Heavily worked by dealers who pick the horses up cheap and sell them to slaughter." Sonora could see the kid in jeans riding the gray quarter horse down the dirt chute, patting the horse, telling him he'd be okay. "A man showed up at the auction last Tuesday afternoon when Joelle disappeared. Times work out, and he was seen by two or three different people, at least. Had a horse and a trailer he was trying to sell, package deal."

"Sold it to slaughter," Crick said, drumming a finger on the tabletop.

"No, that's the weird part. From what I can tell, he had two offers from dealers—I think they were more interested in the trailer than the horse. But he wouldn't sell to them."

"Can't be our boy, he'd be desperate to sell."

"There's criminal precedent for stupidity," Sonora said.

Sam put a hand on the back of her chair. "Whoever it was, he sold the horse and trailer to a Barbara Adair, runs a riding program pretty close to there, in Loomis. We were thinking maybe our man wants to keep track of the horse. Keep it under wraps, then go back and buy it back later on, when things cool down. If the horse was worth going to all this trouble for, it'd be hard to send it off to the killers."

Crick nodded slowly. "Get up there ASAP. I'll talk to Rick Martin, he works that area. You'll have a clear shot, no jurisdiction trouble. He's a straight shooter."

"If the horse isn't there. Even if it is. Hal thinks we should get a warrant, go look through what they have at Bisky."

"Let him do his legwork. We have our own priorities." Crick drummed his fingers. "Was the child sexually assaulted?"

Sonora shook her head. "No sign of that whatsoever."

There was a moment, as if all of them let out their breath.

"So you don't think we're looking for Mr. Stranger Danger?" This from Mickey.

Sam waved a hand. "Mr. Stranger Danger isn't going to take a horse. This thing was set up. The guy had a trailer, he knew what he was doing."

"We've got some weird inconsistencies." Crick held up a thick finger. "If this killer is after the horse, why involve the kid? If the killer is after the kid, why involve the horse?" Another finger. "Why the attack on Donna Delaney? Hours apart like that—it's got to be connected. And why go back to the barn and mix it up with Blair when they got to know there'll be cops all over? Why plant that finger in the riding glove?"

Mickey took the last gulp of his Jolt Cola. "I myself think the kid had to be incidental. They couldn't know she was going to fall off that horse and hit her head. Then when she does, the killer thinks she's dead, or too much trouble dead or alive."

Sonora was not sure why Crick was looking at her, and it made her nervous. She pushed her thumbs against the edge of the table. "Not to change the subject, but I'll tell you what bothers me more than anything, and that's the crime scene."

"Primary or secondary?" Mickey asked.

"Secondary. Halcyon Farm, where Joelle was buried."

Crick leaned back in his chair. Folded his arms. "What's bothering you?"

"First off, she's wrapped in a blanket. A blanket that can lead us right to the killer—everybody watched O.J. The whole world knows about fibers. But there she is, bundled like a baby, arms across her chest, face wiped down with a wet wipe.

We're talking placement. Intimate insight. This is the most honest direct piece of communication we're going to get from this killer."

Mickey tipped his chair backward, scratched the back of his head with unbecoming vigor. If he'd been her child, Sonora would have told him to put his chair back down, before he fell backward and got hurt.

"You know what you're saying, Sonora?" The chair legs went down. Mickey must have read her mind. "Only two types of killers are that careful with placement. Stranger Danger fetish types, guys who want her found, because they have remorse."

"And parents." Sonora looked around the room. Hard faces, unreadable. "I think we ought to go with Dixon Chauncey."

44

THE WAITRESS SET a platter down in front of Sonora, moving quickly, like it was hot. Sonora unrolled the white cloth napkin, glanced across the table at Sam.

"Study the art," she told him. She stirred her coffee. Opened a tiny white bucket of cream.

She was having her favorite breakfast at Cracker Barrel—grilled sourdough toast, hash brown casserole, one egg cooked medium, a large orange juice, and coffee.

Sam used his fork to cut a wedge of pancakes, scooped up a strawberry, and dipped it into a puff of cream. "Dixon Chauncey wouldn't do something like this, he's too squishy."

For some reason, the word *squishy* brought the attention of a young man and woman having what looked to Sonora like a power breakfast of cell phones and bran. The woman arched one well-plucked eyebrow.

"Yes, he's squishy. But that wouldn't stop him. There are lots of squishy murderers out there." Sonora took a bite of sweet sourdough toast. Sweet. Crunchy. Perfect.

Sam put a piece of bacon on her plate. "Name three."

Sonora looked from her plate to his. The bacon was his, the strawberry pancakes were his, the platter of scrambled eggs were his. Sonora had learned to accept that men could eat this way and not gain weight, while women could go up two jean sizes on lettuce. She put the bacon back on his plate, and he tossed it right back over.

"Eat it." More a growl than anything.

"Quit testing me, you know I love to eat."

"It's one of the things that makes you the light of my life. Quit worrying, what are you—a hundred? A hundred three?"

"Oh, yeah, I'm sure." He was sweet-talking her. He was jealous of Hal McCarty, and he was sweet-talking her. And it was working. She was actually being charmed by bacon. Sonora took a sip of juice. She could resist bacon. "Study the art, Sam."

"Quit saying that, Sonora, you're like Annie when she's chanting."

"I hate it when they chant."

"So stop."

"But it does work." She smashed the egg yolk, and it swirled over the fried whites. "Salt, Sam. Pass it over."

"Pepper?"

"What would be the point?" She sprinkled salt. "Think about the comfort level of the killer, Sam. It's immense, is what it is. You got Joelle taken right in sight of her mobile home, then dumped and buried a mile or two away. This is Dixon Chauncey's territory. And it's overplanned and clumsy, a neophyte murderer, a squishy murder."

"I didn't say the killing was squishy, I said Chauncey was."

The woman with the plucked eyebrows gave Sonora a sideways glance. But her attention was forestalled by a waitress bringing a fruit cup.

"Come on, Sam, look at the *care* involved in her placement. Blanketed, bundled, hands crossed over her chest, face wiped down. That's remorse, Sam, admit it."

He crunched bacon, and a sprinkle of crumbs leaked onto his tie. He didn't notice. Sonora decided to let him wear them for now. He could go around looking ridiculous until he admitted she was right.

"Try this." Sam shoved a fork piled with pancake, strawberry, and cream across the table.

A perfect bite. Not possible to resist.

Sonora went for it, Sam holding a hand under her chin to catch the inevitable spillage from the overloaded fork. Fed her the strawberry that landed in the egg yolk and left a pink swirl.

Wonderful. Sweet thick pancakes, the texture of the berry, the salty tang of egg. While she was chewing, Sam jumped in.

"What's the trigger, Sonora? Why live with a kid fifteen years and then kill her?"

"I have teenagers, I can explain."

"Serious. Why *now*? Why, when all that stuff is going on with Delaney, when your bud McCarty is all over the place."

"He's not my bud."

"That's not my point."

"Okay, Sam, but lookit. She wasn't sexually assaulted, right?"

The woman at the next table set her fork down with audible click. There was a banana on the tines of the fork. Sonora wondered how she made the click with the banana on there.

"But where's the horse? Tell me that. And how does Chauncey know Joelle's going to fall off? And why doesn't he finish her? Why bury her alive in a pile of manure?"

"Maybe he thought she was dead."

"You're reaching, Sonora." He threw the bacon back on her plate. "Finish your breakfast, we'll be late for school. They're probably halfway through lunch by now, anyway. You believe Annie's lunch period is at ten forty-two A.M.?"

"I believe everything you tell me, except—"

"Yeah, yeah, you made your point."

45

His name was Madrigan, and he was not unattractive. Six two, at a guess, dark haired, with big shoulders. He was the assistant principal at Joelle Chauncey's high school, and he had the squinty-eyed apologetic look that a certain class of alcoholics take on—as if they've forgotten so many names, faces, and promises, that "I'm sorry" comes as often as hello.

His eyes were bloodshot, face florid, nose thick and clown-like and shot through with broken blood vessels. His handshake was firm, and there was intelligence in the eyes.

He stood up from behind his desk, a large man, clothes loose and comfortable, flesh firm, as if he'd been eating healthy, working out, trimming down. A man with a past, on the upswing now.

"Madrigan. Vice principal."

Sam introduced them, flipped the ID, but Madrigan waved it away.

"Mrs. Clarkson, out front. She told me who you are." He waved them toward the chairs.

Uncomfortable chairs, unfortunately—plastic seats and metal legs. The office was stark, straight out of the concrete-block-walls-and-yellow-linoleum school of design that gave schools and other public buildings the cheerless look of prisons.

A framed photo on the right wall caught Sonora's eye.

Madrigan, younger and lighter, sunburned and sweaty in a fishing boat that looked worn but competent, boat docked in a swampy inlet that said low country.

A long hard way from Cincinnati.

The permanent tan that burnished Madrigan's arms, neck, and face belonged much farther south. This man would get along well with Sam.

"You're here about the Chauncey girl. Joelle?"

Sam nodded.

"I saw it on the news. I heard today that her . . . that her body had been found. What on earth happened?"

"We're still in the early stages of the investiagation, Mr. Madrigan." Sonora watched his face glaze over, knew exactly what was on his mind. It wouldn't hurt to scotch the rumors, for Joelle's sake, and her family's. "We would guess, at this point, that she was not sexually molested. That's unofficial."

Madrigan took a deep breath, let it escape slowly. "I appreciate very much your telling me. One imagines the worst."

Sonora did not comment. She could imagine worse. She did not want to.

"Mr. Madrigan, what's your enrollment here?" Sam asked.

"Eleven hundred forty is our intended capacity. We've got more like fourteen hundred, give or take."

"So you probably didn't know Joelle."

Madrigan laid his palms on the top of the orderly desk. There were piles, files, and computer printouts, but all were stacked with a method, and there was no slop.

"I try to know all my students. But Joelle in particular. She was one of my projects, one of the ones I watched."

Sonora glanced at Sam, who was flipping the tape over in the small black mini-recorder. "Why Joelle?" she asked.

Madrigan frowned. "She's the kind of child I try and look out for."

"And what kind is that?" Sonora got a look from Sam. Time

to shut up and be patient, the man would get to the point in his own good time, please God.

"She's the kind of kid that comes around, seems to need the attention. One of the ones who usually slips through the cracks. Held back at least one grade, schoolwork mediocre to poor, not a whole lot of friends or motivation. Her test scores would surprise you, they're very high. Definitely a low achiever. Sort of dreamy and unfocused, just getting by.

"Some of these kids, you know, they move around a lot, one school system after another. They get behind, and if they do catch up and get settled in, they move again. It's hard, I know from my own experiences when I was a kid."

Something in his voice, in his eyes, caught Sonora's attention. She had the feeling that this man had led an interesting life. She would bet that he'd served in Vietnam, that at night he lay awake wondering about exposure to Agent Orange. She wondered about the journey that had led this man to the assistant principal's office in a small high school on the outskirts of Cincinnati.

That he was sincere and caring was clear. That he was different, never a square peg, was equally clear. She was surprised he'd survived the administrative prejudice and narrow-mindedness of the Central Office.

Madrigan looked up at the ceiling, thinking. "Joelle just didn't seem to click, to tune in to school. She was preoccupied, there were other things on her mind. She couldn't seem to concentrate, didn't seem to join in. She seemed very much apart."

Sam crossed his right foot over his left thigh. "You think it was a phase? Discovered boys, maybe?"

Madrigan's face was hard to read. "Possibly. She was at that age."

"But you don't think so?" Sonora said.

Madrigan shrugged.

Sonora leaned forward, made eye contact. "Mr. Madrigan, this is a murder investigation into the death—the brutal death—of a child at your school. Speak candidly. Tell me what's really on your mind. Your instincts, your theories, your gut feel. If it doesn't pertain, it'll go no farther than this room."

Madrigan glanced at the recorder. Sonora hoped he was not going to ask them to turn it off. She guessed that he wouldn't. That if he talked, he would stand behind what he said.

"Some children seem to live . . . the way I think of it is, children under a shadow. They worry. They fall asleep in class. Their minds are on other things."

"Are you talking about abuse?" Sam asked.

Same old tune, Sonora thought. Different lyrics.

But Madrigan was shaking his head. "With Joelle, no, I don't think so. Some of the kids have genuine worries. A sibling pregnancy, family money problems. Illness, impending divorce. I admit there were times with Joelle when I wondered. She made a lot more trips to the emergency room or the clinic than is normal.

"But I checked it out, decided the ER trips were more because her father was overprotective. I guess—you've met the guy, I'm sure."

Sam was nodding.

"Normal childhood things—most parents would let them go, or treat at home. Joelle's dad would haul her off to the ER, get upset. He usually took it worse than she did."

Sonora glanced at Sam.

Madrigan waved a hand. "I always got the feeling that Mr. Chauncey was trying to be an absolutely perfect parent. He was very hard on himself, very intense. We had conferences a couple of times, and I usually spent most of the time reassuring him, instead of talking about Joelle."

"What was he worried about?"

Madrigan raised both hands. "Everything. Nothing. I tried just talking to Joelle a couple of times. She's always happy to talk to me, but she was shy about personal things. I didn't want to push."

"Any teachers she was close to?" Sonora asked.

Madrigan's face settled back into the apology. "Not that I could tell. Like I said, she was slipping through."

"What about her grades? They go up or down the last couple of weeks?"

Madrigan leaned forward, picked up a computer transcript off the top of a pile, offered it across the desk. "We haven't had a grading period yet this year, but these are from last semester."

Sonora took it, Sam looking over her shoulder. A D in algebra one, a C in social studies, D in chorus, F in home economics, C in biology, A in freshman English. No comments from anyone other than the chorus teacher, who found Joelle "a pleasure to have in class, but needs focus."

"What happened with the English grade?" Sonora asked.

Madrigan took the transcript, studied it, shrugged. "I have no idea."

"Did Joelle have a locker?" Sam asked.

The hallway was redolent with cafeteria cooking. The heating system was running, and Sonora could smell floor wax beneath the odor of fresh-baked rolls and pizza.

Madrigan led them into a connecting hallway lined with metal lockers, painted orange. "Three forty-seven," he said, bending down.

Joelle Chauncey had a bottom locker.

It was hard to open, mainly because it was crammed with books and ragged-edged paper, torn out of spiral notebooks.

A bell rang, followed by a moment of hushed expectation, then classroom doors swung open and children streamed out.

So many of them, all in a hurry, wearing loose low jeans, platform shoes, heavy backpacks.

"She's got a couple of buddies, doesn't she, who go by the nicknames of Pistol and Bits?" Sonora reviewed the journal entries in her mind. Pistol and Bits.

Madrigan looked blank. Sonora permitted herself a small

surge of superiority, that she could come to this man's school and reel off the nicknames of students, nicknames the principal did not know. All in the legwork. Relentless. Focused.

"The kids I'm thinking of are Maggie Billifano and Josh Elam."

Pistol and Bits, Sonora thought.

"Let's head back to the office, and I'll double-check to make sure, but they're sophomores, so unless they're in band, they'll have A lunch. They should be in the cafeteria or hanging around the gym. Ms. Flutie?" He turned, held up a finger. Bent close to Sonora. "This is Joelle's English teacher, from last year."

She was a thin woman, with yellow blond hair, and would look brittle in another ten to twelve years, but the gauntness was youthful now and all the rage. Her skirt was long and slender, and the white blouse was translucent, exposing a full slip and demi bra with a large square yolk of lace at the top of the blouse, like a bib.

Sonora winced. It wasn't that she did not like lace, she simply preferred it where it belonged, on underwear and tablecloths.

Ms. Flutie wheeled toward them, one eyebrow raised. She gave Sonora and Sam a brisk thorough look. Glanced at her watch. Looked to the principal for direction.

"Yes, Mr. Madrigan?"

He folded his arms and leaned against the wall next to the packed lockers. Smiled.

It would take a hell of a woman to resist that smile, Sonora thought.

Ms. Flutie wasn't up to it. Her voice softened. "How can I help you?"

"It's about Joelle Chauncey."

Flutie's face went blank, but Madrigan's funereal tone of voice made an impression, and the woman took half a step forward.

"Of course. The student who . . . Joelle was in my second-hour English class last year." Flutie took a breath, as if she'd passed a test. She seemed on the verge of walking away.

Busy, busy, Sonora thought. "She made an A in your class, even though she wasn't doing so well in her other ones."

Ms. Flutie nodded. "It was dropping there toward the end of the year. I was surprised she was able to maintain it."

Sonora did not like the tone of voice. She had dealt with the Ms. Fluties of the world many times, often over her own children. Joelle Chauncey was expected to get a C, and Ms. Flutie had done everything she could to see to it.

But Joelle hadn't. She wondered why.

"What was your impression of Joelle? Troubled, or—"

"Joelle was never very *attentive.*" Flutie tucked the yellow blond hair behind her ears. "She was always off in never-never land, she'd miss turning in homework, she was rather apathetic."

"Her chorus teacher said she was a pleasure to have in class," Sonora said.

Flutie's smile was tight. "She wasn't unpleasant, she just wasn't there, in her mind, anyway. But the child could write— give the devil his due. Position papers, research papers, essays. The biggest grade of the semester was over a topic paper, on current events. The students take a subject from the headlines, gather research material from periodicals—newspapers, magazines," she explained to Sam and Sonora, as if Cincinnati's finest might not know what a periodical was. Teacher-speak. "And I have to say that in this case Joelle fired right up. I couldn't *not* give her that A." Her tone of voice implied that she'd tried. "She did a truly outstanding job, but then by the end of the semester, her work dropped off again. I was quite disappointed."

No, Sonora thought, you were not.

"For a while there, she was quite the little firebrand."

"What was her topic?" Sonora asked.

"I suppose I could look it up." Ms. Flutie lifted her chin, tapped it with a long narrow finger. Her nails were rough edged, chewed to the quick. "Missing children, that's what it was. Missing children and adopted children searching out a birth parent. Too broad, in my opinion, I really wanted her to go in one direction or the other—in fact, I specifically instructed her to do so, and I had to take points off when she didn't. But all in all? A fine job. I saw some genuine writing talent, raw and unformed but there. There was a contest, statewide, and I strongly considered sending her writing in. If she had stayed within my guidelines—but Joelle, most people don't realize, was a child who did exactly what she wanted at all times. She's capable of a lot more than she's giving."

"Not anymore," Sonora said.

46

JOELLE CHAUNCEY'S two best friends were on their way out of
the cafeteria when Madrigan caught them in the hallway. He
introduced them to Sam and Sonora, let them know, in an
understated way, that their help would be appreciated but that
they were under no obligation to talk to anyone. He offered all
of them the use of his office, and Sonora could tell that Sam
was on the verge of turning him down, when the school secre-
tary appeared, summoning Madrigan to a plumbing crisis in a
boys' bathroom.

They stood alongside the brick wall in back of the cafeteria.
The smells wafting through the open windows took Sonora
back to her own school days—the warm yeasty smell of fresh-
baked rolls, mingled with the aroma of boiled greens, and the
modern addition of pizza from the pizza line.

She checked her watch. Ten forty-five A.M., and A lunch was
already over. The bewildering illogic of school schedules was
one thing that had not changed since Sonora was a kid.

Josh Elam was tall, and it seemed to embarrass him. He
slumped, head low, and Sonora could see that the hunched-
over posture was a habit. His hair had been shaved up the
sides and left thick at the top, and his acne, while still a presence, was clearly under control. Another three years, and he

would win the fight. He stood close to Maggie, whose hair was a deep and artificial red with a dashing streak of lavender in the bangs.

"I guess the two of you heard what happened to Joelle." Sam's voice was low key and sympathetic.

They nodded and looked embarrassed, as if they were not sure how to act.

"We're sorry for your loss," Sam told them.

They nodded again, but there was a general feeling of relaxation, like they'd been holding their breath and were letting it out. Sam's quiet, heartfelt validation of their dignity and grief struck the right note. Sonora decided to let Sam work this one. He was clearly on the right track. With kids this age, they could learn a lot or they could learn a little. It was all in how it was played.

"You guys got anything on the guy who did it?" This from Maggie, but Josh's eyes were on them, flat and angry.

"Yeah, we've got some ideas, but we've got more investigating to do."

If he'd been talking to adults, Sonora felt sure Sam would have said "information gathering." Most teenagers had had all the "information gathering" they could stomach by their sophomore year.

"Who you lookin' at? Can't say?" This from Josh, almost timidly.

Sam shook his head, agreeing. "No, sorry, I can't. I could get into all kinds of trouble if I talked about it before I was sure of my footing. But I'm after it. Joelle seemed like a good kid."

They both nodded.

Sonora tried to stop grinding her teeth. Patience. Getting a teenager to talk was as tricky as getting a butterfly to land on your fingers.

Sam leaned back against the brick wall. "Either of you know her dad very well?"

"A little," Maggie said.

Sam folded his arms. "He can't seem to come up with any thoughts on who did this to Joelle."

Maggie looked at Josh. Rolled her eyes. "He wouldn't."

"Why do you say that?" Sonora asked.

Josh shook his head. "The guy's lame. I know that sounds harsh, with his loss and all. But it's the truth."

"Was he close to Joelle?" Sam asked.

More shrugs. Nobody was admitting anything.

"Joelle have a boyfriend?"

"Not that we know of." Maggie went wide-eyed and innocent. Josh shook his head in total support.

It was the answer Sonora had expected, and she was surprised, because they were clearly lying. She glanced at Sam, wondering if he knew. His own daughter was younger. He had not yet run smack into that studied, wide-eyed innocence.

Sonora's formula was that the amount of charm exerted was directly proportional to the likelihood of a lie. "That's not what I hear."

Maggie and Josh gave her blank looks and big eyes. Even a smile from Josh, which pretty much clenched it. Looks were exchanged. They began gathering books, ready for flight.

Sonora waved a hand. "Look, if you want to walk away, go ahead, you don't have to talk to me. But I've been a homicide cop a long time, and even though I didn't know Joelle, I saw what her killer did to her, and it was bad. Whatever details you heard—this was worse. The only good thing is that she wasn't sexually assaulted."

They were hooked now, Maggie in sudden tears. "I thought they raped her."

"No," Sonora said. "She was unconscious right away, and she didn't suffer."

The children moved closer together.

"I'm going to catch this guy, with or without your help. But if you know anything, that would be great. It could make my job easier, help me catch him faster. You don't have to tell me *everything.* You're afraid we'll start looking at the boyfriend, and yeah, I know there was one. Well, you're not dumb, you know that's one place we'll go, if only because he can help. He's probably your friend, and you don't want to rat him out.''

This brought a small startled laugh.

"What?" Sonora said.

Maggie looked apologetic. "It's just nobody says 'rat them out' anymore.''

As if it mattered, Sonora thought. "I do, but hey, I'm old. And you know what I mean, don't you? I don't happen to think a kid did this, as a matter of fact I'm sure not. You tell this guy—tell him to come talk to me if he wants to. It'll make him feel better, I guarantee it. Maybe he knows something, maybe he wants to help. But meanwhile, tell me what you do know, what you don't mind saying.''

They stared at her. Hard as hell to know what was in their minds.

"You mean, like, did she have enemies? She was only fifteen." Josh laughed a little, then remembered himself. Sonora reminded herself that a lot of this was nervousness.

She folded her arms. "Which one of you is Pistol, and which one of you is Bits?''

The look of shock was replaced by laughter, part nerves, part genuine amusement. Sam and Sonora waited them out.

"You going to let us in on it?" Sam asked.

Another exchange of looks. Maggie glanced into the cafeteria window. "Not here.''

Josh and Maggie led them to an oak tree between a green Dumpster, a dirt running track, and an asphalt parking lot in back of the school. They settled in the grass, cross-legged, and Sam and Sonora sat down with them.

The kids looked comfortable. They wore loose jeans four sizes too big and huge T-shirts. They did not seem concerned about grass stains.

Homicide was hard on clothes.

The girl, Maggie, was talking.

They had been a threesome, Josh, Maggie, and Joelle. A

twosome now. "See, the big thing you need to know about Joelle, was how smart she was."

"Genius, man," Josh was nodding. Smiling a little.

"But she hated school, and she hated the work, you know, like homework. And it wasn't like at my house, where they ground you if you don't bring home the grades. I mean, her dad got upset and all, but he didn't really do anything—"

"Except pile on the guilt," Josh said.

Maggie nodded. "And she was sneaky as hell. That girl got away with stuff."

"My hero," Josh again.

"And she'd like, you know, mess with people." Maggie leaned toward Sam. "She didn't get along with her dad. He made her do all the work around the house and go to bed early, and he got after her if she talked on the phone late at night, like, he was totally unreasonable."

Sonora and Sam automatically looked to Josh, whose turn it was to speak, according to the rhythm. He grinned at them. Stayed silent.

"Plus he was snoopy," Maggie said.

Sonora could see that she was just warming up.

"He'd go through her stuff, her *drawers,* her backpack, and lie to her and tell her he didn't. So she starts setting little traps for him."

Josh bowed his head, emitted a series of low masculine chuckles.

"And he's reading her journal! That she had to write for Flutie's class! That really did it!

"And see, she had all this stuff to work out, and I'm talking about really adult-level stuff here, not kid areas. Stuff. And so she starts keeping two of them, journals, you know? One for her dad and Flutie, and a, like, private one in her locker."

"She was a good writer," Josh said. "She could have written songs. Only she had to move it."

"Move what?" Sonora said. One moment she was following, the next she was lost.

Maggie gave Josh a wary look, but it was his turn to talk, and he didn't notice.

" 'Cause one time she was sick, you know, with bronchitis, so her dad came and picked up all her assignments and crap. And Mr. Madrigan gets her books out of her locker, so it was a real close call. Her dad almost got that good journal, you know, the real one? So after that, she keeps it in Maggie's locker."

Maggie stared at the ground.

"Who's the boyfriend?" Sam said.

"It's this guy, goes to Rembrandt, whole other school. She met him at the mall or something."

"Yeah, he works at Chick Fillet."

"You know his name?" Sam asked.

*"Bry*an," Josh said.

"She only mentioned him, like, a million times a day," Maggie told them.

"Last name?"

Josh looked at Maggie. "Simpson?"

"No stupid, that's Bart. *Martin.* Bryan Martin. They used to meet down at this secret place—I'm not exactly sure where it was, she never would tell. It was a farm somewhere by a pond, and some kid, like, got killed there a whole long time ago."

Sam gave Sonora a look.

"That stuff you were talking about—that Joelle had to work out—"

Maggie snorted. "She wasn't a drug dealer, okay? And she didn't, like, go with the gangs. She didn't declare."

Josh started up again with the chuckles.

Maggie wrapped her arms around her knees. "I don't know for sure the details, I just know it was a home thing, with her dad."

"Was he abusive?" Sam. Ever so delicate.

"Ick, no, not *that* kind of stuff, she would of *told* me, she'd of gone right to Ms. Clifford if that was it. We get lectured on that in health and everything. It was like . . . she had this big decision. Something to do with her dad. And she didn't want to cause him a lot of grief, 'cause even though he was really really lame, he was, you know, good like a parent. I mean, he took care of her and all. She wasn't going to just cause him all this grief because he wouldn't let her talk on the phone after eleven. Which I thought was totally mature on her part.''

"But you don't know what it was?''

They shook their heads. "She didn't want to say. She got secretive. She didn't want to get him in trouble.''

Josh fingered the zipper on his jacket. "Plus she wasn't sure yet. She had some stuff to check out.''

"No, Josh." Maggie flipped her hair back yet again. "She knew for sure, 'cause I saw her like a week ago, and she was *completely* freaked. She said it was like reality just shifted. I mean, whatever she found out, I think she kind of just went after it, like a quest, and then when it turned out to be real, it was too much.''

"And you think it had something to do with her dad?''

"I just don't know for sure. She kind of would not talk about it. Like, once she knew, she had to keep it to herself and deal with it.''

Sam nodded. "About that journal.''

Maggie got up, dusted off the back of her jeans. "It's in my locker.''

Sam gave Sonora a hand up. "Was Joelle close to any of her teachers?''

Maggie shook her head. "She liked Mr. Regal, her algebra teacher, but that was last year.''

"She flunked algebra,'' Josh said.

"No, she didn't, and she still liked Mr. Regal. But he's at the middle school now, I'm pretty sure.''

"How about Mr. Madrigan?''

"The *principal*?'' Maggie looked at Josh. Something funny yet again.

"What now?'' Sonora said.

"It was like a bet,'' Josh told them. "He keeps a bottle of Baileys Irish Cream in his middle drawer, and like, she was hanging around him a lot so maybe she'd get a chance to take it. Those Baileys bottles are the biggest trophies in the whole school.''

''Now she'll never get it.'' Maggie's eyes turned red, and Josh put an arm around her.

Sam got his keys out, looked over his shoulder at the school, the hordes streaming from the redbrick buildings into the square windowless gymnasium.

''Poor suckers,'' he said.

''The students or the teachers?''

''Either. I've seen prisons that were better equipped and more cheerful.''

''At least they get to go home at the end of the day.''

He unlocked the passenger door for her, headed around to drive. ''What do you think, Sonora?''

''I think it's weirder than shit, Sam.''

''What's weirder than shit?''

''That Joelle hung out at the Kidgwick place where the Randolph boy was murdered, that she was fascinated by the case and wound up buried there herself. You think it's fate or karma or something?''

''No, hon, I think it sounds like the killer knew her very well.''

She looked at him. ''Coming around to my way of thinking, are you?''

''I'm getting there. Let's head up to that barn where you think the horse was sold. Follow that up once and for all. Here.'' He handed her the journal. ''Read to me on the way.''

''I get carsick, Sam, I'll throw up.''

''Read fast, and hang your head out the window.''

47

Sonora opened the window halfway. Good air circulation would give her more time to read before she got sick. She shivered. Definitely sweatshirt weather.

They passed an exit, and the BP Oils, Shell stations, McDonald's and Burger Kings gave way to pasture. She pictured herself riding Poppin over the hill.

Sam glanced at her sideways.

"I'm reading already," Sonora said. She opened the spiralbound notebook, the front cover a picture of a cartoonish Cinderella wearing a blue ball gown that floated around her feet like a cloud.

> . . . *I've been thinking about families a lot, what makes a family and all that. Is it the blood and gene thing, is it living all together because you don't have a choice, is it all of the above? If this was a multiple choice test, I'd mark C, all of the above.*
>
> *If I stir things up, Poppie could go to jail. I don't even like to think about that. Poppie in jail???? He couldn't take care of himself in a million years. Say it. He'd get raped. He'd have to be a wife or something to another prisoner, some big-muscle guy, like a Nazi or something. I dreamed the other night that Poppie was sitting across from me at a table in one of those prison visiting*

rooms, and he was crying and saying he forgave me. If I tell, I'll
see that face for the rest of my life. And who am I going to tell?

A white Mazda 926 passed them. Sam, unconsciously, in-
creased his speed. "Why'd you stop?"

Sonora swallowed. "I'm getting sick, Sam. What could she
have found out that would put Chauncey in jail?"

"Don't throw up yet, keep reading, and then we can find
out."

She flipped pages. "There's not much more in here, this is
a new notebook."

"Read."

"I'm skimming. There's a lot in here about Bryan."

"Don't read that part. Is this our exit?"

Sonora craned her neck. "I think so."

"No, it's not. Why am I asking you? You get lost in the
bullpen."

"I wasn't lost, I just got turned around."

"Read."

Sonora pushed the button and closed the window.

"Keep the window open in case you need to throw up. If
you're cold, you can have my jacket."

She had a jacket of her own and he knew it, but she took his
anyway, because she just might throw up, so it was safer to wear
his. It was an older one, scratchy but familiar, and she pulled it
over her, inhaling the fragrance that was Sam. She knew his
wardrobe almost as well as she knew her own. This was not his
best-looking blazer, but it was the most familiar, and her favorite.

She laid her head against the glass, closed her eyes.

"Read, Sonora."

She flipped through more pages. Her stomach wasn't going
to last much longer.

I talked to Poppie. I was worried about Mary Claire and
Kippie. They have mothers somewhere even if mine is dead, like

he told me. I can't believe she's really dead. I'll never find her now. He says sometime he'll take me to see her grave.

"This doesn't make sense," Sam said. "Why does she think they have different mothers? Didn't he tell us her mother died when Joelle was a little girl, that she had breast cancer?"

"I suppose you *could* explain it."

"Like how?"

"That she was little when her mom died so he told her she went on a trip or something."

"Why lie about how she died?"

"Breast cancer is scary."

"I don't buy it."

"Me either. What do you think is going on?"

"Hell if I know."

"Anything else?"

"Bryan, Bryan, Bryan. Let's see." She flipped a page. "Bryan, Bryan . . . oh, here."

If what Poppie says is true about Mary Claire and Kippie's mom, maybe I should leave it alone. It's kind of unbelievable that he would rescue us like that. Like a litter of lost kittens. I told him—

"Told him what? This mother thing is bugging the hell out of me." Sam looked at her. "You're chalk white, Sonora, want me to pull over?"

"Fast."

"You awake, Sonora?"

Sonora slumped sideways, head against the door, feeling the cold air on her face. "I am now. Sorry about the jacket."

"It'll dry clean. Want me to stop and get you something?"

"Not unless it's a bullet to the brain."

"We're almost there."

She chanced a quick look out the window. Lebanon, Ohio.

"Watch for it, Sonora, Four Wishes Farm—it should be on our right."

"I'm not watching for anything."

They passed a sign for Camp Swaneky and Fort Ancient. Camp Swaneky? Saw the Turtle Creek Cemetery, and then they were past Lebanon and out into the countryside.

They passed a large new high school, a subdivision under construction, then a small sign painted red, shaped like an apple. "Four Wishes Farm—owner/trainer/instructor, Barbara Adair."

"Why an apple?" Sonora said.

"You want an apple? Think it'll settle your stomach?"

"No, Sam, just never mind."

He gave her a sideways look, slowed the Taurus, and bumped down the gravel road that led to a small one-story white house, circa early sixties, and a big black barn with red doors—freshly painted.

"Don't be cranky."

"I can be cranky if I want, I'm sick."

An oval riding ring circled by a white fence, paint peeling, was in heavy use—six little girls, ranging in age from eight to thirteen, trotting their horses.

They wore black velvet helmets, some had black knee-high riding boots, and some wore boots that zipped along the side and covered the ankle. One wore tennis shoes and jeans, an aberration among the rest who wore Lycra riding pants and sweatshirts. The girls were posting, and they looked new at it, rising and falling in an awkward exaggerated motion that had to be hard on a horse's back.

Sam pulled the car to the side of the road. Sonora got out, moving slowly. Her legs felt like jelly, but it was good to get out of the car.

"Hello," she said, trying to get the attention of the woman in the center of the ring. The woman had red hair, shoulder length, clasped back in a ponytail. She wore beige breeches and knee-high black rubber boots, and a blue flannel shirt that hung down across the back of her pants.

She gave them a look, then went back to her barrage of instructions. "Shelby, you're balancing on the reins. . . . Jan, get your heels down, think toes up. . . . Kim, go, go around— no, you pass to the inside, always. *Girls. Always, always* pass to the inside."

Despite the constant corrections there was no observable change in the actions of the riders, who seemed to have their hands full, going around and around in a cloud of beige dust.

One of the horses coughed and dipped his head forward violently, pulling his small rider out of the saddle and up on his neck. She grabbed the horse's mane for dear life.

Sonora looked at the horses with a new eye. They were scrawnier than her own Poppin, ribs showing like washboards along their sides. Their heads were down, movements slow, with the exception of one gray who looked like he was going to take off and jump the fence at any moment. The little girl on his back had a wide-eyed look that begged for someone to let her get down.

Sonora contemplated saying something, then changed her mind.

Sam rested a hand on the fence. Lightly. It did not look like it could support much weight.

"Excuse me, miss? We're looking for a Barbara Adair."

The woman gave Sam a look that mingled disgust with surprise. She did not answer. "Kim, hold him tighter, and *lean back.*"

Sonora nudged Sam. "Let's try the barn. Maybe there's an office."

Sam nodded, headed for the barn just as a woman in blue jeans and Roper boots led a solid black mare out of the barn. The horse was dancing, head up, black saddle glistening with polish and oil.

The woman was tall. She put her left foot in the stirrup, bounced on her right toe three times, and swung her leg over and into the saddle.

The horse trotted forward. The woman took the left rein and turned the horse's head, circling until the mare stood still.

"You wouldn't be Barbara Adair, would you?"

She shook her head. "I'm just a boarder. Barbara's in the back in the foaling stalls with the vet, looking at Songbird."

Sam smiled. "Could you point us in the right direction?"

The woman smiled back, and Sonora chalked up another conquest for Sam.

"Just go on in the barn, and go through the feed room back out the other side."

The mare danced sideways, the woman raised a hand at Sam and picked up the reins. Sam said thanks, and Sonora followed him into the barn. Behind them, the mare was still circling.

This barn had dirt floors, churned and spotted with droppings, and rows of tiny stalls, thinly bedded with straw. Sonora looked into the stalls as she went by. It was dark inside, dust thick in the air along with the pungency of ammonia. Some of the horses were tacked up—saddled and chained to the wall, waiting with their hind leg cocked for afternoon duties.

"Anyone here?" Sam called.

A horse nickered.

Two stalls in the center had their doors open wide. In one, Sonora saw saddles and bridles mounted on the wall, and Fiberglas and Tupperware trunks tucked back along the sides. The next room held feed bags and trash cans, a small refrigerator, and a microwave oven that looked like one of the first Amanas off the assembly line.

"She said through the feed room," Sonora said.

"Let's check the stalls first. See if we see the mare." Sam took the right side, Sonora the left.

"Sam, I'm not sure I'd recognize her if I saw her."

"Look for a brown horse with a big belly and a mane that lies to the left. Man." She heard him rustling. "From the looks of these horses, that feed room is a myth. My God, you poor thing, look at you. Don't they serve dinner around here?" He reached a hand through a stall window, petted a soft nose.

Sonora moved up the hallway, slower than Sam, thinking that for some horses there might be fates worse than slaughter.

She would not want Poppin to wind up in a place like this. She would have to be careful if she sold him.

"Anything?" Sam said.

"Come look at this one." She pointed, and he doubled back, studied the horse a long moment. Gave her the smile where his eyes crinkled up.

"That's a gelding, Sonora."

"Oh."

"Sonora—"

"Not another word, Sam." She headed for the feed room, tripped over the cracked wooden arm of a wheelbarrow that was resting, for no obvious reason, beside the microwave oven. The wheelbarrow went sideways, tipping into a can full of feed.

Which set the horses off. She heard a whinny, some snorts, and a hopeful nicker.

"Can't take you anywhere." Sam pushed on a door that led to the outside. The door stuck, and Sam kicked it, leaving a black smudge along the bottom, one of many other smudges. The hinges creaked, and they were back outside, blinking in the sunlight.

They exited into a small grassy area. Along the right-hand side was a neat row of horse trailers, a white one, rusty, a blue stock trailer, and a white Sundowner gooseneck with maroon trim.

Sonora headed straight for it, looked at the license plate on the back. "Bought out at Richard's, Sam—that's a Cincinnati dealer." She climbed on the wheel well, looked inside.

Dried horse droppings, spilled swatches of hay, kernels of feed. Along the top ledge, a dirty white lead rope. "This looks like the one, Sam."

"Help you folks?"

Sonora jumped down off the wheel well, heard Sam ask the voice if she was Barbara Adair, heard the voice agree that she was.

"I'm Detective Delarosa, this is my partner, Detective Blair. We're from Cincinnati PD."

The woman took a quick backward look at the trailer, studied Sam's ID.

"I knew it was too good to be true. My trailer was stolen, wasn't it?" She was a petite woman, small-boned, wavy blond hair and wire-rim glasses. She wore black breeches and a sweatshirt that said "Four Wishes Farm," with the pink logo of a cartoon horse blowing out the candles on a birthday cake.

"Where'd you pick the trailer up?" Sonora asked. "Do you have the bill of sale?"

The woman shifted her weight to her left foot, absently patted the gray mare she held at the end of a lead rope. The mare stomped her foot, shook her head.

"It's been going like this all day, you know. Mare didn't take, one of the kids falls off her horse and breaks a collarbone. My dad always said things come in threes, and by golly, there you be."

A man walked out of a stall. He wore jeans, rubber boots, a blue work shirt. "Sorry, Barbara."

"She had *me* fooled."

Sonora moved next to Sam, kept her voice low. "What does she mean, the mare didn't take?"

He bent close, his voice soft. "It means she got knocked, she just didn't get knocked up."

"Catch her on the next one." The man looked at Sam and Sonora, but Barbara did not introduce them.

"You got time for one more?" she asked. "I've got a gelding I think is developing navicular."

The man hesitated. "Let me look at him next week. I was supposed to be at Ten Acre Farm an hour ago."

Adair nodded. "Okay. I'll send you a check toward the balance."

The man thanked her, lips tight, and headed around the side of the barn.

Did anybody in the horse business pay their bills? Sonora wondered.

"Ms. Adair—" Sam was pulling out the tape recorder.

"Let me put this mare away." Adair turned the horse expertly, unclipped the lead rope, and let the mare trot into a dark outdoor stall, locking her in behind a red metal mesh sliding door.

Adair leaned up against the side of the barn, bent her knee, and propped herself up with a foot. "I'd invite you into my office, but if I do, we'll be interrupted every three seconds."

"Here is fine," Sonora said.

Adair looked at her. A speculative look. "So, what's the deal with the horse trailer?"

Sonora handed Sam a fresh tape out of her purse. "That's what we're asking you. Where'd you get it?"

"Aquitane Stockyards. Outside Cincinnati."

"When?"

"Oh, let's see, two, three days ago. Tuesday."

"You remember what time?"

Adair smiled and shrugged. "Late afternoon sometime."

"You get a bill of sale?" This from Sam.

Adair shrugged. "Nope."

Sam nodded. "Can you get more specific about the time?"

"Lessee." The woman touched her upper lip with the tip of her tongue. "Before five and after two."

"What were you doing there?" Sonora asked.

"Selling Girl Scout cookies, what do you think?"

"I think you were receiving stolen merchandise. I'm wondering if you make it a habit."

"I wasn't receiving, I paid for it."

"How much?"

Adair could no more have forgone the smirk than she could stop breathing. "Fifty dollars."

"Fifty dollars. For a gooseneck four-horse trailer in prime condition." Sonora looked at the trailer over her shoulder to make sure it was actually in such good shape. It was. "Ma'am? This didn't seem unusual to you?"

"It was a package deal. I had to buy the horse."

"What horse?"

"Guy who sold me the trailer had a horse that went with it. Saddlebred mare in foal. Chestnut."

"How much did you pay for the horse?"

The smirk again. "Fifty dollars."

"Where is the horse?"

Adair waved a hand. "Sold her."

"Already?"

"I don't want her here eating her head off. I've got fifteen acres and twenty-seven horses. Last thing I need is another paddock pet taking up space."

Sam got in ahead of her, asking Adair to describe the mare.

"Chestnut, about fifteen three hands, probably fourteen, fifteen years old. She had a frieze brand. On the left."

"Did her mane lie to the left?"

Adair frowned. "Could have. Can't say I noticed."

Sonora was frowning. Adair had paid one hundred dollars to her six hundred twenty-five and gotten a horse *and* a van.

Sam leaned up against a black fence. "A package deal? The guy insisted?"

"Oh, yeah."

"He say why?"

"Didn't want the mare sold to slaughter. I think the van was thrown in to sweeten the deal. He said he'd lost his job and was selling the mare and the trailer because he couldn't afford the horse anymore. You know, a hard luck thing. He said that the horse was a family pet, and he didn't want to sell her to the killers. I mean, the guy was pathetic. I can't believe he stole them, I wouldn't have thought he'd have the nerve. A shy type. You know."

"Squishy," Sonora said, trying not to look at Sam.

"But he was picky about who he sold to—the dealer would have given him more money than I did. You sure this is the right guy?"

"Can you describe him?"

She rolled her eyes. "God, I don't know. Average. Not particularly attractive, but not gross."

"Hair color?"

"Dark, I think. I'm not sure."

"Fat? Thin?"

"In the middle."

"If you saw him again, do you think you'd recognize him?"

She scratched her cheek. "Yeah, sure, maybe. See, he had on one of those dorky hats with the flappers on the ears. You know the kind?"

Sonora knew the kind. "Who'd you sell the mare to?"

She shifted her weight. "A Saddlebred barn up in Wisconsin, they show and train and do lessons. She's long gone, but she's in good hands."

"Got the bill of sale on that one?"

"Ah, no, I gave her to the guy in trade. Owed him on some stud fees, so I gave him the mare as partial payment."

"Okay, Ms. Adair. We need you to get in our car and take us to whoever you sold her to. We're investigating the homicide of a fifteen-year-old victim, and *we know* you're going to do everything you can to help."

She looked at them. "I don't have time to go with you."

"You'll have to make time," Sonora said.

Adair shifted her weight back and forth. "Actually, I guess the horse is still here."

"You guess that, do you?" Sonora said.

"Guy hasn't had a chance to pick her up."

"Do you understand what obstruction of justice is?"

"Look, I didn't lie, I did trade her. Guy just hasn't had time to pick her up yet, and I forgot she was still here." Adair waved a hand to the outdoor stalls. "That one over there. I mean it, I forgot the guy hadn't been by. This is a big barn, I can't remember every little detail."

"Of course not." Sam gave her an encouraging smile.

Sonora turned her back on them and headed for the stall. The woman had sold the horse to slaughter, or was planning to, maybe after the birth of the foal. If she waited. Somebody like the Horseman's Buddy was slated for this mare's future.

Sonora looked through the rusty grilled mesh of the stall door, saw the vague shape of a horse standing nose to the back wall. The stall was very dark. The smell of horse and urine was loud enough to make her eyes water.

She opened the door carefully, stood just inside.

She did not know whether to laugh or cry. The mare's stomach was swollen with the pregnancy, and her coat was coarse-looking, mud streaked, mane windblown and snarled with mats. Hard to believe this one animal had set off a series of crimes including fraud, murder, grand theft auto, and various violations of traffic laws. She looked hungry, cranky, and very much in need of a friend.

"Talk to me, baby," Sonora murmured. "We'll put alfalfa in the witness box if you'll testify." The mare took a side step toward her, then changed her mind and backed away.

This too would come in time.

Adair came into the stall in a flurry that sent the mare farther back into the dark, urine-soaked corner. "Are you really doing it? You're taking my trailer?"

"We could arrest you first," Sonora said.

"What for?"

Sonora looked at the mounds of worm-infested manure, the scum-filled water bucket, no more than one third full, the lack of bedding over the uneven dirt, the absence of light and ventilation, the complete lack of food.

"We're not just taking the trailer, Ms. Adair. We're also taking the horse."

"You can't do that!" Adair's wail sounded like a temper tantrum winding up.

Sonora looked at her over one shoulder. "You want to come along?"

"*Hell*, no."

"Then get this horse some feed and hay while I arrange transportation. And rinse out that water bucket."

"I'll do that," Sam said.

Adair gave him a sour look. "Much obliged."

48

Sonora went to the barn, alone, at dusk. Poppin was in his stall, finishing his dinner. She felt a twinge of disappointment. She'd hoped to give him his dinner herself.

He put his head out the open Dutch window, dribbling grain over the wooden ledge and onto the ground. His ears were forward. He looked curious and friendly. Sonora rubbed him on the forehead, stroked the rub mark over his nose. He bobbed his head but did not pull away.

Joelle Chauncey's final journal implied ongoing discussions with her father. Had this been the trigger that had gotten her killed? What could have been so sensitive that he would kill her, when he had faithfully parented her all these years? Multiple mothers would not put a man in jail.

Sonora took a dirty lead rope from a peg next to Poppin's stall. The cotton was thick, it felt good in her hands. She slid the stall door open, and Poppin was right there, trying to get his head through the opening.

She clipped the lead rope to his halter, glad Hal had insisted on leaving it on, since she had no idea how to get it on or off. Shoved the door open and led the horse out.

She was nervous, stomach tight. She'd never handled the horse alone. There at the other end of the rope, he seemed bigger than he had in the stall.

She headed out the barn door, hoping the horse would come along quietly.

She led him out into the pasture, constructing scenarios in her mind. Suppose, for the sake of argument, Dixon Chauncey had killed Joelle, the trigger being whatever was alluded to in the journals. There were still problems, and even with Sam coming around to her point of view, she was still uneasy. Because *expecting* someone to fall from a horse and die from their injuries was stretching it. Even for Dixon Chauncey.

The psychology was not so bad. It would be something Dixon Chauncey could set up and stand away from. Perfect for a man as terrified of confrontation as Chauncey was.

But why take the horse?

And yet. Taking the mare put the suspicion on Bisky Farms—where there were tensions and dirty dealings already. Easy enough to get a blanket, and incredibly stupid of the mythical Bisky killer to wrap the child's body in a cooler from the farm.

Could she picture Vivian Bisky pulling off such a cold-blooded murder? Actually, yes. Maybe she'd been a cop too long. She could picture people doing all kinds of things.

And stupid perps were a fact of life, which did wonders for the homicide clearance rate. So it wasn't something she could rule out.

A jerk on her arm pulled her backward and to a sudden stop. Poppin had selected a clump of clover and short green shoots of tender grass to munch. Sonora let him eat for a minute, wondering what his criterion was, why one clump of grass was passed over for another.

He moved toward her, chewing, and she scrambled away, wondering how long it took to teach a horse not to step on its human.

Sonora gave Poppin a rub on the shoulder. Even if Dixon Chauncey had killed Joelle, vague and suggestive journal entries were not enough to take to a grand jury, even with the prosecutor in their corner. And after convicting the lead district attorney of murder one last year, Sonora did not have a prosecutor in her corner.

People were never grateful.

Poppin's head came up, and he froze, eyes on the horizon. Something out there he didn't like.

Sonora looked over the hill, saw nothing that should alarm a horse, even one like Poppin, who had so far proved sensitive to the bright yellow of a clump of daisies, the flutter of a butterfly, and the truly terrifying spectacle of a plastic grocery bag. If horses told horror stories, Sonora was convinced they'd use demon plastic grocery bags to scare the foals.

Poppin decided he'd had enough, for whatever reason, and headed toward Delaney's fields. Now that his head was up, Sonora kept him going, circling ever closer to the break in the fence where Joelle Chauncey had taken her final fall.

Poppin had other ideas.

Forty-two minutes later, Sonora, who had checked her watch at the outset, had sweat drenching her temples and the hairline at the base of her neck, but she had gotten Poppin across the fields, and he was now grazing nervously near the broken fence line. At which rate, she figured, it would take her only the better part of the night to get him back to the barn.

She was beginning to see an amazing number of similarities between horses and teenagers, not limited to but including a refusal to listen, a language barrier, and a personal agenda that bore no relation to her own.

Horses could be put in their stalls, teenagers could be sent to their rooms, and both could be counted on to trash their living quarters when left unattended.

Sonora looked out over the horizon. What light there had been was quickly draining away. She could not accomplish much now, going over the crime scene in the dark. She kept hold of the lead rope, while Poppin, head to the ground, ate grass like a horse who has not been in good pasture for some years.

Which, for all she knew, might well be the case.

The sky was midnight blue now, smudged with dirty pink

streaks of cloud. She could see stars, a rare treat for a city girl. The wind was just enough to brush Poppin's tangled red mane and dry the sweat on her neck. She was wearing her favorite gray sweatshirt, inside out, like she really liked it, a loose pair of jeans, and her latest Reeboks—a bad choice for barn time, she should have put on an old pair. If her checkbook ever recovered, she'd buy some barn boots.

Sonora breathed in the smell of horse and felt an inexplicable wave of happiness. It was a rare and quiet moment. The cicadas were loud, countryside white noise, and she heard the staccato squeak of a bat.

A light went on in the Chauncey trailer, then another. It looked snug and homey, all windows glowing except one, which she guessed was Joelle's bedroom. How were they doing, the Chaunceys? How were Mary Claire and Kippie handling the bottomless loss of an older sister?

And she knew that in spite of his pitiful dyed hair, his cigarette offerings to acquaintances in the hopes of future friendship, his shuffling head-down walk, his kicked-puppy smile, Dixon Chauncey was trying to do all the right things.

The trailer would be clean, the bathroom would smell of Pine Sol. The children would have a hot home-cooked meal, they would have clean folded clothes for school, home-packed lunches, supervised study time for homework, and help with their math.

She should manage her own household so well.

A man like this did not kill children. A man like this did not bury them alive.

What was she doing, trying to pin a heinous murder on the male equivalent of Donna Reed? Even Joelle, in her true journals, had seen the worth of this man.

This man had not amputated Donna Delaney's index finger and stuffed it into a riding glove. This man had not terrorized a barn, and a tough nut like Delaney. Surely the killer and the cutter were one and the same.

Sam had called this one. The focal point of the investigation should shift to Bisky Farms.

It was full dark now, and all Sonora could see of the trailer was those yellow glowing lights, the center one flickered with a bluish purple that meant a television screen. The bicycles would be lined up to one side, the front porch clear of toys.

But because she was a cop, her mind kept moving, ignoring the new conviction that Dixon Chauncey was exactly what he seemed, a devoted, meticulous, hard-luck kind of guy trying to raise three, now two, children on his own. And in her mind's eye she saw the Weed Eater, propped up in front of the trailer, on the porch next to the bikes.

Had the Weed Eater been in front of the trailer the night Joelle had disappeared? Sonora was sure that it had. Even Dixon Chauncey would not come home and trim borders when his oldest daughter was missing. And he was not the type to leave his tools in front of the house for days on end, like others that Sonora knew.

She tied Poppin to a fence post with a knot that would make a man curl his lip, but she was alone and it was dark, so she did it her own way. She moved slowly in the dark, so as not to alarm her horse, who took exception to the noise of her feet in the grass, and to keep from turning an ankle in the uneven field. Looked for the fence post six feet from where Joelle Chauncey had come off her horse.

Frustrating, not to be able to see. She ran her fingertips slowly down the rough wood, catching a splinter in the ball of her thumb.

And even though she'd been half expecting it, she felt a chill and a tingle in her spine when she touched the thin plastic line of Weed Eater tape, tied to the post twelve inches up from the ground, shin level on a horse.

Sonora heard the howl and bark of a coyote, the horn of a train. She glanced at the mobile home, wondering if the Weed Eater was still propped out front.

She had answered one question. Which was how Dixon Chauncey could be sure that Joelle would come tumbling off that horse.

49

By THE TIME Sonora got Poppin untied from the fence, the wind had kicked up, and lightning flashed on the horizon, a seam of brilliance in a thick night sky. The barn lights brought them in like a beacon.

It did not take her the better part of the night to come in from the fields, as she had feared, and in fact Poppin was so eager for his stall and his flakes of hay, and for the handful of grain that he mysteriously knew she would give him as a treat, that they went back much more quickly than Sonora intended.

She was able to keep up, just.

She had been in enough barns lately to appreciate how clean and open this barn was, how it smelled of Pine Sol and cedar shavings, hay and the musk of horse.

She turned on all the interior lights as she led Poppin to his stall.

He rushed the doorway, knocking her sideways, and she let go of the lead rope rather than be dragged in. Her wrist hit the doorjamb, smashing her hand between the wood and the shoulder of the horse.

''Shit,'' she said, which did not faze the horse. She held her wrist to her side and went into the stall, grabbed the lead rope. Poppin was snuffling his food bowl and did not care to be disturbed, but she did not take no for an answer. She dragged him out into the aisle.

The rain started, thumping on the tin roof of the barn. She listened for a moment, thinking there was no other sound quite like it.

Rain and dirt blew into the barn, and Poppin snorted and took off.

"Whoa, you son of a bitch." Sonora zigzagged up and down the aisleway, trying to keep him under control, thinking that people who complained about being walked by their dog ought to try being led by a horse.

"Shorten your lead rope, and let him move around you in a circle."

Sonora looked over her shoulder. Saw Hal.

She nodded, not bothering with hello, focused on the lead rope, the horse, and not getting stepped on, and the fear in the pit of her stomach went away, the relief in Hal's presence overwhelming. She felt safe again.

It was totally a girl thing, and she was surprised how good it felt to be in the company of one of those rare men who made her feel that way.

"You talked to Crick yet?" he asked her.

"No." She had the horse circling. "Now what?"

"Wait till he stops. When he does, pet him. You and your partner got a good reason for trying to blow my investigation?"

"I have no idea what you mean by that." But she did. They had thrown Delaney to the wolves. "And what do you mean, pet him? How about I break his neck?"

"Don't you want him to stop?"

"Of course I do."

"Then pet him. If you break his neck when he stops, he's not going to want to stop for you anymore." He leaned against the wall, arms folded. "Donna Delaney is about to have a stroke."

"How so?"

"Spare me the look of sweet innocence. Vivian Bisky is not a happy camper. Donna's thinking along the lines of, if they cut off my finger last week, what are they going to do to me tomorrow?"

"That's called pressure. Use it. What if this horse doesn't ever stop?"

"He'll wear out eventually."

"So will Delaney." She remembered their conversation about Arabian endurance. If the Horseman's Buddy had been within reach, she'd have broken *his* neck.

"Yeah, that's what I was thinking. I'm pulling her in tomorrow. Going to make a sweep of it, early in the morning. Warrants for Vivian Bisky, Donna Delaney, and Claude Vincent."

"Vincent. Why don't I know that name?"

"Big strapping South African. Thick blond hair, wears it long. Recently treated by an under-the-counter medic who happens to owe me a favor, for damage to his left eye and a bullet wound."

She looked at him. "You found my guy!"

He nodded.

"And you didn't tell me?"

"I'm telling you now."

"Where is he?"

"Tucked in his bunk, I hope, and under surveillance. We'll be knocking on his door before sunup. The TRC specializes in that early-morning adrenaline rush."

"Before your perps get their coffee? I always heard you guys were *bad*. What about the brother Bisky?"

"Cliff? He's big and fat, he smokes cigars, he falls asleep in meetings, and his wife is ugly."

"So you're not bringing him in?"

"He's out of town. It may interest you to know that Vincent is an illegal alien employed by Bisky Farms. I'm figuring he was stashing the finger in the riding glove the day you tripped over him in the barn. Likely he's the one who did Donna in the first place. Which may mean he did Joelle. He could be your guy."

She shrugged. "I don't think so."

"You don't think so? Why don't you think so?"

She told him about the Weed Eater tape. Finding the mare. The journal entries.

He shook his head. "If Chauncey's been a good father all these years, why kill Joelle now? Why cut off Donna Delaney's finger?"

"He didn't do that. That was the Bisky people. Your guy Vincent, just like you told me, and I want you to know I'm delighted to have shot him."

"Too much coincidence here, Sonora."

"Did it ever occur to you that Chauncey picked this time to take advantage of all the stuff between Delaney and the Biskys? It gives him a built-in villain to point the finger at."

McCarty shoved his hands in his pockets. "You ought to have consulted with me about Delaney."

"Look, while you're searching for the evil horse sponge artist and the equine fraud con, I've got a fifteen-year-old victim who was buried alive with blunt trauma to the head."

"Your horse just stopped."

"Don't try and change the subject." Sonora looked to her horse, who had come to a halt, weight forward, and she petted his neck and told him what a good boy he was till his head came down and his lower lip quivered.

Hal stepped close, rubbed Poppin's neck. "There you go. A relaxed, obedient horse. How do you like training?"

She gave him a look. Her children would have been nervous about a look like that, but Hal did not seem worried.

"I like training just fine."

"Good thing. You got your work cut out for you with this one."

She led Poppin back to the stall, stopped him two feet away. But the horse was on his good behavior now, with McCarty in the barn, and he went in politely without rushing and stood docilely while she unclipped the rope.

No chains, no screams, no beating. Was there a way to apply this to children?

She checked his water, got him a handful of grain, ignored

Hal's comment about spoiling, and gave Poppin two thick flakes of hay, shaking them out in the corner so that it looked like a huge pile of food.

Poppin snatched a mouthful of hay, then rushed to the window to munch and visit. Sonora rubbed his nose, pulled a stick of hay from where it hung between his lips.

"He's friendly, you have to give him that. Are you sure you want to get attached to him?"

She looked over her shoulder. McCarty had climbed up in the loft and was shoving hay bales. "Look out below." He rolled three bales, one after the other, over the edge, and they fell with soft thuds, spreading into flakes, raising clouds of dust.

"You're thinking I ought to sell him?"

"I'm thinking horses are expensive and time-consuming. You're going to have to board him out eventually, pay vets, farriers, have his teeth floated, not to mention hay, grain—"

"Yeah, yeah."

"I'm sure the Horseman's Buddy would take him back."

"Go to hell."

"Yes, ma'am."

"I'm allowed to have a life, aren't I? Can't there be more to the day than work, and bills, and children?"

"Yeah, more work, more bills, and manure." He sat on the edge of the loft. "Come on up, why don't you? I'll show you where the good hay is. If you've got a minute."

She looked up at him. "I take it I'm invited to the morning festivities?"

"We're using your office." He was swinging his legs, giving her that smile. He wore a gray sweatshirt, big and loose, over jeans.

She'd fed the kids before she left. Cooking again, country ham, corn on the cob, and eight little dinner rolls from the Pillsbury Doughboy. Mother of the Year.

"I've got a minute."

The bottom rung of the ladder was the kicker, especially with McCarty watching. Graceful was hard when you were trying to bring your knee above waist level, and she was thankful she had worn loose-fit jeans, like everyone else in her generation.

McCarty cocked his head, watching her. Stood over her as she came up the last rung, gave her a hand. It was dusty in the loft, dark and warm. The rain was loud on the roof.

Something about the way he took her hand. A tentative quality she thought of as a query.

Testing one two three—is she willing?

She had not felt nervous like this in ages. She was not sure she liked it. Butterflies in the stomach were not a pleasant thing. She could be safe at home.

"See this hay over here? See this scummy stuff on the top? It's moldy. Don't feed it to your horse or your children."

She nodded, looked at the hay.

"Over here is the grass hay. And this is a timothy-alfalfa mix. *Your* horse won't eat the grass hay. He likes the more expensive stuff."

Sonora did not want to admit that all the hay bales looked the same to her, so she committed their locations to memory. Bad hay, right back corner; grass hay, left center; good stuff, far left and central. She would just give Poppin the good stuff.

McCarty looked up at the roof. Patted a hay bale and sat down. "Rain's still coming down pretty hard. Might as well wait it out."

She sat next to him, and he gave her that funny half smile, leaned close, picked sticks of hay off her sweatshirt.

Now was the time to pull away, if she was going to.

She watched him, wondering what he would do next. She felt oddly quiet and scared. She was not quite sure what she was afraid of, just that lately she was afraid.

He leaned close to kiss her, a long slow brush with his lips. He pulled back, just an inch, to double-check, to give her the opportunity to scream, run away, or file a lawsuit. When she chose none of the above, he snugged his legs next to her, put his hand on the back of her neck, and kissed her properly, slowly, sweetly, and confidently.

She did love a confident man.

He was clearly one of the ones who enjoyed the kissing part, who liked to take his time. He sucked her bottom lip into his mouth, and she leaned closer in. He wrapped his hand in her hair, and his other arm went around her shoulders, and he enveloped her in a tight, lush hug. The size of him, the strength of him, the confident safe maleness of him, was warmth and tingly pleasure.

They seemed to fit well, her head in the crook of his shoulder. She did not resist or pull away when he rolled her off balance, catching her in his arms and cushioning her before she hit the stack of hay bales behind. Her instinctual ease in trusting him in this small thing surprised her.

She abandoned all the scary feelings, listened to the pressure of his fingers as they moved under her sweatshirt, touching the border of the white lace demi bra before he unfastened the hooks in back, and she felt his palms, large and square, on her bare skin.

He was rougher than she was used to, enthusiastic, and very well versed in the dance.

He had done this before, many many times before, and it was a smooth transition from jeans to no jeans, sweatshirts in a tangled heap. He had a blanket stashed, and a package of condoms, and he spread the blanket and smiled, acknowledgment that yes, he'd been lying in wait. She felt sexy, elusive, and desirable.

He was heavy on top of her, and his chest was broad, arms thick in the way of well-muscled men, thighs wide and firm, basketball calves—men often had the best legs.

He was gratifyingly responsive when she let her hand travel to that first touch, a pause when he did not move a muscle, except to smile and make a noise in the back of his throat to let her know she was on the right track.

She pressed a palm into his chest, and he lay beside her willingly, and she loved the way he smiled and laughed when she ran her tongue up and down his body.

He smelled good. Clearly he was fresh from his shower,

which was not fair, she had not had time to prepare. She wanted a long soak in the tub, to rub lotion all over her body, to find the right combination of silk and lace, and then make him hers.

Next time.

He laughed suddenly. Put a hand on the top of her head. "Better stop. Oh, God, no, really."

"I don't want to stop."

He took her shoulders and brought his face to hers.

And then at last he settled his body over hers, and once more she felt the weight of him, pressing her down. She put her arms around his neck, holding him tight and pulling him close, and he worked her slowly, roughly, like a man who does not know his strength. She could have made him go easy with the right word, but found that she wanted to do no such thing.

The phone woke Sonora at six forty A.M. She opened one eye. This early it had to be a body.

Or Hal?

She smiled. The sun was just starting to come up. She had a pretty new white eyelet bedspread. And the start of a by-God normal relationship with a very attractive man who was—

The phone rang again, and she picked it up.

"Good morning, Sonora."

"Hal?" She tried to keep the sleep out of her voice.

"No, you can call me *Sam*, because that's my name. Sam."

Sonora raised up on her left elbow. "What's up, Sam?"

"I'm in the office."

"This early?"

"You expecting maybe Hal McCarty? He usually call you at six thirty Saturday morning?"

"They're serving warrants with the pancakes this morning, Sam, I thought he might need to get in touch. Isn't that why you're in so early?"

"Yeah, sure, so where the hell are you?"

"On my way."

"Anyway, Sonora, since I had a minute, I ran McCarty through the system. Since I thought you might be getting interested."

"No, Sam, I always think it's best to stay away from coworkers."

"Just as well. You do know he's married?"

"Who? McCarty?"

"Yeah."

She lay back on the pillow, thinking what a fleeting thing happiness was.

"That so?" Conversational. Sam was rambling on about something. She threw all three of her pillows, lovingly encased in new pillow shams, across the room.

Her arm was as good as ever. One of the pillows caught the desk lamp, which crashed to the floor.

"Sam, one of the kids is having a temper tantrum, I have to go."

50

WHEN SONORA walked into the bullpen at seven fifty A.M., she was not in a good mood. She had cooked the children a hot breakfast. Okay, grilled chicken sandwiches were not the average morning meal, but you had to work with what was in the freezer. She'd fed hers to Clampett, because her appetite was a thing of the past, and she'd left the kids' food in Reynolds Wrap for whenever they'd crawl out of bed, which she guessed would be sometime between noon and two.

Lucky them.

The interview rooms were lit, doors shut, and she felt a pang. Everything was moving along without her. She was being left behind.

She was halfway to her desk when she saw the huddle, Crick and Sam over her own desk, invading her space before she got her first cup of coffee.

"We expected you earlier," Crick said.

"I will remind you that I have two children who need breakfast in the morning."

The staccato cadence of the words, and the tone of voice, caused one of those sudden sweeping silences in the squad room. She turned her back on everyone while they got over it, headed for the coffeemaker, which she refused to clean no matter how dirty it got. She had realized a couple of years ago that the men were not expecting her to clean it, they just didn't notice it was dirty.

There was her mug, lipstick stain on the side. Woman in residence.

She filled the cup, added as much cream as she wanted, almost too much, it was a very light brown. On impulse, she helped herself to Molliter's Swiss Chocolate Fat Free flavoring. An entire spoonful.

She stirred, taking her time, and took the first perfect sip while everyone waited. Then she turned back to Crick and Sam, trying to quell the "bright ingenue" look that was coming over her face no matter how hard she tried to make it stop. I do not have to smile, she told herself.

"Bring me up to date," she said.

"We're getting ready to go three-way. Hal with Donna Delaney, Sam with Vivian Bisky, and you with Claude Vincent. You need to ID him anyway, if you can."

"That one you can sort by his injuries." Gruber off in the corner. Giving Sonora the thumbs-up.

Sam did not look at her. She did not look at him.

"How do you want to work this?" Crick asked. "You want someone in there with you, or will it go better if you're alone?"

"Alone," Sonora said. "Where is he?"

"Two," Crick said.

She nodded, grabbed her cup, and went down the hall.

She didn't exactly kick the door in when she entered the room, but neither was she quiet. Claude Vincent was not fazed. He looked tough, particularly with the patch over his left eye. In her mind she repeated the police officer's prayer—*Please, God, let him be stupid*—and sat down next to him in a chair, invading his space.

She grinned at him. "How you feeling, Claude?"

He gave her a look. Bored.

She took a drink of coffee, and from the way he watched out of the corner of one eye, she knew he wanted a cup. This was the hardest part of interrogation for her, the Martha Stewart instinct, which was Provide hospitality no matter what.

She leaned back in her chair, playing with the edge of the mug. "Don't say you don't remember me, Claude. That would hurt my feelings. How's the leg?"

He squinted, and she was aware of his thought processes moving. This one would be cake.

"You don't recognize me, Claude? You can't be serious. The guys have been laughing their asses off about our little tussle in Delaney's barn, and I've still got the bruises. I have to thank you, man, you've done wonders for my credibility around here. Hey, are you a natural blond? 'Cause I love the color."

A deep blush of rage rose like high tide from the base of his neck to his face.

"Do you have high blood pressure?" she asked. Seriously curious.

"I want a lawyer." His accent was rather attractive.

Sonora stood up. He'd said the L-word.

"Good idea, Claude, 'cause you're looking at the death penalty over that little girl. I'll see you later."

He was a slow mover, possibly due to the bulk of his muscles, because it wasn't the bulk of his brain.

"Wait." He was used to giving one-word commands.

She turned but kept heading for the door. "What do you mean, wait? You want a lawyer or don't you?"

"You have mistakes. I am not here about some little girl. I don't know little girls."

Sonora wondered how old he was. Early twenties maybe. Somewhere he had a mother.

"Look, you got a choice here, Claude, and I can't make it for you. If you want a lawyer later, that's cool. If you want one now, we can't talk anymore, it's against the law. Now, it sounds to me like what we've got going is a misunderstanding, maybe even a case of mistaken identity. You know what that is, Claude? I mean, I'm not trying to imply you're stupid, I'm thinking about the language barrier."

"My command of English is excellent."

Sonora smiled. "Good for you. So, okay, what's it going to be, my friend? 'Cause you asked me for a lawyer. Which means this conversation is over, and you get locked down until we get a Legal Aid kid down here. Unless you've got an expensive lawyer, which means you still get locked down for a couple months at least till we get all this straightened out. Because bail is something you will not get when it comes to the brutal murder of a little girl. You're here on a temporary visa, and you're a major flight risk, and no judge in his right mind is going to let you out of the orange jumpsuit and chains."

"There is no little girl."

"Claude, I'm asking you one more time, then I got things to do. You want a lawyer, or you want me to grab you a candy bar and a Coke, maybe a cup of coffee, whatever, and you and I sit down like civilized people and get all this straightened out?"

"You have the Baby Ruth?"

"Baby Ruth it is. What to drink?"

"Cherry Coke."

She got herself a candy bar too, what the hell, she was mad at the world anyway. Reese's cups. She liked the bright orange wrapper, and there was nothing quite like peanut butter and chocolate. They both got intent on opening candy wrappers and popping soda tabs. She had managed a surprising camaraderie with this guy over chocolate.

"Ah," he said, mouth full of chocolate, caramel, and peanuts. "The Reese's cup, this is good too."

It reminded her of Jean-Claude Van Damme, the way he talked, only this guy wasn't nearly as smart or good-looking.

She broke him off a piece of a Reese's cup—the sacrifices she made to earn a living—and was touched when he responded with a chunk of Baby Ruth.

She took a sip of Coke, it was cold and wonderful. Pah on coffee. "I just don't get it. I can't picture you doing something like that."

He looked uncomfortable and was clearly struggling to figure out which crime she was referring to.

"Was it an accident, you know, because you really just wanted the horse?"

"Yes, the horse I wanted, but I get it other ways. I tell you there is no girl."

"Let me refresh your memory, Claude. Joelle Chauncey was the girl *riding* the horse. Tell me it was an accident. Tell me that you didn't mean for her to get hurt. Believe me, it'll make a big difference."

"But I tell you there was no horse."

"Oh, come on—"

"No. Delaney has the horse, and this horse is Bisky property."

"Which horse are we talking about?"

"The mare, Sundance, she is in foal to Big Blue Baby, who has blood from We Had It Coming, very good lines these are."

"And she's owned by the Biskys?"

He waved a hand. "By the client of the Biskys'?"

"Yeah, yeah, I'm with you. How did Delaney get the horse?"

"Is business arrangement." He leaned across the table. "The Bisky people, they have the beautiful show barn, you've seen it?"

Sonora nodded.

"They have overrented the stalls, you understand this?"

"Rent them out to more than one horse, collect all the board fees you want."

"And big board fees, these are. One thousand a month, just board. Fifteen hundred to foal. More to train. Mr. Bisky, he calls this bread-and-butter funds."

"So he farms the horses out."

Vincent took a large swallow of Cherry Coke and picked a fallen peanut up off the table. Sonora pulled another candy bar out of her jacket pocket and laid it in front of him. Payday. He picked it up, said "Oh, thank you," opened it, and gave her half.

This guy was amazing.

"It is a bad business, this. These places are bad—I have grown up with horses, they are where I will spend my life."

If you're not in prison, Sonora thought.

"And the Delaney people, they do not feed or worm these animals. The pasture is very bad. This is true also in my own country. People are not good to animals if there is money involved. I have worked and studied with many farms—it is a hard way to make a living. Money is so hard, even good people do bad things. From here my plan is to Kentucky, then to Ireland. They have more horses per capita than anywhere in this world."

"I get you, Claude. There's no doubt—look at your hands there, look at the calluses—you've studied and worked hard. Probably done a million and one odd jobs."

He nodded.

"I mean you cleaned stalls, and—"

"No, I have done that, but I have learned to train, studied the nutrition—"

"Probably even worked with a vet, haven't you?"

He sat up straighter and smiled. "Yes, this is true, for many years."

"Probably get board certified, if they'd let you."

"I could pass every test. Dr. Vooherman, he let me take care of even some high-dollar horses."

"Even the hard stuff? Like surgeries? That advanced?"

His smile of pride was a ray of sunshine in Sonora's heart. She wished she'd looked at his feet earlier, but he was a hunk, she would bet anything that his shoes matched the print outside Delaney's window. They had their finger ripper.

"So what happened with Delaney?"

He tapped a finger on the table. Clearly thinking. Coming to a decision. About what, Sonora could only imagine.

"Delaney will not give back this horse. Bisky, he tells her the client is coming to town, I think this is unexpected, and Delaney says no horse unless she gets more money. It is blackmail. Bisky, he thinks she is waiting for this opportunity. She has taken such bad care of others that he is deciding not to use her again, and he thinks she has figured this out and wants to stick him for what she can.

"She will not give back this horse, so there are some visits and much argument, and a payment of money, they are in agreement. And then the horse disappears with this little girl. And Bisky"—he leaned closer—"he is out of town, but he calls the sister, and they are angering like you cannot say. They think Delaney has done this so she will not give back the horse. This little girl who disappears, she is the daughter of Delaney's man who cleans the stalls. They think Delaney just has moved the horse and the girl awhile. And the sister, Vivian, she does not like to be beaten down, not by a Delaney woman. They never do get along, both are strong and mean."

Sonora nodded.

"So she has the idea for me to do."

"Do what exactly?"

He sat back and shrugged. "Apply the pressure. Just tough phone calls and such."

"And such." Sonora leaned back too, a big believer in advance and retreat when you were trying to catch a man or a horse. "The riding glove was inspired."

He tried very hard to look blank.

"But not very nice. You scared some of the children. I bet you were following orders."

He did not seem to know where to look, at her or the floor.

"But you know, scaring kids is one thing. Killing them's in a whole other league."

"I have killed no one."

"See, Claude, we're going to have to sort out what you did and didn't do. What you did to Delaney—in your favor, she was blackmailing your boss. And it's not like you were irresponsible. She could have bled to death when you made the cut, except you made sure to stitch her up."

"Yes, I am most careful, there is almost no bleeding, no pain."

"The ER doctor was pretty impressed."

"It is in the sharpness of the knife."

"You used a scalpel, didn't you?"

"Yes, I believe strongly the right tool for the job."

"How'd you get her doped up? Didn't you come in through the window?"

"She is doped already. In the beer. Sleeping hard."

"Who was helping you out with that?"

He got that wary look she never liked to see in the interrogation room. It was a look that often shut things down. She'd been too direct. No choice now but to go with it.

"Hey, Claude, don't be the sucker who takes all the heat. You made sure she didn't bleed to death, you stitched her up. You're almost clean here, but we need somebody to hang. Don't risk your future for somebody else."

"It is Vivian."

"Vivian Bisky?"

"Yes. She goes ahead to give more money, is what she says, but the truth is she puts chloral hydrate in the beer. And I go in and do the job."

"Did she make it easy for you, leave the door unlocked?"

"No, I have to do that through the window."

"She did that on purpose, you know that, don't you? We couldn't have gotten you for breaking and entering if you'd gone in through an unlocked door. She's rich, she knows the law, and she wants you at risk. So then what happens?"

"This little girl, she is a very big deal, and the Biskys are most nervous. The brother is in Florida and will not come home and leaves this all to Vivian."

"What'd she do?"

"She says keep the pressure on Delaney, then after the girl is found dead, she says, pull out and back off. This is much too hot."

"And she was right too. Whoever did the girl—we give the death penalty, here in Ohio."

"I have nothing to do with little girl."

"Here's what you need to do then. You need to give us hair and blood samples, so we can rule you out. You don't have a problem with that?"

"No, no problem, I invite you."

"Good. The business with the girl, that's all a mistake, so

I'm going to help you out. Let's do it like this.'' She shoved a legal pad and a pen across the table. ''You write out a statement. Keep it simple, tell it in your own words. Explain everything just like you told me.''

''I do not know.''

''It's brave and loyal of you to want to protect people, Claude, but you're going to have to use your head if you ever want to make it to Ireland. Vivian Bisky is the one who had the big idea. She's the one who wouldn't even unlock that door, and if you don't think that was on purpose, you were born yesterday, which you weren't, right?''

''Right.'' His response was slow. He looked at the paper. The pen. Shook his head like a wet dog.

Sonora pointed to the tape recorder. ''Look, we got all this on tape already. Writing it out is for your benefit. So you can add stuff if you need to, say why and that you're sorry. I'm trying to clear the way for you, okay? As best I can? You just write it all down and sign it, to let the judge know you were cooperative—that kind of thing carries a lot of weight. A *lot* of weight. And then an apology.''

''On the paper?''

''Let's do it up right, Claude. I want you to make an apology to the lady you hurt, to Donna Delaney. You write this down, then I'll take you out in the bullpen, and you can tell her you're sorry in person. That should take care of about everything. It's the Biskys who are at fault here, they're the ones making the money. And it's not like you didn't give the finger back, right?''

51

SONORA GAVE VINCENT one final look, saw his blond head bent over the yellow legal pad like a child at his homework, and headed into the hallway, shutting the door softly.

Ran, literally, into Hal McCarty. She stared at him with her mouth open. She'd been so into the interrogation of Claude Vincent, she'd forgotten Hal. Her warrior juices started to ebb. Two seconds ago she had been all the way up, now she was all the way down.

His smile faded, and he took her elbow, guiding her into the corner, as if they were not under the casual observation of about ten other detectives in the bullpen.

"Tell me what's wrong." He spoke quietly, and it was annoying that he seemed to know exactly what she was thinking.

"You didn't happen to bring up that you were married, Hal."

His face went stiff, and Sonora found herself wondering if he had a lot of little moments like this one.

"I figured you knew. I figured you'd run me through the computer, check around. You didn't ask."

"You didn't tell. And you don't wear a ring."

"I'm working undercover."

"I'll say."

He laughed and grimaced, shook his head. "I'm really taken with you, Sonora."

"Are you happily married?"

"I have a wife and five kids."

"Five?"

"A combined effort. Two of mine, two of hers, one of ours."

There was an obvious affection in his voice when he spoke of them, and she wanted to scream, *God, I don't understand men,* but she did. They were just like her.

She had a flash of envy for the private moments between the two of them. That would never do. It was a requirement that any man in her life adore her.

"Listen, Hal, casual sex just doesn't do it for me. And God knows I've tried."

He laughed again. She gave him a small smile. After all, he hadn't *lied* about being married. Listen to yourself, she thought. Was it genetics or plain stupidity, the way women, herself included, found excuses for men?

"Look. I still want to see you. You're very . . . different."

"Yeah, I just bet. Come on, McCarty, we got work to do." And she had no choice but to work with him.

"What, I'm McCarty now?"

"There's worse things I could call you."

"I'm not letting you go. Not unless you want me to."

"Business, Hal. I need you to help me pull off a reverse lineup."

"What's going on?"

"Just that I'm one hell of a cop. Try to keep up."

52

Nᴏɴᴇ ᴏꜰ ᴛʜᴇ ᴡᴏᴍᴇɴ would talk.

Vivian Bisky already had an attorney, a chunky blonde with a sweet face and a killer reputation. Dead in the water, for the time being.

Donna Delaney, lips tighter than the bandage on her hand, would not say a word. Not to Hal, not to Sam. Sonora was dying to give her a try.

They had Donna in the bullpen, sitting in front of Sam's desk. They'd rounded up every available female and scattered them throughout the office, to give Vincent a good choice.

Sonora led him out of the interrogation room. Steered him toward Sanders. Molliter was getting it all on videotape, and she wanted to go out of her way not to influence him.

Vincent frowned and moved away from Sanders, heading toward Donna Delaney. He stood over her, frowning.

She glared at him.

Sonora's heart was pounding. If Delaney kept up the prison yard stare, Vincent would never come through.

He looked at Sonora, and she knew she had him. She smiled benevolently and nodded to reassure him.

"I wish to make the formal apology."

Delaney's head went up. She stared up at him, eyes narrowed into slits. "What?"

"For the finger of yours which I have unfortunately cut off, and then returned. I am telling you that I am sorry, and that this is not something that should be taken personal."

Delaney's mouth opened, and she made a small noise but no words were intelligible. She looked around the room, at Sonora, Gruber, Crick, and then back to Vincent, who looked down at her, holding out a hand, as if he expected to kiss and make up.

"Son of a bitch."

She was saying it again.

Crick, sitting at Sanders's desk, looked at Sonora and nodded. Gave her one of his very rare smiles.

53

SONORA LOOKED at the faces around her—Sam, McCarty, Crick. Gruber, just for the hell of it, because he wanted in, because he had a good mind, because he was available. How many times had they gone over it? It was beginning to feel like a prison, this case.

Sonora rubbed her right eye, smearing mascara. "I want to bring Chauncey in. I know I can sweat him."

Crick rubbed his chin, making a scratchy sound. They were all tired, all had spent the better part of the day trying to get something out of the women. All had spent the better part of the day getting nowhere.

"Okay, Sonora. Bring him in." Crick's voice was thick with fatigue.

"Really?"

"You think he'll do anything but cry?" Sam said.

"Take a vote," Gruber said. "Everybody who thinks he'll cry, say aye."

"Aye." Sam.

"Aye." Gruber.

Crick looked at Sonora.

"Yeah," she said. "He'll cry. So what? After he cries, he'll confess."

Crick shook his head. "I don't think so."

"Why not?"

Gruber waved a hand. "My take? This guy, he cries to get sympathy and to escape dealing with whatever is bugging him. It's like a weapon. I mean, it's a chick trick. He ought to be ashamed."

"Gruber, you're a Neanderthal."

The door to Interview One opened. Mickey breezed in. Took a look at the empty pizza box, the crumpled coffee cups, the soft drink cans and wads of yellow paper from the legal pad.

"Looks like the Spanish Inquisition," he said. "Any luck?"

"Sonora brought down the finger ripper." Gruber laughed. "Best reverse lineup *I've* ever seen. It was beautiful, really, you ought to have been here."

"Hey, while you guys were sitting in here eating junk food, I've been doing a real cop's work."

Sonora looked up. "What?"

"We drained the pond. Drained it. Got all the way down to the muddy bottom."

"What'd you find?"

"Not as much garbage as you might imagine. Old shoes. A couple of notebooks—you said that kid kept a journal?"

Sonora nodded.

"Ink's blurred, if they were hers. Illegible. I might be able to bring some of it up later. A BB gun, a dorky hat with flaps over the ears—"

"Whoa, whoa," Sam said. "That woman, Barbara Adair, who bought Sundance and the trailer. She said the guy that sold it to her had a hat with flaps on the ears. All the witnesses mention that stupid hat."

"Makes a great disguise," Gruber said.

"You get hair from the hat?" Sonora asked.

Mickey stood up straight and glared at Sonora. He seemed to be swelling like a show dog. "How can an artiste such as moi *not* get hair from a hat?"

"What's it look like?"

"Black. Dyed. And a half-used spool of Weed Eater tape. Got hair from the blanket, from the cap, from the trailer. Dixon Chauncey. Defense can argue the ones from the blanket, maybe even the cap, are legit. But not the trailer."

Gruber rubbed his hands together. "Forget these bitches. Chauncey's our man."

Sam and Sonora looked at Crick.

He nodded. "And Counselor Bristol, being what he is, keeps Saturday hours till the workload comes down. So go to the DA's office and do it up right. Then bring this guy in."

"What about his kids?" Sonora asked.

"Make formal arrangements."

She bit her lip. No other choice.

Gruber looked up. "Need any help taking him down?"

Sam shook his head. "Come along if you want to. But be sure and bring extra hankies."

Crick stood up. "He's going to cry me a river now."

54

SAM WAS DRIVING fast. Sonora dug out her cell phone, called the DA's office, got put on hold and flooded with Muzak. As soon as anybody down there knew it was her, she got put on hold. They likely circulated memos, blah blah blah; and give Detective Blair hell whenever possible.

"Sonora?" Sam said.

"I'm on the phone here."

She waited. The female voice came back, finally.

"Sorry to keep you waiting, detective."

"That's okay, I always wanted to know all the words to 'Mack the Knife.' "

The woman did not respond. They must have put that on the memo too. Don't laugh at Detective Blair's jokes.

"I spoke with Mr. Bristol—"

"So he's still in the office?"

"Yes, but he's leaving soon. He says if you're not here in the next fifteen minutes—"

"We'll be there. Tell him to please wait, as we'd hate to have to disturb his evening at home." Sonora cut the connection.

"So, you're mad at me now?" Sam asked.

Sonora looked at him. "Mad about what?"

"About me running McCarty through the computer."

"Sam, just stick to business, okay? We're breaking a case here."

"You're mad."

"I'm not mad."

"I'm just trying to look out for you, Sonora."

"Sam, are you happily married?"

"Yeah, so?"

God, she hated it when he said that. "Then leave me alone."

"Sonora, I want you to find somebody, I just want it to be the right somebody. I worry about you."

"My God, you're the reincarnation of my mother. Let's have lunch and trash Dad."

"Look, if you want to do that married man thing—"

"Sam? Not that it's any of your business? But I'm not going to sleep with McCarty." She was like a kid with her fingers crossed behind her back. *I'm not going to sleep with McCarty because I already did.*

They drove.

"You have to admit, Sam, McCarty is an attractive man."

"I wouldn't know." He went through a yellow light, just as it turned to red.

"Come on, you don't think he's cute?"

"I'm a guy. I don't know if a man is cute."

"Hey, nobody's asking you to give up football or turn in your dick. I mean, he's a good-looking guy. McCarty is. Don't you think?"

No answer.

"Okay, Sam, speaking professionally, like you were describing a suspect. Is he cute or not cute?"

"We still on McCarty?"

"We still are. Answer the question."

Sam wiped his forehead. "The suspect could be described as . . . attractive."

"To women or just men?"

"Fuck all y'all."

* * *

Security let them in through the front door. Their footsteps echoed in the dark hallway. Gone were the late nights and camaraderie that had been the hallmark of this office when Gage Caplan had been in charge. He'd been very good at his job—good with the younger attorneys. It was no wonder Sonora was not popular down here, the man was undoubtedly missed. It was his habit of murdering pregnant women and dismembering their bodies that had gotten him in trouble, as such a habit often will. Other than that, he'd been an all-around guy.

Light shone from behind the frosted glass of Bristol's office door. Any other attorney would have left the door ajar, acknowledgment that he was expecting them.

Not Bristol.

Sonora considered just walking in, but she decided to make a genuine effort to get along. Be a trouper. Do the job. She wanted to pull Dixon Chauncey in. Get Mary Claire and Kippie out of his tear-stained hands.

Sam knocked. They waited.

Heard the squeak of a chair, soft footsteps, then the door opened. Why not shout "come in" from the desk?

Not Bristol.

He looked at them from a three-inch crack. Frowned, voice soft. "Detectives." He left the door open and crossed back to his desk.

He was the kind of man who ironed his jeans and disapproved of people. He was thin. He took nourishment, not enjoyment, from his food. He smelled sweetly of cologne. On his desk was a picture of his wife—no children. She looked unhappy.

No mystery there.

Bristol's hair was very short, just shy of a butch cut, coming to a point at the back of his neck. He wore glasses with wire frames, and his nose was sharp, like a beak.

"Please. Have a seat."

Sam and Sonora exchanged looks, took a chair, faced him across an immaculate desk.

"What is it I can do for the two of you?" Bristol was soft spoken. His words held a sympathetic understanding that was not matched by the tone of his voice or the look in his eyes.

He had started in juvenile. He had, by reputation, been fond of grinding any child unlucky enough to come under his purview into a fine dry ash and scattering them across the juvenile court system. He was every mother's nightmare in court. He had no children of his own, which did not stop him from having views on exactly how they should be raised and, more important, punished. He liked holding people's fate in his hands.

Sam did the talking. Bristol listened with infinite patience, hands folded in his lap. Occasionally, Sonora would find him sneaking a look at her.

She braced herself for the barrage of questions that would come after Sam was through. But Bristol just stared at them. He sighed, stood up slowly.

"Do either of you want coffee?"

"No."

"No, thanks."

He went to the coffeepot that sat on a marble-topped table he had likely brought from home. The coffeemaker rested on a white circle of lace, next to a brass spider lamp, small light blazing.

Bristol bent at the waist, filling the cup. He took his time, carefully measuring out a teaspoon of sugar as if it were the most important thing in his life. He was in a world of his own, focused solely on that cup of coffee. Still bent, one arm rigid by his side, he took a sip. He straightened swiftly, a look of resignation crossing his face. The coffee had failed him.

He turned to Sam and Sonora. It was their turn to fail.

"I can't help you."

They stared at him a long minute.

"What do you mean, you can't help us?" Sonora asked.

He sat down behind the desk. Lips in a tight little bow. "Really, detectives. This case is a mess. Motive? Journal entries from an unruly, ungrateful teenage girl who probably resented being told to come home for curfew. You have this war going on between these two horse farms, you've even caught the man who mutilated one of the principals, and yet you look to the *father* as the killer. The girl was fatally injured when she came off that horse. Are you seriously telling me that she was the intended target? Why not shoot her and have done? This makes no sense at all."

"There are other children involved," Sonora said.

"Yes, that is uppermost in my mind. You want to rip them from their home on your gut instinct?"

"That, plus the evidence," Sonora said.

Bristol looked at his watch. "You've made me late for my dinner."

"Look—"

Bristol held up a hand. "Stop and think, detectives, stop and think." He did not raise his voice. Sonora would have liked it better if he had. "This man has been all over the eleven o'clock news, this is a high-profile case. If he was Mr. Nobody with a record, I'd say pick him up in a heartbeat. This is a middle-class widower, bringing up three children—"

"Two now," Sonora had to interrupt.

"He has a steady job and, more important, the sympathy of this entire community. He turned down Montel Williams!"

Sonora wondered where Bristol got his information.

"He doesn't come in until the case is so solid, it could be tried by an idiot."

Sam kicked Sonora before she could say a word. She stayed quiet. It was hard.

"Come back when you've made your case."

"And meanwhile those other two kids are at risk," Sonora said.

"If that's what you believe, detective, then you'd better get to work. Cross your t's and dot your i's."

And blacken yours, Sonora thought. She looked at Sam, who inclined his head toward the door. She knew what he was thinking. If you can't go through, go around.

So much for cooperation.

They drove back in silence, both staring straight ahead. Not a word, till he pulled into the parking lot at the Board of Elections building.

"Where'd you park?" he asked.

"Just let me off here."

"You're upset."

"I'm worried about those kids. Aren't you?"

"Am I uneasy? Yes. Do I think they're in immediate danger? No."

She opened the car door. "See you tomorrow."

"Come on, Sonora. Don't be mad at me anymore. You know I love you."

She closed the door, looked in at him through the open window. "Thank you, Sam. Now don't ever say that again unless you plan to follow it up."

"With what?"

"Sex. Love. Commitment."

"How about two out of three?"

"Sam, I just want to say that your timing really sucks."

55

SONORA AWOKE to the sound of a train, the wail of the horn. Had she been asleep? Halfway, maybe. The train sounded the horn again. She looked at the clock. Two A.M.

She remembered standing in the pastures at End Point Farm, hearing the train in the distance, wondering if they would find Joelle Chauncey alive or dead.

Had the child been alive then?

The ME did not think so. Sonora had called Stella and asked, only to find out from Eversley that Sam, Hal, and Mickey had all called with the same question.

There was no escape from the mental image that replayed over and over in her head.

Joelle on horseback, rounding the corner, horse cantering across the beaten-down dirt pathway, dark hair flying out behind. A moment of happiness. Both girl and horse, together in the rhythm and pace, unaware of the strand of Weed Eater tape, stretched across the path, and the man who waited for the fall.

Sonora knew that man was Dixon Chauncey.

Had he watched? Had he turned away? Had Joelle screamed, or had it happened too fast?

Anyone could use Weed Eater tape. Weed Eater tape did not

prove beyond a reasonable doubt that Dixon Chauncey had killed Joelle. A dyed black hair in a dorky ear flapper cap did not prove that Dixon Chauncey had killed Joelle.

And much as she hated to admit it, Bristol had a point. The case was full of holes. She would have to fill them in.

She had spent all day yesterday, Sunday, re-reading the journals, going through Joelle's things. What she had to have was a motive.

What she needed to do now was find out why.

Sonora got out of bed. Put on her favorite navy sweatpants and her little gray T-shirt, layering it over with the big black sweatshirt she liked to wear inside out. Her newest and whitest Reeboks.

She would bake raspberry muffins for Heather and Tim's breakfast, and then she would go to work.

The outpatient and emergency parking lot at Jewish Hospital was about two thirds full, most of the cars with parking stickers that indicated staff. Sonora found a good slot, right up front, and she locked the car up tight, hospital parking lots being one of the three most dangerous places in the world, the other two being ATMs after dark and downtown parking garages.

A paramedic unit was parked in the emergency entrance, lights flashing. Someone else's drama. She passed the smokers, huddled together in the small outdoor terrace to which they had newly been sentenced, passed through the automatic doors into the harsh yellow-white light of the lobby.

The hospital was hot and heavy on a courtesy campaign, one thing accomplished by the influence of HMOs, and the receptionist actually smiled.

"Gracie on shift?" Sonora asked.

"Gracie?"

"Gracie Fletcher." Everybody knew Gracie. This one must be new. "This is her shift," Sonora said, not sure but hoping.

"Oh, yeah, I'm sorry, I'm brain dead tonight. She's in the break room, nuking a Lean Cuisine."

"Thanks."

Sonora headed down the hall. Turned a corner and saw Gillane walking her way, head down.

She leaned up against the wall, folded her arms, watched him unaware. Same jeans, same Ropers, a white T-shirt, lab coat, and ID. All alone in the hallway, he looked exhausted and maybe a little down.

"You always wear jeans to work?"

Clearly she had caught him unaware, and his eyes crinkled up when he saw her, that smart-aleck half smile.

"Woman, a vision in sweats. Love the hair—no, I'm serious, I bet it took you three seconds to stick it up in that clip." He walked toward her, talking. "But it's almost . . . artistic." He touched the hair that had come loose. "See how it spills down every which way? Is this your favorite sweatshirt?"

"Yeah, so?"

"I have one just like it that's my favorite, only I don't wear mine inside out." He touched her cheek. "Bruises, fading."

She put a hand up. "You should see the other guy."

"You're up late tonight. Or is that early this morning? Is anything wrong?"

"I'm working."

"Good. I have those lab results for you."

"Finally."

"Come on, they're in my call room. Plus, I have a secret stash of Twinkies."

She had to walk fast to keep up with him. "*Twinkies?* I can't eat Twinkies. I ate bacon already this week."

"These Twinkies are magic Twinkies. They have no fat and no calories when eaten by a woman wearing sweats." He smiled at her in that way men have when they're glad to see you and don't care if it shows.

The call room had a single bed, no windows, a desk. A laptop computer glowed on the desk, next to, of all things, a harmonica, and a guitar was parked next to the wall.

Gillane opened the bottom desk drawer. Pulled out a box, already open, and tossed her a cellophane-wrapped Twinkie.

"I'm not keeping you from your work?" Sonora said.

"Slow night, Cricket. This ain't Parkland."

"Parkland?"

"Just a little hospital in Dallas."

"Why do you call me Cricket?"

"I told you, after my favorite horse."

"You said dog."

"Ah, you remembered. I was testing you."

"I have a horse," Sonora said.

"You have a horse?"

"My first one. I bought it a few days ago."

"I didn't know you rode."

"I don't. I ran across this gelding, and I just had to have him."

"Oh, that it were me." He studied her a minute. "Are you telling me that you spontaneously, without agonizing and shopping and researching and asking ten of your best friends for advice, went out and willfully bought a horse? On the spur of the moment?"

She snapped her fingers. "Just like that. And I don't know a damn thing about horses, but I'm learning fast."

"I bet you are." He frowned. "You should never tell me this sort of thing. I've been married three times already. And I'm Catholic."

"You are?"

"Well. Call me Catholic lite."

She tried not to laugh. "What's that got to do with any-thing?"

He glared at her. "Do you think it's easy? Not falling in love with a woman who goes out one afternoon and comes back that night with a horse?"

"Most people don't see it that way, believe me."

"Most people are idiots. This calls for a Twinkie."

They sat side by side on the bed, opening Twinkies. He

looked at her, smiled, started bouncing up and down on the mattress.

"I'm going to excuse your weirdness, Gillane, on account of it being four o'clock in the morning, and because I want a favor."

"Favor?" His mouth was full of sponge cake and cream.

"I want you to take that little laptop of yours and pull up some medical records for me."

"That would be naughty."

"But you could do it?"

"Oh, honey. With the greatest of ease. We're all one big conglomerate medical computer bank, and when the queries come from the inside, they're assumed to be legitimate. What is it you want to know, anyway?"

"Blood types. On Dixon Chauncey and his kids, Joelle, Mary Claire, and Kippie."

"They ever been patients here?"

"I don't know. Does it matter?"

"Probably not. You wouldn't have any social security numbers?"

She reached into her pocket. "Right here."

"She comes prepared." He reached for the laptop, took another bite of Twinkie. Attacked the keyboard. "Am I assisting in a real live police investigation?"

"Yep."

"Wow. Can you deputize me?"

"Raise your right Twinkie."

He complied.

"You're a deputy."

He tapped the keyboard. Looked at her. "What is it you're expecting?"

"One of the children isn't his."

"No. Shocking. Here it comes." He frowned.

"Well?"

"I'll be damned. None of them are."

"None of them?"

"Nope. And Joelle isn't blood sister to the other two. Mary Claire and Kuppie."

"Kippie. Who's related to who?"

"More like, is anybody related to anybody."

"And?"

"Possibly the two youngest, possibly not. Nobody else. What, are you going?"

"I've got to go home and sleep for ten minutes, get the kids to school, go to work, and catch a killer."

"She brings home the bacon, fries it up in a pan. No, stop, you can't go yet, I've decided to court you." He grabbed his guitar. Looked at her soulfully and started to sing "Woman" . . . John Lennon.

She threw a Twinkie at his head.

56

SONORA SAT in front of the computer, eating bite-size Tootsie
Rolls a mile a minute, drinking from a can of Coke, glaring
into the screen. She was still in sweats, had gone to an ATM,
that blessed modern convenience, and stopped by the house
long enough to put the kids on the alert. Emergency money in
the secret box, stay in touch by phone, and call their grandmother.

The case was breaking.

The children had been sleepy but were experienced in the
drill. She was touched when Heather gave her the bag of Tootsie Rolls (Sam's Club size, God knew where she had gotten it),
and her son had given her back her Eagles tape to listen to in
the car, so she could relax and think.

Like many other cops before her, she turned to the National Hotline for Missing Children, said a prayer for Adam
Walsh and his parents, and fired up the search.

Waiting.

Waiting.

Her eyes blurred, and she rubbed them. She did not feel
tired. She felt powerful. She hoped Dixon Chauncey was sleeping peacefully in his bed. It would be the last time.

When the information came through, she caught her

Sam lowered the fax, so she could read without being on her toes.

"Sam, can we cross-reference here? Missing kids snatched by a live-in or fiancé?"

"That'd be about ninety percent."

"No, not biological parents, Sam. He's not the real father. I got to talk to Crick."

57

CRICK WAS on the phone, but he motioned her in as soon as he saw her hanging shyly by the door. She went in slowly, sat down while he wrapped up the conversation, then got back up again.

Impossible to be still.

"Catch you later." He hung up. She closed the door and sat on the edge of the seat, leaning forward. "Sergeant. Let me be blunt."

She saw a tiny flicker of smile touch the edge of his mouth. If the two of them had understood one thing about each other from day one, it was that they both preferred blunt.

"I want to go get Dixon Chauncey right now."

"Now, as in this minute?"

"This very second I want to get in a car and pick him up." Sonora was sweating, though it was cold in the room. She pushed the sleeves back on her sweatshirt. Realized she had not taken a shower, put on makeup, or taken her hair down from the clip Gillane had sworn was artistic.

She was running on high-octane fuel—Twinkies, chocolate, coffee, and Coke. The end of the chase.

"I feel really strong about this."

"Instinct or ulcer?" he asked.

"Both." The ulcer visited her only occasionally now, and always on the downhill run.

Crick slid his chair forward and leaned across the desk. "You know the time constraints, Sonora. You know how long things take, even with the fax, the phone, the computer."

She was nodding, nodding, nodding. "Sergeant, my mind tells me you make a lot of sense. I just . . . I don't know. I feel like we really need to get him now. Sam just got a fax, it's definite, this guy grabbed Joelle eight years ago when she was seven."

"Why?"

"Her mother broke up with him, so he took the kid and disappeared."

Crick rubbed his chin. He was weakening just a little, she was just not sure it was enough. "We talked about this, Sonora, several times. You don't think he's been hurting the kids."

"No, I don't. But he killed Joelle—clearly she'd figured things out."

"Or he was afraid she was going to."

"Whatever. If he's cornered, he'll kill."

"He won't miss that funeral tomorrow," Crick said.

"That's what Sam thinks."

"Don't you?"

"It fits the pattern."

"But you're still not happy?"

She shook her head. How could she word this? "I think it is very important that we get him right now." Brilliant, she told herself. Head-of-the-debate-team stuff.

The look on Crick's face told her she had presented him with a dilemma. He tapped a finger on the edge of the desk.

"Sonora, did I ever tell you about my uncle George?"

She did not answer, because all she wanted to say was fuck your uncle George, and she did not think that would go over.

"He had hunting dogs, lots of them. One in particular, the youngest, drove him nuts, because he considered this dog the best in the pack, but he was always so antsy to get after the kill that he'd take off and run like hell, sometimes before he had the scent.''

Sonora lunged across Crick's desk, surprising him and her. ''Now. *Right fucking now.*''

''Get out of my face, detective.''

She took a breath. Stood up. She'd lost, and it felt like the bottom dropping out of her stomach.

''Go do your job, Sonora. It's on my head now. I'll let you know when.''

58

SONORA BRUSHED by Molliter in the hallway on her way to Interview Two.

"Hey, what happened to the dress code? Or you working undercover now?"

"Yeah, since yesterday." Idiot.

"You seen my Swiss chocolate coffee stuff?" He was tall, thin, red haired. They had a history of not getting along, but he was religious and always trying.

"Yeah, I took it." She walked away. She actually hadn't taken it, but she wished she had. "Go tell Crick about it, Molliter. He can tell you about his hunting dogs."

"You're losing it, Sonora. You are off the deep end these days."

Another voice, calling her name. Gruber. She turned, saw him holding the phone, his desk behind hers.

"Come back over here, you got a call."

She went back to the bullpen, sat on the edge of Gruber's desk. "Detective Blair, homicide."

"Detective Blair, my name is Linda Sinclair, I'm private, and I work out of Oakland, California."

The woman sounded like she was in her fifties, like she was smart, like she had her shit together.

"How can I help you, Ms. Sinclair?"

"I specialize in missing children, detective."

Sonora narrowed her eyes. Took a pen out of Gruber's shirt pocket. He handed her a scratch pad, gave her a wink. Some days she loved this man.

"I've been working for a client whose infant son was taken nine years ago."

"Ma'am, I don't know how you got my name, but—"

"We've been looking a long time. You have kids, detective?"

"Yes to all of your questions. But I don't think my situation is connected to yours."

"Please hear me out."

A simple plea, no ego.

"I don't want to be rude," Sonora said. "But I'm going to give the phone to one of my associates. I'm on a deadline here, and—"

"You're the lead detective, and I'll keep it down to three minutes."

Sonora balled her fist. "Okay."

"This woman's child was snatched by her boyfriend of eight months, Wilbur Pandlin. Five eight and one half inches tall, dirty blond hair, blue eyes. Bad posture. Very timid. Nobody you'd ever suspect."

Sonora took a breath. "You got his prints?"

"Yes."

"Send them."

"The child—he was just a baby, six months old. Male. He'd be about ten right now. I can get you a computer-generated image of what he might look like, or send you pictures of his brothers."

"I . . ." God this was painful. "Ms. Sinclair, I won't need your pictures. I have no knowledge, at present anyway, of the involvement of a ten-year-old boy."

"I see." There was a long silence, and Sonora could picture the woman, slumping at her desk. "Forgive me. We've been looking for this man for a long time."

Sonora scooted farther back on the desk, was vaguely aware

of Gruber rescuing a cup of coffee from behind her back. She crossed her legs. "Tell me about it."

Sinclair took a long breath. "She met him, my client, on the tail end of a nasty divorce that pretty much wiped out her bank account. She lost everything except her kids, which was where she put up her fight. She's back on her feet now. She's quite a lady.

"Her ex was mentally and physically abusive, and she was at a pretty low ebb when she met Wilbur. He was a welder."

"A welder?"

"Yeah, that mean something?"

"Maybe. Go ahead."

"She was crazy about him at first, so she tells me. She says he was the most nonthreatening man she had ever met. Between you and me, I think that was the major attraction. In six weeks they had moved in together, and she said it was like they'd been married for fifty years. I'm thinking that was part of the problem too. He never argued with her and did everything the way she wanted, but she usually wound up doing things his way, because he made her feel so guilty all the time. After a while she felt like she just had another kid, and she was being manipulated, and she asked him to move out.

"She says he cried, but she stayed tough. She remembers thinking that he would call her again and be hard to get rid of. But nothing for two weeks. She didn't call him, he didn't call her. Then one morning he shows up on the doorstep while she's ready to head off to work. Says he left some stuff in the bedroom, could he go in.

"She says sure, but hurry, she's got to get the other kids to school and go to work, and the baby needs his bottle. He says I'll give the baby his bottle, you get the kids off to school, then you can meet me here, get Stevie, and lock up the house.

"She's in a hurry, she says okay. Dumb yes, in retrospect, but he timed it pretty well, she's under pressure. And remember she's shared her bed, her home, and her children with this man for seven months and thinks she knows him pretty well. He's never hurt the kids—in fact, he's been a model father.

"So she comes back for her baby, and you know the rest of the story. At least, I hope you do."

Sonora was very afraid that she did. "Send me those prints, Ms. Sinclair."

59

SONORA SAT in Interview Two, head in her hands. Another set of parents were on the way, these close to home, out of Cleveland.

"What's the matter, Sonora?" Sam put a hand on her back.

"I'm just waiting for those prints. What do you think of her story? The Oakland PI, Sinclair?"

He sat on the edge of the desk in front of her. "I think it's creepy as hell. But it's got that ring about it, you know?"

"I know. What did that lady in Cleveland say?"

"Same deal, different details. Took her two-year-old. Age and description sound like Mary Claire."

"So where did Kippie come from?"

"Don't know yet. This is weirder than hell. Why take the kids and keep them?"

"Rage," Sonora said.

"You should eat, you look awful."

"I'm full of Tootsie Rolls." The ulcer was agony.

"Wait here." He disappeared, came back with Gruber's bottle of Mylanta. "I know you."

She took the Mylanta. Felt guilty for getting mad at him yesterday. She put her head up. "I wonder how much of this Joelle had figured out."

Sam shook his head. "I think she knew he wasn't their real father. Imagine this kid's childhood. Dad gets a girlfriend, loses the girlfriend, keeps her kids."

"That's why she was so obsessed with missing children and finding birth mothers. She must have known her mother was still alive somewhere, or suspected it anyway."

"Okay, Sonora, I get why he takes the kids, I just don't know why he keeps them."

"Rage makes him take them. Gloating makes him keep them, they're like trophies. Fear makes him kill them."

"Why not kill the woman? Why not stalk her?"

"He's afraid to stalk, Sam, he can't stand the tiniest confrontation. This man must be afraid every day of his life. He wakes up with it, he sleeps with it. I'd like to know how such a creature gets formed."

Sam gave her a look. They both knew the answer to that one.

Sonora rubbed the back of her neck. "But look what taking the kids gets him. Her attention. For the rest of her life, she thinks about him, wonders about him, hopes he'll show up. And revenge. She hurt him, and boy is she going to pay. What's the worst thing you can do to a mother?"

"Take her child."

"Like Sinclair said, I bet these are all strong, assertive women. He's attracted to that. He's afraid of it too."

"I noticed he was attracted to you, Sonora."

"Don't say that."

"Didn't you feel it? Wasn't that why you left the other day, when he was crying?"

"I know I could get a confession out of him, Sam."

"You will. Bide your time."

"He likes strong women, for whatever reason. And he does everything for them, everything they want, and they still throw him out. Rage, Sam, the only way he can express it, and they'll pay for the rest of their lives."

"Plus he gets off on the martyr thing. The single father."

"He's a sympathy junkie. You've watched him. He loves every bit of the attention."

"He'll get a lot when we take him down tomorrow."

"Crick still wants to do it after the funeral?"

"Between the hearse and his home," Sam said.

"He wants all that media?"

"He says we'll get it anyway, might as well control it."

Sonora frowned. "Something's wrong here."

"What do you mean?"

"Shut up, shut up, don't talk to me, I almost had it." She stood up. Something at the back of her mind. "Go over it again, everything you just said."

"The hearse, controlling the media—"

"Shit, shit, shit, Sam, that's what it is." She was jumping up and down. "Oh my God, Sam, think for a minute—*Montel.*"

"Montel Williams? The talk show host?"

"Dixon turned him down. Didn't you think that was weird? Mr. Attention Getting Sympathy Junkie turns down national TV? What possible reason could he have, except he's afraid he'll get caught? He's worried about getting recognized. Sam, don't you get what this means?"

Sam looked up. "He's not going to be at that funeral tomorrow."

"No, because he's afraid. And Sam, fear. Fear makes him kill."

60

THE DRIVING ARGUMENT didn't come up; Sam was the best, and Sonora knew it. They slapped the siren on the roof and booked. Crick was alerting and organizing uniforms, putting the SWAT team on standby, though they were under strict orders to prevent a hostage scenario.

They should be so lucky, Sonora thought.

McCarty was on his way, riding with Crick. Gruber and Sanders were en route. But Sam and Sonora would go in first. Don't escalate, Crick had told them. As if they needed to be told.

It was a long drive in, and Sonora sat, almost doubled over, eating one Mylanta after another, face grim. She could not get it out of her head, a man who would not sell a horse to slaughter but would put children in harm's way.

What had made him the way he was, what kind of a mold had formed him? What made him afraid to lift his head, what made him plaster a hesitant smile over a welter of anger so sore that he would take a child for revenge? What engendered this perverse mix of anger and fear?

Two miles out, they took down the siren and slowed their pace. Sonora chewed the end of her hair and crunched Mylanta tablets.

The farm looked just the same as always, battered down and beautiful. Sam turned down the familiar gravel drive, and Sonora shook the Mylanta bottle into her hand, only to find it empty. They had worked it out on the way over. Leave the car out of sight. Give Sam time to go around the back, along the tree line, and out of sight, then Sonora would hit the front door.

Move fast, backup was right behind.

Sam parked the Taurus in the parking lot, which was empty. It was four o'clock, the dead time of the day. Sonora saw horses peering from the little barred windows. She thought about Poppin, in the barn next door.

She did not shut the car door completely. The sound of a car door carried. She did not want Dixon alarmed.

"Got your gun?" Sam asked her.

She held up the Beretta, tucked it into the back of her sweatpants. The elastic was loose, she had been losing weight. It was going to fall down the back of her pants if she wasn't careful.

She did not share this with Sam. "Go," she told him.

He looked at her over his shoulder. "Just remember, Sonora. There is nothing more dangerous than a coward in a corner."

"I'm not afraid of this guy."

He grinned. "Me either. But you just remember what you told me. Fear makes him kill. This is the man that buried a fifteen-year-old girl alive in a manure pile."

"Then let's go nail his sorry ass."

"I'm gone."

She watched him go to the right of the fence line, sticking close to the trees. She counted to a hundred—a full hundred, Sam had made her promise—but she counted very fast.

She took a shortcut through the barn. Delaney's office was unlocked, empty, motes of dust thick in the streaks of daylight. The barn was dark and cool. She did not turn on any lights but went through the wash rack to the outside, made her way around the small round paddock, and went over the rusty white gate.

The trailer seemed so very quiet. The bicycles were still in front of the mobile home. The Weed Eater was gone. Sooner or later she would get her hands on that Weed Eater.

Please God let them be there.

Sonora knocked on the door. Waited. Heard absolutely nothing. Logically, the children were home from school, and Dixon Chauncey was working his shift at Procter and Gamble.

Logically.

She thought about knocking again. Decided against it. Quietly tried the lock. It was the kind in the door handle, it did not amount to much. She put her ear to the door, listening. Heard a toilet flush.

She should knock again, announce her presence. "Knock knock," she whispered. "Anyone home?" She paused. "Guess not."

Sonora took a breath and kicked in the door.

It was easier than she imagined, or she had enough adrenaline in her system to make it seem that way. She went in with her gun drawn, no point giving it a chance to fall down the back of her pants, crouched, saw Dixon Chauncey in the hallway, coming out of the bathroom, khakis, no shirt, using a powder blue hand towel to dry his hair. Sonora hesitated. She almost didn't recognize him as a blond.

He froze, eyes huge, turned, and ran. Hot pursuit.

She fired a shot over his head and ran him down in the bedroom, Joelle's bedroom, where he bounded up on the bed and tried to unlatch the window. She caught him around the middle and pulled him down. Momentum took them off the bed and onto the floor. And all the while a small part of her mind registered how quiet the house was, and she prayed that the children were staying after school.

"Down, down, stay down."

"Please, let me go, I haven't done anything."

She kept screaming at him to get down, and it confused

him, as it was supposed to, so that he took the path of least resistance and stayed down, as he was supposed to.

She rolled him to his stomach, knee in his back. Grabbed his arms and had him cuffed in a matter of seconds. Really, her best time so far.

"Dixon Chauncey, you have the right to remain silent." She stopped, took a breath, heard the pounding of feet on the front porch. "If you give up this right—"

He began to cry. "Please, will you just tell me, what did I do?"

61

CHAUNCEY WAS at the kitchen table, head bowed, hands cuffed behind his back. His eyes were red, and the tears flowed freely.

"Please. It's cold in here." His voice had an intense, throbbing quality. King of the Drama. "If you won't give me my shirt, can I please just have a handkerchief or a Kleenex to wipe my nose?"

Sonora, watching him, thought that she would like for him to wipe his nose, but that there was no way in hell she would do it for him, and she'd have to let him out of the cuffs if he was going to do it for himself.

The rest of the team, except her, Sam, and McCarty, were taking the mobile home apart. There was no sign of Mary Claire or Kippie. Chauncey's clothes were packed, but not the girls'. He was leaving without them. Sonora had a very bad feeling in her heart.

"Where were you going, Dixon?" she asked.

"Nowhere."

"Why'd you dye your hair?" Sam asked.

No answer.

"Why'd you pack your bags?" from McCarty.

Dixon shrugged.

Sonora folded her arms. "Come on, Dixon, why'd you pack those bags?"

"We were going away after the funeral. The three of us. After Joelle, I just didn't want to stay here anymore. I was getting my things packed today, and I was going to do the girls' things tomorrow."

"Where are they? Where are the girls?"

"I told you. In school."

Sonora shook her head. "School's out. And I called the school. I called them on the way, Dixon. They said they hadn't been there all day. The principal told me. Are you saying the principal was lying?" She was making it up, but he bought it. She could see it in his eyes. "Why weren't they in school, Dixon?"

"I don't know. That's where I thought they were."

"Did they catch the bus? The bus driver didn't see either one of them. You think I'd come out here and not check this out?" She was shouting. He lowered his head.

"I drove them."

"You drove them?"

"I drove them."

"Why?"

"We got up late. We got up late, so I drove them."

Sonora took Sam into the hallway. "You came in from the back. Did you see his car?"

Sam frowned. "I don't think so. No, I didn't."

"Me either." She started back into the kitchen. Crick came in from the back bedrooms. "Anything?" she asked.

"He's packed, the kids aren't. Somebody's been wrapping presents."

"Presents?"

He held up a snippet of Muppet Baby wrapping paper. A receipt from Toys "R" Us. "He bought a lot of stuff."

"What the hell," Sonora said. "His car is missing."

"He said anything?"

"Bullshit and lies and more bullshit and lies." She started back into the kitchen, and Sam grabbed her arm.

"Sonora have you noticed that he only cries when the rest of us ask him something, but he gives you answers?"

She looked at him.

"You told me yourself, you thought you could get a confession." Sam turned his attention to Crick. "He likes strong women, he wants to be—sorry, Sonora—I think he wants to be dominated."

"That is so disgusting."

"I think the rest of us should leave the kitchen, leave the mobile home. We'll be outside. And I think you should go in there and, you know, whatever."

"Dominatrix," McCarty said.

Sonora glared at him.

He smiled. "Should have brought a dog collar and a leash."

Crick put a hand on her shoulder. "Get in his face like you did in my office. Find me those two little girls."

Sonora was pissed when she went back in the kitchen, she did not want to do this, and she let it work for her. She kicked the table, and Chauncey jumped, head up, eyes wide and, God help her, excited.

"Are you mad at me?" he asked.

Mad at him? Was she mad at him?

"No, I'm mad at them, they're all leaving, and I have to baby-sit you till the uniforms come."

She turned her back on him. Let him listen to the footsteps as everybody left the mobile home. The thundering herd.

"I'm sorry," he told her. Softly.

She turned around. It was those eyes that got her, those fever-blue eyes that watched her till she had to look away.

"Quit looking at me. You hear me, Dixon? Quit looking at me."

He obeyed instantly. Head down. Taking a peek out of the corner of one eye.

"I said quit looking at me."

She was in his face, and his head jerked and sank deep into his shoulders.

"I'm sorry. I'm sorry."

"You shut up. Just shut the hell up, Dixon, and don't you say one word, not one fucking word, till I tell you to."

He nodded, quivering.

Listen to yourself, she thought. You're the mother of two lovely children, and you make a heck of a meat loaf, and listen to yourself.

Cop first. She wished Gillane was here. He'd understand. He would think it was funny. He would tell her to see the light side, and he would feed her Twinkies.

"They're not your kids, are they, Dixon?"

Nothing.

She smacked the back of his neck. "You answer me when I'm talking to you. They're not your kids, are they, Dixon?"

He bowed his head. "No."

"No, *ma'am*."

"No, ma'am."

"You going to start crying again, Dixon? Go on, Dixon, cry. Cry."

The waterworks came. Along with choking sobs. She did not like this. She wanted to do anything but this.

"You didn't drive them to school, did you?"

"No. No, ma'am."

"Where'd you drive them?"

"I can't."

"You can. You can, Dixon, you can, and you will."

"No, no, I can't, it's too late, I can't tell you."

Too late, too late, it echoed in her head. She had to know, she had to move quickly.

She grabbed the back of his chair and wrenched it sideways, and he howled and went down on the floor. She stood with a foot in his rib cage, hunched over to scream in his face.

"Where'd you take the girls?"

His sobs made the words unintelligible, and she was on her

knees so close, she could smell his breath. He dared a look, and she slapped him.

"I told you not to look at me, and I meant it."

"I'm sorry, I'm sorry."

"Where are the girls?"

"At the storage facility."

"Which storage facility?"

"It's on . . . I can't remember the name of it. A side street." He did not look at her, and his voice was small. "I'll show you. Put me in the car, and I'll show you."

62

SAM DROVE, with McCarty up front, and Sonora sat in the back with Dixon.

She did not have to tell him to keep his head down. She did not have to tell him not to look. It was like a secret, their sly secret.

The tears slid down his cheeks, and his nose ran, and he hiccuped at irregular intervals. The siren screamed, and people stared. Dixon liked that part, Sonora could tell.

"It's too late," Dixon whispered.

"Drive faster," Sonora told Sam.

The storage units were new, beige metal, no more than eight minutes away. The land was scraped raw, some of the units still under construction. Sonora saw Sam looking at her from the rearview mirror. She knew what he was thinking. Homicide cops dreaded the calls to storage units. These things were never very pretty and were often very ripe.

"Too late," Dixon said again.

McCarty jerked around and looked at Dixon. "Don't say that again. Not one more time."

"You better be straight on this, Dixon. You take me to the

right place, or I'll wash my hands of you and turn you over to the guys.''

"I'll do the right thing. I'll show you. In your car.''

"In my car?''

"In your car. Can you take off the handcuffs? They're hurting.''

"I'd just as soon break your neck.''

He nodded. Accepting. As always.

Sam stopped the car. "Get out of the backseat, Sonora, and let me have some time with him.''

Sonora shook her head. Looked at Dixon. "Where?''

McCarty leaned over the seat and touched her knee. "Get out of the car. I'll talk to him. I don't like you back there with him.''

"Dixon,'' Sonora said.

He wet his lips, eyes so bright and hard, and she looked straight at him and did not turn away. Something about the way he looked at her made her queasy, but she did not turn away. He held the gaze a long time, as if he would look into her eyes forever.

"Where?'' she said.

Dixon inclined his head. "Over there.''

"The number?''

"I can't remember.''

"Show me, then.''

His head came up, eyes wide. "I don't want to go there. I don't want to see them.''

McCarty, clearly, had had enough. He was out and had Dixon's back door open in a heartbeat, picked him up by the scruff of the neck.

"If you don't want to see them, you better close your eyes, 'cause you're leading the way, you son of a bitch.''

Sonora took a breath, followed, glad it was out of her hands.

Chauncey led them around the back and down a long row to the garages on the left, third from the last.

"Give me the key,'' McCarty said.

Chauncey said something, too soft to make out.

"I said—"

"Forget it." Sam rounded the corner with the crowbar from the back of the trunk. He wedged it under the thin metal door. McCarty went to help, and Sonora kept an eye on Dixon.

She heard sirens, saw Gruber and Sanders drive up, Crick coming alone. The garage door gave way to the crowbar just as Sonora became aware of a movement out of the corner of one eye. She was never sure whether she was so in tune that she sensed the move before he made it, but Chauncey was booking.

A moment's inattention, her fault, underestimating the prisoner, her fault again. She ran like a son of a bitch, cussing herself, cussing Chauncey, and he headed over a hill, behind the last row of storage units. She heard shouts, knew the garage door was going up on Mary Claire and Kippie, wondered if anyone was backing her up.

Chauncey was moving incredibly fast or she was out of shape. She pulled her gun out of the back of her sweatpants, fired into the air. Yelled halt after she fired, glad no one was there to notice seriously out-of-sequence police action.

"Stop! Don't make me shoot you."

He knew where he was going. She reminded herself that he knew the area and she didn't. He disappeared around a rise in land, and Sonora saw a chain-link fence and a down-at-the-heels car lot. The name of the lot was familiar, featuring regularly in reports from vice.

She felt a catch in her side. My God, the man could move. There were children unaccounted for, she had to bring him back. Alive, if possible, which was not going to be easy, she was a terrible shot, she could easily kill him.

Sam's words of caution flicked through her mind as she felt the body slam that sent her flying off her feet, gun spinning out of her hand. He was waiting for her.

He could have run then, but he wasn't through with her. She squirmed and looked for the gun, saw him doing the same, spotted it eight feet to her left.

She never knew if he didn't see the gun or was in too much

of a hurry. The first kick caught her square on the temple, bringing a rush of darkness and light speckles, and an ungodly ache. She was aware that he was kicking her again, and she tried to curl away from him but could not seem to move. She did not see the kick that caught her in the left side, but she felt her ribs crush, felt the incredible jolt of disbelief and shock, and gasped, trying to fill her lungs.

She heard, rather than saw, his feet on the chain-link fence. Climbing in handcuffs. He was getting away.

She crawled toward her gun. Please, God, just give her the breath and the aim to shoot him down dead.

A cacophony of noise brought her head up, and she opened her eyes, blood dripping down the side of her face. Heard a scream, heard the growl of dogs, Rottweilers, a pair, and the clang as Chauncey tried to scramble back up the fence.

The gun felt solid in her hands. Chauncey screamed, a noise she thought she would remember for the rest of her life, and then she heard shouts, and Sam's voice, and guns going off. Someone was shooting the dogs.

And then McCarty or Sam, one of them, she wasn't sure which, tried to pick her up, which brought a wave of agony, but she did not care, because she was safe, and Chauncey wasn't.

McCarty described it for her later, sitting beside her in the hospital, holding her hand.

It had been dark in the storage unit, much too quiet, the smell of exhaust thick in the air. The car's interior lights were on, the two little girls slumped in the backseat.

The car doors were locked, and Sam had gone after them with the crowbar. Sonora had watched McCarty's face as he described it. Two little girls, so quiet and so still. Mary Claire still wearing her little round spectacles, John Lennon granny glasses, and Kippie slumped beside her, head in her sister's lap. Their lips were cherry red. They were clean, hair combed neatly, both wearing brand-new dresses, lacy socks, and black patent leather shoes. Placed, just like Joelle, by a loving father.

They had been surrounded by torn wrapping paper, ribbons. McCarty remembered each one, the death toys, he called them, a Tickle Me Elmo, a Wedding Bells Barbie, a Slinky, *Rugrats* coloring books, and a new box of crayons. Two juice boxes had fallen to the floor, apple juice, one hundred percent fruit concentrate, from Mott's.

Sam made it in first, handed Kippie, still warm, to McCarty, and Mary Claire to Gruber. The girls had not seemed to be breathing.

Crick had seen that help was on the way, and there were sirens, and a red fire department truck was at the top of the hill, coming down, and McCarty had heard gunfire, looked up, and seen that Sonora and Chauncey were gone.

He took her hand then and kissed her, and she always wondered what would have happened if Sam and Gillane had not rounded the corner bringing flowers and Twinkies.

63

Sonora walked up the hillside, turned her back on the drained, muddy pond at Halcyon Farm, stood about one hundred yards from where they had found Joelle Chauncey's body. It felt good to walk without having to stop and catch her breath every three steps.

It was ending as it had begun, a farm at dusk, horses in paddocks under a violet autumn sky.

She had come to bring the Kidgwicks a gold necklace Mickey had found when they drained the pond, a necklace that Sonora thought might have belonged to their daughter. No one was there. There was a for-sale sign at the end of the road—the Kidgwicks were moving on.

Joelle's mother was going to be a trump on the witness stand. She'd taken her daughter's body home to Seattle, had faced Chauncey with a steely-eyed look that had security searching the woman's purse with the utmost care. Sonora had given her copies of the journals, the originals held in evidence.

Mary Claire had gone home to a mother so overwhelmed, she could barely speak. They were still looking for Kippie's parents.

It was the apple juice that had saved Mary Claire and Kippie, apple juice laced with sleeping pills to make them drowsy, to smooth their way. The drugs had slowed their metabolism, reduced their intake of oxygen, kept them alive.

Chauncey had parked them in the garage, given them presents to open and play with while they waited for his supposed return, put a tape in the car, *Sleeping Beauty*, still in the slot when Mickey took the car apart.

Sonora had borne the brunt of a thousand and one dominatrix jokes and now had a collection of dog collars left anonymously on her desk.

Sundance had been returned to her grateful owners, and Hal had read them the riot act till their gratitude was gone. Under his careful supervision, the mare had picked up weight by the time the truck arrived to ship her home to a farm in Nashville, Tennessee.

Their undercover investigation blown, TRC had decided to press charges against Donna Delaney and Vivian and Cliff Bisky. Sonora was not optimistic, but she wished them well.

She walked up the drive, moving slowly, her speed these days, looking out over the fields.

That she was the incidental cause of Dixon Chauncey's maiming would haunt her—not because she felt guilt but because she did not. She knew in her heart that she could have brought the dogs down, or at least tried.

Chauncey would now show a face to the world that was a jigsaw of misplaced features and thick ropy scar tissue, a face that would bring a rush of revulsion and pity, a voice, hoarse and high pitched, an obvious effort from vocal cords damaged beyond repair. He could now effect the instant sympathy that he had spent a lifetime trying to achieve.

The prosecutor's office was asking for the death penalty, a proceeding Sonora could have stopped with a word. She wondered if she owed him that, in exchange for the maiming. The prosecutor, eager to secure information from Chauncey about other children, unaccounted for, had been willing to make a deal with Chauncey's lawyer, until Crick, with Sonora's cooperation, assured him that they could get whatever information they needed from him without resorting to deals. The prosecutor, in the midst of a public thirst for blood, had agreed.

Sonora stopped to rest, thinking that her job had made her hard. She had a new and uneasy self-awareness when she was home, helping Heather with the impossible math, dealing curfews, and making moment-to-moment decisions with Tim—do I punish, do I give this freedom, do I handle this latest transgression with a laugh in lieu of a frown? In some strange way, the awareness of her hard edges gave her a new perspective, an easier attitude, an inner knowledge that these were small matters in the scheme of all things evil, and the cloud of anger over minor annoyances was refusing to rise these days.

Before, she might have sold that new horse of hers. Now she had no hesitation in keeping it.

She looked at the necklace in her hands. She wanted no reminders. She would have liked to toss it back into the pond, but her side was dealing agony now, and she very much wanted to go home.

Sonora paused at the top of the road. The house with the back porch was empty, the porch swing gone. There was no one in sight, just cows, and horses on the horizon.

She looked over her shoulder, tossed the necklace behind her, looked away, and then back again.

She squinted, wondering if she saw what she thought she saw, there by the pond—a boy and a girl, slender and young. Likely it was nothing more than a trick of the dusky light, the distance, the sunset glare in her eyes, and wishful thinking.

ACKNOWLEDGMENTS

My thanks to George Smock, horse educator, who has the rare and priceless ability to teach people and horses to work together, for advice and suggestions and, incidentally, for helping with my own Hell Z Poppin, Empress and Cracker Jack. Any mistakes I made are entirely my own.

To Sue Mardis, wife of Sergeant Roy Mardis, Lexington, Kentucky, Police Department, who died in the line of duty working one of his dogs to bring in a killer. My thanks to you for sharing your knowledge of Roy's groundbreaking work with bloodhounds.

To Sandy and Boyd Haley of Naibara Arabians, for spending an afternoon answering my questions and talking horse. Many thanks for your hospitality.

To Kay Campbell and Amy Wilson for research assistance, conversations on plot, and backup at the barn during those moments of adrenaline rush at the paddock gates when the horses came thundering in. The jury is still out on which one of us can climb a fence faster.

To Benji McEachin, who knows how to throw a dinner party.

To Lynn Hanna and Eileen Dryer, for expertise in things medical.

To Jackie Cantor at Delacorte, who gets it.

To the gang at Hodder & Stoughton: George, Phil, Stewart, Carrie, Camilla, Georgina, Breda, and all of the fabulous sales reps. You guys really know how to throw a book tour.

And always to the usual crew, Matt Bialer, Maya Perez, Stephanie, Marcy, Jim Lyon, Steve and Cindy Sawyer, and the world's best kids, Alan, Laurel, and Rachel.